About the author

Claire Allan was born and reared in Derry, where she still lives with her husband Neil and two children, Joseph (5) and Cara (ickle tiny baby).

When she is not fending off the baby sick, she works as a reporter and columnist for the *Derry Journal*.

Her addiction to handbags has been replaced by an addiction to pink dresses following the arrival of her baby girl.

Jumping in Puddles is her third novel. You can find out more by visiting her website **www.claireallan.com** or her blog **www.diaryofamadmammy.blogspot.com**.

Also by Claire Allan

Feels Like Maybe

Rainy Days & Tuesdays

Published by Poolbeg.com

Acknowledgements

First and foremost, I want to thank my family. Balancing writing a book with morning sickness, hormone overload and then a new baby did not make me the easiest person in the world to live with. Thank you, Neil, for understanding and Joseph and Cara, my babies, you help me see the world in a whole new light every day.

Thank you to my parents, sisters and brother. As always your support is overwhelming – from proofreading to attending signings with me and waiting in the wings. Thank you.

To all the Davidson, McGuinness and Allan clans – thank you. It's nice to have an inbuilt fan club.

I'd like to thank my writer friends for their continued support, advice and encouragement. In particular I'd like to mention Sharon Owens for her wickedly wonderful sense of humour, Anne Dunlop, Clodagh Murphy, Trina Rea, Keris Stainton, Fionnuala McGoldrick and Emma Heatherington.

To the management and staff of the *Derry Journal* and Johnston Publishing – thank you for support and free plugs aplenty. Special mentions go to Erin, Mary, Catherine and Bernie.

Thanks to all the booksellers and journalists who have worked so hard to put my book out there and encourage people to read it. Special thanks to Eason, Foyleside and Hughes & Hughes Dublin Airport who have been amazingly supportive.

Thanks to all the readers of my blog, diaryofamadmammy.blogspot.com, for their feedback and encouragement and thanks to Evie for suggesting the name Robyn for one of the characters. It really suits her.

And to you, lovely reader, thank you for picking this book up!

As always I want to thank those who believe in me enough to put my work out there. To my agent Ger Nichol and Niamh, Sarah and all the team at Poolbeg, with special thanks to Paula Campbell who steered this book in the right direction and who didn't mind at all when I took a horrible bout of morning sickness at a very inopportune moment. Thanks also to Gaye Shortland who can see the wood for the trees.

Finally, I can hand on heart say this book would not have been written without the support of several friends who dusted me off more times than enough and encouraged me to keep going. First of all to the ridiculously talented Fionnuala Kearney – thank you from the bottom of my heart for all your support and the kitchen island story. And secondly my VBF Vicki, who didn't let me give up on it.

For
Granny McGuinness
With much love and admiration

1

Niamh

THINGS I HATE ABOUT MY HUSBAND:

* He likes pea and ham soup – I mean, who in their right mind eats something which looks like snot?

* He waits until he gets to work to shave, so that when he kisses me goodbye in the morning I get stubble rash.

* He drives too fast.

* He died because he drove too fast. Stupid bastard.

* No one else has bought pea and ham soup from our local shop since he died. And I've no way of telling him I was right that he was the only person in Donegal who ate the blasted stuff.

* He never said goodbye. And the last kiss we had was a stubbly one . . . and I had morning breath.

* He makes me cry.

* * *

1

THINGS I HATE ABOUT MY EX-BEST FRIEND:

* Caitlin hasn't spoken to me since Seán died.

* She doesn't answer the phone when I call.

* She is a bitch.

* She won't tell me why she has become a bitch.

* * *

Niamh had doodled on the top corner of her page. It was a strange picture – her artist's impression of a tin of pea and ham soup. She knew she was obsessed but if she stopped thinking about tins of soup she might just have to think about everything that was so terribly wrong in her life.

Like the fact her husband was dead – and she was now a widow with three-year-old twins. And that her best friend in the whole world had turned into a psycho-bitch from hell precisely half an hour after her husband was buried in a graveyard in the arse-end of nowhere.

And, of course, she now lived in the aforementioned arse-end of nowhere – their dream home, where it was all to begin and become fabulous. Except it hadn't begun at all, it had ended.

This was to be her Wisteria Lane. She was happy to leave the rat race of Derry behind and become a kept woman in their perfect home, with the porch swing and the designer kitchen island. But this wasn't so much Wisteria Lane as Elm Street and her life was the nightmare. The fact that there wasn't actually some psycho with knives for fingers ready to claw her to pieces in the middle of the night was no comfort. She would have quite liked that – at the moment.

Niamh scored through the picture, looked up at three heads bowed over their own notebooks, writing furiously, and she fought the urge to push her pen through her nose till it hit her brain. She didn't even know if it was a painless way to commit suicide, but looking around at her options she thought it might be worth a try.

"Niamh, are you okay?" a ridiculously smiley woman in a long flowing skirt with, Niamh imagined, long flowing underarm hair, asked.

Rolling her eyes like someone half her age in a teenage strop, Niamh nodded. She didn't have the energy to answer that question any more and anyway she had very quickly learned that people didn't really want to know the answer. They expected her to say she was fine. She could occasionally get away with "fine, all things considered" or "fine, given the circumstances" but no one wanted to know that at this stage, three months after her life had changed irrevocably and not in a good way, she woke up every morning seething with rage and confusion wanting to scream at the world and everyone in it.

Nor were they particularly interested in her obsession with pea and ham soup. Even Robyn, the new best friend who had stepped into the shoes of the psycho ex-best friend, had started to openly avoid all discussions on any kind of soup, never mind Seán's favourite flavour.

"I'm grand," Niamh said, and went back to doodling, hoping that Detta O'Neill, the group facilitator, would leave her alone if she looked busy enough.

She hadn't wanted to come here. She'd done it to keep Robyn, her mother and her GP happy. All had been understandably concerned that Niamh had seemed to give up the day Seán died – putting her life on hold in a haze of grief and anger.

"Don't take this the wrong way," Robyn had said, almost afraid to meet Niamh's eye, "but you should think about some form of counselling, or support."

"I thought that is what I had you two for," Niamh said, looking at her friend and her mother as if they had betrayed her. Had they become tired of her grief? Should she have moved on by now? Surely three months was wee buns when it came to loss and longing?

"Of course you have us," her mother had soothed, "but, darling, we feel we can't reach you sometimes. And it doesn't help that we're up in Derry and you are all the way down here."

"It's only an hour away," Niamh pouted.

"That's a long way when you are worried about someone," Robyn said, "and you seem to have become a hermit since – you know – since. And you never get out and talk to anyone."

"These two keep me busy," Niamh said, gesturing to the corner of the room where Connor and Rachel were playing contentedly with their Bob the Builder toys. "I don't need anyone else."

"Of course you do," her mother said. "You must be lonely."

It would, Niamh realised, have been churlish to reply "No shit, Sherlock" to her mother's concern, but counselling wasn't going to ease her loneliness – not unless the counsellor was planning on coming home and stroking her back gently each night in bed just as Seán had done. That kind of loneliness wasn't going to go away.

"Look," her mum said, standing up and moving to switch on the kettle, "I've been talking to Dr Donnelly and she has given me the name of a woman here in Rathinch who is starting a support group for lone parents."

"But I'm not a lone parent!" Niamh shouted. How she hated that title. She was a married woman, who along with her husband had planned her family with scary precision. The twins were conceived in May, born in February, raised in Derry until they were two and then the family moved to their dream home on the Donegal coastline. It was a home she and Seán had designed together, built together and were ridiculously proud of. They had pored over interior-design magazines, taped every episode of *Grand Designs* and made their house the envy of the village. They had done it all together.

Niamh hadn't made any decisions as a "lone" anything and she shrugged off the title now. It was right up there with "widow" in her most hated terms in the world ever.

"Look, we'll leave you her number. She's Detta and Dr Donnelly said she's a dote. Think about it, pet. What harm can it do?"

Niamh shrugged, walking out into the perfectly manicured garden and staring out at the grey sea at the bottom of the path. As the wind whistled around her, she hugged her cardigan and her grief around her.

Talking to Detta couldn't do any harm. After what she had been through lately, nothing could ever harm her again.

And of course her options were limited. She knew her mother was like a dog with a bone and wouldn't leave her alone until she was joining in nicely with village life and at least putting forward an impression of calm and happiness to her new neighbours. It was either the Lone Parents Support Group, Niamh had realised with a sinking feeling, or the knitting club. And Niamh didn't do knitting.

2

Ruth

THINGS I HATE ABOUT MY EX-HUSBAND:

* He used to fart in bed and shout "Smell that!" as if it
  was something to be proud of.

* He never bothered with the kids, not unless I threatened
  him with no dinner if he didn't take them out for an hour.

* I can't remember the last time he told me I looked good.
  Occasionally he told me I looked nice and we all know
  "nice" means "Actually I don't give a feck what you are
  wearing."

* He didn't give a feck what I was wearing, because he
  was too busy worrying about what Laura was wearing.

* He was shagging Laura. I would say "having an affair",
  but we all know it was just shagging. The bastard.

* And now they've run away with each other. Well, fair
  play to them, I hope they are very happy together and I
  really hope she likes smelling farts.

* Oh, all that other stuff too. But we'll not talk about that.

* * *

This class was going to be a new start for Ruth Byrne, she had decided earlier that day after Detta O'Neill had persuaded her to come along and join in. She'd had enough of moping about the house and wailing about the fact James had walked out for a new life with that slut down the road.

The kids had become sick, sore and tired of her wandering around like a lost soul. When she told them earlier that she was considering coming to a confidence class aimed at lone parents, they had practically kicked her out the front door.

It was strange, Ruth thought, or maybe not strange at all, that the children actually seemed that bit happier now that James was gone. There had been tears at first, admittedly, and a good deal of confusion, but now they just seemed to be getting on with things. If Ruth was honest with herself, she had noticed her three children laughing more recently. She didn't want to think about what that meant about their relationship with their father.

Their quick recovery from his departure had helped ease her guilt – the guilt that it must have been something she had done that pushed James into the arms of another woman. She must have been so bad that he didn't even seem to think twice about leaving the home they had built together or the three children they had been raising together. Christ, Matthew was only eight. He needed his daddy, but Ruth – she berated herself – had managed to push her gorgeous son's daddy away. And after all she had put up with too. She really must have been much, much more worthless than she thought.

She felt tears prick in her eyes. Looking around the room, she wondered if the group could really be a benefit to her.

Detta looked in her direction and smiled. Of course Detta knew her – they had gone to the same school all those years ago, before Detta had left for her new life in the bright lights of Dublin. Detta also knew all about James and his new woman. Then again, with a population of around 700, everyone in bloody Rathinch knew about James and Laura and their escape into the sunset.

Her cheeks started to burn. She wasn't sure any more that this had been a good idea. She looked around at the three other heads bowed over their notebooks and tried to reassure herself that each of them must be feeling as nervous as she was.

Taking a deep breath, she settled herself and smiled back at Detta, who was talking to that poor critter whose husband had been killed in that awful accident. There's worse off than you, Ruth, she said inwardly and continued to write, turning her thoughts back to her husband – sorry, *ex*-husband – and her feelings towards him.

She wondered, if she did actually crack one day and beat him over the head with her frying pan, could anything she wrote within the confines of this group be used in evidence against her in a court of law?

She made a mental note that she would talk to Detta afterwards and ask her if it could be an unwritten rule that anything that was said in the community centre stayed in the community centre. A bit like a hen or stag weekend, only with less drink and more chocolate biscuits.

She would like to think this group would work. She could do with some friends. For a long time her life had revolved solely around James, the kids and home and her part-time job. She couldn't say she'd had much time for friendships. She would watch programmes like *Sex and the City* and crave that closeness with a group of female friends. She had to admit she was also quite jealous of all the rampant sex everyone but her seemed to be having. She was thirty-seven for the love of God – she was supposed to be in her sexual prime.

Ruth choked at the thought that it had been at least five months since she'd had sex and, if that was her peak, she realised she might as well run off to the convent now.

She blushed as she thought that, actually, if any of the sex she had had with James marked the best sex she would have in her life she would definitely be better suited to life in the cloisters.

3

Liam

THINGS I HATE ABOUT THIS FECKING COURSE:

* I'm only here to keep my mother from sending the priest round to counsel me.

* I'm the only man here. Now I know how Robin Williams felt when dressed up like that woman in *Mrs Doubtfire*. I'm one step away from support tights and fake boobs.

* And there's Ruth, James's wife. Christ, I hope she doesn't want to talk about the "situation". I don't want to talk about it to anyone.

* I should be writing why I'm angry at Laura. I'm not – well, I am – but if she walked in here now and asked to come home I would let her.

* I don't understand why she left. I loved her from the day we met.

* * *

This just didn't seem right. Liam considered himself very much a man's man, so how on earth had he found himself in a room full of women talking about feelings, emotions and relationships?

He'd felt sick when he'd come through the door that evening. If he was honest the first thing he wanted to do, as the cold sweat broke out over his body, was to turn and run for the hills.

Still he had promised his mother that he would give it a try. She had morphed into the world's most over-protective mother the day Laura walked out. But instead of helping him cope with the misery of the last few months, she seemed to make it worse.

"Stop looking at me like that," he'd scolded when she'd arrived earlier that day.

"Like what?" Agnes said, wounded at the harshness in his voice.

"Like I've got some terminal illness or something. I'm managing, Mother."

"But it's not right," she said. "You here, on your own, with a child to care for. That woman is an affront to womanhood."

Liam rolled his eyes. Sure enough there were certain variations on this theme but almost every conversation with his mother included at least one barbed remark on what a god-awful bitch his wife (he refused to use the word ex) was.

"How on earth is Poppy going to cope with no mammy?"

"She has me," Liam said. "And we get on just fine. And besides, Laura isn't dead. She's just down the street!"

His heart had lifted a little at the thought of his precious daughter – so precocious and full of life – as determined as Laura had ever been. At five years old, she was missing her mother terribly, even if she *was* only down the street. As a consequence Liam had been overcompensating wildly for her disappearance. She would want for nothing, he promised himself.

"It's not right," Agnes sniffed, sitting down on the sofa, running her finger along the coffee table for signs of dust. To her chagrin, her son seemed to be coping with his household duties just fine. "I was talking to young Detta O'Neill today at the church hall. She is starting a new course for single parents. I know she's a bit flighty and all that but she seemed to think it would be a great way for people to mix and make friends. I told her you would go along."

"I will do no such thing," Liam replied.

"Yes, you will, and it will do you good," Agnes replied and Liam knew from the steely look in his mother's eyes that saying no was not an option.

As luck would have it, he bumped into the very self-same Detta O'Neill as he walked to work after his lunch break. She was wandering down the street, staring at the sky, her golden curls hanging loosely around her neck. With her flowing skirts and permanent smile she looked very much like a rose among the thorns of Rathinch's female population. Most of the other women in the village walked around with their lips pursed like cats' arses as they whispered gossip beneath their breath at every given opportunity.

Detta didn't look like the gossiping type. In fact, as she noticed him and smiled, waving and crossing the street, she looked like the friendliest face he had seen in a long time.

And she persuaded him, with her curling hair and her flowing skirt and her non-cat's-arse kind of a face to come along and sit in a room with a load of definitely cats'-arsey women and chat about his fecking feelings.

* * *

As expected, when he walked into the church hall it hadn't

taken long for things to take an "all men are bastards" turn.

"How are you feeling tonight?" Detta had asked.

"Angry," the woman he recognised as Niamh Quigley answered. "Angry and tired."

"Anger's a good part of the healing process," Detta had answered in a soothing tone.

"It's not so good for my china though," Niamh sniffed with a half smile.

She wasn't fooling Liam though. Even though a smile danced on her lips there was such a deep sadness in her eyes that Liam almost felt as if he was intruding on her grief by looking at her.

"Well, I'm fecking angry too," a young girl with jet-black hair stated. "My boss gave me grief for needing to go home early today because the baby was sick. What was I supposed to do? The crèche won't keep them if they're vomiting."

She was young enough to be his daughter and yet she had a child of her own. Liam shifted uncomfortably in his seat.

"Of course, Ella's daddy doesn't have such worries. He's just getting on with his life. You wouldn't even think he had a child."

"We're not all bad," Liam wanted to shout, but he didn't. He kept quiet, put his head down and hoped that if he didn't speak this whole thing would be over as soon as possible – just as he hoped that if he kept quiet and didn't make a fuss about his wife running off with yer man from up the road, this too would all be over soon and Laura would be back where she belonged.

4

Ciara

THINGS I HATE ABOUT MY LIFE:

* Everything. I didn't want a baby. It wasn't my fault I got pregnant. He told me he loved me.

* My mum. She hasn't looked at me the same way since I told her I was pregnant. I miss her and how we used to be. She used to be my best friend.

* Sometimes I think she loves Ella more than me.

* The fact that no man will ever, ever look at me again because I'm seventeen and have a baby and sure who wants spoiled goods?

* This place. There is no *craic* to be had in Rathinch. How is anyone here supposed to have a life? Me and Ella are going to get out of here as soon as we can. I'll show everyone.

* * *

Ciara sighed and sat back in her chair chewing her pen. This was so not her scene. There was nothing about this that appealed to her but it was either come here or spend another night in with her mum and Ella, with her mum watching her every move and commenting on every little thing she did with her daughter.

She had been serving in the shop earlier when Detta came in to get some milk and invited her along.

"It's going to be all about being positive and strong in yourself as a lone parent," she'd said while Ciara rang in through her shopping.

Detta was nice, Ciara thought. She hadn't been one of the crowd who whispered behind her back about getting pregnant and she had actually cooed over Ella when she took her out in her pram. Some of the other old biddies had crossed the road to avoid her or tutted at her as they walked past.

She had long since been tempted to start a rumour that it was one of their husbands who had impregnated her, but she wasn't sure they wouldn't have taken her and burned her at the stake if she started with any of that nonsense.

"Who's going to be there?" Ciara asked, mentally trying to figure out who in the village was single with kids at the moment.

"I'm not sure. To be honest, I'm not sure anyone is going to be there. I spoke to Niamh Quigley – you know, from the big house up the road. She said she might make it."

Ciara nodded. She felt sorry for Niamh – she always looked so sad when she walked through the village with her twins. The old biddies crossed the road to avoid her too.

"If you came along it would really help," Detta pleaded and Ciara agreed – all she would have to do was ask her mum to baby-sit.

* * *

"I'll check, you know," Lorraine Boyle had said, looking her daughter up and down with a look of curiosity on her face.

"You can ring Detta and check if you want. I've nothing to hide," Ciara said defiantly, bouncing her baby on her knee. Her mother may well have mellowed and now doted on Ella, but she watched Ciara's every move waiting for her to slip up and reveal who the daddy was – but there was no way that was ever going to happen. Not a chance.

* * *

Ciara had arrived five minutes late and looked around the room at the village's other lone parents. Sure enough Niamh was there, and there was Ruth and Liam. The scandal of their partners running off with each other had long been the main topic of conversation for the gossips who gathered in the shop.

Ciara felt sorry for them too – to have everyone talking about their misfortune like that – but then she reminded herself, if the locals were talking about them they weren't talking about her, and that had to be a good thing.

She smiled a quick hello and sat down. Detta said hello, welcomed everyone and handed out some notebooks.

"Let's get started," Detta said in a strange sing-song voice she hadn't used in the shop earlier. She had some oil burning in the corner of the room but it failed to cover up the faintly mouldy smell of the floorboards.

"I want you to write a hate list," Detta said.

Ciara had raised an eyebrow suspiciously. Glancing around her, she noticed her other three group members had raised their eyebrows too. There was funky symmetry to it.

"A hate list?" Niamh had piped up.

"Yes, a list of things you hate about your life. I find with things like this that people have a lot of 'hate' or discontent they need to get out of the way before they can start being constructive and moving on. So I figured, as we might not all want to spill to each other just yet, sure we can just write it down and be done with it."

Ciara sighed. She didn't fancy writing a hate list. Part of her was worried if she started she wouldn't stop, but Detta just smiled – a mad hippy kind of a grin from behind her blonde curls – and it was clear she was very excited about the notepads and shiny new biros she had just handed out.

But then, Ciara thought with a grin, this was the woman who had obviously gone slightly bonkers in Eason earlier buying up every shred of coloured paper and glitter pens to make overly bright and colourful signs to advertise the one thing the rest of the village was ashamed of.

But as Niamh, Ruth and Liam all bowed their heads and started writing, Ciara realised she didn't have much of a choice other than to start writing herself, or at least if she wanted to fit in here, even a little bit, she needed to write. She didn't want to make them all think she was just some stroppy teenager from the outset, even if she was, in fact, just some stroppy teenager.

5

Niamh sat on the porch of the house, on the swing she'd insisted Seán buy, and pulled her cardigan around her as she sipped from a glass of wine and listened to the wind whistle in the trees and her children breathe softly through the baby monitors.

She was trying to process the day which had just passed, and the fact that she had attended one of those happy-clappy support groups she had always mocked in the past.

* * *

"Let's get started," Detta had said, rubbing her hands together with a sense of anticipation. Niamh had looked down at her list, hoping she wouldn't be asked to read it aloud. She was here for support, yes, but she didn't really fancy being here for some ritual humiliation. Besides it was okay for her to write bad things about Seán, but she wasn't ready to have anyone else think badly of him. It would be the worst type of betrayal.

She would sink Caitlin for a penny though, so she took a deep breath and waited for Detta to ask her to start talking.

"Now that we've got that out of the way, all your anger

and hurt for tonight, we can actually do something productive," Detta said. "Now take your lists and tear them up, as small as you want, and throw them in the bin. You've let that go now, we don't need to go there again tonight. Let's just introduce ourselves."

Niamh took a deep breath – what seemed like her first breath in about five minutes – and started tearing up her list. She was allowed to be angry, she reminded herself, but once that subsided her grief would crash in again.

"You all know me," she said, her voice shaky. "I'm Niamh and I'm thirty-three. You know I have twins. No doubt you have seen us down on the beach." She gave a half smile. This felt mildly like she was on some weird Donegal version of *Blind Date* and Detta was Cilla with her "What's your name and where do you come from?" nonsense. She took a deep breath and continued. "And you will no doubt know that my husband died three months ago when he crashed his car driving home to us."

If she said it fast, it didn't sound so devastating.

Liam, Ruth and Ciara nodded, before looking downward. Niamh was used to this look, used to people not really knowing what to say in reply to: "My husband died in a horrendous car accident and my life is fucked."

"I'm here because my mother and my friend think it will help. I know I'm in a different position to the rest of you and, well, I'm not sure what good this will . . ." Much to her shame she started to cry, fat, wet tears plopping on the blank page of her notebook making the lines run into each other.

Detta walked over and sat beside her, while Ciara rustled through her bag for a tissue. "I always have tissues. Ella throws up a lot," she told the room before handing a crumpled Kleenex to Niamh. "Don't worry, it's clean," she added with a smile.

Niamh felt herself warm to her. The poor girl couldn't have been more than sixteen or seventeen and here she was in a room filled with old fogies who had all made an unholy mess of their lives.

"Thanks," Niamh mumbled, blowing her nose loudly into the tissue and putting it in her pocket.

"Look, it's okay to cry," Detta said, rubbing her shoulder. "I can't imagine what you have been through."

Niamh wanted to hug her. It seemed for the last three months everyone and his mother had been telling her how they *could* imagine how awful it must be, when all she could think was there was no one who really knew how it felt. But she decided against the hug. It was bad enough that she had already cried in front of these people. Whatever would they think of her? The flaky woman from the big house who burst into tears every time someone spoke to her. What a way to make friends and garner the admiration of her neighbours!

Liam spoke next: "My mother insisted I come here tonight," he said, red-faced. I suppose you all know my story too – well, at least I'm fairly sure you know it, Ruth, eh?" He laughed nervously, Ruth joined in, her laughter sounding forced.

Ciara bit back a giggle and, smiling, winked at Niamh.

* * *

Niamh smiled now at the memory of the wink Ciara had given her as Liam and Ruth explained their weird connection. She had smiled back. It was only a small smile though – she didn't feel she was allowed anything more, except when the twins were about when she absolutely had to pretend that everything was, as that annoying purple dinosaur her kids loved so much would say, A-okay. She was great at it though – she would have made a wonderful *CBeebies* presenter if bright colours had suited her.

When the session had finished she'd felt at least she had one ally, and possibly four, in this godforsaken village and given that it seemed her friendship with Caitlin was pretty much past the point of rescue, she would take any ounce of friendship she could get.

The loneliness was the hardest thing to deal with. Everyone else had moved on, it seemed. Even if they pretended to still be interested she could see their eyes glaze over that little bit when she talked about *that* night and her husband and her grief. She couldn't be angry with them and she couldn't say she really blamed them. There were nights – like tonight – when she wanted to shut thoughts of it all out herself. She wished at times that someone would erase every memory of Seán from her life and that she could move on and away without the gut-wrenching grief eating into her soul.

"Fuck it," she said aloud and pulled her knees to her. "I don't want to feel like this any more. Seán, do you hear me? I don't want to do this! I didn't ask for this and I didn't want you to go."

She threw the remains of her wine onto the lush green grass and, slamming the door behind her, went inside and climbed the stairs. She walked through to the twins' bedroom and felt their hair damp with sweat. Lying down beside Connor, curling into his tiny body, she fell asleep.

It was okay to cry, but she didn't want to cry any more.

6

Ella woke early and Ciara tried to keep her patience. She was tired though and she knew by the time she finished her shift at the shop she would be totally wrecked. Her old friends would be hitting the town tonight – while she would be hitting the hay.

Glancing at the clock, she saw that it was five thirty. It was much too early to be awake and dealing with a gurning child. She lifted her daughter from her cot and tried to soothe her. She'd only been crying a matter of minutes when the bang came on the wall.

"Ciara, could you try and settle her, please? I need my sleep," Lorraine called gruffly.

Ciara took a deep breath and started counting to ten. Her mother was a decent enough support but after ten months of interrupted nights she had finally snapped and told Ciara she was on her own with the early rises. Ciara could understand – her mum worked hard all day – but then, so did she. She hadn't gone back to school after having the baby. She couldn't face being the talk of the playground and, besides, she fancied her hand at earning a bit of money. Then again, if she had known just how much Lorraine would make her stand on her own two feet she might have taken her chances with double maths.

Groaning at the thought of another day under the beady and watchful eye of her boss, Mrs Quinn, while out of her head through lack of sleep, Ciara walked down the stairs and opened the fridge. She took a long cold slug of Diet Coke. She normally wasn't the tea-and-coffee-drinking sort, and by God did she need the caffeine hit right now! If there had been a gallon of Red Bull anywhere in the house she would have downed it as quickly as she could.

Half an hour later she found herself in the living room watching some brightly coloured puppets singing a song about rainbows on TV, Ella now sound asleep beside her but her own mind much too awake, thanks to the fecking caffeine, to drift off herself.

How sad was it that a meeting in a community centre, with people twice her age, had been the height of her social life this month? She thought of Niamh – she seemed lovely, kind but sad. Then she thought of Ruth and Liam – it would be lovely for them to one day get together.

Chiding herself for having romantic notions, she slid down on the floor beside the sofa and watched Ella sleep – the soft rise and fall of her chest.

What good would having romantic notions do? She was already spoiled goods. The boys from her school hadn't looked at her sideways since she'd got pregnant and she couldn't imagine they would again. She had stretch marks now – dirty big pink lines running up her stomach. There were even a couple on her boobs. And, dare she say it, her boobs sagged. She was fecking seventeen and her boobs sagged. What would they be like when she hit forty? She'd be in serious danger of tripping over them.

Besides, Ciara was pretty sure she didn't ever want another boyfriend anyway. Giving birth had put her off any notions of having sex of any description, even just touching anyone again. To be honest, having sex itself – that one time – had put her off the notion of doing it again. No man was ever getting near her again. Ever. It was no big deal. It certainly wasn't the be-all and the end-all that it seemed to be in the movies. She cringed remembering how she'd tried to make the right noises to sound like she knew what she was doing, but in all honesty it just felt clumsy and sore and not in the very least bit sexy.

She switched over and watched MTV for a little before getting dressed for work and setting about feeding her daughter – hoping that she wouldn't sick up on her before they left the house. Her other uniform was in the wash and she was on a warning already for coming to work in her own clothes even though it was only the poxy village shop. It was hardly bleedin' Tesco.

Sighing, she strapped Ella into her buggy and walked out into the misty rain – making sure not to bang the door as she closed it. As she walked along the shorefront towards the crèche, she saw school children, some her former classmates, come out their front doors, dressed in uniform and swinging their bags from their shoulders, smiling and chatting with their friends. She put her head down and walked on. She wasn't in the form to chat to them this morning and have them coo over Ella, saying how cool she was. Ciara knew that babies were far from fashion accessories – in fact, instead of making you super cool, they were more likely to make you the ultimate drudge.

Dropping her daughter off, she checked her watch to make sure she wasn't late for work. Then she ran down the street and wondered if she would see him again today.

She never knew if she really wanted to see him – Ella's dad

– but she had a longing in her all the same. She might feel worse after he blanked her and went on about his life as if nothing had happened between them and they didn't have a child together, which was his usual tactic. She chided herself once again – romantic notions about the village Lothario-in-training were not going to get her very far at all.

7

"So is it all crackpots and loonies then?" Eimear asked, biting into a slice of toast her mother had just buttered for her.

"No and don't be so rude," Ruth chided, buttering another slice of toast for eight-year-old Matthew who was lost in an episode of *Ben 10*.

"Ach, I'm only joking," Eimear replied, tightening her school tie. "I'm sure it was mad *craic* hearing all the scandal. Was your one whose husband died there?"

"What happens in the group stays in the group," Ruth replied, feeling rather proud of herself for refusing to be drawn into idle gossip.

"Aye, but was she there? That was really sad. We were talking about it in school. She has two wee wains, doesn't she? But I heard she was loaded and I heard she got mega-bucks after he died. That car she drives is gorgeous. I'm going to have personalised number plates just like hers when I'm older. Lucky cow."

Ruth rolled her eyes. "I'm sure she would rather have her husband with her than piles of money."

Her daughter snorted. "Aye, right!"

But she knew it was pointless discussing it further with Eimear – who, given recent experiences in her own life, would have been only too happy to see her own father wiped out in a car accident so she could live off the proceeds of his insurance. Not that James ever had insurance, or made any financial provision for the future – or for the present for that matter. She hadn't seen a penny off him since he walked out.

"And was yer man there? *Her* husband? Poor fecker."

"Eimear, language!"

"I said feck, not the *other* word," Eimear said, rolling her eyes. "Calm down, Mother! Seriously, there are worse things I could be doing."

Her daughter stood up, pulling her hair into a high pony-tail before taking one last bite of toast and going to call Thomas, who was still spiking his hair in the bathroom.

"I'm not being late for school today because of you and your hair! No one notices it anyway. They can't see past your zits," she shouted at the bottom of the stairs.

"Eimear, would you leave your brother alone!" Ruth called, her blood pressure rising. Her daughter was sixteen going on forty-three – thought she knew it all and thought everyone else was just enthralled with her opinions. She was a right madam these days and while Ruth loved the bones of her there were times when she secretly fantasised about wringing her pretty little neck. Poor Thomas was only fourteen and hit with what seemed like a double dose of puberty hormones which were raging through his puny body while Eimear had seemed to blossom into puberty – no gawky teenager phase or problem skin for her. Ruth often wished she would cut her brother some slack.

"You're a mega meanie!" Matthew called as he put on his school coat and pulled his bag onto his back. "Leave my brother alone!"

Eimear just stuck her tongue out and called again to Thomas, storming on ahead of him as he wandered down the stairs, half a jar of gel in his hair.

As Ruth pulled on her coat to take her youngest son to the school at the other end of the village she wished for one moment that she had someone else there to act as peacekeeper between her brood – not that, when she thought about it, James was ever much of a peacekeeper – in fact it was usually the exact opposite.

Once Matthew was deposited at school, Ruth walked home and let herself into the blissful peace and quiet. She wasn't due to start work for another two hours and so it was the perfect time to catch up on some housework, or sort out the mountain of bills piling up on the hall table. But all she wanted to do was sit down, put her feet up and cry into a cup of tea.

Most of the time she stayed strong, but when push came to shove she was a thirty-seven-year-old woman cast out on the world again – single, with three children, a mountain of debt and a plethora of grey hairs which seemed to be on a mission to multiply on a daily basis. Thirty-seven wasn't old, she knew that, but on days like today, even though last night she had felt so positive coming away from the meeting, she felt ancient.

She had been so convinced she was headed for her happily ever after when she married at twenty-one. Her mother had told her, the very morning of the wedding, that it wasn't too late to call it off and Ruth had laughed. She loved James – so madly and deeply that she knew she could never love anyone like that again.

And she had beamed all day. In every photograph of that day she was glowing amid her layers of lace and netting.

Everyone commented that she was a beautiful bride, that she had never looked better. Yet now when Ruth looked at the pictures she saw a child staring back at her. When Eimear started with her teasing and flicking of her hair Ruth could see in her the same hopeless naïvety that she'd had at that age and it scared her.

Ruth sat back in her seat, switched on the TV to watch some warring couple battle it out on the *Jeremy Kyle Show* so that she could at least comfort herself with the knowledge her life wasn't as much of a train wreck as that of those poor souls. The washing could wait until later, and as for the bills – no amount of number-crunching was going to change the fact that financially she was up a creek without a paddle. Ruth knew she would have to start making begging phone-calls to lenders soon and that she would in all likelihood have to give up her part-time job in the doctor's and find something which paid more – a lot more.

Ruth couldn't believe her life had come to this. Her pocket-money job – the one that was supposed to pay for her luxuries – had now become her sole source of income. No doubt if the good people of Rathinch knew that James Byrne – him in his high-fallutin' office – wasn't offering a bean to his family they wouldn't believe it.

She rubbed her eyes and stared around her. If the worst came to the worst she could Ebay some stuff – God knows they had enough tat lying around here. Her wedding ring was worth a few quid, as were the many bracelets and necklaces he had bought over the years as peace offerings. They could go. She had no need for them any more and could take no joy from wearing them.

If things got really bad she could sell her car – battered and bruised (mostly of her own making, admittedly), it was her pride and joy. But she would do what she could to keep her family provided for until she got the courage up to drag James through the courts for child support.

Watching the latest row erupt on the TV, Ruth allowed herself to smile. She wondered if Rathinch was ready for its first hooker yet.

She could just imagine the neighbours' faces as she touted her wares in the front-room window – all fishnet stockings and tarty red lipstick and then maybe she could get herself a slot on the telly with all the old biddies from the town shouting at her for scaring the tourists away.

She shuddered as she imagined the clientele – a couple of farmers and Billy the fisherman who always smelled of haddock. Nope – she would pick up the paper later and scan it for a job a little more suitable and she would phone James again, and try and bring up the tricky subject of child support again – just as she did every week. Maybe, she thought with a smile, she should enlist Eimear to ask for her. Her bolshy daughter wouldn't take any nonsense from her father, or anyone for that matter. Ruth wondered where on earth she got her gutsy personality from. It certainly didn't come from Ruth, and that was for sure.

She rinsed her cup under the tap and made her way upstairs to start getting ready for work. Glancing in the mirror she shuddered. She was certainly a far cry from the gorgeous young bride she had been years before. Her hair was cut in an unflattering bob, greying at the temples. It was not a good look – and not at all helped by her growing mountain of wrinkles. When she smiled she realised she was in danger of her eyes disappearing entirely amid a mass of loose skin. Her clothes were a little too tight – something she was not at all impressed with, given that the label read a 16.

And, to add to her woes, she had one of those apron-type bellies thanks to three pregnancies and an addiction to Maltesers. She gave it a good jiggle for good measure. Sure wouldn't she look just sweet in red nylon stockings and suspenders as the village tart?

8

The postman arrived while Niamh was cooking breakfast on her AGA. As usual the twins tore off, falling over each other to get to the letters first.

"Calm down!" Niamh called as the stampede battered towards the door.

"But, Mummy, it's my job to bring in the post!" Connor yelled.

"No, Mummy, it's mine, it's mine!" Rachel yelled back and Niamh couldn't help but smile even though she knew that it was all bound to end in tears, just as it always did.

"Can you not share?" she shouted, walking to the hall in time to see their three-year-old heads collide over a pile of letters.

The three-second silence came next, followed by a joint wailing and screaming as both toddlers scampered down towards their mother at lightning speed, clutching their letters in their podgy hands.

"There, there," Niamh soothed, smothering their heads in kisses until the sobs subsided and they dropped their letters in favour of the brightly coloured characters jumping around on the TV screen in the playroom.

Still sitting on the hall floor Niamh flicked through today's haul. Thankfully she was no longer reduced to a sobbing wreck by letters addressed to Seán, and due to the insurance payouts the credit-card bills didn't fill her with dread. In fact, ironically, she could now spend more money than she had ever had in her life. In any other circumstance she would have been happy as a pig in the proverbial, but now even the allure of a guilt-free Lulu Guinness purchase failed to lift her spirits. In so many ways, it felt as if her life was meaningless. Apart from the children there was no one who wanted anything from her. She sighed as she sorted through the post, stopping at the handwritten note in a floral envelope.

Caitlin's handwriting was as recognisable as her own. She took a deep breath and tore it open, wondering if it could offer some sort of explanation for her off-the-wall behaviour lately.

Trying to focus on the words written in front of her Niamh started to feel very, very angry. How dare she? How fecking dare she?

Lifting the phone she furiously tapped in Robyn's number, her anger rising with each second. She walked into the kitchen, away from the children so they wouldn't hear her tirade of expletives.

"The cheeky fecking bitch wants me to stay out of her life," Niamh said as she heard Robyn lift the receiver. "She hasn't spoken to me in three months and then I get a fecking card to say she wishes me well but she wants nothing more to do with me! No explanation − just a fecking card with a fecking flower on the fecking front saying she wishes me well. What the hell is that supposed to mean? Wishes me well? She can stick her fecking good wishes up her fecking arse. In fact, feck that, I'm so annoyed right now she can stick her fucking good wishes up her fucking hole!"

Robyn sighed. Niamh could hear the squeak of her chair as she sat back in thought. That was just so Robyn, Niamh thought. She didn't leap in, all guns blazing, shouting the odds. Maybe that is why Caitlin hadn't taken Robyn off her Christmas-card list just yet, while it was clear that Niamh herself was never going to be invited around for drinks and nibbles again.

"I don't know what is going on with her," said Robyn. "I can talk to her if you want, but I'm not sure it would do any good. She hasn't given me any hints either."

"But why?" Niamh said, cringing at the whingeing tone in her voice – aware she sounded like a spoiled child. To her disgust tears sprang to her eyes. This was all getting to be too much. It was bad enough she had lost Seán – why did it feel like everything else was slipping away from her too, most of all her sanity?

"I'm going to have it out with her. Right now. I'll phone you back."

Niamh was vaguely aware of her friend protesting wildly on the other end of the phone as she hit the end-call button but she didn't care. The red mist had descended and she wasn't going to put up with this any longer. She had done nothing – absolutely nothing – to deserve being treated like a cold snotter by the person she considered her oldest and dearest friend.

That friend should have been making herself available, as Robyn had been doing, to listen to sobbing mad phone calls at all hours of the morning and night. That friend should have worn a track between Derry and Rathinch over the last three months with an endless supply of wine, chocolate and Balsam tissues.

That friend should have been a friend. Full stop.

With her hands shaking, she battered the number into the phone and waited for Caitlin to answer. After four rings it went to answerphone. The same happened when she called her mobile. Damn fecking caller ID. If she hadn't been worried about scaring the life out of the children she would have bundled them in the car, driven at full pelt up the road to Caitlin's riverfront offices and demanded that she explain herself.

The last time they had spoken to each other had been at Seán's funeral. Caitlin had been perfectly turned out as always. Even through her grief, Niamh had felt like Nora Batty, sagging in her mourning clothes beside the perfectly preened and coiffed Caitlin in her Armani suit.

Caitlin had been upset. Niamh could still remember the look of devastation on her face – how she had dabbed at her eyes with a delicate lace hanky while all Niamh had was a crumpled Kleenex which was in danger of disintegrating in her hands.

"I can't believe he is gone," her friend had muttered, air-kissing her, and Niamh had wanted to scream.

She was all for air-kissing – in the right place at the right time. She had attended plenty of parties and business conventions in her day when kissing was de rigueur, but you do not air-kiss your best friend on the day she buries her husband.

She picked up the phone and dialled another number: the switchboard of the PR firm Caitlin worked in.

"Can I speak to Caitlin O'Kane please?" she asked, drumming her fingers against the worktop viciously.

The receptionist replied politely and patched the call through and again it went to answerphone.

"Hello, Caitlin. It's Niamh here. Niamh Quigley. Remember

me? I just wanted to say, you do not fecking air-kiss your best friend on the day she buries her husband."

She slammed the phone down and poured a glass of water, hands still shaking. She wasn't sure what that had achieved but she at least felt better for it.

9

Liam stood in the bathroom of his offices at the builder's yard and looked in the mirror. He noticed the slight spread of his stomach and vowed to get back to the gym when he could. Just because Laura had left there was no need for him to let himself go. And the better he looked, the more she might want him back. Sure, hadn't she found him the sexiest man in Rathinch at one stage?

The night before had been strange. Despite his misgivings he had wanted to feel comfortable and when Detta had talked about healing their hurt he had felt a moment of hope – the first that he had felt in a long time. But then the girls – sorry, women – had started talking and had stopped just short of stating that "All men are bastards."

Liam knew he wasn't a bastard. He wasn't perfect – he was man enough to admit that, but he hadn't made life unbearable for Laura. They had been happy. Yes, she was younger than him and he had spent a lot of their time together wondering why she had chosen him. Greying round the temples, he had the look of a rather weather-worn George Clooney about him – Clooney without the Hollywood sheen. Laura had often told him she loved how he looked, his physical strength, his burly stature, but that, he conceded, had been a long time ago. Laura hadn't been happy in a while. She had lost her sparkle and Liam hated that he hadn't acted on that when he noticed her light dimming, but he had been too busy at work – trying to make her happy by bringing home a decent wage. And when, after a while, she started smiling again he was too caught up in how well his business was doing to think that it could be down to anything other than his success and the mountains of new clothes and handbags in her wardrobe. Until the day she left, and that was the same day Liam promised he would do anything he could to get her back.

After all, he hadn't done anything wrong. It had been "one of those things" – a falling out of love on her part. He certainly hadn't fallen out of love with her. Still, unless he gave up building houses and extensions in favour of counting money in the bank and wearing pastel-coloured pullovers which accentuated his professionally whitened teeth, he figured he had feck all chance of getting her back.

She'd made that clear on one of the many occasions they had met – her with the intention of making arrangements for Poppy – him with the intention of doing everything in his power to get her back.

On the first visit, he'd brought her flowers. A bunch of gorgeous wild blooms, fragrant and romantic. They wouldn't look out of place in a Flake ad as the gorgeous model ran through a barley field before collapsing in a chocolate-induced coma.

She had smiled, a little sadly, left them on the table in front of him and arranged to pick Poppy up every Thursday from school for some quality time.

On the second attempt he brought perfume – Chanel No.5, her favourite – and some chocolates. She hadn't smiled. In fact, she had shaken her head and he'd had to fight back the tears.

"Tell me why?" he asked, opening the chocolates himself.

"It just happened," she replied.

As he bit into a caramel crunch, he wondered how affairs just happened. It wasn't like he never had a woman look at him. There had been a series of randy housewives who had practically thrown themselves at his feet – whether it was through lust or the thought of a discount on their loft conversions he didn't know. He always said no. He knew right from wrong. He knew who he loved.

He would have asked her how affairs "just happened" that time but he didn't have the strength.

On the third visit he brought her wedding ring, polished and cleaned at the jeweller's.

"I'll keep it for when Poppy is older," Laura said. "To show her mummy and daddy did love each other once."

"We still could," he said.

"I love James."

His heart caramel-crunched at those words.

He silenced the "but whys" in his head and cursed the day Laura had come home to say she was going to be working on a big legal case up at the bank. She'd been so excited that he couldn't help but be excited too for her. And after she started trailing up the road each day, briefcase swinging from her shoulder, smile on her face, he saw her light up and felt even more in love with her than ever.

Until the day of the note on the worktop.

He would have said he never saw it coming, but in hindsight he probably did. Maybe he should just be happy that she was happy again. Didn't Sting or some other such gobshite sing about that? If you love someone, let them run off with the bank manager and leave you like a cold snotter on your own. It went something like that, anyway.

God, if the fellas in the yard found out about this they

would have a fecking field day. He wouldn't be able to show his face any more. Sighing and breathing in, patting his still relatively flat stomach, he strutted back to his desk and set about making the orders for the new build.

Just then the phone rang and he lifted it, shaking thoughts of Laura and his train-wreck of a life from his head as he tried to put his best professional foot forward.

"Liam Dougherty speaking, what can I do for you this fine morning?" he said jovially, fully aware that clients old and new responded well to his down-to-earth manner.

"Son," Agnes said, "I just wanted to check on you and see if you needed anything. I'm cooking a stew for my lunch and I thought I might drop some over for your tea."

His heart sank in that special way it always sank when he heard his mother's dulcet tones on the phone. "Thanks, Mum, but I'm fine. I'm taking Poppy out for tea tonight. We thought we might go into Letterkenny and grab a pizza or maybe up to Derry for a McDonald's."

"That's not proper food. I'll bring dinner over and then at least that wee pet will have one good meal in her today," Agnes sniffed.

Liam felt his blood pressure rise. "Mum, we're fine. She's having a good lunch at school and then I promised her a special treat tonight. Maybe we'll come over tomorrow for dinner? Would that be okay?"

"No, no, that won't do," she tutted. "I'll come over to you and that way I can get stuck into the cleaning and the washing."

"Mum, there is no need. I'm on top of it, and besides I'm thinking of getting a cleaner in to make life a little easier." As soon as he said it, he knew he had said the wrong thing. Agnes Dougherty would not tolerate a cleaner in her son's home. Oh, the shame of someone else hoking through his personal belongings when she could be having a good nosy herself!

"Why on earth would you need a cleaner when you have me? Sure I'm free and I can do a better job than any cleaner. God knows I'd do a better job than Laura did – that girl wasn't exactly house-proud, was she? I mean, the cobwebs in your light fittings, it's a wonder Poppy doesn't have asthma and eczema and all those other nasty illnesses. I mean, really, Kim and Aggie would have a field day in your bathroom."

Liam rolled his eyes at the phone. "Mum, you are too old to be cleaning my house. You should be relaxing and enjoying yourself, not running after me and Poppy. We don't want you tiring yourself out. We need you too much."

He hoped his soft-soaping would be enough to put her off but he should have known that his mother would not be deterred so easily. She seemed only too happy to slot into the void that Laura had left and Liam knew it was only a matter of time before she would suggest that she move in and help full-time. She had already expressed her disgust with the fact that Poppy was attending an after-school club.

"Sure she could come down to her granny's and keep me company?" she had said and it had taken a great deal of gentle persuasion before she had dropped the issue. Liam had talked her round by having Poppy visit each Sunday afternoon. He hadn't the heart to tell her that spending any more than three hours watching the *EastEnders Omnibus* with her doting granny would have sent Poppy loopy. The after-school club was much more fun than knitting lessons and recitations of the Rosary every afternoon.

"Look, I'll come over and clean," she insisted. "How about this weekend we set about decluttering? I'll get a few boxes from the supermarket. Maybe we can box up some of madam's stuff and send it on to her and her new man?"

Liam sighed. "Mum, we'll not be decluttering this weekend or any weekend. Now, I'm going to get a cleaner in and then with the extra time I have we'll spend a bit more time together. I don't want to hear any arguing at all."

Agnes hung up with a grunt and Liam's heart sank to his boots.

Fecking women. He sat back in his chair and felt completely emasculated. Between his mother, his wife and that floaty-skirted hippy Detta O'Neill he was pretty bloody sure he was in real danger of turning into a fecking woman one of these days.

10

It was Monday morning and Niamh was standing apprehensively outside the door of Seán's law firm. She hadn't been back since he died. She had spoken to Kevin, his partner in the law firm a few times, and of course he and the rest of the staff had come to the funeral and sent a massive display of flowers – despite the fact she had asked for family flowers only. But then, she guessed, Seán had spent more time at the office than he had at home. And the law firm liked to keep up appearances.

She didn't resent his devotion to his work while he was alive, because when he was home he dedicated every second to her and the children, revelling in the role of perfect husband and father, but now that he was gone she couldn't help but think of all the times he could have been with her.

If she had known what was going to happen, she would have spent more time drinking him in – remembering the feel of his hands, the softness of his lips, the strength in his body, the feeling of him inside her. But, she thought, wiping a tear away and locking the car, she wasn't ever going to feel him inside her again.

She had made an extra effort that morning, washing her hair, blow-drying it and using her straighteners. She had dressed to impress – in one of the designer suits Seán had bought her when she was still working for him – and had used more than just some loose powder for make-up. Her eye-liner had felt alien in her hand as she slicked it on while Rachel sat on the edge of the big sleigh bed, mesmerised by her mother's transformation.

"You look pretty, Mummy," she'd said and she ran to wrap her chubby arms around Niamh's neck and kiss her cheek.

"And so do you, princess," Niamh had smiled back "Now are you both ready to go and see Granny? She's told me she's going to bake buns this afternoon and she needs two very special helpers."

"But, Mummy," Rachel said, her eyes wide and her expression serious, "baking is for girls. Connor is no good. He always wants to eat the mix before we put it in the bun cases and then he cries when we don't let him."

"Now, Rachel, you have to be patient with your brother and let him learn so he can help."

"S'not fair," Rachel huffed, crossing her arms defiantly.

She had been used to getting her granny to herself – Connor always went to Daddy's office instead but Niamh didn't think for one second it would be appropriate to take him in there now and have everyone stare at him like he was a little boy lost.

Niamh resisted the urge to snap back that life wasn't fair. Her daughter was only three for God's sake and her life had been turned upside down too and Niamh knew she was getting off easy if the only thing causing her daughter upset was having to share licking a bowl when making buns with her favourite granny.

Now Niamh straightened her skirt and walked to the law firm door. She felt odd buzzing the door to be let in – like she was visiting a house she no longer lived in, in a place where she no longer fitted.

Kevin wore a suitably sombre expression as he hugged her. Despite the seriousness of the situation. Niamh had to force back the urge to laugh. His face looked almost constipated with the effort of dealing with her.

"It's good to see you, Niamh," he said, inviting her to sit down at the boardroom table.

He buzzed through to reception for coffee to be brought in and they exchanged some meaningless chat about the weather and the traffic while waiting for it.

"How have you been anyway?" he asked then, dunking a Rich Tea into his coffee, lifting the soggy biscuit to his mouth and slurping it – as if he didn't have a care in the world.

For a split second, she fantasised that he would choke on his biscuit and she could stand above him and say, "Pretty shit actually, how about you?" as he breathed his last.

Niamh had learned pretty damn quickly that very few people actually expected or wanted you to answer this question truthfully. They didn't want to hear how there were days when you actually wanted to crawl out of your body to escape the feeling of dread.

"Fine, things are fine. You know, getting better."

"It will be tough for a while yet," Kevin said, imparting the words as if they were new to Niamh and as if she should be grateful for him sharing that information with her. He always was a cocky, annoying bastard.

"Yes," she said, "it will."

"And I suppose today won't be easy, will it?"

If stating the obvious was an Olympic sport, Kevin would no doubt be a gold-medal winner.

"No, it won't," Niamh said, "but it has to be done."

"I don't like putting you under pressure, but life has to go on. It is what Seán would have wanted."

Niamh was pretty sure, however, that if you had sat Seán

down and asked him what he would have wanted, his answer would not have been to be dead, buried and have his wife and former business partner about to pack up his office into boxes so that someone new could start working in his precious company, making all his money and schmoozing with all his clients. Nope, Seán really, really would have hated all this.

"And you know, he would have wanted the business to go on. He would have been delighted with the new man we've hired. He's young, full of enthusiasm. We're totally on the same wavelength as to where we want the practice to go. You know, Seán left some pretty big shoes to fill but the new guy should do a good job."

Niamh wondered why Kevin was telling her this. She wondered why on earth he thought for even one second she would care to hear about the young man who would be slipping into her husband's shoes and sitting on his chair in his office talking to his clients. She wondered why she didn't just tell Kevin to fuck off, but then what would be the point? He would always be an asshole. Plenty had told him to fuck off before now and plenty would in the future and he would remain blissfully unaware of just what a prick he was. Yes, watching him choke on a soggy Rich Tea would really, really make her happy about now.

Niamh just nodded. "We should really get started," she said, her heart heavy.

Seán's office was just as he had left it – down to the moulding teacup on the desk. Someone could have at least tidied that, Niamh thought before wrapping her hand around it trying to feel some hint of him.

She sat down at his desk and looked at the piles of paperwork in front of her. Doodles on dusty paper. The only things which had been moved were his open court files – couldn't have the firm losing business now, could they? She saw the picture of her with the twins when they were less than twenty-four hours old, smiling at her from his desk and she felt her heart swell with love for her gorgeous Seán. Touching it gently, she consoled herself that this would have been one of the last things he saw before he got into his car on that fateful night.

Kevin bustled back in, handing her boxes to store away her husband's possessions. "I can help, if you want," he offered, not catching her gaze, and when Niamh said it was fine, that she could manage on her own, he looked distinctly relieved.

A coward as well as a complete eejit, it seemed.

When the door closed she opened the drawers and started shuffling through the paperwork – the salt sachets from the sandwich bar across the street and the piles and piles of letters and Post-it notes.

She should sort them all meticulously, but her heart wasn't in it. She just piled the boxes high and decided she would look at them another day – just as she would sort through his clothes another day and pack away all traces of his life. She would do it in the comfort of her own home, not in the coldness of this office where she was now convinced all the secretaries were standing with glasses against the door dying to hear her break down and sob.

Seán had loved this place. Niamh used to joke that he loved it more than he loved her and of course he would smile and say it just wasn't possible. She was his best girl and sure didn't he just work hard so he could take her away from all of "this"?

Piling yet more paperwork along with family photos into a sturdy cardboard box on the table, and dusting down the desk – the desk she had once made love to Seán on top of – she sighed.

It has to be a lie, she thought to herself, that it ever gets easier. It never will.

When the boot of her silver Mercedes was filled with boxes, she walked across the street to the Sandwich Company where Robyn was waiting to share a coffee with her.

"Was it awful?" her friend asked, standing up to kiss her on the cheek.

Niamh nodded, flopping into the seat and staring at a broken nail which was annoying the hell out of her.

"It was weird that he wasn't there. I felt like I was letting him down – packing up his life like that."

Robyn nodded, reaching across the table and rubbing Niamh's hand. "I'll get us some coffee and you can off-load as much as you want over some carrot cake."

Niamh nodded and sat up, rubbed her eyes and set about reading the paper while Robyn fought her way to the top of the queue for two large cappuccinos and some fine carrot cake with healthy dollops of fresh cream. She figured that she deserved it, as did her friend.

Niamh and Seán used to come to this cafe every day for lunch. It wasn't the most romantic of spots, but they would chat about life in and outside of the office and make plans for the "great escape" to Donegal.

"What more could you ask for?" Seán had asked, smiling as he stole the last of her chocolate cake.

"Hey, Mister," Niamh had teased, "I'm a pregnant woman – bearing the fruit of your loins – could you leave my bloody cake alone!"

"What's mine is yours, and yours is mine," he teased, reaching back for a second bite – and narrowly avoiding the stab of her fork. He never realised that getting between a hormonal woman and her chocolate cake was never going to be a good idea.

They had walked back to the office hand in hand, her

stomach round and heavy and she remembered feeling so very excited about everything that was still to come.

"There's nothing that can't be made better with carrot cake," Robyn muttered as she sat back down.

Niamh looked at her friend – well, it was more of a glare really – and Robyn quickly apologised.

"No, no, I'm sorry," Niamh stuttered. "It's been a tough day and I know you didn't mean any harm, and if I'm honest carrot cake does make things marginally easier to take."

"Atta girl!" Robyn smiled, sitting back and breathing out. "So what now? Straight to the dump or recycling depot? Or should we just hit the shops for a bit? You could do with some new clothes to perk you up."

Niamh felt her clothes loose around her frame – stress having made weight drop off her – and smiled. "I think the shops would be good. I can pick up something for the twins as well."

"But we must make sure to be back at the dump before four unless you want to be hauling all that rubbish out to Rathinch with you."

Niamh blushed. She knew Robyn would be disappointed in her. "Actually I've not finished sorting through it all yet," she said.

"Have you even started?" Robyn asked softly.

"Well, it's in boxes," Niamh answered. "And I threw out the old packets of salt and the cup where a new breed of penicillin was growing. I'd like to think of that as a start."

"You know you have to do it some day so I won't go over my notes to you, but if you need help, you know where I am."

"Yes, thanks, Robyn. You are a superstar."

"Of course I am," said Robyn, sipping from her coffee cup. "How about we give it a wee go this weekend?"

"I thought you said you weren't going to go over your notes?"

"I'm not," Robyn said with a smile. "But a gentle nudge won't hurt. It's most likely there is little important there and you don't need business papers and old letters cluttering up your house. It will play havoc with your feng shui. Wouldn't it be nicer to get to the things you really want? The things that remind you of Seán more than a pile of rubbish does?"

Niamh had to admit her friend had a point and, as she sipped her own coffee and took a huge bite of carrot cake to make her feel better, she found herself agreeing with Robyn that this weekend she would start to sort out her husband's belongings.

11

On Tuesday Ruth was sorting through the prescriptions Dr Donnelly had left out for collecting when she saw James walk through the door.

Arse, she thought. This was the last thing she needed – so far her day had been going well. She hadn't found any extra grey hairs or found her favourite bra had popped its wire in the machine. She had even felt a little teeny tiny bit chipper as she walked to work that morning, telling herself she was a strong and confident woman who could do this single parent malarkey with no problem. "Wee buns," she had said aloud as she pushed her way through the door into the surgery.

But now it felt different. James had that effect. He made wee buns feel like big fecking insurmountable mountains. Her heart thumping, she found she had to put her hand to the desk to steady herself before she spoke to him. She didn't actually think people ever did that – steadied themselves. She had seen people walk out of the doctor's office, weeping and wailing at whatever news had been imparted to them, but not many had steadied themselves, so physically shaken they could barely stand.

It had been three weeks since she'd seen her husband –

since he had called to the house on the pretext of seeing the children but had actually only wanted a good look around to see what she was getting up to.

He didn't want her – he had made that clear in the harshest and most painful of terms. But he did not want anyone else to have her either. And he didn't want to think for even one second that his influence was gone entirely from his marital home.

He had shared three short, stilted conversations with his children before collecting yet more of his belongings and bundling them into the car. He had barely spoken to Ruth except to ask her if she knew where his cufflinks were. He had a dinner, you see, with Laura and her friends and he wanted to look his best. He had smiled when he asked her.

"Can I help you?" Ruth said now, finding her voice.

James sniffed and moved closer to the receptionist's desk, while the few patients still milling about that late afternoon strained to hear what was going on. He leant over the desk and tried to get a look at the confidential records his wife was working with.

She pulled them away and took a deep breath before meeting his gaze.

"I wanted to talk to you about taking the kids away over Hallowe'en," James said.

"I'm at work, James," Ruth answered with a calmness she hoped didn't betray the growing sense of panic she was feeling.

"Yes, well, I was at work too but I was passing and thought I'd call in. I'll pick them up on the Friday and drop them back on Sunday."

"We have plans," Ruth said, almost in a whisper. "They want to go up to Derry to the carnival and I promised I would take them."

James took a deep breath, and then as if he was talking to a three-year-old he rolled his eyes and spoke slowly. "I will pick the children up on the Friday and return them on the Sunday. Laura has it all arranged."

And he turned and walked away.

Ruth knew she should have told him where to go. She should have been honest with him and told him the kids wouldn't want to go away with him and Laura. She should have told him there was no way Laura – a woman who had left her gorgeous little girl – was ever going to tuck her precious Matthew into bed. She should, she thought, have given him the finger or kneed him in the balls, but she didn't and as Mrs Quinn walked up to collect her script Ruth bit back tears and felt as if she had let him win again.

"No man's worth crying over, dear," Mrs Quinn said, "and the one who is won't make you cry."

"I'll take your word for it. Now here you go. The doctor has asked you to come back to see her before re-ordering again."

* * *

As predicted there was all holy hell when she broke the news about the Hallowe'en trip. She told the children as they ate their tea and watched as one by one their faces fell. She felt as if she'd just bought them a puppy and given it a good kick for their viewing pleasure.

"But, Mammy, I wanted to go Derry and see the fireworks! Sam from my class saw them last year and said they are brilliant," Matthew pouted.

"Well, I don't care what *he* wants," Eimear spat. "There is no way I'm going on holiday with him and *her*."

Thomas didn't say much at all, and perhaps that worried Ruth more than anything. He rarely talked about his father's departure – in fact he had become quite withdrawn since

James had left and when he looked at her, with that sadness in his eyes, she could weep because he reminded her so much of her own reflection.

When she left them at home to walk to the community centre, everyone was in rubbish form. Eimear had tried the hysterical-crying-till-she-almost-puked route. She had always been remarkably good at that but, unfortunately for her, Ruth was well used to ignoring this particular tactic. Matthew had opted for the altogether more manipulative baby of the family/puppy-dog-eyes combo. Thomas had just pounded up the stairs and put on some interminable racket which was allegedly music. Ruth had slapped on some foundation – powdering over the cracks – and headed out the door, stopping just short of slamming it behind her.

She thundered into the community centre, trying to smile at Niamh though truthfully it was more of a grimace than anything resembling a friendly greeting. She was angry at James but angrier at herself for allowing him to control her.

She should have said no when he came to the health centre – and she definitely should have said no when she saw the reaction from her children, but instead she had smiled and told them it would be fine and that they would have a nice time with their daddy. Ruth slammed her handbag onto the desk and sat down defeated.

"Tough day?" Niamh asked softly.

"Something like that," Ruth said, taking a deep breath to calm her breathing.

"There's a kettle in the kitchen. I'll make us a cuppa while we are waiting for the others – I think we're a bit early."

Ruth looked at the clock: it was just ten to seven. At least her rage would do wonders for her figure, she thought wryly. Although she'd left at her usual time, she had made it down to the community centre in record time.

"That would be grand," she said, smiling as Niamh made for the kitchen. "The sugar is kept in the press below the sink," she called, "in case you need it."

"Naw, I'm sweet enough," Niamh called back, popping her head around the door. Ruth stood up and walked to the kitchen, leaning against the door frame for a chat. "Sorry for the dramatic entrance. I've had a rubbish day with my ex. Sometimes I wish he would just drop –"

She stopped herself before she said it, but noticed Niamh's expression change just that little and instantly wished the ground would open and swallow her up. Sometimes she swore she had been born with her foot in her mouth.

"God, I'm sorry. Me and my big gob. I'm such a stupid cow."

Niamh paused and reached out to Ruth, touching her arm. "Don't worry about it. I had plenty of days when I'd have gladly wished Seán off the planet too. I know you don't really mean it."

Ruth smiled back, and just stopped herself from saying "Oh yes, I do," in a pantomime style.

When the kettle was boiled and the tea brewed the two returned to the main hall where Ciara was just arriving, soaked from a fresh shower of rain.

"Jesus H Christ," she muttered, pulling her denim jacket off and slipping it on the radiator. "It's pishing down out there."

Ruth sat back and resisted the urge to tell the young girl she should get herself a proper coat for the winter. She had to remind herself that she was not talking to Eimear and even though there was little difference in the two girls' ages, Ciara had a lot more on her plate than her daughter did. Eimear wouldn't have a notion if she was presented with a baby, a dirty nappy and a box of wipes.

"The kettle's boiled," Niamh said. "Grab yourself a cuppa and get some warmth into you."

"I'm grand," Ciara said. "I'll get a can from the vending machine. I'm not a hot-drink person."

Detta arrived next, not swearing but clearly not impressed with the rain either. "God, it's a bad night. We'd better not sit too long in case it gets much worse."

Ruth noticed Niamh shiver and knew it wasn't from the cold. If she remembered correctly it had been teeming down the night Seán's car had gone off the road. Change the subject, she told herself, while trying to think of something to say which wouldn't make Niamh think of her dead husband.

"I wonder if Liam will make it tonight," she said.

Detta sat down. "I hope we didn't scare him off – poor creature, stuck with all us women yapping on. He must have felt a little odd."

"We're all in this together though, aren't we?" Ciara said. "I hope he does come back. He looks like a nice man. He definitely didn't deserve what that wife of his did to him."

Ruth felt herself blush. She chided herself. Why did she feel responsible for Liam's misery as well as her own just because it was her husband that Laura had chosen to run off with? It was ridiculous that she tied herself up in knots like this all the time.

"No, he didn't and nor did I," she said, trying to keep the childish tone out of her voice. "And now that fecking pig of a husband of mine has gone and made things so much worse."

"How do you mean?" Liam asked, walking through the door and looking alarmed at news of any developments with Ruth's ex-husband and, by association, his wife.

Aw fuck, Ruth thought. This was not going well at all, was it? Perhaps she would have been better off taking her chances back at home with her three children – hear no evil, see no evil and pure huffy teenage-girl evil.

* * *

It had been bad enough when Agnes showed up at half past six while Liam was sitting down to a plate of stew and ushered him out the door. He had hoped to give the group tonight a miss and watch the football instead, but Agnes was most insistent. He was to go and talk to that "lovely Detta O'Neill woman" and leave her to have some "quality time with her granddaughter" – which he knew was code for "nosy around the house to her heart's content".

And now, after getting a soaking just by walking from the car park to the hall, he had to listen to the women of the group gossiping about his wife and her latest carry-on.

Liam's heart had sunk as he walked into the hall and heard Ruth say things had just become worse for her. He had been hoping Ruth might say things had improved for her – that perhaps James was making noises that it had all been a huge mistake and he dearly wanted back into the family fold.

When he should have been shouting orders to his project manager on the site that afternoon he had been imagining a scene where Laura walked back into his – their – house and told him it had all been a horrible, horrible mistake. He would, of course, fold his arms around her and tell her that she was welcome home and that she had been missed. And then he would take her upstairs and shag her senseless. There was no doubt he was missing the intimacy he once shared with his wife.

He sat down on the plastic seat in the community centre, gratefully accepting the cup of tea Detta put in front of him, and as Ruth explained how James was planning to take Laura and his children away for the Hallowe'en break he felt sick.

There was no good outcome to this, he thought. If they were planning on taking Poppy with them – which had not even been mentioned – he would have to cope with his daughter playing second, third and fourth fiddle to James's kids. And if they weren't taking Poppy with them – well, that just might break his precious daughter's heart.

"I'm sorry," Ruth said, "I assumed they would have told you. James could barely hide the glee from his voice when he spoke to me earlier."

"No, no," Liam answered, shaking his head, "they haven't told me anything." It was embarrassing really, to be the last to know.

Looking downwards he tried to find his composure. Jesus Christ, he couldn't cry – not here, in front of the women. They would all think he was some kind of freak.

Taking a deep breath, he sat up straight in his seat. He had to change the subject and fast. He had to retain his cool and calm exterior. He was a man. A dude. An alpha male. He took a bite of a chocolate Hobnob and said: "Right, Detta, what's on the agenda for tonight?"

Detta appeared to take a deep breath and give him an odd sort of a look before she started talking. Liam couldn't help but wonder if she was wondering what she had let herself in for. He knew she hadn't long returned to Rathinch after spending the last ten or more years in the big smoke of Dublin. While the capital city had more than its fair share of junkies and crackheads, the madness levels of this delightful village was just that one step beyond.

"Well," Detta said, "I thought tonight we could write some letters to ourselves."

Liam snorted. He didn't know if he had it in him to write again and this was all just feeling a little bit too much like new-age mumbo jumbo and if there was something Donegal men didn't do, it was new-age mumbo jumbo.

"Now, now," Detta said, seeing his grimace, "it will be fun, honest to goodness. Well, maybe not fun – but you might find it useful."

Liam wondered just how helpful it would be. He also wondered if she would make them tear the feckers up again, because if so there was a good chance he could get away with a couple of wee doodles instead of pouring his heart out. It might not be in the spirit of the group, but it still held a certain appeal.

Detta stood in front of them, handing out the requisite spiral notebooks and blue biros, and began to chat.

"Can we all try this exercise," she began, her voice suddenly more mellow, "Write yourself a letter. Imagine it is a year from now. What would you have hoped to have achieved? Do you think you will feel stronger? That your children will be doing okay? Do you want romance?"

All four snorted at the thought of romance and Liam found himself laughing – a deep belly laugh and as the others joined in he relaxed. Okay, he'd rather be down the pub supping a pint of Guinness but this wasn't the worst thing he could be doing. At least they were all, one way or another, in the same boat as him.

"You never know what the future holds," Detta chided.

"Oh yes, I do. As long as I live I'm never going near another man again," Ruth said.

"I'd rather turn gay," Ciara chimed in with a look of disgust on her face.

Although he was shocked to see one so young talk so openly, Liam could not help but smile. He didn't want new romance either – he wanted Laura back and if he had his way it would happen.

Detta looked at them pleadingly. "Just give it a go, please," she said, before walking to the corner of the room and putting some god-awful panpipe music on the small CD player she had brought with her and lighting an incense stick. The smell mingled with the scent of the musty floors and the damp coats, and Liam wondered if Detta had taken her share of drugs while in Dublin.

But damn it, there must have been something in the incense because despite his reservations Liam soon found himself pouring his feelings out on to paper. Seems that once he stopped doodling and started writing, it was hard to stop.

It wasn't hard for him to lose himself in imagining where he wanted to be this time next year. It was the same place he had been for the last twelve years until James Byrne had stolen his wife out from under his very nose.

He resisted making the letter a list of his own shortcomings – all the things he knew he had done which had pushed Laura away. Instead he wrote a love letter – one he knew he should have written for Laura last year, or every year, or every day for that matter so that she never, even for one second, felt undervalued.

"So what do we do when we're done then?" he asked. "Is this something else for us to tear up?"

"No," Detta said. "No, we're keeping these. Or at least I'm keeping these."

Liam felt sick. He was happy to pour his heart out when he thought no one else – except perhaps for Laura – would read it, but Jesus here was Detta O'Neill saying she was going to take his innermost thoughts and keep them. She would probably read them before she went to sleep, give herself a damn good laugh at how sad he was.

He realised he must have been looking as outwardly horrified as he felt inside as Detta quickly reassured him that his letter would be held in the strictest confidence.

"Don't worry. I have four envelopes here. I want you all to put yout letter in an envelope and then address it to yourself. I'm going to lodge them in a safety-deposit box in a bank in Letterkenny and then in one year's time we are going to get the letters out and have a read. It's my sincere hope that when we look at the letters you will have the happiness you want, even if it won't be what you think it is right now."

Liam snorted, and shifted in his seat. How could Detta, or anyone in this room, know what he wanted? He knew full well that she could put those bloody letters in the safe-deposit box for a week, a year or ten years – but how he felt about Laura, what he wanted to make him happy was never, ever going to change.

And as he looked around the room he wondered would any of them get the things they wanted to make them happy. Ciara – she was so young and yet had such responsibility on her shoulders while Ruth looked much older than her age. He wondered how she managed with her three kids. As for Niamh, how would she ever get over her loss?

* * *

All in all, it had been a shit day. He felt bereft as he left the community centre that evening – an emptiness so deep that he just wanted to pack it away and never feel anything again if it meant that he wouldn't feel as bad as he did right now.

The rain was still falling, lashing down, and he saw Ciara, her denim coat wrapped tight around her body, make a dash up the street. Rolling down the window of his car, he pulled up alongside her, not sure if his actions would earn him the reputation in Rathinch of being a pervy old man.

"I'll give you a lift if you want," he offered.

Blinking rain from her eyes, Ciara nodded gratefully and got into the car.

"Thanks, Mr Dougherty," she said, pulling the seatbelt around her.

"Liam. Please call me Liam. I know I'm old enough to be your father, but there's no need to stand on formality. Jesus, sure we are all crackpots together, aren't we?"

Ciara nodded, pulling her dark hair back from her face. "It's a strange set-up all right. I'm not sure I enjoyed that letter-writing thing. I mean, God, what chance do I have of getting all the things I need to make me happy in a year? Unless I win the fecking Lotto."

Liam nodded, unsure what to say.

He drove Ciara home and let her off outside her house. A woman he recognised as Lorraine Boyle, Ciara's mother, was hovering by the door, a look of thunder on her face.

As he drove off, he wondered was anyone in this godforsaken shite-hole of a village in danger of being happy any time soon.

12

"What time of the evening do you call this? And what the feck are you doing getting out of some old man's car? Is he the father? Jesus, Ciara, tell me he isn't the father! Is that why his marriage broke down? Oh God, we'll be a laughing stock. Oh Ciara, love, what have you done?"

Lorraine's face looked ashen as she put her hand to her forehead in a "woe is me" pose and sat down on the sofa. Ciara was used to these over-dramatics and in some ways she wished she could tell her mum who Ella's daddy was, but as he refused to accept it, she didn't think there was much of a point.

The truth was, all she had to do was so much as breathe in the same air as any male inhabitant of Rathinch and Lorraine would start secretly planning how to pluck a hair from his head for a sneaky DNA test.

"Mum, Liam – Mr Dougherty – is at the support group too. He just gave me a lift because it was raining. I'm sorry I'm late back, but we all got chatting a little more than we thought and no," she said with a sigh, "he is not Ella's daddy. Has she settled okay?"

Lorraine looked up with an expression Ciara couldn't

quite determine. It might have been relief. It might have been resignation. It might just have been boredom. There were only so many times you could have the same conversation, or so Ciara thought.

Lorraine took a deep breath. "Ella is asleep. She took a full bottle and I changed her nappy. She got her wind up no problem. Was a little gurny going off to sleep but there hasn't been a peep since."

Ciara looked at the baby monitor in the corner for some sort of reassurance that what her mother had said was true and then she offered to go and put the kettle on.

"No, pet, I'm going out, remember? I have to meet one of the girls from work. I shouldn't be too late but could you make sure not to wake me in the morning? I'm planning on letting my hair down and I don't want to be disturbed."

Ciara nodded and Lorraine gave her a peck on the cheek before heading off down the path, looking more than ready for a drink or two. Ciara made a hot chocolate and a couple of slices of toast which she ate while watching a re-run of *Father Ted*.

"This place makes Craggy Island look like fecking Las Vegas," she said aloud before climbing the stairs to her bedroom where Ella was sleeping in her cot, her hair damp with sweat and her cheeks rosy red.

As she got undressed for bed her phone beeped to life.

It was a text from Abby from school – the only one of her old friends to talk to her as if she still had a brain in her head.

"How was the Mad Mammies' meeting?" she wrote.

Ciara smiled and texted back, "Gr8. Not quite lk da clubs, but craic was gd."

"Will I come ovr?" Abby replied.

Ciara thought about it for a moment. It would be nice to have some company, but given that it was now close to nine thirty and Ella would be waking during the night at some stage, all she really wanted to do was fall into bed, watch a bit of telly and drift off.

And although she knew it was unlikely her mum would be home this side of one o'clock, she really didn't want to subject Abby to Lorraine after a few vodkas and Cokes. Her mum was fine most of the time, but with a few drinks in her she would only launch into her unholy ranting about how Ciara had ruined her life by having a baby so young.

"Trd," she replied. "Txt u 2morro. Mayb go 2 Lttrknny on Sat?"

Ciara was due to be paid on Friday. She would have just enough left over after paying for the crèche to treat herself to a new top in Letterkenny – and she would need to go there anyway to buy some new babygros for Ella who seemed to be going through the world's fastest growth spurt.

As she climbed under her duvet she thought of how, just two years ago, she was at school, still relying on her mum for money and able to nip over to Abby's in the evenings and not worry about being too tired for work the next day.

Back then she thought that Ella's dad genuinely cared about her as well. She thought she was in love, and that he too was in love with her. Sighing at the memory she switched off the bedside light, put the telly on low volume and snuggled down to relax.

* * *

She had done her pregnancy test in the toilets in the shopping centre. She had almost died of mortification buying the damn thing – certain that the old biddy behind the counter was thinking all sorts of nasty thoughts about her. She hadn't told anyone that she was going to do a test, not even Abby who knew she'd had sex. She had got the bus to Letterkenny first thing on that Saturday morning on the pretext of picking up a book for the school reading list.

She was grateful that there were no longer any plastic, see-through bags to be had in the shops. The brown, heavy paper bag had hid its contents well, especially when also thrust to the bottom of her handbag. Until, that is she locked herself in the toilet cubicle and began to undo the wrapping.

The noise had seemed magnified and she had wondered whether to just do it fast – like ripping off a plaster and to hell with who heard – or slowly peel the plastic wrapping off. Instead she waited until she heard toilets flushing around her and opened the wrapping bit by bit each time it got noisy.

Inside the box there was a useful, and hilarious, diagram of a girl holding a stick between her legs with a "stream of urine" passing over it. Ciara would have laughed, phoned the girls to tell them about it, even – if it hadn't been so serious and so scary.

I would have to be the unluckiest fecker in Rathinch to be pregnant, she thought to herself as she tried to position herself so that some pee actually went on the stick and not, as she feared, all over her hands.

"It's probably just stress," she uttered under her breath.

She had read that stress could make your period late. Maybe not a full week late, but late all the same.

She peed, getting only the tips of her fingers wet, and then sat staring at the stick and willing it to let her know that she wasn't pregnant.

As one line appeared, followed by another, she realised she didn't know what that meant. With all her faffing about, and smiling at the peeing lady on the box, she hadn't actually read to the end – the crucial pregnant-or-not-pregnant bit.

Two lines she thought that could well be two words: Not Pregnant. Surely one line would mean one word: Pregnant.

It was simple, easy logic. And she breathed a tentative sigh of relief as she reached for the test box and looked at the instructions to confirm what she knew – or at least hoped – in her heart.

* * *

For once she was on time for work. Ella had behaved and allowed Ciara to dress her without screaming blue murder and she had been calm when they reached the crèche, not squealing after her mammy like she so often did. Ciara had therefore arrived in work, in full uniform, a full two minutes early.

"Will wonders never cease?" her craggy-faced boss declared as she set to work pricing a delivery of eggs and milk.

"I'm not that bad. Not all the time," Ciara chided, kneeling down by the fridge.

"No, not all the time. Just most of it," Mrs Quinn said, from her high stool behind the counter – where she would sit all day, doing little but chatting far too much, passing comment on everyone and everything that went on in Rathinch.

"That Detta O'Neill was in earlier. She was asking after you. Wanted to know if you had got home okay last night? Are you going to that wee group she has set up? Lord, I don't know, in my day we just got on with things. We didn't need to sit around and have a group hug if times were tough. Then again, in my day," she said with a sniff "there weren't that many of us running around with babbies at the age of seventeen either."

Ciara took a deep breath, although she feared if she counted as high as necessary to resist the urge to slap the stupid cow, she might just pass out.

Mrs Quinn would have Ciara and the rest of the lone parents burned at the stake on the village green if she could get away with it. She would be only too happy to sit on her high stool while her fellow old biddies gathered round and discussed it for weeks in advance. She might even be tempted to get her old Singer sewing machine out and make some bunting especially for the occasion.

Fecking witch, Ciara thought, *is your coven meeting tonight?*

It was this inner dialogue which got Ciara through the day. Occasionally she would dream that she had the nerve to actually say out loud what she was thinking, but she knew she would have to bide her time. She needed her job – and she really wanted that shopping trip with Abby to Letterkenny at the weekend so there was no way she was going to let rip just yet.

Besides, if Mrs Quinn knew everything – exactly *who* was also a parent but just didn't admit it yet – she would probably choke on the brandy balls she spent her days sucking.

13

Niamh's mother had agreed to take care of the twins on Saturday while her daughter sorted through the reams of paperwork she had collected from Seán's office. She had offered to help, of course, but Niamh had told her it would be more use to her to have the twins out from under her feet.

"Just take them to Wains' World and let them run around until they are knackered. At least they will go to bed for me nice and early, because I'm sure I'll need a glass of wine when I'm done."

"Are you sure, sweetie?" Mary had asked gently. "I can get your dad to take them and then I'll help you with it all."

"No, Mum, it's fine, honest. Robyn is here. But you can stay for dinner if you want. You can help me drink that wine. Stay over if you want."

"Sounds good – especially the part about the wine," Mary replied.

"And you're sure Daddy won't mind?"

"After helping me with the twins all day, he'll be wrecked. He'll enjoy the peace and quiet. A couple of Buds and he'll have an early night."

Niamh smiled, her dad was nothing if not a creature of habit.

Niamh thought back to her childhood, when she would creep down the stairs long after bedtime and hear the strains of his favourite ballads filter through the heavy wooden door. She would sit there for a while, the crack of light taking away any fear she had of the dark and then she would open the door, creep in and sit on her daddy's knee. He never told her to go back to bed. He would just wrap her in his arms, his breath warm and scented with beer, and sing to her gently until her eyes became heavy. She would wake up again in her own bed, blankets curled up on her chin, cosy and warm, and she would feel so very secure and loved.

As Niamh replayed this memory in her head a sob caught in her throat. Rachel would never – could never – experience such a thing with her daddy. It was yet another thing that she had been robbed of – that they all had been robbed of.

The pain of that realisation winded Niamh and she could not even speak to tell her mother how she felt.

"Niamh, darling, are you still there?" Mary asked.

Her daughter fell to the ground sobbing.

Robyn, who had been in the living room, poked her head around the door, saw her friend crying and came and took the phone from her.

"It's going to be a tough day, Mary," she said, her voice breaking, and then she hung up, sat down by Niamh and rocked her gently in her arms until the tears subsided.

* * *

Niamh and Robyn were sitting on the floor of the home office, drinking green tea while they decided which box to open first.

"I know, I know – I'm a stupid oul' bitch sometimes. God, I can't believe I had a meltdown like that."

"It's going to happen, you know," Robyn said. "It's going to hit you at times when you least expect it. I read that it takes a year and a day to accept a loss – you have a lot of first experiences to go through without him, the whole 'this time last year' nonsense."

"If it only was a year and a day," said Niamh, filling up again. "I can't help but think that everything in our lives will be tough – will be a reminder of what we could have had. When the twins start school, when they graduate, when they get married. It's all things they should be doing with a daddy by their side and which I should be doing with Seán there holding my hand."

Robyn set her teacup on the floor and rubbed her friend's hand. "I know, darling. It's just not fair, is it?"

"No, it berluddy well isn't!" Niamh huffed, blowing her fringe from her face. Wiping her tears on the sleeve of her jumper, she steadied herself. "Well, it's not fair and it's completely shite but no amount of crying is going to bring him back, so we might as well just get on with sorting this lot out."

"Atta girl," Robyn soothed and took the lid off the first box.

To be honest it felt strange going through this stuff. Almost irreverent – as if they were doing something they shouldn't.

"Seán would hate it if he knew I was snooping through his things," Niamh said, sorting letters into different piles for filing, shredding and dumping. "He always hated snooping."

Robyn nodded.

"Serves him right though for being a stupid bastard and crashing his fecking car then, doesn't it?" Niamh added with a half smile and Robyn laughed.

"I suppose it does."

"It's not very exciting though, is it? I mean you would think we could find something interesting like a surprise eternity ring he had bought me and never given me, or a winning lottery ticket."

"Nope, only letters, tax information and Post-it notes. God, Seán liked his Post-its, didn't he?"

Niamh smiled, remembering their home office as it was, covered in dozens of little yellow pieces of paper which all fluttered in the draft whenever she opened the door. When she would bring Seán his evening cup of coffee, he would get annoyed when two or more of them fluttered to the ground. Niamh had always teased him, telling him he should really get a better filing system, but he couldn't be swayed.

"Sometimes," she said with a half smile, "I swear he loved those Post-its more than me."

She lifted Seán's diary, a thick black leather-bound affair and flicked through the pages. Seeing his scrawl, the pages divided with yet more little yellow pieces of paper, Niamh felt for a second as if he was with her. He was sitting behind her, his hands massaging her shoulders as he always had done and she closed her eyes and breathed in the echo of him. Robyn was sorting through more paperwork, oblivious to her friend's thoughts.

"Hey, gorgeous," Seán said, kissing her neck.

She leaned back into him, feeling the warmth of his breath on her shoulder – smelling his aftershave.

"I've missed you," she muttered.

"I know," he replied. "But I'm here, you know. I'm always here."

Blinking herself back to reality, she traced his handwritten words, the very proof that he had lived. She wished he really was there, behind her, his arms wrapped around her. Turning the pages she reached May 19 – their wedding anniversary. He had written in their booking for Harry's, and below was the number for the florist he always used. Niamh smiled at his predictable nature. He never deviated from the plan. It wasn't in his nature.

She flicked forward to July 17, her birthday. Again there was a booking for Harry's written in and a reminder to call the florist. Below it Caitlin's number was written and Niamh realised that her ex-best friend, who of course had still been her best friend at that time, must have had some hand in choosing the charm bracelet he had bought for her. Instinctively her hand reached down to the sterling silver links around her wrist, the solid heart and small handbag. He had promised to add to the charms with every birthday, Christmas and anniversary that passed.

She flicked on. August 23. The day he died. A few appointments were scrawled in, phone numbers, figures, reminders of what to do the next day. He couldn't have known he wouldn't be there after that.

Turning the pages on, she saw another Post-it and a familiar handwriting – one she knew as well as her own – stating in big letters that she couldn't wait for that weekend.

That weekend.

The weekend Seán was supposed to be in Dublin on business.

Supposed to be.

Niamh felt the bile rise in her stomach and, while Robyn ran to help, she found herself heaving her guts up over the pristine white toilet in their pristine en suite in their pristine house.

14

This was bliss, Ciara thought as she handed over her change to the surly-faced bus driver and climbed on board, headed for her meeting with Abby in Letterkenny. For once she didn't have to try and haul a buggy with her or sling an oversized changing bag over her shoulder. Instead she had the smallest of small bags – one which only had enough room for her mobile phone, purse and a very non-baby-friendly lip-gloss.

Lorraine had been in a good mood that morning and had offered to look after Ella not only while Ciara went into town, but also while she got herself ready.

As she straightened her hair, pop music blasting from her stereo, Ciara almost didn't know herself. She was able to wear her long, dark hair how she used to love it – straightened and round her face as opposed to pulled back in a scrunchy to save her from getting it pulled from her head. She had even pulled on a nice top and her best jeans, and left her boring old flat, buggy-friendly shoes on the floor in favour of her nicest heeled boots.

Looking in the mirror, she knew her tummy still sagged that little bit but, ignoring that, she felt she looked good. No one would necessarily know she was a seventeen-year-old mum of one. She looked and felt for that day like every other seventeen-year-old heading out shopping on a Saturday afternoon. The only difference was that she would be bringing nappies and vests home for her baby, but no one in Letterkenny need know that. The shop assistants could just think she was doing a favour for her mother or something.

No, today was going to be Ciara's day and as she sat back on the bus and slipped the earphones from her ipod into her ears, she breathed out, determined to enjoy herself. She could barely remember the last time she had gone into town sans daughter. It probably wasn't all that long after she did that fecking pregnancy test in the shopping-centre loos.

Abby's face had been a picture when Ciara broke the news. In fairness it was fairly obvious to anyone that something was very, very wrong as soon as Ciara stepped out of the loos. Instead of heading into yet more shops to try on yet more impossibly tight tops she had insisted they go for a sit-down and a drink. She was aware she was sweating profusely and she felt sick. She didn't know if that was the shock or the morning sickness, or just the thought of breaking the news to her mother. She felt as if she might just faint.

"Are you okay?" Abby had asked as Ciara sipped gingerly from a glass of water, shunning her usual Diet Coke.

"Oh fuck, Abby. I'm fucked. I mean really fucked. F.U.C.K.E.D. Fucked."

"Fucked?"

"Fucked."

Abby looked worried and sat back in her chair, regarding her friend for a moment before sitting forward again. "When you say fucked, what exactly do you mean?"

"I mean that in every sense of the word, my life is now fucked. Oh Abby, what am I going to do?"

Abby just looked baffled and it took a while for it to dawn on Ciara that she hadn't told her friend she was pregnant. The only words running through her head for the last ten minutes had been "I'm pregnant", but thinking them and saying them out loud were two very different things and for some reason her mouth could not articulate what her brain was thinking.

"Oh Abby. Jesus. I'm dead. Mum is going to kill me. Ben is going to kill me. *I* might as well just kill me."

"You're scaring me now," Abby said, face growing serious. "What is it, Ciara? We can get through it."

"Pregnant," Ciara blurted. "I'm pregnant."

"Fuck!"

"Exactly."

Ciara smiled as she recalled that experience – not because it was particularly pleasant but because she at least knew for a fact there would be no repeat of such drama this time around. This was going to be pure teenage fun, without so much swearing, nausea and tears.

The journey flew by and Ciara could barely hide the grin from her face as she stepped off the bus and walked to the place she had planned to meet up with Abby. It did feel a little odd not to have a buggy in front of her but she just held on tighter to her impossibly small bag and gave her head a shake now and then to show off her glossy hair.

Abby was uncharacteristically on time and let out a squeal of delight on seeing her friend. Despite feeling a little past the squealing with delight stage – a sixteen-hour labour dampening her desire to squeal ever again – Ciara grinned and ran to give her friend a hug.

"It's great to see you. I can't wait to hit the shops."

"How come you didn't bring Ella?" Abby asked, looking behind her friend just on the very bizarre off-chance she had secreted her child somewhere on her person.

"Mum agreed to mind her. Or should I say, Mum offered to mind her. I nearly died of shock, but I wasn't arguing. I was just too happy to get out of there for a bit."

"I'd have loved to have seen her," Abby said with a sigh, hooking her arm in her friend's. "But I know you need time out."

"Call in and see us any time after school," Ciara said. "It's not like I've any mad social life to be going on with."

"Not even the Mad Mammies group you go to?"

Ciara looked at her friend and smiled. "We're not mad. We're just all left on the shelf. And we're not all mammies. There is a daddy there too."

"Is he hot?"

Ciara choked. "It's Liam, Mr Dougherty, from the builder's yard. He's old enough to be my da."

"He would be a very hunky da. My mum thinks he's gorgeous and I bet he has money. He could keep you in fancy bags and shoes for the rest of your life!"

"Could you imagine the scandal in Rathinch?" Ciara laughed. "You know, it would almost be worth it to see the look on Mrs Quinn's face when we sent her the wedding invite."

"But what is it like? Seriously? Is it all huggy-feely? Mrs O'Neill's a bit far out, isn't she? I can't decide whether I think she is really cool or mad in the head."

"She's probably a bit of both," Ciara replied, matter of factly. "But she seems nice enough – a bit funky even – and it's good to have people to talk to who know what it's like."

Immediately she noticed the wounded look on her friend's face. It drove her mad. Abby was a great friend but sometimes she just didn't get it that she would never really understand what it was like to be a seventeen-year-old single mother. The lucky cow was still at school, having a blast and planning to go off to college soon. Ciara could barely even plan an afternoon out at Letterkenny without it turning into a full-scale military operation.

"Abby, don't be like that. Trust me, I'd rather be out with you lot but at least I know with the Mad Mammies, and Daddy, I can talk about nappies and baby poo without shocking them."

"Well, if it gets me off the talk of the exploding nappies, then that's just fine by me," Abby said and peace was once again restored.

The pair giggled as they walked from clothes shop to shoe shop. Ciara didn't even care that she didn't have money in her purse to buy all the things she wanted, she was just enjoying the company. Looking around at all the other little cliques of friends out shopping together she felt very much part of the in-crowd and when Abby suggested they rest their feet in McDonald's she slipped into her seat, delighted for once not to be having to hunt out somewhere to heat a bottle or warm up some disgusting baby goop. Not that Rathinch had much in the line of chic cafes or fast-food spots. There were a few tourist-friendly seafood restaurants which would baulk at the sight of her pulling her screaming baby in through the door in her buggy, and there was the Country Kitchen, which did a great line in scones and gossip. Apart from that there was the chippy which was closed every Tuesday and Thursday and it only served fat chips, not the tasty little fries she loved so much.

Abby carried down a tray laden with food and Ciara set about tearing open salt sachets and dousing her fries in tomato sauce.

"I almost forgot to tell you," Abby said, taking a slug from her Coke. "You should hear the latest scandal about Ben Quinn."

"My Ben Quinn?"

"Yes, shit, sorry, Ciara. Here I am gossiping away about your Ben Quinn. I'm a complete tit. Sorry."

"Abby, just tell me what the scandal is with Ben," Ciara said impatiently, pushing her longed-for fries away from her.

"Well, it's not with him, not really. It's more who's after him now. You'll die when I tell you."

"You'll die if you don't tell me," Ciara said gruffly.

"Eimear Byrne. She's been making the maddest play for him. You wouldn't believe it. Everyone is talking about her and how she has no shame."

"Just like me then," Ciara said, face blushing.

"No, you weren't as bad as that. You thought he loved you."

"I bet Eimear thinks he loves her too. God, her mum will go nuts if she finds out." Ciara was thinking of her new friend Ruth.

"Why would she? She doesn't know what he did. No one does. She'll probably be all delighted. Sure doesn't everyone think the sun shines out of his ass?"

"Oh crap," Ciara said, knowing full well that she might just have to talk to Ruth herself and take some of the shine off Ben Quinn's halo.

15

Niamh and Seán had driven to Rathinch on a sunny day. The sky had been clear apart from a streak of fluffy white cloud and the dappled roads to the quaint village gave Niamh a warm and cosy feeling. It was as if Bord Fáilte had taken the scene right off a postcard and recreated it just for the thick Northerners looking for somewhere to spend their money.

When they arrived and walked down the main street, past all the little coloured houses, Niamh could not help but break into a chorus of "The Coloured House Song" from Balamory.

"I didn't think places like this actually existed any more," she said to Seán. "It's all so quaint and lovely. I swear to Christ I expect to see John Wayne chasing Maureen O'Hara up the street any second shouting for his 'tae'."

Seán laughed, a deep throaty laugh and as he turned to look at her the sunlight glinted off the frame of his glasses and all she could see in the shadow was his wide, bright smile and she felt happy.

"It is a bit twee, isn't it? Like Darby O'Gill's going to run down the road any second. Makes a big difference from rush hour on the Strand Road back in Derry."

"As long as Darby doesn't bring those blasted leprechauns with him. They scare the shit out of me." Niamh shivered and Seán pulled her close.

"Nothing can touch us here, Niamh. This is our dream. Can you imagine how amazing it's going to be? No rush-hour traffic – not for you anyway. Pity me – I'll still be booting up that road every day."

"You don't mind, do you?" Niamh asked, wrapping her arms around his waist and looking him straight in the eyes as they stood in front of the twee coloured houses in the glorious sunshine.

"Of course I don't. I have wanted this all my life. House in the country. Two amazing children. Sexy wife. No one could want more!"

Of course he *had* wanted more. The house in the country wasn't enough. It had to be the best damn house in the country. With a sweeping driveway, sandstone walls and balcony opening off the master bedroom, it was the envy of the village. Seán had wanted it to be like that, and if Niamh was honest she had too. She loved it. She felt all Lady of the Manorish and posh when they moved in. As she had clacked up and down the marble floors in the hall each morning she had thought of just how much they had and just how very perfect it all was.

* * *

Niamh had thought the hardest thing she would ever do was bury her husband. In the days after the Gardaí had knocked on the door – bringing the parish priest with them even though Niamh hadn't set foot in a chapel since the twins' christening – she thought nothing would ever be as difficult as those first days without her beloved Seán.

No words, she thought, could ever hurt her as much

as "I'm terribly sorry, Mrs Quigley, you had better take a seat."

Her heart, she had sworn, would never shatter as much as it did as she broke the news to two confused three-year-olds that Daddy had gone to heaven and wasn't coming back.

She assumed her body could not physically ever ache as much as it did the day the sobs wracked her as she saw her beloved husband's coffin lowered into a cold grave in Rathinch.

"Never assume anything," she remembered her daddy saying. "It makes an ass of u and me!" Then he would laugh, so proud of his joke.

Niamh lay on the bed – staring out of the French doors which led to that shagging balcony. The sun had started to fall and though there was still a trace of light across the sky, it felt as dark as midnight.

After she had thrown up she had stumbled in there and lain herself down. Robyn had followed, her face a picture of concern, and Niamh had handed her the Post-it that she had been clinging on to for dear life.

As realisation dawned across her friend's face, Niamh felt a tear slide down her cheek. She felt her stomach churn, again and again – her mind struggling to take in what she had seen. As her brain told her it couldn't mean what she thought it did – that Seán had been having some sort of affair with her best friend – her heart broke with the realisation that it couldn't mean anything else.

She curled up into a ball, hugging her knees to her and fighting the urge to give up there and then. Her life had been a lie, she realised. Everything about her and Seán and their perfect life had been a pretence. Everything from the top-of-the-range cars in the driveway to the swimming pool in the garden. Who the fuck needed an outdoor swimming pool in Donegal anyway, she raged. It was all one big, fat, ugly lie.

For all she knew he hadn't been working late the night he died. He might have been shagging Caitlin.

The thought that hers weren't the last lips he kissed crushed her and she knew that if he was here, right now, she wouldn't be able to stop herself from slapping him across that face and beating the life out of him.

"If he wasn't already dead, I swear to Jesus I would kill him now," she sobbed.

Robyn knelt down by the bed and took her hand.

"I can't believe it," Robyn said.

"But it explains why Caitlin hasn't been in touch, doesn't it? Oh God, Robyn, how could he do it? How could she do it? They were my life, I don't know . . ." her words trailed off amid a fresh torrent of tears and Robyn simply sat stroking her hair and soothing her as best she could.

When Niamh's mother arrived, with the twins each carrying their Tupperware boxes filled with buns, Robyn had got up and explained gently what had happened. Niamh's mother put the children to bed, telling them Mammy was sick and then she came into the bedroom where her daughter was lying staring out of the window into the black sky.

"Niamh, darling . . ." she started but Niamh didn't turn to look at her. She didn't want anyone to see the humiliation which was etched all over her face. God, what would people think? Seán gave her the perfect life. They had it all and yet she couldn't be the perfect wife to him. She wasn't enough. She would never have the chance to be enough again. He had betrayed her in the most devastating way possible.

"It's okay," her mother whispered, pulling the throw from the bottom of the bed around Niamh's shoulders to stop her shivering.

Niamh tried to find the energy to reply but she couldn't. Her fight was gone, she realised. She had spent the last three months grieving for a man who didn't really exist. She had sat each night cradling his jumpers to her, trying to catch a hint of his smell. She had kept his toothbrush in the mug by the sink, his shoes in the cupboard under the stairs. She had countless imaginary conversations with him where she imagined him as heartbroken as she was at having been separated from her. When things were at their darkest, Niamh had at least consoled herself with the notion that she had been loved so very deeply . . . and now it seemed that she hadn't been loved at all.

So she closed her eyes and drifted off to sleep.

* * *

When Niamh woke she heard her mother and Robyn chattering downstairs. She knew that she should probably get up and go to talk to them. The old Niamh would have put on her pink Timberland boots, marched downstairs, driven to Derry and kicked some serious arse. Robyn and her mother would have been left quaking in her wake as she opened a big old can of whoop-ass on her former best friend. (She always got a little carried away and American when angry.) She had never been one to shy away from a confrontation in the past. Seán had always said he loved her fire. Well, by Christ if he was alive now he would be feeling her fire, right in his cheating knackers.

Niamh drifted back off to sleep and dozed fitfully for a few hours before she realised she was hungry. She pulled her dressing gown around her and padded downstairs into their luxury kitchen. Opening the fridge and taking out a bottle of wine and some ham, she set about making herself a snack.

The gentle hum of conversation was still coming from the living room, so she tried to make as little noise as possible but she should have remembered her mother had ears like a bat.

"Niamh!" her mother called, before walking into the kitchen and flicking on the light.

Of course Niamh realised she must look a sight. Connor had managed to smear Weetabix down her dressing gown that morning and while she had intended to put it in the washing machine she hadn't quite got round to it. Her face was swollen and scourged from crying and her hair was stuck to her cheek on the side where she had been lying.

She was still wearing her jeans and jumper under it all, and yet she was freezing.

"I don't want to talk about it, Mum," she said. "I just want to eat something and have a big fuck-off drink of wine."

"Niamh –" Her mother reached out to her.

"No, Mum," Niamh replied with steely determination. "I really don't want to talk about it. I can't talk about it. I just want to have a drink, and something to eat and to get on with things because, trust me, if I go to pieces now, that's it."

16

Ruth poured herself a glass of cold Chardonnay and reached for the box of Maltesers on the sofa beside her. Flicking on the television and the DVD player, she heard the first strains of "Be My Baby" play and settled down to watch *Dirty Dancing* for the one-hundredth time. If real life was ever getting too much, an hour spent with Patrick Swayze and his snake-like hips would bring her round.

Thomas and Matthew were upstairs, lost in some Wii game or other and, as she hadn't heard any shouting or loud bangs in the last fifteen minutes, Ruth assured herself they must – for once – be playing nicely and she decided to leave them to it.

She took a long, cold gulp of her wine and popped another Malteser in her mouth, curling her feet under her and sliding down into the soft creases of her battered old fabric sofa.

The headache that had been threatening all day was starting to lift, thanks to the two paracetamol she had taken half an hour before – just after Eimear stormed out, slamming the front door so hard that the glass panels rattled. It was a wonder the house was still standing at all these days.

"If you break those, you'll pay for them, young lady!"

Ruth had called to the closed door, but she couldn't bring herself to go after her daughter and challenge her head on about her behaviour. Ruth knew why she was pissed off – there had been no movement on the Hallowe'en plans despite at least four major-league tantrums from Eimear and the breaking of at least three of Ruth's good plates accidentally on purpose.

The day before, at work, Ruth had sent James an email. She couldn't face ringing him, or going to see him and having a scene so she figured the written word was her best bet. It had surprised her how her fingers had hovered nervously over the keys as she typed. She wasn't a confrontational person by nature and it was rarely she would have questioned James. He had been the chief earner while she raised the children, so it was only fair he made the lion's share of decisions about their family, she had reckoned.

She had to think this one through carefully. She didn't want her ex to think she was being a spiteful bitch by turning down a free holiday for the children – it was just that the kids had been through enough upheaval already this year and they had all made it clear that when it came to the Hallowe'en celebrations they would much rather be at home with their mum, piling into her clapped-out Astra and driving to Derry for the fireworks. Then Eimear would go on out with her friends and the boys would come home with Mum, singing spooky songs and telling ghost stories as they drove along the winding roads back to Rathinch.

Instead now she would be in alone, with Patrick Swayze on the telly, feeling wracked with guilt that her children were spending a night with James and his tart. There would be no fireworks – well, not the traditional kind anyway – with James. He still treated the children as if they were pre-schoolers. Matthew went along with it – he worshipped the ground his daddy walked on – but Eimear and Thomas weren't as easily placated.

James,
First of all thanks for offering to take the children away for Hallowe'en. The thing is, the children and I were kind of hoping to spend the evening together. We had made plans already and that doesn't mean we don't appreciate your offer, but we'll have to say no on this occasion.
Ruth

It had struck her that the email was very formal in tone but she didn't want to let one ounce of emotion escape. She didn't want James to know that he had upset her by storming into the doctor's that day because she knew that if he thought such a confrontation annoyed her, he would be likely to do it again and again and again.

That was his way.

She had hit the send button and waited for a response, but James liked to play games and she should have known that his answer wouldn't be immediate. She had jumped every time her email refreshed at work, trembled every time the phone rang, and while she sorted through the prescription she kept one eye on the door – just in case. It's a wonder she didn't end up giving someone the wrong advice, or the wrong prescriptions.

Her answer had come just before Ruth left work for the day. It was one small sentence which put her squarely in her place.

Change of plan. I'll be picking them up at five on Thursday.

That was it and Ruth knew from past experience that James would not be entering into discussion about it again.

She sighed and rubbed her temples. Maybe the headache

wasn't going away after all. Knowing her luck, it was going to turn into a blasted migraine.

Having lost interest in Patrick, Ruth lifted her glass of wine and moved to the kitchen table where she sprawled the large newspaper out in front of her and started to search through the jobs section.

The problem was she didn't have the damned qualifications most of them were looking for. Yes, since Matthew had started school she had been working part-time with Dr Donnelly, but it seemed experience counted for nothing these days and it didn't help that she didn't actually want to leave the doctor's practice where she knew all the patients by first name and some of the regulars just by the sound of their voices on the phone.

"You know James should be giving you child support," Dr Donnelly had offered sensitively that morning over coffee.

Ruth had smiled to hide her blushes. "We get by just fine."

"You can't on the wages I pay you," the doctor had replied. "The children are his. He should be handing over money for them."

"He has promised me a cheque at the end of the month," Ruth lied.

The truth was, since James walked out on them he hadn't offered her a single cent. The two boys needed new shoes but she would have to eek that money out of her Christmas savings – yet he was happy to whisk them away on a luxury weekend with his fancy woman without caring if they had things they actually needed, like food on the table and a roof over their heads.

Dr Donnelly had rolled her eyes. "Don't let him away with it, Ruth. Maybe you could get something drawn up in the courts."

Ruth had nodded and stood up, brushing the biscuit

crumbs from her skirt. "Maybe," she replied in that half-hearted way she usually reserved for the children.

She couldn't imagine James responding kindly to a court summons – in fact she was pretty sure how he would respond and no one would walk away smiling.

Downing her wine, Ruth felt tears sting in her eyes. How had her life become such a mess?

"God grant me the courage to change the things I can, the serenity to accept the things I can't, and the courage to know the difference," she whispered.

* * *

In a perfectly shitty end to the day's proceedings, Eimear didn't come home until just before one. Ruth had been pacing up and down the living room, and had even gone for a walk along the shorefront just to make sure her sixteen-year-old wasn't lying dead in a ditch.

With no signs of Eimear, she had returned home, her head spinning a little from the fresh night air and the half bottle of wine she had downed.

Her worry was mixed with anger – that her daughter could have such a blatant disregard for her and her rules. But when Eimear walked in, Ruth found herself throwing herself at her, tears pouring down her face.

"Thank God you're okay! Where the hell have you been?"

Eimear looked at her mother, glassy-eyed, and smiled. "Nowhere. Just forgot the time. You know, my watch wasn't working."

Ruth wasn't sure – Eimear wasn't slurring her words – but there was just something about her that piqued her suspicions.

"Have you been drinking?"

"No!" Eimear protested, moving to the sofa and flopping down with neither style nor grace.

"Don't lie to me, Eimear. Have you been drinking?"

Eimear rolled her eyes in an overdramatic fashion. "Calm down, Mum. I only had a couple and I am nearly seventeen. All my friends are drinking."

"So that makes it okay then?" Ruth raised her voice, the relief at seeing her daughter now replaced by the very real desire to give her a good smack. "It's okay to go out, get drunk, come home at stupid o'clock in the morning just because your friends are doing it?"

"You are too protective, Mum. I'm not drunk. I had a couple of drinks – not a skinful and it's a Saturday night – so it's not like I have school."

"For all I knew you could have been lying dead somewhere. I won't tolerate this behaviour, Eimear. You are still only sixteen and you are still under my roof and while you are here you will do as you are told."

Eimear looked at her mother and started to laugh. "Oh Mum," she said, getting up and hugging her mother half-heartedly. "You're funny when you're angry. Calm down and go to bed."

She let go of her grasp and walked into the kitchen while Ruth stood staring into space, willing herself to find the strength to deal with her daughter's moods without losing her temper.

Ruth turned, taking a deep breath and walked into the kitchen. She switched off the kettle and the toaster, throwing the bread Eimear had been toasting into the bin, and turned to her daughter.

"Listen to me, Missy. You pull another stunt like that and it won't be funny. As it stands, you are grounded until Thursday when your dad will pick you all up. Give me any more lip and I'll take your phone off you as well. I will not have you treating me like something you dragged in on the bottom of your shoe. I am your mother and I deserve your respect."

Eimear's face darkened, her clear blue eyes tightening into a scowl. "Respect? Don't make me laugh! If you'd had any respect, Mum, you wouldn't have let him get away with it all these years, would you? And you're still letting him get away with it. You are pathetic, Mum, and it's no wonder he ran away with someone else!"

She stormed up the stairs, slamming the door loudly as she went, and as Ruth heard Matthew cry out from his sleep she wiped the tears from her eyes, painted on a smile and climbed the stairs to soothe her child.

17

The following morning Niamh painted on a smile. It was amazing what a good slathering of Clarins Beauty Flash Balm could do, she thought as she stared at her reflection in the mirror. She greeted the twins with a cheery good morning and pulled them close to her.

"Are you all better, Mammy?" Rachel asked, her eyes wide with concern.

"Nearly," Niamh answered.

"You should take some Calpol. It makes me better when I'm sick," her daughter chimed, putting her hand to her mother's forehead to check her temperature. "Hmm, you are a wee bit warm, Mammy. Do you want me to get you a blanket for the sofa?"

Niamh couldn't help but smile at her daughter's caring nature.

"No, darling, I'm fine. You know, actually, I think a walk along the beach could bring me round. Fresh air works wonders."

At the mention of the beach, Connor looked up from his Bob the Builder toys, let out a yelp of delight and jumped to his feet. "I'll get the hats and coats, Mammy," he said, heading for the coat cupboard in the hall and starting to pull down everything that came to hand.

"Can Granny come with us?" he shouted.

"I think Granny is having a wee lie-in. Sure it will be fun just the three of us, won't it? We might even stop in the cafe for a bun and juice afterwards."

Niamh was wise enough to realise that just after ten was a quiet time in the cafe. The breakfast bunch had gone on to church and there would be an hour's lull before they poured back out again filled with the Holy Spirit. She wanted to make sure that she talked to as few people as possible.

Wrapping the kids up in their gorgeous Kidorable raincoats, scarves and hats, she led them out the door towards the beach. It was dry and bright and, as the fresh air filled their lungs, the kids delighted in seeing their breath puff out as steam.

"Look, Mammy! It's magic – I'm a dragon!" Connor shouted, standing still and bending over so that he could concentrate all his efforts on breathing "smoke".

Rachel stopped to laugh at him and seemed horrified as the steam billowed out of her own mouth. "But, Mammy, I want my smoke in me," she wailed, reaching her chubby hands to catch it and Niamh felt herself break into a smile.

Whatever had happened some good had come out of her life with Seán.

The children ran on ahead of her, hurtling away from her with the enthusiasm only children or those high on sugar have.

"Slow down," she yelled, a wide grin across her face as she tried to keep up with them. She realised as her legs ached that she had let herself go. Even though the weight had fallen off her, it obviously hadn't been replaced with muscle.

The lack of sex too, she thought with a sigh, would have contributed. She and Seán had always wanted each other, always been eager to jump into bed and enjoy spending time lost in each other. That made it all harder to understand, Niamh thought as she caught up with the twins amid the sand dunes. There had been no signs – not one – that he had been with someone else. Surely she would have known. Surely there would have been some dampening of his ardour. Surely he would have started taking more care over his appearance. He would have made furtive phone calls. He would have come home late from work more and more. There should have been a faint whiff of perfume on his clothes, but there wasn't. And Niamh should know. Every night since Seán died she had taken one of his shirts to bed and breathed it in as she tried to sleep.

She felt a hint of bile rise up, the shock of what she had learned hitting her again in the stomach and she fought the urge to fall to the sand and get the children to bury her in it.

"Aw, feck it," she whispered, wiping away a stray tear and sitting down close to where the children were making sand castles and laughing as they kicked them down.

* * *

The person who invented power-walking is a masochist, Ruth thought as she pounded along the beach trying to blow the cobwebs from her head. And the person who invented power-walking on a beach is a masochist with a death wish.

She knew that Eimear would be asleep for a while yet, so she decided to give the plasterwork in her house a break and vent her frustration on the beach instead. She had felt buoyed by her lightning-speed walk to the community centre the previous Tuesday night, so she figured the walk along the beach would be a breeze. She was wrong. As her feet sank into the soft sand, her calf muscles burned and her face blazed with the exertion. She was so unfit it scared her. She actually started to worry she would pass out there and then on the sand and risk a mercy dash by Greenpeace to save her.

"Come on, keep going," she urged herself, stepping out. She knew that all she had to do was break through the pain barrier – but as it stood the pain barrier was in real danger of breaking through her.

It had, she realised, been months since she'd even attempted any sort of fitness regime. Rathinch was not known for its gyms or leisure facilities. The most the inhabitants usually got was a stroll along the beach during the summer months and even then it wasn't a brisk walk – more a dander among the dunes, dodging tourists and hastily made sand castles.

For Ruth the dander often ended in the chippy (except on Tuesdays and Thursdays). There was something about the smell of the salt in the air that made her crave a fish supper like never before – liberally dosed with salt and vinegar. Thinking of it now, her tummy rumbled. The effects of last night's wine had left her ravenous. Thanking her lucky stars that it was too early for the chip shop to be open, she powered on, determined to get to the end of the beach without the need for the cardiac ambulance. She was just turning to walk on the more ankle-friendly terrain of the village Main Street when she saw Niamh and her twins playing in the sand in the distance.

Grateful for a chance to stop her walk and catch her breath for a few seconds, she called over to her new friend shouting a cheery hello. She hadn't, of course, been close enough to realise that Niamh was crying when she shouted over to her. If she had known, she was ashamed to say, she would probably have walked on and hoped to get away unnoticed.

"Are you okay?" she asked Niamh, realising almost as soon as the words had passed her mouth that her question was stupid. Of course Niamh wasn't all right. People who are all right do not sit on the beach in the buck-freezing cold crying into their designer pashminas.

Niamh looked up, blinking against the light, and hastily wiping the tears from her eyes. "Oh, I'm fine, Ruth, honest," she said, her voice wobbling.

Ruth stood for a moment – not quite sure what to do. She'd had a grand total of two conversations with this woman – save the times she had arrived at the surgery with the children. She could not force her into sharing a confidence and, anyway, there might not be a confidence to share. The woman had lost her husband. Although Ruth would gladly dance a jig at the news of James Byrne's demise, she knew that Niamh and Seán had been madly in love and that his death had been a cruel blow.

"Well, if you're sure," she offered half-heartedly and started to walk off, just in time to hear Niamh break into a fresh flurry of tears and the twins, who up until now had been building sandcastles, oblivious to their mammy's distress, start to wail too.

"Mammy, what's wrong? Don't cry, Mammy," Connor pleaded and Ruth found herself turning back and kneeling down on the sand beside the children.

"Mammy is fine," she soothed. "She just has some sand in her eyes and now I'll help her get it out, so you two go on and play. That's a cracker-looking sandcastle you just built – do you think you could knock it down for me?"

The twins looked at Ruth and then at Niamh, who managed a half smile and nodded in the direction of the sandcastle, "On you go, Dizzy and Muck, knock it down now for Mammy and then build the best one ever!"

They took off down the sand and Niamh mouthed a grateful "thank you".

"Look, tell me to feck off. You wouldn't be the first and you won't be the last, but if you need a listening ear I'm told I'm very good."

Niamh nodded and started to spill out her secret as Ruth sat open-mouthed in complete disbelief.

Of course Ruth was used to hearing all the gossip in the doctor's. She knew what was wrong with whom, and why and what cream they had to try to make it all better. There was little that shocked her. She could listen to talk of thrush and piles and chronic constipation without so much as raising an eyebrow, but this left her speechless. And if it was a shock for her, she could only imagine how much of a shock it was to Niamh. Feck. This was huge. Massive. And she knew she had to handle it just right.

She did a lot of nodding and hand-rubbing – skills she had also perfected at the doctor's and then she offered to join Niamh and the twins for tea and a bun at the cafe. She couldn't imagine what Niamh was going through. At least, with James, she had known he was a bollocks long before he had walked out. His leaving was just confirmation to the world at large of what she'd known at home for a long time. There was no way she would have put Seán Quigley in the same league. She might never have spoken to him but she had often seen the couple walking along the beach, the twins running on ahead of them while they walked along hand in hand like something out of the lifestyle pages of a Sunday newspaper.

She was sure she had the look of a rabbit stuck in the headlights as Niamh walked towards her with a tray laden with juice for the children, sticky buns and some steaming hot coffees.

"Thank God it's not too busy. I must look a right state," Niamh said through red-rimmed eyes.

"You look fine, sweetheart," Ruth replied, her hand

reaching instinctively to her own lined face. She knew her eyes were red-rimmed too from lack of sleep and worry. Glancing at her watch she realised that Eimear would probably wake soon and if she wasn't home to play the role of the strict disciplinarian, her daughter would probably head out to get up to God knows what mischief.

"I'm not keeping you back, am I?" Niamh asked, cutting through Ruth's thoughts.

"Oh no, not at all. It's just my eldest is giving me some trouble at the moment and I'm worried she'll be up to all sorts if I'm not back soon."

"God, you must think I'm a selfish fecker," Niamh said, "ranting on about my problems. Is there anything I can do?"

"Unless you have any hints and tips for keeping a sixteen-year-old in check, preferably without the use of a straitjacket, I doubt it." Ruth ran her fingers through her hair. "It's probably just a phase – she's been through a lot lately with James leaving and all . . ."

"I know, poor thing. It must be tough for all of you. Look, I'm much calmer now – on you go and I'll see you on Tuesday night at the centre."

Ruth downed her coffee, and wrapped her scarf around her neck. "I'm sorry to run off like this," she said apologetically.

"No, you've been a godsend. Thanks for listening and if I can return the favour any time, well, you know where I am."

* * *

Walking back up the hill towards her house, Ruth wondered how it was that shit things happened to good people. She thought of Niamh and her kind heart and wondered why life was so rubbish sometimes, and then she thought of herself.

She was a good person. There were times when James would have had her believe she was far from good, at anything, but she knew she had never willingly hurt anyone or anything in her life. So why, she wondered, was she now dealing with the Bride of Chucky in her house?

Sighing, she put her key in the door and braced herself for another round with Eimear.

Matthew was sitting on the sofa in his Spiderman pyjamas munching toast. For a second Ruth's heart soared. Perhaps Eimear had woken up a mature grown-up and had made toast for her baby brother, but when Thomas walked in shortly after with a fresh plate of toast her heart sank again.

"Is Eimear awake yet?"

"No," Thomas answered gruffly.

"I tried to wake her, Mammy, but she shouted at me to piss off," Matthew added solemnly, delighted that he had been able to use a swear word by proxy. "But Thomas made me toast and gave me some juice."

Matthew nodded in the direction of his plastic mug on the floor and turned his attention back to the TV where some mutant somethings or other were knocking fifty shades of shit out of each other. Thomas, Ruth noticed, was trying not to look interested and failing. She smiled. He might be her big son at fourteen but there were times when he was still a little boy at heart. She didn't dare say that to him though – he'd be mortified and would in all likelihood sulk for a month afterwards and she had enough stroppy teenagers in her house already.

Ruth walked to the kitchen and pulled out the ironing board. She might as well use this time, when the children were occupied, to get the kids' clothes organised for the weekend.

James, of course, hadn't deigned to tell her where they were going so she had to make sure she had things ready for every eventuality. She wished she could look forward to it.

Ordinarily four days alone in the house would seem like heaven – with books to read, wine to drink, films to watch and no noise at all to contend with, but instead she was worried how things would go. James wouldn't tolerate Thomas's shyness and he most certainly wouldn't tolerate Eimear's moods and no doubt he would come home accusing her of mollycoddling Matthew.

Feeling another headache starting, Ruth poured a glass of water and reached into the cupboard for some paracetamol. As she turned around she saw Eimear, a picture of misery, standing in the doorway.

"Can I have two of those please?" she asked sheepishly and Ruth poured another glass of water.

"Can we not fight today, Mum? I don't feel well."

Ruth nodded and took hold of her daughter's hand. "Okay, sweetheart. I don't want to fight but we have to sort this out because neither of us can go on like this."

Eimear nodded and sat down, her face a whiter shade of pale.

* * *

But Eimear sneaked out again that night and did not come home until gone twelve. Ruth spent another evening walking the floors, calling mobile numbers and trying to find her daughter.

That had topped off what had been a pretty shit night anyway. Matthew had put his foot down that there was no way he was going away with James for the Hallowe'en break and had lost the head when Ruth had told him that not only would he be going but he would be going a whole day earlier than previously planned.

"But I want to stay with you, Mammy," he had pleaded, eyes wide.

Ruth had wanted to assure him that she wanted him to stay with her too, but she wasn't sure if that constituted taking sides. She didn't want the children thinking bad of their daddy – or more to the point she didn't want James blaming her for their bad attitude.

She had cried once Matthew had been settled and then decided to ask Eimear to nip out and get a DVD. The two of them could curl up on the sofa and watch some soppy chick flick as a way to build some bridges after the previous night's furore.

"Eimear," she called softly from outside her daughter's bedroom door.

There was no answer.

She knocked and called again. "Eimear, darling. I know you are raging at me, but c'mon. Let's watch a wee film together. If you want we can get some chocolates in or a frozen pizza?"

No answer again.

Ruth was feeling fragile enough as it was and she really didn't have the strength to cope with one of Eimear's huffs, so she rattled the handle to the room and walked in.

Of course her daughter wasn't there. The room was a pit and Ruth could see, at least, that she had not run away. Every item of clothes she owned was scattered on the furniture and floor. There was make-up scattered on her dressing table, cups and plates Ruth had long thought broken sitting on the floor.

Ruth felt her heart sink and her hackles rise. Where had she gone so wrong with Eimear? They used to be like two peas in a pod and now they were at war with each.

"Give me strength," she had muttered before walking downstairs and starting her efforts to track Eimear down.

When her daughter had stumbled in, there was no question whatsoever in Ruth's mind that this time she had been drinking – and quite a lot by the look and smell of her.

"What the hell has been going on?" Ruth shouted, her resolve to play this in "good cop" style dissolving entirely.

Eimear struggled to make eye contact, her face pale. She started to sway and flopped down on the sofa. "I'm fine, Mum."

"Well, I'm not," Ruth shouted back, just as a familiar sour smell assaulted her nostrils.

"Have you been sick? Is that sick on your dress? Jesus, Eimear, what have you been up to? Have you no respect for yourself?"

"Ha!" Eimear snapped. "I don't think you can talk to me about respect, Mum!"

"Oh yes, I can, and I'll tell you now, young lady, if I have to sit on your knee for the next week until your dad comes and picks you up for the weekend then I will. Because you won't be leaving this house and you certainly won't be drinking anything else and you should only count your bloody selfish little arse lucky that I don't tell your dad what you've been up to because then, believe me, you would know what was sticking to you!"

Eimear looked at her mother, her mouth gaping open and shut as if she was trying to find some smart teenage putdown but instead she just burst into tears.

"Why don't you just tell him, Mum? If you hate me so much? Just tell him!" and then she ran up the stairs and despite an hour of pleading and crying at her bedroom door, Ruth couldn't talk any sense to her.

18

"Daddy, can we go up to Derry for Hallowe'en?" Poppy asked over breakfast on Monday morning. "Jamie and Oran from my class are going up and they say there's going to be fireworks and music and everything."

Poppy's enthusiasm for life was infectious and Liam found himself smiling and nodding. "Of course we can, sweetheart. We'll go up straight after school if you want."

"Yes!" Poppy said in an American accent, punching the air, and Liam laughed. "But, Daddy, we'll have to get a costume and everything."

Liam sighed. Laura normally organised the costumes. A talented seamstress, she was a dab hand at whipping up a princess dress or a fairy costume in a matter of minutes. Liam didn't have a notion – his entire knowledge of Hallowe'en costumes was when his mother would hand him an old curtain as a child and tell him it was Dracula's cape. He had a fair idea such half-hearted attempts wouldn't go down well with Poppy, who had dressed as a Barbie Princess the year before, complete with dainty heeled shoes and a glittery home-made tiara.

Oblivious to the panic that was rising in her father's gut,

Poppy blethered on. "This year I want to be Dorothy from the *Wizard of Oz,* or Gabriella from *High School Musical,* but I think I want the ruby slippers. Jessica had ruby slippers last year and they had proper clicky-clacky heels like Mammy wears and everything."

At the mention of her mammy, Poppy's face paled just a little and she looked down at her breakfast before pushing it away.

Liam stared at her from across the breakfast bar – such a grown-up head on young shoulders – and felt a surge of anger towards his ex.

"Daddy, do you think Mammy will make my costume this year? I bet she'll be too busy. Do you think we could go to Tesco and buy one? I think we can get one for cheap and I don't have to be Dorothy. I can just be a witch. I don't mind."

Liam sighed. "You'll be Dorothy. I'll get you the best damn Dorothy costume in Donegal. You mark my words."

"It's okay, Daddy, I don't mind," Poppy said, jumping off the stool and starting to put on her school coat.

"Listen, girlie. I'm not going to let you down." He stopped himself just before adding "like your mother did". He had vowed not to badmouth Laura no matter how much he wanted to. Poppy had been through enough without getting stuck in the middle of an unholy row between her two parents.

In her typical style his daughter changed the subject, stopping him from dwelling on his relationship meltdown. Now that she had been assured that Hallowe'en wasn't going to be a washout, she had much more important things to talk about – like clothes and shoes. Not much of it made sense to Liam but he just smiled and nodded while she chatted the whole way to school. He wondered how he would cope in a couple of years when the chat moved on to seriously girly subjects like boys and, God forbid, periods. Christ, the thought of having to buy sanitary towels in the local shop brought him out in a cold sweat. Please God Laura would be back by then and it wouldn't be a problem.

When he had dropped her off, with a sly kiss on the cheek because big cuddles were no longer cool for a five-year-old girl, he called into the Country Kitchen Cafe for a cooked breakfast. Nothing beat a couple of sausages, rashers and some fried bread to start the day. He looked down at his waistband, however – he had vowed to eat better, thinking that losing a few pounds could possibly win Laura back. She used to scoff when he went into the Country Kitchen for breakfast.

"Sure I've got a pot of porridge on the stove. That's much better for you," she would say and in turn he would smile and say that nothing was better for him than feeling he had a belly fully of runny eggs and bacon.

"I'm a working man, love. I need to build my strength up."

"That may well have been true in the days when you were actually lifting and carrying on the site, but given that you spend most of your days now sat on your rear in the office, I'm not convinced."

"I've the constitution of an ox."

"That's what I'm worried about," Laura had said, pouring a glass of cranberry juice for herself. "That you'll not only have the constitution of an ox, but the figure of an ox too."

Liam had sighed every time they had this conversation and smiled, kissing his wife on the forehead and heading out anyway.

As he ordered his usual and opened the paper for a read, he wondered if Laura would still be with him if he had managed to keep on the porridge? Surely it wasn't as simple as his expanding waistline. He still had a nice bit of muscle tone, even if he did say so himself. Sure James fecking Byrne was skinny as a whippet. Wimpy skinny. How anyone could find him attractive was beyond Liam entirely.

The bell above the door pinged and running in out of the rain was Detta O'Neill, looking suitably frazzled.

"By God, it's pelting it down out there today. So much for the Indian summer we were promised," she said to the young girl behind the counter.

"It is nearly Hallowe'en, Mrs O'Neill," the girl replied, "but there does seem to be a big change in the temperature all right."

"Indeed there is. Now could you get me one of those gorgeous treacle scones, smothered in butter, and a big pot of tea, please?"

The girl nodded and Detta turned to face Liam, who smiled at her while he tried to hide behind his paper. But as he was sitting close to the fire, Detta made a beeline for him.

"You don't mind if I sit here, do you? I'm chilled to the bone."

Liam felt his heart sink a little. It wasn't that he didn't like Detta – he thought she was a great woman altogether – but he knew that if they were seen chattering away it would just feed the gossipmongers of Rathinch. He was already concerned enough about taking Ciara home after their last meeting. All he needed now was a reputation of being a sleazy old man. However, he couldn't really say no, could he? So he nodded and moved over a little bit. Perhaps a reputation as the village Lothario wouldn't be a bad thing? It would show that skinny snotter James Byrne anyway.

"So how are things?" Detta asked, drying her face with a napkin.

"Ach, not so bad. Off to work later."

"Have you plans for Hallowe'en then? From what I can tell half of Rathinch is going up to Derry."

"Yes, well, Poppy is looking to take a run up. Now I just have to put together a 'Dorothy' costume in the next few days or face her wrath. I tell you, that one gets her temper from her mother."

Detta smiled. "I have an old sewing machine not doing much in my spare room. I'm sure I'll be able to whip something up. I used to be quite the seamstress in my day."

"I couldn't ask you to do that," Liam said, sipping from his cup of tea.

"You're not asking, I'm offering, and you should know by now not to say no to a Rathinch woman."

Liam laughed. He admired the fact that Detta took no prisoners – she said what she meant instead of playing silly little games. He also realised he was unlikely to get as good an offer again and he wasn't exactly all that handy with the needle and thread.

"Okay, then, and thank you," he said.

"Great. I'll pick up some material and call around this evening."

Looking around her, Detta saw that the cafe was relatively quiet and leant towards him. "So I'm guessing then, from how you're talking, that Laura and James haven't included young Poppy in their holiday plans? Is the wee poppet okay with that?"

"She is very resilient. God knows, I don't think I have her forgiving streak. I'm going to talk to Laura about it all today – you know, find out what's going on in her brain. I just don't know how she could leave our little girl like that."

Feeling his voice wobble, the emotion getting the better of him, Liam took a breath and straightened himself in his chair. He would have to remember this was not the community centre on a Tuesday night. This cosy little cafe – with its roaring fire and pictures of the great and the good of Rathinch staring down from every wall – was Gossip Central to the villagers and it would not do at all to be seen losing his cool here.

Detta just sat back, and smiled gently. "I hope you get some answers, Liam. For what it's worth I don't understand it either, but then Lord only knows what is going on in her head at the moment. She always struck me as quite sensible – I can't see what the appeal of your man is."

"I wouldn't say that to Ruth if I was you," Liam replied, with a smile.

"Well, I don't think Ruth wants him back. She might look as though she is hanging on by a thread, but if you ask me she's doing better without him. But still, we shouldn't talk about people behind their backs. How is work going anyway?"

* * *

It had been two weeks since Liam last saw Laura. It was strange, he thought. He was so used to seeing her every day – to hearing the minutiae of her day's work – that he could hardly believe the majority of their conversations were now conducted via email or over the phone.

Opening the door to the solicitor's office where she worked as a paralegal, he felt sick to his stomach. Clodagh, the well-meaning receptionist, looked at him and turned a delightful shade of pink. Where before she would have struck up a conversation with him should he visit, chatting nineteen to the dozen about Poppy, now she seemed stuck for words.

Liam couldn't say that he blamed her. There weren't many things you could say to a forty-seven-year-old Donegal man consigned to the scrapheap.

"Is Laura in?" he asked and Clodagh nodded before lifting the phone and dialling her extension.

"Liam's here," she chirped, then put the phone down and gave him a half smile. "She'll be out in a minute. Have a seat."

She used to always laugh when she called Laura. "The love of your life is here," she would giggle before chatting some more with him while he waited. It would be churlish – not to mention extremely embarrassing – for him to make a scene about Clodagh's lack of flirtatious banter so he walked to the seats, sat down and started flicking through a well thumbed copy of *Ulster Tatler*.

When the door creaked open he looked up and his heart skipped a beat. Strange that he had never really understood that sensation until the first day he laid eyes on Laura Casey and every day since his heart had skipped a beat when she smiled at him. She was standing there in a tailored red skirt-suit, her blonde hair twisted into a loose pony-tail. She gave him the same half smile Clodagh had, except the warmth was missing from her eyes.

"Are you free to talk for a few minutes?" he asked.

Laura looked at her watch and then at him. "Well, I've a client coming in soon, but if you make it quick."

He followed her into the office. She took her seat behind the desk and he sat down on the opposite side, feeling very much as if he was about to start discussing an upcoming appearance in the circuit court rather than his concerns for their daughter.

He took a deep breath. "Look, there is no point in me beating around the bush, especially if you're seeing someone soon, so I'll come out with it. This is about Poppy. I know you're going off this weekend with James and his children and I'm assuming that Poppy is not part of that excursion, and well, I just wanted to know what was happening."

Liam was impressed with his use of the word "excursion". The lawyer-y setting was obviously rubbing off on him in a good way. He hoped Laura would be equally impressed with the coolness of his tone. She didn't like melodrama – especially not from him.

Laura sighed. "James's kids are having difficulty coming to terms with the separation. They miss him desperately."

Liam bit back a snort – that was certainly not the impression Ruth had given him at the support group meetings – and besides, what about how much Poppy was missing her mum?

"We thought if we take them away now, I could take her somewhere the next weekend – just me and her. It would be too much with James' kids too."

"You know she'll think she's less important than them."

Laura rolled her eyes. "Don't be ridiculous, Liam. Sure don't I take her out one night a week and at weekends and ruin her stupid?"

"She'd prefer it if you lived in the same house as her." Liam had dropped his voice to a whisper, even though there was no one else in the office.

Laura sighed and for a second – just that briefest of moments – he thought he was getting somewhere with her. He thought perhaps he'd finally found her heartstrings and given them a good old twanging.

"I'd prefer she were in the same house as me too," she said, her eyes pooling over with tears, "but, Liam, she's a daddy's girl and always has been. I might be many things, but I'm not so cruel as to take her away from you. You know that's why I left her and I'll do my best to make it up."

He wanted to shout. He wanted to tell her that her best was simply not good enough – not by a long shot – but when he saw her, Bambi eyes dripping tears, her face wretched with emotion, he couldn't shout. He couldn't give out to her at all.

Laura was right, Poppy was a daddy's girl – through and through. From the moment she was born she had craved her daddy's attention more than anyone. She would settle quickest on his chest as he cradled her after his long day's work. When she started crawling she headed straight for him, pulling herself up on her pudgy legs to him and he would walk, never tiring, bent double with her little hands in his. Even when she became steady on her own two feet, she would walk beside him, hand clasped in his.

That's not to say she didn't love her mother – the two could be thick as thieves as they plastered each other in make-up and glittery lip-gloss, but when she wanted that extra feeling of security it was her daddy she had called for.

For Laura it had been the best thing to do to leave Poppy with her daddy when she left. The wisdom of Solomon.

"Come home," he said, almost pleading.

"You know I can't," she said, her tears drying almost instantly.

"Why not?" he asked – as much for himself as for Poppy.

"I don't think here and now is the place to talk about this. This is my place of work."

"Well, when can we talk then, Laura? Because we do need to talk." He hoped his voice had an ounce of coolness in it.

"I'll call you when we get back," Laura said, standing up and walking to the door. "Tell Poppy I love her," she added, showing him out and turning on her heel to walk back into her office, leaving him standing like a wet rag in the hall.

He took a deep breath, pulled his tummy in and walked out of the building, trying to hold his head as high as possible.

* * *

Detta was a natural with Poppy, Liam realised as he watched his daughter twirl in front of his friend in her blue gingham dress.

"Daddy, don't I look pretty? Aren't I like the very real Dorothy?" Poppy beamed. "You are indeed," Liam replied, sitting back in his chair and beaming with pride at his daughter.

"Ach no," Detta smiled, "you can't be Dorothy yet – you don't have the ruby slippers."

Poppy's face fell and she let go of her dress and stopped twirling.

"Don't worry, pet," Detta said. "I just happened to be in Penneys earlier and saw these sparkly pumps." Lifting a bag from under the table she took out two shiny red shoes and Poppy's smile was restored.

"You needn't have done that," Liam blushed. He wasn't used to random acts of kindness. There weren't many of those about at the builder's yard. You were lucky if one of the tight feckers included you on the bun run without demanding a euro from you for your bap.

"Sure it's nothing. It's only Penneys – nothing fancy – and we can't be having Dorothy without the ruby slippers."

"But how did you know her size?" Liam asked, amazed because for the life of him he couldn't remember it himself.

"A woman knows these things," Detta said.

"Glad someone does. I'm useless at the details," he confided, wondering what it was about this woman that made him spill out his innermost thoughts. It was really quite disconcerting – how he couldn't seem to shut up when she was about, even though he barely knew her from Adam.

He'd seen her around the village recently. She was a hard one to miss. With her bright coloured skirts and long cardigans, and her hair blowing wildly in the wind, she caught everyone's attention. If he wasn't still so madly in love with Laura he would have found her attractive – in a windswept and interesting kind of a way.

He knew he didn't know much about her – her life, why she had been away from Rathinch for so long and indeed why she had come back. It was rare, Liam thought, that when anyone left Rathinch they came back. This place had invented the brain drain.

Poppy stopped twirling and climbed onto her daddy's knee. "Daddy, you are best daddy in the whole world," she said, before turning to Detta. "Do you know he is taking me up to Derry for Hallowe'en and we are going to see the fireworks. Would you like to come with us?"

Poppy's enthusiasm was overwhelming, and Liam couldn't help but think it wasn't the worst prospect in the world. It was the least he could do after Detta's sewing efforts anyway, so he nodded that she was more than welcome to join them on their night out.

"You know, I think I would like that and," she smiled, looking at him, "maybe we could ask Niamh and the twins, and Ruth and Ciara too for that matter. I think it's about time we had a group outing. I could bring the old mini-bus."

Liam's heart sank to his boots. It wasn't that he didn't think all the ladies were nice in their own way but the thought of a couple of hours in a mini-bus with them and a heap of wains was intimidating. They'd no doubt be up for sing-songs and all that old nonsense. He could feel a headache starting at the back of his neck already, but looking at Detta and Poppy who were now dancing around singing 'Ding Dong the Witch is Dead' together, he knew that just like on every other occasion in his life he would give in to female pressure.

* * *

Poppy was in bed and Liam was still muttering about how exactly he'd like the Wicked Witch to die when the phone rang.

"Is that you, son?" his mother asked and he bit back the urge to answer that no, it wasn't, it was Daniel O'Donnell and he, Liam, had actually run off with some seventeen-year-old down the road and wasn't planning on coming back – ever.

"Yes, Mum. Are you okay? It's late," he said instead.

"I heard that – that – *thing* you were married to is swanning off for the weekend with her fancy man!" Her voice was dripping with indignation.

Liam sighed, sat down and prepared himself for at least fifteen minutes of defending his wife to the woman who had taken against her from the first time they'd met. He rubbed his temples and he couldn't help but wish just for a second that she would give it a rest. She meant well – he knew that – but she didn't often achieve her goal of wellness.

"Yes, Mum, she is going away with James, and his children too for that matter." He figured he might as well pre-empt her next piece of juicy gossip.

"And Poppy? Is she taking her own daughter with her?" Agnes was almost apoplectic with anger by now.

"No. She is going to take her away on her own some time."

"Oh son, you know I never liked her – but now, well, now I hate her, and God forgive me for saying this, but I wish you had never met her. The only good thing she ever did was have that wee girl."

Liam sat back and tuned out of his mother's tirade. He knew that she was wrong. Laura had done so many wonderful things during their time together. She had made him feel like a real man – had looked after him, cared for him, loved him. She made him laugh till his sides ached. She made him feel proud to be alive when she was by his side and she had been the best possible mother in the world to their daughter.

He knew she had changed – and he couldn't understand why – but he couldn't give up on her now. He could not let the last few months, no matter how they had humiliated and crushed him, override the years they had spent together. He wished his mother would understand that but he knew when it came to her and Laura he was fighting a losing battle.

He let his mother rattle off a long list of Laura's faults and then replied, with as much control as he could muster. "Yes, I know you don't think much of her, but we've talked about the weekend and it's fine."

The worst thing he could do now was let Agnes know that his heart was breaking. She would be moved in before he could say "No, thank you" and have the armchairs of his prized leather suite covered in her blasted doilies. His canvas prints would no doubt be replaced by Sacred Heart pictures and musty old watercolours and he would not be able to breathe out without her commenting on it and praying for a safe intake of breath to follow.

It was half an hour before Agnes realised he wasn't biting and ended their phone call. Liam walked to the fridge, pulled out a cold beer, sank back into his chair and switched on the TV. Bloody Sky, he paid a small fortune for it and there was still nothing on. Surprisingly, that was one of the things he missed about Laura the most – just sitting chatting together in the evenings. Not the sex. Though at the time he'd had a niggling suspicion she was chatting to avoid the sex. She would tell him about life in the office and he would tell her about their latest building project. Of course, she never bothered to tell him she was shagging somebody else, but then that probably wouldn't have gone down well over a bottle of wine in front of the fire.

He remembered the day she had told him, or at least the day he came home to find the note by the phone. It was such a fecking cliché. He cringed when he remembered it, and also cringed when he thought of how he had smiled when he saw the letter, thinking it must be some romantic little love note. He had lifted it and walked to the kitchen, pouring himself a tall glass of milk from the fridge and sitting down at the breakfast bar. And only then had he opened the letter, and found himself in the middle of what he could realistically describe as his worst nightmare.

Dear Liam,
I'm sorry to do this to you and I'm even more sorry to do it in this way.

By now you may have guessed something is wrong. God knows, things haven't been great between us for a long time and you must have felt, like I have, that living here lately has felt like living in a pressure cooker.

The thing is, I've met someone else. I know that sounds awful and you probably won't believe this, but I didn't mean for anything to happen. But we've fallen in love and I tried, honestly, to fight what I was feeling because you are a decent man and I have never wanted to hurt you.

I've realised though that life is for living and I wasn't being fair to you, or me, or Poppy, to keep living a lie. She deserves two happy parents and to be raised in a happy home.

I've gone – not to him. I need some time to think.

I've not taken Poppy. I know she adores you and I would hate to mess her around when I'm so uncertain of what is going to happen. Please let her know I love her.

I hope you understand.
Love,
Laura

It was the "*Love, Laura*" bit that Liam really couldn't understand. How could she love him if she was prepared to rip his heart out as he sat at the kitchen counter drinking fecking milk? His heart started to thump as the realisation of what he had just read started to seep in. His stomach sank to his boots as a rush of adrenalin flooded through his veins. He realised, as he knocked the milk over, that he was shaking.

Now, as the memory flitted through his mind, he wondered just for the briefest of moments why he kept defending her. What she had done was indefensible.

He hadn't been aware of any tension, but then he wasn't perhaps the most sensitive of souls.

Yes, perhaps Laura had been a little quieter but she had been working longer hours and he thought she was just tired. He had offered to rub her feet, her shoulders or whatever else might have taken her fancy many times to ease the strain and while she had refused, he had just thought this was because she was stressed with work. He never, for one second, thought that she could be in love with someone else.

Flicking through the TV channels he thought about how deeply unhappy he was with his life and while he was dreading the thought of it, he realised that he didn't have anything to look forward to apart from the bus run to Derry,

As long as no one expected him to dress up – because there wasn't a bloody chance he would be dressing up as anything. He was a grown man, for God's sake.

19

"Sure you can bring the wee one up in her buggy and we'll all help you mind her," Ruth urged as she sipped her tea in the community centre.

Ciara wondered was it extremely sad that she was ridiculously excited at the possibility of a trip out *at night*.

Lorraine would probably say she was being very irresponsible – keeping Ella up late and bringing her in the cold night air among the throngs of people who crowded into Derry to see the fireworks. But then, as Lorraine frequently reminded her, Ella was Ciara's responsibility alone and surely if she wanted to take her daughter on a trip to Timbuktu it was her decision and hers alone.

"You don't think she'll get too tired?" she asked, hoping Ruth would assure her it was not at all irresponsible to go with her gut feeling on this.

"Well, I imagine she'll be knackered all right – and Niamh's two will be as well, but they can sleep on the way back." Ruth seemed determined. Her face had lit up at the thought of the bus run, which Ciara could understand. She knew her friend wasn't looking forward to spending Hallowe'en without her children.

"Is Niamh coming tonight?" Liam asked, looking at the clock. It had gone seven thirty and Niamh would usually have been there by now.

"I saw her in the shop today, but we didn't really get a chance to talk," Ciara said, shrugging her shoulders. "Maybe she wouldn't be up for a trip to Derry?"

"Nonsense," Detta said, sitting down. "Of course she will be, and if she isn't then we will just have to do our best to persuade her – just like we will you, missus."

Ciara smiled. She wasn't going to need much persuading. Of course all her old school friends were going. Abby had talked about nothing else the whole way home from Letterkenny on Saturday. She was delighted with the sexy schoolgirl costume she had bought, but worried her dad wouldn't let her out of the house in it. She had schemed with Ciara to leave the house in something more suitable and pick up her real outfit from Ciara's house before getting on the bus.

Ciara had felt completely jealous that she was going to miss out on all the *craic*, and while traipsing up the road with the rest of the village's lone parents was not the way she really wanted to do it, it was better than nothing.

"Okay then," she smiled. "I'll go. What will I dress Ella up as?"

"I saw a wee bumble-bee costume in the Post Office earlier. It would be gorgeous on her," Ruth said with a smile.

"Well, that's us sorted then," Detta said with a grin. "We'll just check with Niamh when she gets here and then I'll make sure the mini-bus is ready to go. It should be a laugh."

"If you want," Ruth offered, "you can come and stay with me after – you know, if your mother wouldn't mind? Detta, you could come back too? I hate being in the house by myself and sure we could make a night of it."

Ciara wondered was there something actually wrong with her, a seventeen-year-old feeling a flurry of excitement at the thought of a night out of the house with some middle-aged women.

"Oh fine then," Liam chirped good-heartedly, "you plan your girly night and I'll see to myself."

"Sure can't Liam come too?" Ciara asked, cheered by their banter. It was refreshing not to be wailing over notepads and writing letters to themselves for once. The only thing taking away from the *craic* was that Niamh still hadn't arrived.

"Everyone can come," Ruth answered. "We'll even bob for apples if you want."

"I'd prefer to bob for vodka," Detta grinned.

Ciara laughed and wondered would it be at all possible for her to sneak in a couple of Bacardi Breezers. Though Lord knows, since Ella was born eleven months before, she had rarely touched a drink and she was likely to pass out after half a glass. A cheap date, and old before her time – this wasn't exactly how she had imagined her teenage years.

"Right, well, it doesn't look as if Niamh will be joining us tonight, so we might as well get started," Detta said, cutting through her thoughts.

Ciara was relieved to see no sign of the dreaded notebooks.

"Well, you'll be delighted to know that tonight we won't be writing letters," Detta said. "I thought that, as well as talking about Hallowe'en, we could also have a good old natter about what brings us here anyway – our kids."

"God, I thought I was coming here to escape all that," Ruth said, a grimace on her face.

"Things not so good?" Detta said, sitting down opposite her and adopting her best listening-ear pose.

"Well, to be honest, they aren't awful but Eimear is giving

me a few headaches at the moment. She seems intent on going off the rails."

Ciara felt herself blush. The memory of her conversation with Abby was still fresh and she was willing to bet that whatever Ruth thought her daughter was up to, things were likely to be much, much worse than that. If Abby was right, and Eimear was throwing herself at Ben Quinn, then she, Ciara, had a notion Ruth would have more than headaches to deal with in the near future. Baby-shaped headaches, most likely.

Ben Quinn was gorgeous. Every girl in school was madly in love with him and on the outside he could be charming. Ciara had been flattered when he'd shown an interest in her, but she'd found out quickly he was just using her. He treated her appallingly and she still burned with shame when she thought of their last encounter.

He'd called her a slut, a slag and a whore. He hadn't wasted the opportunity to throw in as many insults as possible and he'd left her crying on the beach. She had known, of course, he wasn't going to be happy about the baby but she couldn't have guessed just how unhappy he was going to be.

As she had dressed that night, she had planned it all out. She would tell Ben and he would offer to support her and then they would, together, tell her mother and while there was every chance there would be some screaming and shouting, it would all work out in the end.

She had tied her hair back from her face and put on her nicest, most flattering pink T-shirt with *Little Miss Naughty* on the front. She thought it was rather ironic really, the T-shirt, but she figured if she approached it all like it wasn't the worst thing in the world, it might not be.

They had strolled hand in hand up the beach and he had told her how much he loved kissing her. She had smiled, and run her fingers through his hair which did, she remembered, have just a little bit too much gel in it.

When they were far enough away from their friends she had told him, in awkward, short sentences, that she was pregnant and he had erupted with rage.

"I'm not going to do this," he said, his face dark. "I have plans. And don't even think about telling anyone I'm the daddy 'cos I'll tell them all you're a slut."

And he had wasted no time in doing just that: in a pre-emptive strike of extreme shit-headedness he told all their friends he had dumped her because she had been sleeping around. She didn't have the strength to argue that she hadn't been and sure wasn't she carrying his baby to prove it. She just got on with it.

No, Ben Quinn was Bad News. With a capital B and a capital N.

Looking at the worry on Ruth's face, Ciara knew she was going to have to say something – but she didn't know that anyone would believe her. Only the very unlucky few saw the side of Ben she had seen that night on the beach – the rest of them thought he was the catch of Rathinch.

She took a deep breath, vowed to sleep on it, and proceeded to tell the group how Ella had been a wee dote that evening.

* * *

"Did you have a good night?" Lorraine asked as Ciara walked through the door. She was sitting on the sofa, feet up on the battered footstool, drinking from a bottle of beer.

Ciara flopped down beside her and looked at the TV. Some cheesy American-style soap opera was on and Lorraine was clearly engrossed.

Cuddling close to her mother, putting her own feet up on

the sofa, Ciara replied: "It was fine, Mum. They're going to have a Hallowe'en party on Friday. I think I'm going to take Ella and I might stay over in Ruth's after."

She looked at her mother and chided herself. She felt as if she was asking for permission, which was completely nuts. She was a mother herself – if she wanted to go to a party with her middle-aged friends then she would go to a party with her middle-aged friends!

"Sounds nice," Lorraine answered, gazing at the TV.

"It does, doesn't it?"

They sat in silence for a few minutes more.

Ciara looked at her mother who had one hand resting on the remote control and the other wrapped around her bottle of beer. Her hair was curled, hanging softly around her face and she had a look of concentration on her face. There were lines there – but she was still young. Still up for a bit of *craic*. It suddenly hit Ciara that it was wrong that she'd even been thinking about telling Ruth all about Ben when her own mother didn't know.

"Mum?" she started, her heart thumping in her chest.

"Yes, pet."

"Can we talk, please?"

"Just give me fifteen minutes," Lorraine said, raising the bottle to her lips. "I want to see the end of this. And then I'm all yours."

* * *

Ciara remembered the last time she had a big talk with her mother. She still cringed at the memory – at just how awkward it had been.

"Can I make you a cup of tea, Mum?" she'd asked, her mouth dry. She fancied a cup of tea herself. It was what you did in stressful situations, wasn't it? Drink tea. Sweet, milky tea.

"I'm grand, love," Lorraine answered, staring up from the novel she was lost in. "I've just had one."

"Are you sure?" Ciara asked. She realised she was putting off the inevitable but right now the inevitable was giving her the heebies.

"I'm sure," Lorraine replied, putting her book down and looking at her daughter. "Are you okay, love?"

Ciara instinctively put her hands to her stomach and then realised that might look completely obvious and returned them to her hips. But her hands felt like butter and slid across her body uncomfortably, trying to find a place where they gave nothing away. She realised, of course, the irony in not wanting to give anything away considering the bombshell she was about to drop.

She opened her mouth to speak, but instead of a coherent sentence she bubbled out a huge watery sob.

"Oh Jesus, Ciara, what's wrong? Are you hurt? Has someone hurt you?" Lorraine's eyes flashed with protectiveness and she jumped from her seat and grabbed her daughter into a hug.

It should have been comforting, but it was mildly suffocating. Between the fluffiness of her mother's blue jumper and sobs wracking her body, Ciara wondered if she was just about to pass out. She pulled her head back and swallowed hard, gulping at air. She had to do this, and she had to do it now. There was no easy way to get around it.

"I'm okay, Mum," she said, sitting down.

Lorraine sat beside her on the faded leather sofa and took her hand. "You don't look okay, or sound okay," she said softly.

"Oh, Mum," Ciara replied. "Don't kill me. I'm pregnant."

* * *

There was no blue jumper this time. Ciara guessed her mother was fully expecting her to tell her she was up the stick again. Much as she tried to be supportive and understanding, Ciara always felt her mother was waiting for the next disaster to strike.

"I want to talk to you about Ella. And Ella's daddy," she said.

Lorraine switched off the TV and looked at her. "I was wondering when this would come up."

"I know, and I'm sorry, Mum, for not telling you. But he told me no one would believe me."

Lorraine looked aghast. "He didn't, you know, rape you? Did he?"

"No, no, Mum. Nothing like that," Ciara said, fiddling with the zip on her fleece jacket. She watched her mother sag in relief. "But he told me that he would make sure everyone knew I was a slag and you were disappointed in me enough, Mum. I didn't want you taking his side too."

"As if I would," Lorraine said, dejectedly.

"You were pretty mad."

"And so would you be, madam, if Ella there came home one day and told you the same."

The thought made Ciara's stomach turn. "I suppose," she said. "But I did think I loved him, Mum. And yes, I was stupid. I can't say I wouldn't do it again because then I wouldn't have Ella but, you know, I wish it wasn't him and I wish I was a whole lot older."

"No point in wishing," Lorraine said. "I wish I was a size 12 with Cindy Crawford's body and Julia Roberts' smile but it isn't going to get me anywhere."

"But he's a pig, Mum. He's a selfish pig."

"Does he – this pig – have a name then?"

"It's Ben, Mum. Ben Quinn."

Ciara had obviously heard the expression "you could have heard a pin drop" before, but now she knew what it meant. Her mother's jaw dropped in an exaggerated manner. The shock was plain to see and she knew what was coming next.

"But he's such a nice boy."

"No, no, Mum. He's not a nice boy. He is a pig. Can I swear?"

Lorraine nodded silently.

"He is a fecking pig. He told me that if I told everyone he was the father he would tell them I had slept my way round the school. He would kick up such a fuss and no one would believe me. He was nasty, Mum. He called me every name under the sun."

The silent nodding had turned to a silent shaking of the head.

"The wee bastard," Lorraine said, eventually. "I'll kill him. I'll fecking kill him."

She stood up and for a moment Ciara wondered if her mother was indeed going to rush out and kill him, right there and then.

"Much as I would love you to kill him, Mum, please leave it. He's not worth it. And I'll tell you something, Ella does not need him in her life – not when she has us. I'm only telling you because he is working his charms on someone else and I have to warn her. I didn't want to let you down by leaving you out in the cold on this."

Ciara's face was blazing because now, after almost two years of keeping this to herself – afraid of her life her mother would be further disappointed in her – she could see what she should have seen all along. Her mother's loyalty would have always been to her over the village stud. That started a whole fresh flood of tears.

Lorraine agreed, reluctantly, to leave things as they were

127

for the moment and the pair cried together for what seemed like hours.

"I'm sorry, Mum. I'm so sorry. I should have told you. I should have told you everything. I wish I had."

"No point in wishing," Lorraine said. "No point at all. What's done is done and now we have to move on from here, together."

20

Niamh felt guilty. She looked at her watch and wondered if, just as she was sitting there on the porch drinking her third glass of wine, Ruth, Ciara, Liam and Detta would be bonding in the community centre. But no, they would be finished by now.

She felt particularly guilty when she thought of Ruth, who had been so very kind to her on Sunday when she had been sitting on the beach gurning like a mad thing. Jesus, she was so embarrassed to think of how she must have looked – all those tears, snotters and slobbery sobs. It was not her finest moment – not by a long shot. She wondered whether Ruth had sat in the centre tonight, cup of tea in hand, chocolate biscuit mid-dunk, regaling everyone with the scandal of how Seán and Niamh's marriage was a complete sham and sure wasn't he shagging the arse off her best friend?

In spite of herself, Niamh felt a smile creep across her face. She could just imagine Liam's chin hitting the ground at the coarse use of language and Detta trying to get them to write a fecking letter about it all.

Dear Seán,
Sorry you were such a fecking twat, but then again you died a
horrific death so I guess karma got you in the end.
  Love, or not,
  Niamh and the Loony Lone Parents of Rathinch

Loony Lone Parents, she liked that. If she ever had the balls to go back and face them, knowing that her tears all these months had been a big, dirty lie, she would have to suggest that name. Currently they were only known as "That group yer wan Detta runs" and that wasn't very catchy by anyone's standards.

Niamh sipped from her glass and realised she must be in the numb stage again of the grieving process. She'd thought that was behind her. The two days after Seán careered his car into a ravine on the Derry to Rathinch road she had sat in a semi-comatose state. Yes, she had cried when the Gardaí had called to her house and she had wailed when she identified his body but, after that, until the funeral she had been dead inside. She wondered was it possible she had died instead because she felt nothing, but when her feelings came roaring back as she walked behind her husband's coffin into the church she realised just how much she liked the numb stage. The numb stage didn't hurt. It was kind of blissful. And she could even laugh during it.

It was nice to be back there again. She drained her glass and stood up to walk to the kitchen to polish off the bottle. She knew, from the way she staggered down the hall, that she should stop drinking, or maybe eat something but again she liked the feeling of being just that little bit removed from the reality of her life.

She would regret it the next day, when the twins came running in to her bed, full of toddler enthusiasm and demands for imaginative play, but she didn't really care. She had kept in control of her faculties while her mother and Robyn had been over. She knew neither woman was happy to leave her to go back to Derry, knowing that she was due a meltdown imminently, but they had their own lives to live.

"I don't even know what my fucking life is," Niamh muttered aloud, spilling her wine on the granite counter while pouring it into the glass. She was just reaching for some kitchen roll when her doorbell rang.

"Aw fuck," she said, pulling her hair back from her face and walking to the front door. No one calling at this time of night, to this house in the arse-end of nowhere, could be bringing good news.

Opening the door tentatively, she saw Ruth standing – a concerned look on her face – on the front step.

"Can I come in?" Ruth asked and Niamh forced a smile.

"'Course you can. Come in. I'm in the kitchen – or I was in the kitchen. I'm in the hall now obviously, but I was in the kitchen before," she rambled.

"I heard what you said, but knew what you meant," Ruth said, closing the door behind her and walking down the hall to the gleaming kitchen.

"Want a drink?" Niamh asked, reaching in the fridge for another bottle and lifting John Rocha glass from the cupboard.

"You know, I'd love a coffee," Ruth said softly.

Niamh suddenly felt embarrassed. "I'm not usually such a lush. It's just I needed to let off some steam and this seemed as good a way as any and I don't actually drink all that often. I didn't drink for a full year after the twins were born."

"I love a good drink," Ruth soothed. "I could have filled my own bottle bank after James left, but I'm driving tonight."

"Oh, okay. Well, coffee and maybe I should join you?" Niamh felt herself look to Ruth for some hint of approval.

Suddenly she needed someone to make that decision for her. Ruth smiled and, relieved, Niamh switched on the coffee machine and set two cups out.

"A glass of water wouldn't go amiss either," Niamh said and poured herself a tall glass from the tap.

Sitting down, while the coffee machine bubbled and hissed, she smiled at Ruth again, unsure of where to take the conversation. After all, the last time they had met she had spilled her darkest of secrets.

"We missed you tonight," Ruth said, breaking the silence.

"Oh God," Niamh thought, cringing. After four glasses of wine she had allowed herself to forget she had chickened out of the meeting. "I couldn't get a babysitter," she muttered. "Usually my mum comes down, but she couldn't tonight, you know."

"So it wouldn't be anything to do with what you told me the other day then?" Ruth asked, eyebrows raised.

"No, my mum couldn't come down, honest," she fibbed.

Ruth nodded and Niamh breathed an internal sigh of relief. Hopefully Ruth would take her at her word and not question her further. She went to pour the coffee and open a packet of custard creams.

"Well, you missed some *craic*," said Ruth. "We're all going to have a bus run up to Derry on Friday for the fireworks and that includes you. Now we won't take no for an answer because Detta is getting the mini-bus and Liam and Ciara are bringing their girls. I'll be on my lonesome so I'll be able to help you with the twins and then it's all back to mine for some party games."

Shit, Niamh thought, stuffing a full custard cream in her mouth to buy her time to try and think of some excuse as to why she couldn't possibly go to Derry.

"Gosh, it'll be late, won't it? I don't think the twins would be up for it."

She looked at Ruth. Damn, that raised eyebrow was there again.

"So *that* wouldn't be anything to do with what we talked about the other day? You wouldn't be trying to avoid us? Because, you know, darling, that none of us would judge you in any way."

Niamh choked. They wouldn't need to fecking judge her, would they? She hadn't done anything wrong except love a two-timing arse-wit. But they would judge Seán? And even if he was an arse-wit, she realised with a thud that she still felt an ounce of loyalty to his memory.

"I'm not ready to tell people," she stuttered. "But I don't want to . . . don't think I want to . . . lie about us and pretend it was all perfect." Staring at the glass of wine on the counter, Niamh felt her hand creep towards it. She needed a drink – really, really needed a drink if she was going to talk about this again with someone.

"None of us have had the perfect relationship in case you didn't realise," Ruth said kindly.

Niamh had to fight the urge to shout loudly "But you were different! You weren't me and Seán. We were the perfect couple. We were the Brangelina of Derry!" But of course she didn't. She sat, staring into her wineglass, the smell of the strong coffee making her feel slightly queasy.

"All I'm saying is that you are among friends," Ruth continued. "And none of us are old gossipmongers like Mrs Quinn in the shop. Trust me, if I was a gossip I could tell you a thing or two about Dr Donnelly's patients – but I'm not. And none of this is our business anyway. We are all lone parents, Niamh, and we just want to have a little fun with the children."

Niamh could tell she wasn't going to get out of this. It dawned on her, as she poured both her wine and her coffee into her pristine Belfast sink and poured a glass of water, that Ruth was not the kind of woman who would take no for an answer. At least this trip would get her mother and Robyn off her back. How could they complain or worry that she was going to top herself when she was heading out on jaunts to Derry with the rest of the Rathinch Loony Lone Parents?

"Yes, I would be delighted to join you and the Loonies on the trip," she said.

"Loonies?" Ruth asked with a half smile.

"Well, no offence or anything," Niamh smiled, "but we are the village misfits, aren't we? It's a bit like Stepford here, don't you think? All the little boxes of houses, the picket fences, the quaint shops? I feel like I'm stepping into some kind of time warp when I come here. That's why I liked it at first, I guess. It seemed less scary than a big city but now I feel like we should all be walking about in sackcloth and ashes and shouting 'unclean!' I mean – unmarried parents – how dare we?"

Ruth laughed – a deep throaty laugh. "You do make me laugh, Niamh. I know what you mean but you know people here are just very set in their ways, but feck the lot of them. Anyone who doesn't understand doesn't matter – that's what I say anyway."

* * *

When Ruth had gone home and Niamh had drunk the best part of two litres of water to fend off any hangover the following morning, she climbed the stairs and undressed. She kissed the twins goodnight, stopping to rest her hand on their chests to feel their gentle rise and fall. She whispered "God Bless" in their ears even though she wasn't sure she believed in God any more and then climbed beneath the crisp white sheets of her bed. As she snuggled down under the duvet she drifted off and he came to her again – like he had done many times since he died.

She was always aware it was a dream. That made it easier, she realised, to know that it was all in her head. He was sitting, like he always did, at the edge of the bed looking at her.

"You are an arse-wit," she said and he shrugged, combing his hair back from his face with his hands.

"Explain yourself, Seán," she said, "because I'm really very cross with you."

"It's not what you think," he said.

"Yes, two-timing arse-wits always say that," she raged.

He rolled his eyes. "Think what you want, Niamh."

"Well, you are here to prove me wrong, are you? You're a fecking dream – well, a nightmare really. So just go away, Seán, and don't come back because you are no good to me like this. Just go away."

He shrugged and Niamh woke, face damp with sweat, heart thumping. She sat up in the dark of the room and felt guilt wash over her. How could she have told him to go away and not come back? She wanted him back, even in dreams, just to explain himself and make it all better.

"Oh God, I really, really am going mad. I need to get out of this village and fast," she muttered and lay back down, waiting for her heartbeat to settle and hoping that her subconscious wouldn't take her at her word.

21

Ruth didn't like packing. If she was to list her ten Least Favourite Household Chores, packing would be number 3 – just below ironing (which was generally involved in the packing process at some level) and cleaning the toilet. Packing for three children who were being extremely unco-operative and uncommunicative to boot was even worse again.

"I want anything you need laundered down here now," she shouted up the stairs to two closed bedroom doors and a cacophony of music blasting from Thomas and Eimear's CD players.

"And your swimming suits too," she called. "Dad said the hotel has a swimming pool, so unless you want to sit on the side like saddos you better get those together."

The doors remained shut and Ruth wasn't sure but she could almost swear the music got louder. She secretly thanked God that she had elderly neighbours with well-known hearing problems on both sides or they would have her reported to the Council for noise pollution.

She sat down at the pine kitchen table and wished she had some wine in the house. Although, thinking of the greenish tinge Niamh's face had taken on the night before, maybe she would be safer just sticking to her tea and biscuits. She had already piled as many of the children's jeans, tops, pants, socks and favourite accessories into two battered weekend cases and yet she knew that they would complain that she had forgotten their most favourite items ever and she would be in their bad books. Or should that be even more in their bad books. Although Eimear hadn't gone on the lash since her weekend grounding, she hadn't fallen over herself to talk to her mother. Thomas remained his usual silent self and Matthew had been more clingy than usual.

"Do we have to go, Mammy? Really have to go?" he had asked just that morning.

"Darling, you'll have fun. Daddy says the hotel is really nice and Laura is a nice lady," Ruth said, painting on a smile.

"She's not as nice as you, Mammy. You are more fun than Daddy too."

"Well, of course I am," she smiled, "but you will have fun and you have your brother and sister with you."

"But I'll miss you," he said solemnly, his big blue eyes boring a hole directly into her heart. She wanted to tell him never mind, he could stay, but James would go mad and not only would he make her life miserable for it, he would take it out on the children over the coming weeks. As hard as it was for her to let her children go with James, it was easier than not letting them go and dealing with another of James's Huff Specials.

She was well used to him and his childish ways. She often used to tell people she might as well have four children at home. When Eimear was going through the terrible twos it felt as if James was going through the terrible twenty-twos. But Ruth had known he worked hard – morning, noon and night at the bank doing bankly things of which she had no notion, so she excused him. After all, while he was adding and subtracting and other money things, she was walking along the beach with their children and playing games of hide and seek in the park at the shorefront.

He often told her she should be grateful for the life he had given her. Only now, dealing with the Cold War with her three children, she understood the complete irony of the situation.

Still the tension was doing wonders for her figure. She had pounded along the beach every day that week – even when it was raining. She felt particularly proud of that. Usually a dose of rain had her hurtling for home. Her hair was frizzy enough at the best of times. She didn't want to tempt Mother Nature to give her an Irishwoman's Afro by spending too much time in high humidity. Instinctively, she put her hands to her hair and straightened it down.

She felt nervous about tomorrow. It was never going to be easy to wave her children off with James even though she knew he loved them. He had always loved them. He might not always have shown it, or known how to show it, but he had never hurt them.

Not like he had hurt her.

She took a deep breath and switched the kettle on for the tenth time that day and then she opened the cupboard to see if there were any biscuits left worth munching. Although, being that it was Wednesday and the kids had been on half term she knew she would be lucky to find a mouldy digestive.

Probably for the best, she thought. She didn't want to undo the work of her week of walking. She was tired of feeling like a frump – thirty-seven and feeling about sixty.

She would look at Eimear and see her confidence and her natural beauty and feel like an old hag. She wished she could wear the same skinny jeans and smock tops her daughter wore without looking as if she was carrying a surprise late baby. Instead she wore the cheapest jeans Dunnes Stores had to offer, generally not cut in the most flattering of styles, with whatever sweatshirt came to hand. For work she had a simple uniform of black trousers – of which she had two pairs – and a blue blouse, short-sleeved for summer and long-sleeved for winter. Occasionally, if it was biting cold, she would accessorise her work look with a black cardigan. She was hardly the height of fashion.

But her weight and her wardrobe were the least of her worries now. She had to deal with getting the children out the door without showing herself up or dealing with a complete emotional breakdown from them.

They would have fun. She knew that, but she also knew why they were reticent. She would much rather they were with her, going on the mini-bus to Derry for the night, but she daren't argue with James. His temper was the only thing more legendary than his tightness with money. Only, nobody else really knew about the temper except for her. It was her dirty little secret.

Pouring milk into her mug, she leant against the worktops and touched the side of her cheek gently as if feeling a bruise that was long healed. If Niamh knew what secret Ruth was hiding she wouldn't feel half as bad about Seán being a cheat, Ruth was willing to bet.

Setting up her ironing board to work through the rest of the children's clothes, Ruth switched on the TV to distract herself from the thoughts that were buzzing round in her head.

There was a good drama on, and she lost herself in the ups and downs of other people's lives while trying not to think about hers too much.

* * *

Ruth was exhausted when she arrived into work the following morning. She always got in early to put on the heating, boil a kettle and set out the records for Dr Donnelly of all the patients due to make it in for morning appointments.

139

She had left the children still sleeping, with a note on the table asking them to please get themselves ready while she was at work. James would be calling round for them at five and he didn't like to be kept waiting. The weekend cases were filled and ready for the off and she had left the house gleaming. Her note to the children had asked that they try and keep it in the condition in which she had left it but she knew, as she switched on her computer in work, there would be little chance of that.

Thursdays were her full day at the surgery, but she would ask Dr Donnelly if she could leave a half hour early just to get home and tidy up the worst of her offspring's excesses before her ex arrived. If she ran really fast back up the hill, she might have half a chance of getting it done.

At times like this she wished she could spin around 'a la Wonder Woman and magic a clean house. Better still, wriggle her nose like your woman from *Bewitched* and have it all done for her with no effort at all.

Sitting down, Ruth opened her emails to find one waiting from James. Seems picking up the phone was too much of an effort for him.

Ruth,
Just a reminder to let you know I expect to leave on time tonight. We have a long drive ahead of us. Have the children ready for five.
James

"Oh shag off," she shouted at the computer just as Detta walked through the door.

"You okay?" Detta asked, looking around for signs of anyone else and Ruth turned crimson.

"Ach, you know, computers."

"Don't trust the blasted things myself," Detta said. "I'm all up for as little technology as possible. The old ways were the best."

Ruth looked at Detta and wondered how on earth she had managed to live ten years in Dublin with her aversion to all things modern. She was a rare duck and that was for sure, but she really did have a pure heart.

"Can I do anything to help you?" Ruth asked.

"Oh, I just wanted to make an appointment with the doctor. No rush, you know."

Ruth looked at her computer, clicking the email off and set about taking Detta's details.

"You're not registered here," she said. "I'll need you to fill out this form."

Detta took an ornate pen, decorated with baubles and glitter, from her tie-dyed bag and started writing. "I kept registered with the doctor in Dublin for a long time, but I think I'm finally starting to accept I'm back here for good so I might as well make the change," she said.

"Dr Donnelly is lovely," Ruth soothed.

"Oh I know, she's a dote. She has been a star over these last few months but now I think I'll make it official."

As Ruth wondered just how her employer had been a godsend to this woman, and why, she pushed all thoughts of James and his bullying emails to the back of her head.

* * *

Dr Donnelly did, of course, let her away from work early and she walked at the speed of light home and managed to just about pull things into shape before James arrived. It was no mean feat, given that her three children had taken to throwing themselves at her feet at every opportunity pulling their best "woe is me" poses.

She dared not tell them she was planning on going to Derry

without them. Blood would have been shed – thirty-seven-year-old Frumpy Mummy blood. So she spent that last half hour in their company not only doing her best whirling-dervish routine but also willing her big mouth not to let her secret out.

James arrived spot on time. Ruth was actually surprised it wasn't his usual five minutes early to try and catch her out. He looked her up and down, regarding her with a look of utter disgust, and then grunted at the children that Laura was waiting. Ruth knew though that while in the presence of Laura – who was sitting outside in the car – he would be all sweetness and light. He wouldn't have let his guard down to her yet, she was sure of that.

"I've put Calpol in the bigger case and left the numbers of the surgery and my mobile there just in case," she said.

"I'm not stupid," James said. "I know how to look after my own children."

Ruth nodded. There was no point in biting back.

"They've been a little unsettled. You know, there have been a lot of changes . . ." she offered.

"They will be fine with me," he said. "You'll be fine, kids, won't you? The place we are going is having its very own fireworks display and there is a Jacuzzi and everything."

Eimear's eyes lit up and even Matthew looked mildly excited.

"And Eimear, pet, Laura has booked you and her into the spa for a full makeover. A real girly treat."

Of course at that the battle was won and Eimear skipped off, tapping a message into her mobile, no doubt telling her friends she had the best daddy ever.

Ruth couldn't compete with that. The biggest treat she had managed in recent weeks was a frozen pizza and a family size bag of Maltesers. As for days at the spa, the nearest she got was a trip to the chiropodist about her ingrowing toenail. She doubted Eimear would have wanted to keep her company at those appointments.

The children left and the house fell silent – but in some ways it was noisier than ever. Echoes of her darkest secret rang around in her head.

Eventually she dragged herself from the comfort of her sofa, slipped on her jacket and trainers and headed out into the cold evening air.

It was getting dark. She started walking as fast as she could on the soft sand before moving further down towards the shore to the harder, wetter sand. Her calves were already aching from the effort after ten minutes but there was no turning back – not least because the physical activity was serving to drive the thoughts that plagued her out of her head.

In fact, soon she began to feel quite elated. There was something about this walking which made her feel empowered. She felt as if it was just her, the sand and the sea. She felt close to nature – like she belonged in a John Denver song and eventually she found herself bursting into a chorus of "Poems, Prayers and Promises" as she strode on.

She was just reaching an impressive crescendo of tunelessness when she came across a small figure sitting cross-legged on the beach, staring out at the sea.

"Are you okay?" she called to the dark figure. Locals who would choose to sit on the wet sand on a cold night staring out to the sea were few and far between. It crossed her mind it could be darling Niamh who, having finally flipped her lid, was about to make a run and jump into the black sea.

Heart thumping, she called again "Are you okay?" while at the same time trying to keep a safe distance in case it wasn't some lonely soul but instead an axe-murdering madman waiting for his prey to come dancing along the beach like a buck-eejit singing John Denver songs.

She really wanted to move on. She couldn't be coping with this complication when all she had done was come for a walk on a cool night to clear her head and recover from the tension of dealing with her husband and relinquishing her children into his care. And yet she couldn't walk on and then have some poor fecker on her conscience.

"Excuse me!" she called again, a little louder this time, and moved a little closer.

The long curls draped down the back of the small figure at least made her breathe a sigh of relief. It wasn't Niamh and her sharp, razor-cut bob. A small face looked up – just about the same age as Ruth herself and not looking in the least bit distressed.

"Detta? Are you okay?" she asked, relieved that she wouldn't have to attempt to run away from an axe-murderer on soft sand.

"Ach me, I'm grand. Just balancing a chakra or two."

Detta climbed to her feet, smiling warmly at Ruth. Dressed in loose-fitting yoga pants and figured tracksuit jacket she made Ruth feel instantly frumpy in her Dunnes trainers and sweatpants. Who would have known that under those floating skirts and cardigans there was such an impressive figure? But then again, Detta didn't have three kids.

"Balancing a chakra?" Ruth asked.

"Yoga. It keeps me fit and more than that it keeps me sane."

"Ah, I see," Ruth said warmly. "You need a little chill-out time after dealing with us loonies and our problems."

"We all need a little chill-out time and we all have our problems," Detta replied. "I see you're out pounding the sand yourself."

"Nothing like the sea air to clear your mind."

"Or a cup of tea," Detta said. "Fancy one? We could nip over to mine. I've a brand new packet of chocolate biscuits ready for the opening."

With that Ruth's intentions of ignoring her sweet tooth went out the window and she nodded and the two women set off for Detta's house for some therapy that would be a whole lot less stressful on the muscles than a run along the beach.

Detta's house was not at all what Ruth expected. If she was honest she wasn't sure what she had expected – perhaps lots of incense and bean bags instead of proper chairs. But it was an ordinary house – nothing fancy and definitely with a proper sofa. There were a host of CDs, self-help books and DVDs organised neatly into bookshelves. A couple of pictures of Detta, smiling with a handsome teenager, sat on top of the shelves and Ruth made a mental note to ask Detta who he was. He looked vaguely familiar – and he certainly had made Detta happy. As far as Ruth knew Detta had no brothers or sisters so it was unlikely this young man – who she guessed was around the same age as Thomas – was a nephew. Would it be too nosy of her to ask, she wondered? As she thought about it Detta walked into the room with two cups of tea and glanced at the photos herself. She smiled at them, sat down and looked at Ruth.

"I'll tell you about him one day," she said and she changed the subject.

Ruth knew not to push it any further – sure, didn't they all have secrets they weren't ready to talk about?

22

"Is it tonight, Daddy?" Poppy asked, jumping on the bed and waking Liam from his sleep.

Blinking, he looked at the red glow of the alarm clock beside the bed: 6.30. He groaned.

"Tonight's a long way away, Poppy. Now go back to bed, or climb in here and go to sleep because it's going to be a late night and I want you to be well rested."

"But, Daddy, I'm so excited. I've been trying to get back to sleep for hours and hours and hours but every time I close my eyes I see fireworks or imagine I'm wearing my red sparkly shoes and my brain just doesn't want to sleep."

"But you will be too tired to enjoy it if you don't get a proper rest first," he bargained.

"Okay, Daddy, I'll try."

There was silence for the best part of two minutes before her voice chirped again.

"I've tried, Daddy. Really, really, really I've tried but I can't sleep. I'm too excited."

Poppy sat up and stared at her daddy. Her eyes were still heavy with sleep and her hair was a mess of dark bed-head curls on top of her head, but even in the dark Liam could see the glint in her eyes.

"Okay, darling, you win, but you might want to think about a nap later."

"I will, Daddy, I promise," Poppy said, crossing her fingers over her heart and smiling. "I'll go downstairs and make breakfast. Have we Coco pops? I love Coco pops. Ailish in school prefers Frosties, but I told her that only Coco pops make the milk turn chocolatey, so it's chocolate *and* breakfast so it's good for you."

The chatter continued as she jumped off the bed and padded down the stairs. Liam sat up and stretched. It was going to be a long day and he had hoped that Poppy would sleep until at least gone nine. Every day when she was at school he would have to practically beg her to get up to make it to class in time, but Sod's Law being what it was, now that she had a day off she was up at the crack of dawn.

If he had known she would have woken so early there was no way he would have had that extra can or two of beer the night before.

Rubbing his stubbly chin and yawning, he sighed. These were exactly the kind of times when he would have loved for Laura still to be here so she could take over and he could crawl back under the duvet for an extra hour or two asleep while she did mummy-type things like make breakfast and clean. He groaned as he thought of last night's dinner dishes still sitting by the sink, the remnants of their meal now cemented to them no doubt.

"Put them in the dishwasher as soon as they're done and you won't have to deal with this in the morning," Laura would have teased him. It drove her mad how he could leave dishes beside the dishwasher or in the sink but never think to rinse them off. He had been better since she left but last night, while trying to calm an overexcited Poppy and after an exceptionally stressful day in the site office, he just couldn't find the motivation.

"Daddy," a voice called up the stairs, "is it Hallowe'en all day?"

"Yes, love," he said, heading down to the kitchen.

"Well, can I put on my costume now then, being as it's Hallowe'en all day and all? I mean there's no point in putting on boring old clothes, is there?"

"Now, Poppy, I know you're very excited but I don't think you should put your dress on just yet. Keep it nice for tonight. Now which would you like to do today, come to work with me or go and see your granny?"

Poppy grimaced at the mention of her granny – although in fairness to her she did her best to hide it, turning her face from Liam and opening the fridge to fetch some orange juice.

"Hmmm, I'd really like to go and see Mammy," she said with a sigh.

Liam felt his heart sink to his boots but at the same time he knew he should be wary – Poppy could buy and sell the best of them.

"You know Mammy is away at the moment."

"Yes," Poppy sighed dramatically, "with *his* children. Not me. But I don't mind, Daddy, honest."

As she looked at him, her eyes as wide as that annoying little cat in the *Shrek* movies she loved so much, he had to think quickly. He had to get this just right – tune into the female psyche and deal with it in the best manner possible because if he got this wrong, either his daughter would never forgive him or he would leave himself in the unenviable position of being at her beck and call for the rest of her childhood years, never mind the dreaded teenage years.

"Sweetheart, you know your mammy loves you. And you

know she has promised that the two of you will do something really nice together next week. How about you come with me to work and then we'll both go to Granny's for lunch and then I'll take the afternoon off and you can be in your costume by two at the latest."

Poppy considered the proposal and, realising that was about as good as it was going to get, smiled. "Okay, Daddy," she said.

Liam sighed with relief. That was one crisis averted. Now if only he didn't have to spend the rest of the day appeasing women. He would have his mother to deal with and then the rest of the women from the group. They were nice people though, he thought. He wondered if Niamh would come along. He knew that Ruth had planned to go and see her after she hadn't showed at the meeting but he hadn't seen Ruth since. He had told her that she could call on him after the children left if she needed some moral support but he was kind of glad that she hadn't. He would prefer not to think at all about the fact his wife was off on her jollies with another man and his children while he was fighting a battle of wits with an expert emotional blackmailer with a passion for a fecking Dorothy costume.

"You women will send me to the nuthouse," he muttered as Poppy drank her orange juice.

"But you love us, Daddy," Poppy said, matter of factly, and set about getting dressed.

* * *

Liam was grateful that he could take Poppy into the site office with him. It was one of the perks of being boss, even if he did have to spend the day before making sure nothing questionable was left hanging about. His was a typically male office and there was generally a tabloid left open at page three hanging about, or some rude scribbles on a notebook. The fellas at the office were great when it came to Poppy and would chat nineteen to the dozen to her, but that didn't mean they made sure not to leave the odd snot-covered hanky or half-eaten sandwich festering somewhere.

Liam had taken a good slagging the day before when he donned his rubber gloves and gave the place a good going over.

"All right, Missus Mop!" Paul had shouted as he walked into the office trailing a heap of muck and sand on his boots.

"Jesus, would you watch yourself, I've just hoovered," Liam had chided, which of course had been met with snorts of laughter from the lads.

"I take it the wee woman is coming in with you tomorrow then?" Paul asked.

"Aye, so no farting, swearing, dirty pictures or spitting please."

"We'll be on our best behaviour, Mrs Doyle, don't you worry," Paul laughed, sitting down and resisting his usual urge to put his muddy boots up on the desk and have a read of the paper.

"We'll only be here half the day," Liam said, "so youse can do whatever you want in the afternoon. I've been roped into driving a mini-bus up to Derry for the fireworks."

"Boys' night out, is it? Why weren't we invited?" Paul asked, with mock indignation.

"Not quite. I'm taking a few family groups – you know, some of the kids from the village?"

"Oh aye, are you taking that Ruth one? You could get one back on Laura. Ruth's a fine woman."

Liam had coloured, unsure how to respond. He didn't really want to try and explain to the lads that he was just going for Poppy's sake and that the rest of the village's lone parents were going as well. They thought he was turning into enough of a woman as it was without him admitting he was going to a support group. The slagging would be unbelievable.

"Ach well, you never know," he answered with a laugh. Best to say nothing – there was no way he was going to admit that he still had feelings for Laura or that he was hoping her few days away with James and his three children would make her realise just what she was missing with him. Not that he thought Ruth's children would be a nightmare – but just that a taste of family life again would help her to realise that her own family was worth fighting for. Perhaps that was what annoyed him most about her walking out – how could she not have felt the same desire as he did to fight for what they had?

When he knew she was leaving he had, he was ashamed to say, broken down in tears and sobbed before her. He had gone to her office and asked her to come back. He had even encouraged Poppy to write her mother a letter begging her to come home. He was ashamed of that – when he should have been assuring his daughter that everything was going to be okay, he was embroiling her in his own hurt. That was probably why he spoiled her so much these days – he wanted to make up for that, albeit temporary, blip in his judgement and parenting skills.

"Ah go on!" Paul had said, "You might as well give her a go!"

Liam laughed, but inwardly cringed. He hoped his staff would know better than to talk like that when his daughter arrived.

* * *

Poppy had switched on the computer and made herself at home as soon as she walked into the office. She loved it here – she would sit and have little daydreams about being a grown-up office girl herself. Liam would be tortured with requests for "work" to do. She would saunter to and from his desk with little sheaves of paper for him to sign and mark.

She would also offer to make loads of tea and coffee for anyone who so much as looked as if they had a bit of a thirst on them. Of course, being Hallowe'en and her being in her Dorothy mode, she insisted on doing everything in a pseudo-American accent.

"Daddy, can you pretend to be the All Powerful Oz?" she asked, skipping towards him in her ruby slippers (which Liam had conceded she could wear until it was proper costume time), and he had dutifully donned his scariest and loudest voice as he demanded not one but two Rich Tea with his morning cuppa.

He was just demanding she sit down and do some work, all with his tongue in cheek of course, when Detta walked into the office and burst out laughing.

"Aah, the Great and Powerful Wizard of Oz, I presume?" she laughed.

He blushed. Damn it, this was almost as embarrassing as one of his builders catching him at his playacting, but then again at least Detta knew what he was at and didn't think he was just being an unbearable arse to his daughter.

"And so you must be Glenda the Good Witch then?" he said.

"Or maybe the Wicked Witch? You never know!" she said with a grin. If he hadn't known better, he would have thought she was flirting.

But of course, she couldn't be . . . could she?

"Do you want some coffee, Mrs O'Neill?" Poppy asked in her American accent.

"Now, Dorothy, you are to call me Detta because we are friends, but I don't really have time for a coffee." She winked. "I'm trying to get a few little surprises arranged for later."

Liam's heart warmed as he saw Poppy's face light up. "Surprises? Really?"

"Of course really," Detta said. "But I can't tell you because then it wouldn't be a surprise."

Liam smiled, enjoying the scene that was being played out before him, but then he realised that none of this explained exactly what Detta was doing in the builder's yard.

"So what can I do for you, Detta?" he asked, just remembering to drop the Great Oz voice and speak in the God-given Donegal drawl he was born with.

"I was just dropping the keys for the bus over. Since you have so kindly agreed to drive tonight and save me the bother, I thought I'd give you the chance to give the old girl a test drive first. She can take a bit of getting used to."

"I've driven a forklift in the pouring rain, so I'm thinking this should be okay in comparison," he smiled. "But we'll give it a wee go anyway."

"Grand, sure we'll see you around six. I want to get up in plenty of time to enjoy the *craic* before the fireworks."

By this stage Poppy was almost jumping up and down with excitement. "I can't wait, I really can't!"

"It won't be long, Poppy. Now I'll leave you two to get back to work and I'll see you later for some fun and games."

As Detta left, Paul walked in and winked at Liam. Willing him not to make any inappropriate comments, Liam put his head down and got on with his work.

"Was that Detta O'Neill?" Paul asked.

"Oh yes," Poppy replied. "She's coming with me and Daddy to Derry tonight to see the fireworks."

"Is she now indeed?" Paul asked with a smirk. "You're a dark horse, Liam Dougherty. You'll be getting yourself a reputation. Detta's an even finer woman than Ruth."

Willing Poppy to keep quiet, Liam turned his attention back to work, while doodling on a piece of paper:

REASONS WHY I WANT TO JUMP OFF A CLIFF:

* The boys think I'm the frigging village Lothario.

* Chance would be a fecking fine thing.

* Do I really have to keep pretending to be the Big Fecking Oz for the rest of the day?

23

Ciara dressed Ella in her costume while Lorraine watched, the smile of a proud granny plastered on her face. Ciara had been able to pick up a little bumblebee costume in the Post Office as recommended and she couldn't help but grin to see her wee woman crawl along the floor with her big padded bumblebee bum in the air. She was convinced Lorraine must have used up every square inch of memory on her camera snapping pictures.

"She's as cute as cute can be," she said, grinning from ear to ear.

Things between Ciara and Lorraine had been better in the last three days than they had been in years. They had opened up, talking and laughing, though Ciara still had to do her best to make sure her mother didn't track Ben down and make sure he never got any other girl pregnant ever again. Lorraine had even slipped a ten-pound note into Ciara's hand as she got ready to go out that night.

Lifting her own camera, Ciara smiled and took a few shots, before lifting her daughter to her for a big cuddle. She looked pretty okay herself, she thought, as she smoothed down the white dress she had found in the charity shop and admired the fairy wings she'd also found in the Post Office. Thank God for wee country post offices and their array of bizarre extras. In Rathinch you could buy everything from a postage stamp to a mop and bucket.

Ciara was delighted to still be in possession of a drawerful of sparkly eyeshadows and lip-glosses, even though her chances to wear them now were few and far between. She had gone to town tonight, painting her face like every ounce the good fairy she wanted to be. She even popped a plastic tiara on her head for good measure.

Smiling, she packed a few extra nappies into the overnight bag, slipped her coat on and strapped Ella into her buggy. Then they headed out and up the road to Ruth's house, Lorraine waving them off enthusiastically at the door.

Although it was already starting to get dark and there was a distinct nip in the air, Ciara breathed in and smiled. She was actually going out! Sure it wasn't to a club or a bar or even to Abby's house for a bit of *craic*, but she was going out to do something with friends and she was looking forward to it.

She was sure that Poppy Dougherty would help her look after Ella and the twins would also be great company for her daughter so while she was going to be still on mammy duty, she knew she would also be able to let her newly glittered hair down just that little bit.

"It's going to be fun, isn't it Ella-Bella?" she cooed just as the baby decided to throw her blanket from the buggy onto the ground. "Oh, you little tinker, let me get that for you!" Ciara smiled, moving to the front of the buggy to wrap her daughter back up in her blanket.

As she kissed her gorgeous pudgy cheeks, now red from the cold, she heard a familiar voice from behind her.

"Ciara," he said and she felt herself freeze.

She couldn't deal with this and with him now. She wanted

to just get to Ruth's and get on with her night out – no matter how uncool any of her school pals would have thought it.

"Ben," she said, as casually as her nerves would allow.

"You all right?" he asked with a sniff, scuffing his feet together.

"Fine," she sniffed back.

"The baby looks cool in that costume," he offered.

Feeling strangely protective of her daughter – even though she had made her look a complete eejit by dressing her up like a bumblebee – Ciara put her back to her, covering her from Ben's gaze.

"Yes, she does," Ciara answered, hoping that if she kept her answers brief and to the point, Ben would soon get bored and walk on.

"You look . . . interesting, yourself," he said with a little sneer.

Ciara felt tears threaten to choke her. *Switch on your inner voice*, she told herself, but somehow when it came to Ben Quinn she could never even think of clever putdowns and harsh words. He brought out the very worst in her.

Suddenly she didn't feel quite so cool and trendy any more. Her costume, which she had been so proud of, now seemed cheap and tacky. Funny that, how Ben could make her feel cheap and tacky.

"I have to go, I'm meeting people. Have a good Hallowe'en and I'll see you later," she said, trying to keep the tremble from her voice. She wanted to say more. She wanted to do more – to kick him square in the gonads if the truth be told – but she thought keeping her cool was good enough.

"Not if I see you first," he said in a cocky tone of voice that almost, just almost, gave her the strength to tell him to feck off. He turned to walk away and she waited until he was a safe distance away before giving him the finger.

As she looked at Ella, her gorgeous daughter looked back at her with a look of confusion.

"That," Ciara said, "was a very, very bad man. Well, he's more of a boy, but he's bad whatever he is." She took the plastic tiara from her head and threw it into the hood of the buggy before pushing on up the hill.

Ben had been one of the in-crowd at school. Well, technically he was still one of the in-crowd. It was Ciara who had been pushed to the sidelines. She wasn't part of any crowd now – apart from the gang of saddo lone parents who were mostly all old enough to be her own parents. She supposed she had never really fitted in with the in-crowd, not coming from a home where the latest designer trainers or money for bowling or the cinema was easy to come by. But she had held her own and had been proud of how she had been accepted into Ben Quinn's clique.

She had thought she loved him, although she could now freely admit that what she thought was love was largely based on the songs of Westlife and X Factor winners. It was all about hearts and flowers for her and when Ben started leaving romantic notes in her locker and texting her in the middle of the night she had felt her heart swell with emotion.

He told her she was beautiful and he wanted to hold her hand. She loved the feeling of her hand in his. He might have been only fifteen but his hand was as manly as any she had seen. He even had downy hair on his knuckles. She thought that was so rugged and, if she was honest, damn sexy too. Her heart would flutter when she saw him walking down the corridors at school and when he turned and smiled at her in class, double maths just didn't seem so dull and uninteresting any more.

Ben told her she was funny and evidently he also thought she was hot enough to kiss which was a plus. After all she didn't have the Wonderbras of some of the other girls or the confidence to match. He liked her as she was and that was about as good as it got.

After that night – that first kiss – Ciara had walked home with a smile on her face. When she got home Lorraine had been sitting over a cup of coffee and a cigarette in the kitchen. Ciara had sat down beside her and rested her head on her mother's shoulder, sighing contentedly.

"You look happy," her mother had smiled.

"I am, Mum," Ciara said, getting up to switch the kettle back on to make herself a cup of tea. She liked the smell of coffee, but she couldn't bring herself to drink it.

"There are biscuits in the cupboard," Lorraine said, sitting back and watching her daughter at work. "So what has you smiling? Is there a boy I should know about?"

Ciara poured the milk into her mug and sat down. "It's nothing really. Just a lad at school. He thinks I'm funny."

"Of course you're funny, darling," Lorraine had said with genuine warmth. "A funny wee woman. You've always made me laugh."

Of course if Ciara had known then what she knew now she would have run away from him screaming, but it felt too nice and she stayed with him until she got in as deep as she possibly could. And then it was him, and not her, who had run away screaming.

Arriving at Ruth's house, Ciara put all notions of her encounter with Ben out of her head. Thankfully there was plenty to distract her.

Ruth fell on Ella as if she was the only baby she had ever held in her life.

"Oh my God, would you look at this? Did you ever see anything as cute in your life? Oooh, you could sting me any time, wee bumble bee!" she cooed and was met with a milky burp for her troubles.

"I have a wee cloth here," Ciara offered, reaching into her bag.

"Nonsense, a bit of baby sick never did anyone any harm. I'm one of the weird freaks who doesn't mind at all, wee pet that she is!"

Ciara smiled, relaxed that she wasn't being made to feel her child was a burden or a pain in the rear. "Good, because this one knows how to boke with the best of them."

"My Matthew was the same," Ruth soothed. "But you know, it's true. They really do grow up in a blink of an eye."

"I quite like the sound of that," Ciara said. "Fast forward a couple of years until she is old enough to change her own nappy. It would work for me."

"She's a dote," Ruth smiled.

Ciara rolled her eyes. "Honestly, you wouldn't be saying that at three in the morning. I think that sleeping-through nonsense is a myth." Fighting the urge to yawn at the very thought of her interrupted nights' sleep Ciara sat down, while Ruth continued to fuss over Ella.

"I like your costume too," Ruth said, sitting down across the living room from her. Instinctively Ciara pulled her coat closer to her.

"Jesus, wee girl, if I had your figure I wouldn't be covering it up for anyone," Ruth said with a smile.

Of course Ciara could hardly tell her that it was her run-in with Ben – the object of Eimear's affections – that had brought about her new-found shyness.

"You know, you're right," she said with a smile, standing up to take off her coat before reaching for the tiara from Ella's pram and perching it back on her head. As her daughter giggled and cooed, she spun around.

"Oooooh," a little voice squeaked. "It's Glenda the Good Witch. Hello, I'm Dorothy."

Ciara turned around to see Poppy, complete with plaits in her hair and a small wicker basket, standing clicking her ruby heels together.

"So you are," she said, "and I think this wee one of my mine could be the perfect Munchkin."

"Well," Poppy said solemnly, "Munchkins don't normally dress like bumblebees but we can pretend."

"Of course we can. Now let's sing 'Follow the Yellow Brick Road'," Ciara said, instantly warming to the precocious young girl in front of her who reminded her of just how she had been not so long ago.

"You're very good to amuse her, Ciara," Liam said, following his daughter into the living room.

"I'm sure she's no trouble," Ciara said, dancing from one foot to the next while her own daughter clapped along very much out of rhythm. If truth be told she was enjoying having the chance to act like a complete eejit without anyone thinking badly of her.

"Why don't you all join in?" she asked, feeling as if the weight of her worry was at once gone.

"I'm not really one for dancing," Liam said awkwardly.

"You're obviously not really one for dressing up either," Ruth said with a grin.

"Sure you're not dressed up yourself, woman," he answered.

"Just give me a minute, I will be," she said, running upstairs.

A warm feeling spreading through her, Ciara wondered for a moment what it would be like if Liam and Ruth were her parents and this was what life was always like. Without the costumes, obviously.

24

Niamh had spent the day in a state of utter confusion. She decided one minute to go to Derry with the others, and the next to stay at home in front of a scary movie with yet another glass of wine.

It hadn't helped that at approximately midnight the night before she had woken from her sleep to the very real memory of one of her last nights out with Seán.

It had been Christmas and Seán's law firm was having its annual party. Niamh and Caitlin had travelled down to Dublin to shop for the perfect dress in Brown Thomas and had spent a weekend relaxing in a nice hotel, having every spa treatment under the sun until they returned to the North exfoliated, tanned and waxed to within an inch of their lives.

"You don't mind me coming with you?" Caitlin had asked as they made their hair appointments over a cappuccino and slice of cake.

"Don't be so daft. Of course we don't mind."

"I don't want to be a gooseberry," Caitlin had said, flicking her dark hair from her eyes.

"You're no worse a gooseberry than two toddlers," Niamh had laughed. "Besides, we can't have you sat on your own all night and Seán will most likely be mingling. I'll need you to keep me topped up with champagne and gossip. I'm so out of the loop these days. I never thought I would say it, but I miss the office."

"Like hell you do," Caitlin laughed. "Living it up in your fancy house in the country. What I wouldn't give!"

And they had laughed – a lot.

On the night itself, Niamh had looked stunning. She didn't need Seán to tell her that, but it was nice when he did. He had wrapped his arms around her waist and kissed her neck before running his hands down her chocolate-satin dress.

"Can we not just stay here instead?" he murmured, reaching up and cupping her breasts.

She had to admit it seemed a shame to have a gorgeous hotel suite to themselves all night and not get proper use of it, but she also knew that horny as her husband was, he was never going to miss the chance to network with his law-firm pals.

"I wish," she had murmured, turning around to kiss him. "But you know we can't. Besides there is no way we can leave Caitlin to deal with Kevin all on her own. She'll eat him alive."

Seán had laughed, a deep throaty laugh and had kissed her hard on the lips before lifting his jacket and leading her out of the hotel room.

The night had been magnificent. She had laughed with Caitlin, had too much champagne to drink and had slow-danced with Seán under the mistletoe. When their dance was done he had taken Caitlin out for a dance and she had sat, dizzy with drink, watching them sway around the floor together, laughing and hugging and looking deep into each other's eyes and right then she thought nothing of it – because she trusted them both, implicitly.

* * *

Niamh hadn't told Connor and Rachel that a trip on a mini-bus was even on the cards because she knew she would have to give in to their constant whining and unending renditions of "The Wheels on the Bus".

She had already been tortured into dressing them up. Connor was a very cute Bob the Builder while Rachel was swanning around the house as Cinderella. They were hyper enough without dosing them up on sugar and e-numbers she thought wryly – but then, as she had been such a fecking grump the last week, surely they deserved a little treat.

Picking up the phone she dialled Robyn's number. Her friend had been available to take her many calls morning, noon and night since she had found the Post-it. And while Niamh knew that Robyn wanted to go and have it out with Caitlin in person she respected Niamh's wishes enough to keep her cool.

"Hey, babes," Niamh said on hearing her friend's warm hello.

"Hey, yourself. How are you?" Robyn asked, her voice thick with concern.

"Well, I'm still here. I've not killed myself or dug him up just to kill him again or anything crazy like that." Niamh forced light-heartedness into her voice. She wasn't in the mood for a deep and meaningful conversation and, even if she were, the presence of Bob and Cinders singing a rousing rendition of "A Dream is a Wish Your Heart Makes" would have made it impossible anyway.

"That's always a positive thing," Robyn answered. "But have you hired a hit man for yer one yet?"

"What? And have the two of them living it up together in the afterlife? Not a chance."

"It's good to hear you sounding so calm."

"You mean, not sobbing hysterically down the phone at you for once?" Niamh said, embarrassed at the memory of just such a phone call the night before.

"Well yes, but you know if you need to sob at anyone, I'm your gal."

"Thanks, Robyn. You're a dote."

"So what can I do for you? Given that you want me to hold off on the assassination for now."

"Tell me to wise up and take my children to Derry with the Loonies for the fireworks. They could do with a bit of fun."

"Wise up and take your children to Derry with the Loonies. They could do with a bit of fun. And so could you, for that matter."

Fun? Niamh could barely remember what that meant but she wasn't – not today anyway – going to let the dark moods win. She certainly wasn't going to have fun sitting in while the children slept upstairs so she nodded to the phone before saying, "You know, I will. Thanks, Robyn."

"And if it all gets too much for you, I'll be at home so you can call in. Just do what you can, pet. You need some form of distraction."

"I know," Niamh said "And I'll phone you if I need you, but fingers crossed I can manage one night without a total breakdown."

She said her goodbyes and sat her two children down to tell them the most exciting news ever: that they were going, in a bus, to see the fireworks. At once they screamed – that perfect high-pitched squeal of a toddler – and ran to her to hug her close.

"Oh, Mummy, I'm so 'cited," Rachel said, jumping up and

down in her dress while Connor started to run in wild circles around the living room, ending in a skid along the floor on his knees with his hands punched in the air in victory.

Niamh couldn't help but laugh with them and she set about getting their things ready and setting out for Ruth's house where they would all go together to see the fireworks.

They walked through the village, hand in hand, and sang "The Witches of Hallowe'en". By the time they reached Ruth's the children's cheeks were rosy from the cold and their eyes lit up with excitement at the sight of the rather ramshackle bus in the driveway.

Taking a deep breath, Niamh knocked on the door. I do deserve a bit of fun, she told herself.

The door opened to Ruth, resplendent in a witch's costume complete with long, crooked nose. Connor screamed with delight while Niamh cringed. Oh Christ, she thought, I hope I'm not the only one in civvies. Her heart sank further when she saw a tiara-topped Ciara dancing in the living room with a mini-Dorothy.

"Come along, my pretties!" Ruth beckoned with a curl of her finger and the twins ran into the house to join in the dancing.

"Are you okay, my sweetheart?" Ruth said, this time in her normal voice.

"I'm not too bad. I'm determined not to talk about it. Tonight is just for fun." Niamh thought she saw something – the briefest flash of sadness – across her friend's face but just as she was about to ask Ruth if she herself was okay there was a cheer from the living room and Connor ran back out.

"Mummy, do you think Bob the Builder is a Munchkin because I want to be a Munchkin?"

"I'm pretty sure he is," Niamh replied and followed her son back into the living room vowing that, should she get the chance, she would try and have a quiet chat with Ruth later. It was only fair, given how she had howled over her new friend the week before and, indeed, how she had almost thrown up on her while sopping drunk just a few nights before.

Niamh breathed a sigh of relief to see that Liam wasn't dressed up either. "Glad I'm not the only Hallowe'en Grinch," she said with a smile as she stood watching the children dance with Ruby and Ruth.

"Can we go yet?" Poppy asked, breathless with excitement.

"Yeah, can we go?" Connor chimed in, closely followed by Rachel who was enthralled by the glittery plastic tiara on Ciara's head.

"Not just yet," Ruth answered. "We have to wait for Mrs O'Neill."

"Detta," Poppy said authoritatively. "She said I was to call her Detta and I'm sure she wouldn't mind if Connor and Rachel called her Detta too. She's lovely. She made my dress."

Niamh was impressed. Her sewing skills amounted to little more than a slightly wonky apron in Home Economics at school – and even then the teacher had laughed at her efforts. Caitlin and Robyn had both been outraged and had offered to egg the teacher's car if need be. That was when their friendship had still counted for something – when being a good friend involved pegging eggs at a teacher's house rather than shagging her husband.

"Penny for them," Liam said jovially and Niamh realised she had the most unimpressed expression on her face imaginable.

"Never mind me . . . just thinking of lions and tigers and bears . . ."

"Oh my," he chimed and she found herself laughing.

"Well, in a very non-stalkerish kind of way, it's nice to see you here. We all missed you on Tuesday."

She nodded, and smiled back, "I think I missed everyone too."

Ten minutes later she had forgotten her inhibitions and was, from memory, telling the story of "Room on the Broom" when Detta O'Neill walked through the door, resplendent in an emerald suit, which set against her curls looked stunning.

"I couldn't get the Wizard to come here himself," Detta said, "but I thought, you know, in the interests of gender equality and all that, this might do the job."

Niamh sat there, mid-sentence, and gawped at Detta, impressed she had gone to such efforts and when she saw her children's faces light up she realised that Robyn had been right all along. She needed this – some fun without having to think about what had happened and without having to be "Yer one whose husband was killed in that accident" for a little while. And her children needed it too – a day of not having to miss their daddy or wonder why Mammy was crying again.

Winking conspiratorially at Liam, she laughed. "We are the two odd ones out then. Do we look better for it or complete eejits for not bothering?"

"I'm not sure," he laughed back, "but I'm already dreading next year."

"Ach, look at you two like two big grumps," Detta laughed. "You could at least have been a Cowardly Lion or something!"

"Hey, it was enough of an effort to get Bob and Cinders here sorted," Niamh said and then wondered if she sounded curt.

She was well aware that she had been biting the heads off people a lot these last few months – people who, she knew, were generally just trying to help, but who she had thought were passing judgement on her life. But looking around, everyone was still smiling and laughing with her so she hadn't put anyone's nose out of joint just yet. But, as she reminded herself, the night was young.

"Right, well, you know," she said, "I think we should be making a move soon because the traffic can be a nightmare getting into the city centre and we want to be near the Guildhall for all the fun and games so we don't get stuck in the crush."

"Well, Niamh, as you are from the big smoke yourself I'll take your advice," said Liam. "All aboard everyone!" And he led the way to the rickety bus outside.

Taking a deep breath and climbing on board with the children, Niamh told herself she was not to focus on that stretch of road too much. She was having fun. She would have fun – by hook or by crook and this was going to be the first night in a long time that she was just a mammy. Pure and simple.

"Okay," she said, sitting down and painting on a smile, "who knows 'The Witches of Hallowe'en'?"

"Ooooh, me, me, me!" Poppy chirped before launching into an impressive rendition, which had all the grown-ups fake-quaking in their boots.

"Oh, I can't wait till Ella is that age and a bit of *craic*," Ciara said to Niamh as they watched.

"I know what you mean. They say the twos are terrible, but threes are pretty hard going too. I can't wait till I tell them what to do and they actually listen."

Ruth choked back a laugh, "God, girls, I hate to break it to you, but I'm still waiting for that. Only Matthew pretends to listen to me, the other two are in a world of their own."

"No," Ciara laughed, "don't tell me that! It's supposed to get easier." Turning to Niamh she said, "Is it too late to ask for a refund?"

"Ach, you wouldn't wish her away for the world. I

remember when my two were that little. God, they were hard work – the two of them – but we were about as happy as we had ever been." Almost as soon as the words were out, she wished that she hadn't thought of how happy she had been because she didn't know if it had been a lie. And that, she realised, made her very, very unhappy.

Pushing the thoughts from her mind again – and vowing to get ratted when the whole thing was over – she begged Poppy to sing again and watched with a lump in her throat as the twins joined in.

25

Resentment against James and fears for the children had allowed Ruth's deepest darkest thoughts to surface and swarm about in her head uninhibited. But, if anyone had noticed her inner turmoil, they'd at least had the good grace not to mention it, she thought thankfully as they drove up to Derry.

No one, seeing her in her finest witch's costume, could have guessed at the feelings that were threatening to overwhelm her tonight. Because, no one – not one person apart from her and James – had known what had gone on in her marriage.

He hadn't hit her before they were married. Her joy on her wedding day was real. Her love for him had been too. It was only afterwards, when they were both exhausted as first-time parents, that he let his temper get the better of him. Eimear had been bawling all night and they'd both been exhausted. Being young was no consolation. With a job to go to the next day James wasn't in the form for an interrupted night's sleep and Ruth was worn out from the day in/day out routine of being a new mother to the world's most demanding infant.

"Sort that baby out," James had grunted as he'd rolled over to fall back to sleep.

Ruth had felt tears prick her eyes. All she wanted was a full night's sleep. She had done every night feed to allow her husband a good rest, but should Eimear dare to wake him he was like a bear with a sore head. Of course he'd only be awake until Ruth got up and quietened the baby down, while she was the one walking the floors downstairs, heating bottles and burping their daughter until her eyes were so heavy with sleep she became terrified she would fall asleep and smother her baby.

That night her spirit could take no more.

"Honey, can you do it? I'm so tired," she'd said, her voice breaking.

She felt his body stiffen, his breathing growing deeper, but there was no response and Eimear was still crying.

"Please honey," she pleaded, reaching out her hand to him and stroking his back gently.

He turned around and in what seemed like one swift movement he grabbed her wrist – hard – and pushed her back on the bed. His face close to hers, but all hint of intimacy missing, he told her that Eimear was her responsibility and if she didn't sort the baby out right there and then she could spend the night, along with her child, in the garden. He had pushed her then, so that she fell out of the bed and crashed to the floor and as she fed her daughter shortly afterwards, feeling the bruising on her wrist and her legs, she wondered what had just happened.

They were on edge, of course they were. Their happy existence of just Ruth and James had gone out the window and they were bound to get snappy, weren't they?

He hadn't meant it, he hadn't meant for her to fall from the bed and when she climbed in beside him later he reached over and wrapped his arm around her.

"Sorry," he muttered and fell back to sleep while she lay in the dark and promised to try harder to be a good wife.

The next time was a few weeks later. Eimear hadn't been crying that time, but Ruth had been exhausted again from a day dealing with her. When James came in from work she offloaded her complaints to him until he had asked her to give his head peace. She had sat down, her pride hurt and her temper flaring. She tried to bite back her frustration but a day dealing with a colicky baby had her at the end of her tether.

"So sorry to interrupt your busy day with worries about my sad little life here looking after our baby – who has been crying all afternoon. I'm sorry that I thought you might be interested or supportive or give a damn about what I'm going through."

"I asked you to give my head peace," James said, his fists clenching.

"And I asked you to listen and to give a shit about us!" Ruth shouted, her temper finally breaking. But as her words reached a crescendo, she was silenced by a blow to the side of the face. It was so strong it knocked her against the wall. It was so strong it took the breath from her body and it was a good ten seconds before it came back. Gasping, unable to believe what had just happened, she stood up. Her cheek throbbed, and there was a ringing in her ears. All of this however was eclipsed by the thumping of her heart and the sobbing of her husband.

"Oh God, Ruth, I'm sorry. I'm so sorry."

She walked across the room to where he was sitting and crouched down beside him. Wrapping her arms around him she soothed his tears as he promised never, ever to do it again.

He'd lied.

Each incident had left invisible bruises which would remain long after the lurid purple and yellow had disappeared.

But with every incident she remembered her part in it. She couldn't pretend to be innocent. That night – the first night he had hit her across the face – she had known his temper was flaring. She had seen it from the minute he walked in the door and yet she had pushed him. And she knew, as soon as it was over, that his remorse was genuine. As she had soothed him and he told her he was sorry, he added that she had pushed him over the edge.

"You need to back off a little, Ruth," he'd said later when he had calmed down. "You don't realise how much you can be in my face. You need to give me some space."

From then on, it had just got worse – the list of things that Ruth hadn't realised before James pointed them out to her got longer. She hadn't realised she nagged him too much, or that she wasn't that good a cook. She hadn't realised how she spoke too much in the evenings when he was tired, or how she didn't look half as good as she had when they first met.

He loved her, despite these faults, and she loved him despite his. His temper was something she would have to live with. For better or worse.

She had accepted it and it wasn't as if they were never happy again. He had been delighted when Thomas was born – a proud father of a son. For a while things had been wonderful. Their little family of four seemed to make James happier than he had ever been and he showered Ruth with affection. He'd tell her he loved her and would even do the occasional night feed for his son.

The cracks reappeared when Thomas hit his toddler years and grew into the most affectionate child Ruth could have ever hoped for. A real mammy's boy, he would climb on her knee and smother her in kisses while he shunned James's offer to go out and play football or go and see the diggers up on one of the farms. No, Thomas was much happier reading with Ruth or doing jigsaw puzzles at the kitchen table.

It broke Ruth's heart to see the sadness in her husband's eyes when Thomas ran to her arms instead of to him, but her sympathy was soon tested when he started to take his frustrations out on her.

The only saving grace was that he never took it out on the children. Sure, now that she thought about it, there was a stage when he simply stopped trying to involve Thomas in everything, but he never lost his temper with them, or hit them. That was reserved for her and in a strange way she respected him for that.

But she couldn't really relax when they were in his company without her. She liked to always be there – to act as a buffer – literally – for his bad moods and much as she was sure that he wouldn't act up in front of his new woman, she wasn't sure that if he did Laura would have the same loyalty to her children as she had.

* * *

Ruth broke into a rousing chorus of "We're Off to See the Wizard" as the bus sped out of Rathinch and towards the bright lights of Derry. She was going to enjoy this – if it killed her, and the way she felt right now she thought it might just do that.

"Are you okay?" Niamh asked as the singing finished and Detta started to tell a ghost story.

"I'm not sure," Ruth said with a half smile, "but I'm determined to at least pretend I am."

26

As far as nights out went, this wasn't the worst, Liam thought as he drove the bus to Derry. Poppy's eyes had been alight with excitement all evening and it had done him good to see her so happy. He hadn't seen such sustained happiness in his daughter since Laura had walked out. It was funny, he thought, that he craved his wife back but yet at the same time could be so angry with her for the hurt she was causing, intentionally or otherwise, to their daughter.

Although he hadn't dressed up – and had no intention of ever doing so – he didn't feel like a spare part. If the notion took him, he might even join in the singing in a wee while, although he couldn't imagine being as tuneful as the ladies.

By the time they reached Derry, the children were at fever pitch. Even baby Ella – who hadn't the first notion what was going on – was bouncing up and down like a hyper bumblebee. Poppy had been playing with her most of the way up the road but once they entered Derry and were surrounded by hordes of people walking through the streets in weird and wonderful costumes, they had all become transfixed looking out the window.

"Oh look, it's a Ghostbuster!"

"Look, Daddy, Scooby Doo!"

"Did you ever see the like of that before?"

"Mammy, Mammy, it's Bob the Builder! Do you think it's the real Bob the Builder? Do you, Mammy?"

"God, she must be frozen dressed liked that!"

Liam smiled as he listened to the banter, but preferred to keep his eyes on the road. With zombies and Teletubbies at every turn he wanted to make sure he didn't cause a Hallowe'en Night Massacre.

Pulling into the car park close to the Guildhall, he wrapped his coat around him and persuaded a reluctant Poppy to do the same.

"But Dorothy doesn't have a coat, Daddy," she protested, her bottom lip protruding.

"Yes, but we're not in Kansas any more, pet, and it's freezing here – so unless you want to get sick you need to put a coat on."

Reluctantly she agreed and Liam sighed in relief. Another crisis averted. As they entered the Guildhall Square the sound of cheering rang in their ears.

"Jaysus, what a crowd," he said to Detta, whose eyes were as animated as Poppy's.

"Isn't it great?" she smiled back, pushing her way through the crowds so that her little band of Loonies could follow. Liam had to admit he was impressed with the effort she'd gone to. Her emerald-green suit, with long flowing skirt and frockcoat, hugged her curves wonderfully. Her blonde curls were piled on her head, odd tendrils falling here and there and her green eyes were shining brightly. She looked alive and vibrant and, he admitted to himself, extremely attractive.

There was a band on stage leading the crowd in a sing-song and Liam looked at the crowds of families out enjoying themselves – sons on proud daddies' shoulders, mammies wiping noses and encouraging their daughters to dance like mad things. Liam looked at his friends and saw each of them trying to get into the same spirit, but each was aware, he realised, that something – or someone – was missing from their lives.

Detta looked at him and, he thought, it was as if she could read his mind.

"It's okay to find this a little difficult," she said. "But just look at Poppy and how much she is enjoying it and try to be grateful for the small stuff, eh?"

She gave his hand a reassuring rub and in that minute he felt a flutter of contentment. He wanted to hug her – just to feel the warmth of someone else near him – and thank her for understanding. But then, of course, he remembered he was a big hulk of a Donegal man and it would do no good to fall apart and beg for a hug. He settled for the warmth of the handrub and looked at his daughter and pushed all grumpy feelings aside.

"The fireworks will be starting soon," Niamh smiled.

Liam lifted his daughter up on his shoulders and carried her as close to the stage as he could.

"Are you ready to see some magic?" he asked.

"Oh yes, I sure am," she replied as a bright red firework shot through the sky, popping and fizzing and shattering into a thousand tiny stars which rained down over the River Foyle and garnered a chorus of "Ooohs" and "Aaahs" from the assembled crowds.

It was followed by a shooting star of gold and silver, which burst and cascaded down in the night sky like a gorgeous weeping-willow tree. Liam couldn't help it. He shouted "*Wow!*" louder than he intended because it was nothing short of a wow moment.

When the display was over, and they danced themselves

silly, they crowded – tired and grinning – back into the mini-bus where Detta produced flasks of tea and hot chocolate. She delved into her large bag and pulled out a variety of cookies as well and they sat there, staring over the river and having their snack. This woman put Mary Poppins to shame. Liam had never seen anyone as organised at anything before in his life.

"This has been the best Hallowe'en ever," Poppy said with a yawn.

"Oh, you can't be getting sleepy yet," he told her. "Ruth has games planned back at home. Come on, little lady, the party isn't over yet!"

"But, Daddy, it's past my bedtime. Am I really allowed to stay up late?" she asked, wide-eyed.

"It's a special occasion and of course you can."

"Yes!" she said, punching the air and turning to the twins, who were smeared in cookie all over their dressing-up costumes, and told them proudly she could stay up late as she was a big girl.

"Can Connor and Rachel come to the party too?" she asked.

Niamh smiled. "They'll be tired soon, but we'll see."

"Daddy," Poppy said, hopping onto her seat, "I like your new friends. They are much more fun than Mummy."

If any of the other passengers on the bus heard that comment they chose to ignore it and for that Liam was grateful.

"Yes, we're having fun, aren't we, darling?"

"We are having the best fun I ever had in my whole life. This has been my bestest Hallowe'en ever!" Poppy rested her head against his back and kissed him before returning to her seat and letting him continue with the drive back to Rathinch.

Of course, by now, it had gone nine and he would never

usually let Poppy stay up this late but he could see from the glint in her eye that she was much too excited to even think about going to sleep.

He didn't really fancy going home to a quiet house anyway and was looking forward to the rest of the evening. When the children were finally worn out, Ruth had promised to open a bottle of wine and share some adult time. She had even warned Detta that no notebooks were to be brought out and that this was purely to be a bit of fun. Detta had put her hands up in surrender and said she was looking forward to the wine as much as the next person. Liam smiled at the memory. Damn him, he had smiled at least four times tonight. It was strange feeling even a little happy – but he liked the happiness too. It had been a long time since he felt this contented. In fact, he realised with a start, he hadn't felt like this since before Laura left. Long before Laura left.

27

It didn't take long for the tiredness to hit the children. Ella was first to fall asleep. In fairness she had been asleep from about five minutes after the bus had pulled out of Derry. Liam had marvelled at her downy hair, sweaty against her wee face in her bumblebee costume, as he helped Ciara lift her from the bus. She reminded him so of Poppy when she had been that age and he had a momentary surge of love for his daughter and wished that he and Laura had had another child. Then again, two children would have made this whole sorry situation even messier.

Next to fall asleep was Rachel, curled on her mammy's knee while Connor was running around hyped up on the many Curlie Wurlies he had eaten. He even outdid Poppy who told her daddy she was sleepy shortly after ten thirty.

"You can sleep up in Eimear's room with Ella and Ciara if you like," Ruth said.

Poppy's face lit up again with excitement. "Can I, Daddy?"

Liam looked at Ruth for reassurance that it was fine and she nodded.

"I hate being alone here," she said, "and Ciara and Ella

are staying over anyway so we might as well make the most of it." She then turned to Niamh and said she was welcome to take the boys' room for her and the twins. "I fumigated it just in case," she laughed.

Niamh nodded gratefully. She would really be able to let her hair down if she didn't have to think about traipsing the twins back out to the big house.

"There's a double bunk there. The twins could sleep on the bottom level and you could have the top bunk – that is, if you aren't afraid of heights."

"After a couple of glasses of wine, that might not be a great idea," Niamh had answered, "but I don't mind cuddling in with the twins. That's how we all end up most nights anyway."

"Grand, that's sorted then. The kids can all get some sleep now. Liam, you're welcome to the sofa, but if you want to go on home later I'll bring Poppy round in the morning."

Liam smiled, but realised that Detta was left out of the equation. "What about our esteemed leader?" he asked.

Ruth blushed. "I have a blow-up mattress if you want to stay, Detta," she said.

"I'll be grand to walk home," Detta replied, "as long as Liam doesn't mind escorting me up the road. It's on his way anyway."

"So it is," Liam said, and he smiled. If he wasn't sure that Detta couldn't possibly be flirting with him, he would have thought there was a little spark there.

He tucked Poppy into bed, still in her Dorothy costume which she refused to take off, and stopped by the bathroom. Looking in the mirror he saw his stomach – a little less paunchy than it had been the week before. His diet must be working. His hair was greying around the temples. He still had a thick thatch of hair though – he was grateful for that.

He had shaved earlier, but there was a trace of stubble across his chin and his eyes looked tired. He was sure he had more wrinkles there than he had a month ago – not that he took any notice of wrinkles of course. He was a man. A man's man. But if he did take notice, he thought wryly, he would think he was looking quite good these days. The grey hair and wrinkles actually suited him – in a Rock Hudson/George Clooney kind of way.

Stop it, he thought. This was ridiculous. Just two hours before he had been moping that his wife was off living the happy family life with another man and his children and now he was thinking of Detta and how her smile lit up her whole face.

"Rebound," he whispered to his reflection. "Don't mess this up. You have few enough friends as it is."

He left, his head a muddle of confused thoughts and walked back to the living room where he was handed a cold beer.

"I need this," he said with a grimace and put it to his lips and sat down.

* * *

Ruth offered Ciara a drink and she nodded – not quite sure if she should be accepting or not. After all, she was well aware she was still only seventeen. Much as things had thawed between her and Lorraine in recent days, she knew her mother would go off on one if she so much as thought Ciara was having a Bacardi Breezer or two.

Ruth busied herself opening a bottle and said: "I didn't know whether I should offer you or not, you know, but I didn't want you to think we were treating you like a child or anything."

"I don't drink much," Ciara admitted, "and I appreciate the offer."

Even still she felt weird sipping from her drink, as if her mother would storm in the door any second and do her wounded-swan routine.

"Cheers!" Ruth said, clinking her vodka and Coke against Ciara's bottle and taking a hearty sip. "I don't drink much myself – well, not that much, honest. I just feel a little unsettled with the children being away. Or is that I feel free as a bird?" She took another long drink.

Ciara might only have been seventeen but she was pretty sure from looking at Ruth that she was erring more on the unsettled side.

Niamh walked into the kitchen and helped herself to a glass of wine. "I've been looking forward to this all day," she said, sighing contentedly after her first taste. "Cheers, my dears," she said to Ciara, clinking her glass again.

Ciara smiled. "This is nice, isn't it? Although I do feel like a bit of rebel here. Mum wouldn't be impressed."

"Don't be daft," Niamh said, "You've been running around after your wee woman all day. You've given birth – you deserve a drink! If you can handle gas and air, you can handle a Bacardi Breezer."

"God, gas and air. I love that stuff. I wish Mrs Quinn sold it in the shop. I'd be a total addict."

"It's amazing stuff altogether," Ruth said. "I don't think I'd have got through any of my deliveries without it. It was like being drunk without the hangover the next day."

"I'd take a hangover over stitches in my fandango any day," Ciara laughed.

"Fair point, but we all deserve a drink every day for the rest of our lives if need be – for having survived childbirth. Maybe we should regale Liam with stories of our experiences and put him off us women forever!"

Ciara laughed, and blushed at the same time. She couldn't

imagine anything worse than regaling Liam with her undignified birth experience. She cringed – every part of her cringed, even her fandango – when she recalled her ten hours in the labour ward. It was not pretty – no miracle of birth anyway.

Seeing her horrified face, Niamh laughed. "Don't worry, we're only joking."

Relieved, Ciara took a long drink and smiled. "Thank Crunchie for that. But seriously I'm glad we're all friends now. My nights out with you all are a godsend."

"Even though we are old fogies with dodgy clothes and wrinkles?" Ruth asked.

"Oi, speak for yourself!" Niamh chimed in. "I'm only thirty-three. I've barely a wrinkle to my name and I don't intend on getting any either. I'll hit the botox when the time comes. No doubt about it."

"Can men get botox?" Liam asked, walking into the kitchen, a half smile on his face. "Because I'm thinking maybe a new younger-looking me could help me win Laura back."

"Ooooh, you could go on that *How To Look Good Naked* programme," Detta said with a wink.

Liam blushed a deep red and Ciara thought it was quite sweet really. Liam seemed very shy and she couldn't imagine him stripping off for the TV cameras. Although, if he wasn't old enough to be her father, she could have admitted to herself he was quite attractive in a Harrison Ford kind of a way.

"I don't think anyone needs to be seeing me naked," Liam said and Detta choked on her drink which sent a wave of laughter around the room.

"God, I needed this," Niamh said, sipping from her glass. "Of course, by this I mean a good laugh – not the wine. Although the wine definitely helps."

"Amen to that!" Ruth chimed in.

They made their way to the living room and Ciara sat down by the fire and pulled a cushion onto her knee. Her mother was always teasing her for that – the way she always had to have a cushion on her lap, but she couldn't help it, she felt exposed otherwise. She'd always been that way and was even more so now since having the baby. She felt extra comfortable with a layer of stuffing between her and the world.

She chewed on her lip – the chatter was continuing around her, all the cares of the world gone from her friends' eyes but she wondered what they were all hiding.

Sure, she knew they had their share of heartache, but no one really knew what went on behind closed doors, did they? None of them knew the truth about Ben and she wondered did she have the nerve to tell them? Admittedly that was easier to contemplate now that Lorraine had been so accepting of the news.

"Penny for them?" Detta asked, sitting down beside Ciara and staring into the crackling fire.

"Oh, just thinking," Ciara said. "Life and stuff."

"I fecking hate that stuff," Detta said with a warm smile.

"Me too," Ciara smiled.

"Anything you want to share? I know it's not official group night, but I'm always here to listen. The others are chattering nineteen to the dozen anyway."

Ciara looked across the room and the others were indeed lost in a conversation about films of their childhood. All were currently trying their hand at Dick Van Dyke's dodgy accent from *Mary Poppins* and she couldn't help but laugh.

"I'm okay."

"Okay, but you know if you need to talk I'm a good listener. I've big ears, in case you hadn't noticed. My nickname used to be 'FA Cup'."

"Your ears look fine to me."

"Are you mad? They're mahoosive! When I lived in London for a year they were in danger of getting their own postcode!"

Ciara laughed. "You are funny!"

"But I'm not prying. My nose is perfectly in proportion," her friend replied, rearranging her emerald-green skirt around her ankles.

Ciara believed her. She wasn't like Mrs Quinn with her nosy ways and her acid tongue. There was something about Detta that made her instantly trustworthy – maybe because she was funky and hip with an air of calm about her.

"I was just thinking how much my mum would enjoy something like this," Ciara said, suddenly thinking how much she would like to see her mother relax in the company of others.

"Would she not come along to the group?"

"She doesn't see the point. Anyway, she's fine with things. She's been on her own for a long time. She told me she couldn't ever imagine having a man in her life again. Not long-term."

"And you don't believe her?"

"I think she's afraid of getting hurt. She's had a lot of disappointments in her life."

"I hope you aren't counting yourself among those, young lady, because I'd be proud to have you as mine," Detta said warmly.

Ciara blushed deeper at the compliment. "I haven't exactly turned out how she would have liked – pregnant at fifteen and all that."

"There are worse things that could happen."

"I know. But she had higher hopes for me than this."

"You've achieved a lot, pet. You don't sit around the house

complaining about your lot. You go out there and work and you're brilliant with Ella. God knows how you put up with that oul' biddy in the shop. I'd do time for that one, I swear to God."

Ciara laughed. "I just get on with it and think of the money. She's not that bad if you just keep your head down and get the job done."

"You're a superstar," Detta said with a smile.

"So you are," Ruth butted in.

Startled, Ciara felt her heart sink to her boots. She hadn't realised the dodgy Dick Van Dyke impressions had dried up and that she was now the sole topic of conversation.

"My Eimear would do well to learn from you," Ruth went on. "That irresponsible little madam doesn't know how to get herself up and out of the door without someone prodding her along the way."

Ciara knew that now was the time she should tell Ruth just how much Eimear was likely to learn from her if she didn't change her ways.

She thought back to earlier that evening when she had bumped into Ben Quinn on her walk into the village. She thought of the sneer on his face and his cocksure attitude. She thought of how many times she had desperately wanted to knock that smile off his face. She felt mildly nauseated at the thought that he could do to someone else what he'd done to her – then again, that could just be the excess of chocolate she had eaten on the bus on the way back from Derry mixed with the sickly sweet alcopop she had been drinking.

"I feel a little woozy," she said, suddenly feeling her tummy turn over and she ran up the stairs to the bathroom where she sat on the cool floor and willed her stomach to settle. Her face clammy with sweat, she fell back against the sink and let the cool porcelain soothe her. She was taking deep gulps of air to steady herself when Ruth, accompanied by Detta, popped her head around the door.

"Here's some water," she said, handing Ciara a tall glass.

"Just sip it now," Detta added, kneeling down and reaching out a hand to check her forehead.

Ciara wanted to sink in towards her, but she tried to remain calm. No tepid water or soft hands on her forehead would make this sinking feeling go away.

"Ruth, can we talk for a bit?"

"Sure, pet, no problem," Ruth said, sitting down on the edge of the bath.

Detta stood awkwardly. "Should I go?"

"No, no, it's fine. Honest," Ciara said, pulling her knees to her chest and sitting with her back as straight as she could. "Ruth . . . I need to warn you about Eimear. Or it's more that I need to warn you about Ben Quinn and Eimear."

"Ben Quinn? Why? He's a nice lad, isn't he? I thought he might be a stabilising influence."

Ciara choked. She couldn't help it – when she thought of Ben having a stabilising effect on anything all she could do was laugh.

"He's not a nice lad, Ruth. He's a selfish pig and if Eimear isn't careful – very careful – she could find herself in the same sorry state I did."

"What do you mean?" Ruth asked and Ciara swallowed hard. The best-kept secret in Rathinch was about to be blown wide open.

Detta moved towards Ciara and sat beside her, which Ciara would be forever grateful for.

"Ella's daddy . . ." Ciara began. "It's Ben. He told me he loved me – he made me feel special and attractive and sexy." She could feel herself blushing at the words. How ridiculous to sit here among these grown women and talk about feeling sexy when she was just a young thing?

"We only did it the once. I know, I was stupid. I wasn't careful. I just didn't think I would get caught out. He told me it would be okay. But when I told him I was pregnant he couldn't get away fast enough. He told me he would tell everyone – everyone – that I was lying and that I had slept my way round the village. He's a pig, Ruth, and Eimear doesn't know what she is getting herself into."

If Ruth was shocked by any of what she heard, she did a very good job of hiding it, Ciara thought as she looked across the bathroom at her new friend.

"What a complete fucking bastard," she eventually said, and looked at once stricken. "You don't mind if I swear in front of you, do you?"

"For the love of God, Ruth, Ciara's one of us, I'm sure she's heard worse language than that, and I'm also sure she knows that Ben is indeed a fucking wee bastard," Detta interjected with a soft smile.

It felt good, Ciara realised, to have it out in the open. She didn't know how, or if, that would help Eimear retain her dignity but she was surprised to feel she had gained some of her own dignity back.

"I can't believe you've kept this to yourself," Detta said, rubbing her hand.

"I only told my mum on Tuesday. I knew that I was going to have to talk to you, Ruth, and I couldn't tell you and keep it from her. Before now I didn't see the point. I knew there was no chance he was ever going to admit that he is Ella's dad and if he doesn't want to be in her life, then I don't want to force him. But now, well, when I think he is worming his way into someone else's life I can't let him get away with that. No one deserves to be treated like he has treated me."

Ruth raised her glass. "Amen to that!"

* * *

Niamh topped up her glass and handed Liam another cool beer.

"They've been gone an age," Liam said with a look of concern.

"They sure have," Niamh agreed. "I hope Ciara is all right." She wondered if she should have gone upstairs with the others – but she felt more comfortable here on the sofa with a nice glass of wine. She didn't cope well with sick people or hysterics. She had enough drama in her life, so whatever physical or emotional trauma was keeping them in the loo she was happy enough to let them get on with it.

However, Liam was clearly not as comfortable with being left alone with her and a couple of drinks.

"I do hope they're okay," he said, giving her a pitiful look which made her realise he wanted her to go and check things out and report back. He was a man – a man's man – there was no way he could go barging into a bathroom to make sure everything was hunky dory.

"Okay then," she said with more grace than she felt. "I'll go and chivvy them along, You know, make sure everything is okay."

She took a deep breath, stood up and sat her wineglass on the fireplace before heading for the stairs. Almost as soon as she reached the bottom of the staircase she was greeted with the most raucous laughter she had heard in a long time.

Intrigued, and if truth be told a little jealous, she made her way up to the bathroom and put her head around the door. The colour had returned to Ciara's cheeks and it was Ruth's face which was flushed. Detta was sat on the edge of the bath, her head thrown back in laugher with her blonde curls bouncing as she giggled.

"Men. Bastards. The lot of them!" Ruth said.

"Apart from Liam!" Detta interjected.

"Well, of course apart from Liam," Ruth replied, clutching her stomach.

"He wants to know if you are all okay," Niamh interrupted, still confused about what was going on.

"Oh, we are just men-bashing and plotting our revenge on the world. You know what it's like," Ruth said with a grin. "Men. Can't live with 'em. Can't kill 'em."

Niamh of course knew that Ruth wasn't being deliberately insensitive to her own situation. It seemed however that neither Ciara or Detta knew this and the look of horror on their faces was enough to send Niamh into kinks of laughter herself.

"Oh you are right," she muttered through her tears of laughter, "you are so right."

The baffled look on her friends' faces was enough to knock her laughter up a gear and she struggled to gain her composure.

"I'm sorry," she said eventually, her tongue loosened by the wine, "but if you knew my bollocks of a husband the way I know my bollocks of a husband you would understand why it's all so very funny. Because, ladies," she said, her tears of laughter turning to tears of sorrow, "if he was here right now. I would fecking kill the bastard myself."

Damn it, she thought as she felt a sob catch in her throat. Now she was the hysterical woman in the bathroom that she had been mocking just minutes before.

Ruth stood up from her seat on the toilet and guided Niamh to sit down in her place and then she put her arm around her shoulders and let her cry, while Ciara and Detta took turns to gently stroke her legs and make soothing noises. And yet the baffled looks hadn't left their faces.

"Ach, I might as well tell you. I've nothing to lose from it. Seán's a bastard. *Was* a bastard," she corrected herself. "Last weekend I was sorting through his things and I found evidence, well, proof really, that he was having it away with the person I thought was my best friend."

Niamh had often seen jaws drop in cartoons. She had many mental images of seeing chins clang off floors and tongues loll out in a comic fashion. None of those looked as pronounced as the dropped jaws on Ciara and Detta right at that moment. She could kind of understand Ciara's reaction – she was young with crazy notions of love and romance no doubt – but Detta's was a picture. The worldly-wise Detta who Niamh had come to see as the sage of the village in recent weeks was visibly shocked. She realised then that her veneer had fallen. She was no longer, in their eyes, the perfect housewife. She might have the dream house, the kitchen island and the marble work surfaces. She might drive a top of the range 4x4. The twins might well be dressed from Boden and Vertbaudet and her hair might not be even one strand out of place. The sheets on her bed were the finest Egyptian cotton, her underfloor heating perfect for their real wood floors. Her porch, with its view over the sea, might be the envy of anyone who ever set foot in Donegal. But her perfect life was far from that. She had to admit it: before now, even the tragedy in her life had been perfect. Gorgeous mum of two, widowed when handsome husband dies rushing home to her arms. Insurance policies all in place to make sure she never had to want for anything again. Apart from the handsome husband, that is. And she could grieve while staring out over a perfect sunset on her perfect porch swing, drinking her fecking perfect New Zealand Sauvignon out of her perfect Waterford fecking Crystal glasses.

But here was the reality – a life where, she realised with the sinking of her heavy heart, she was now the object of pity of three other people. People she had considered herself to be better than. People who, although she had wanted to let them into her life, she had considered herself above because, unlike theirs, *her* situation was not of her own making.

But then, all of it was a lie. The nice clothes, cars, marble worktops and everything else. And the biggest lie of all was that she and Seán had been blissfully happy.

"Well, fuck me pink!" Detta declared with gusto, while Niamh leant forward and put her head in her hands.

"I don't know what to say," Ciara said. "I always thought you two were so . . ."

"Perfect?" Niamh said, sitting back and gratefully accepting the cool flannel that Ciara had just wrung out for her.

Ciara nodded while Detta sat shaking her head. "I can't believe it. Oh darling, this must be so hard for you."

Niamh managed a smile. If there was ever an understatement that was the king of all the understatements in the entire world, that was it.

"I can't believe it," Ciara said.

Niamh saw pity in her eyes. She was used to that, people looking at her like she was a poor lost lamb. This was only pity taken up a notch. Extreme pity – the kind normally reserved for beggars or street drinkers or the poor feckers who go on the *X Factor* only to be mocked by the cruel judges.

"I don't think I can believe it myself," she replied. "Or, I don't want to believe it, but you can't argue with the evidence." In her tipsy state she thought for a moment how it would be funny to put on a Lloyd Grossman voice and do her *Through the Keyhole* impression: "Now, who would shag a slut like this?" – except that up until very recently she hadn't considered Cait a slut at all. It wasn't Cait who had a drawer of La Perla underwear. She was much more an M&S girl, while it was Niamh who liked to dress up in fishnets and stockings for her husband. Her cheating fecker of a dead husband.

She relayed the story of the Post-it and of Caitlin's big freeze since Seán died. They nodded, with the extreme-pity look on their face, and asked had there been any other signs. Had he changed his appearance? Worked late? Worked out more? No, Niamh was sure there had been no difference. He always looked handsome, and he always worked late. As for working out more, if anything she realised he had been more energetic in bed. Then again, they do say the more you have sex, the more you want it. Maybe it was nothing more than that. As well as being a cheating bastard he was fecking Michael Douglas sex addict-a-like. She didn't tell them about the Christmas party and how, like the world's biggest tit, she had watched her husband dance cheek to cheek with his mistress.

"I wouldn't have thought it," Detta said. "Is that why you didn't come on Tuesday night?"

"I thought you would judge me," Niamh replied honestly.

"Christ, us judge you?" said Detta. "Would be a bit of kettle calling pot black there, wouldn't it? None of us has an ideal life."

But *I* was supposed to, Niamh wanted to shout. We worked for this our whole life. This was our dream.

"I suppose," she answered.

"We're a right crowd, aren't we?" Ciara said with a half smile. "You must wonder what the hell you have let yourself in for, Detta."

But as Ruth and Ciara laughed, Niamh sneaked a glance at their leader and realised that Detta too must have a secret of her own. She had laughed along with them, but there was something in her eyes that gave her away.

And to her shame, that made Niamh feel slightly better about herself.

This evening was making Ruth feel uncomfortable – very

uncomfortable. Here were two of these women spilling their innermost secrets and she was sitting here, holding hers close to her. She felt as if she should be standing up for the sisterhood and revealing that she was a victim, but then battery wasn't something casually slipped into conversation. "So anyway, did you see *Corrie* last night? I'm a battered wife," or "Yes, yes, the weather's awful these days. And my husband used to knock me down the stairs. Once he broke my arm and we told everyone I'd slipped in the shower."

You couldn't even slip it in comfortably with "Yes, I know your husband is a cheating bastard" or "God, that Ben Quinn is a wee fecker" and then add the awful truth. You couldn't tell people that your husband beat seven shades of shit out of you and while you're here – dressed up as the Wicked Witch of the West – he is off taking care of your children – and you don't seem to mind.

They would think she was mad. The looniest of the Loonies. And, when she put it like that in her own head, then they were probably right. So Ruth sat there nodding and smiling at all the appropriate moments but feeling as if her heart could thud right out of her chest. She wondered could they hear it, and if not then why not? It was deafening in her ears. She pulled her green wig off and sipped from her glass. The shock at Niamh's revelation was starting to subside and the chat was now more light-hearted and from what Ruth could gather largely involved what evil revenge they could take on the ex best friend. Or Ben Quinn. Or better still, the two of them together.

"Ooh, we could be a crack commando unit like in the *A-Team*," Niamh said with a smile. "Taking them out one useless fecker at a time."

Ruth knew who she would like taken out and she wondered would there be some way to have him taken out without telling the others just why.

"The mini-bus is primed and ready for action," Detta replied.

"Youse really are loonies," Ciara chimed in.

"Aye, not bad for old fogies," Ruth said, forcing a smile onto her face. She knew that if she stayed quiet too long they would guess something was up.

"I imagine it's just because we're that bit older that we just don't give a flying damn," Detta said as Ruth stood up and emptied the rest of her wine down the sink.

"I don't know about you lot, but I could do with something to eat," Ruth said. I've some cocktail sausages downstairs. I'll nip down and put them on. Poor Liam will think we are conspiring against him if we all stay up here much longer."

Ciara stood up next and splashed some cold water on her face, while Ruth took a deep breath and walked down to her kitchen.

"I thought youse had all fallen down the loo," Liam said with a grin as she walked back in. On the floor beside him were three empty beer bottles and his face had a cheery glow. He obviously hadn't been one bit bothered by the lack of company.

"By the looks of it, you didn't miss us," she said, glancing at the bottles on the floor.

"Oh shit," Liam said, blushing furiously, "I was okay to drink the beer, wasn't I?"

"Of course you were," Ruth said. "I'm just glad you didn't miss us too much. I'm going to put some food on – would you like some?"

"I never say no to beer or food," he replied. "But here, why don't you let me help you? You've been running around like a mad thing after us all night. You must be wrecked."

"Sure I'm used to running around after three wains all the time. You lot are no bother at all in comparison."

"I wonder how they are all getting on," Liam said.

Ruth felt her heart quicken again. Of course, she knew that Liam was only really interested in how Laura was getting on but she was terrified too of where this conversation could go, given her current frame of mind.

"I'm sure we would have heard if anything had gone drastically wrong anyway," Liam said.

With the same fake sincerity Ruth replied: "No news is good news as far as my lot are concerned."

He followed her into the kitchen. It was strange to realise she felt nervous as they both stood there. She wasn't used to having a man so close to her. She didn't fancy Liam – not that he wasn't ruggedly handsome in his own way. She thought it highly unlikely that she would ever fancy any man ever again – apart from maybe Harrison Ford or Hugh Laurie. But still, having a man in this room with her made her feel nervy. She busied herself taking the sausages from the freezer and setting them out on a baking tray. Switching the oven on, she fished some garlic bread out of the fridge and then tipped some tortilla chips into a bowl.

"We'll not be fit to move if we eat all this," Liam said with a smile, "but at the same time those beers have gone straight to my head. Hopefully this will sober me up. Are you sure you don't mind Poppy staying over?"

"I'm sure she's no bother," Ruth said, putting dip into bowls – anything to stop her from thinking too much about everything in her life.

"No, she's a good girl. I suppose that's what makes it harder," Liam said despondently.

"What harder?" Ruth asked absently.

"You know, her mum going like that. Laura was always a good wife and mother – but she's suddenly happy with a night or two with our daughter a week. I never thought she would have been able to leave her, leave us, like that. It's like she's a different woman."

Ruth shivered. She wondered just how much her husband and his controlling ways were responsible for the change in Laura. But yet when she had seen them together – the one time she had seen them together – they looked happier than she had ever felt with James. She nodded sympathetically. "I just wish we knew what was going on in their heads," she said, thinking that sounded very much like something she should be saying. She felt a little guilty of course for not digging deeper, but she was, she admitted to herself, a big fat chicken with no desire to discuss this further.

"Here, let me help you get the food out," Liam said, reaching for the oven door and Ruth felt a gush of warm air as he opened it.

She felt a little faint, so sat down and fanned herself – hoping that he wouldn't notice. No such luck.

"Are you okay?"

"Too much wine," she replied.

"You've barely had a couple of glasses."

"Cheap date," she said with a smile and then panicked. Would he think she was flirting? Please, God, no. She couldn't handle that. It would all get very messy and embarrassing when she had to explain why her heart belonged to Harrison or Hugh and no one else.

"I'll get you a glass of water," he said, walking to the sink.

She took the water from him and took a few sips. She was that hot and bothered she thought about pouring it over her head to cool herself down – but then she really would look like a madwoman.

"Has anyone told you about the Loonies?" she asked.

* * *

As far as weird nights went, this was one of the weirdest, thought Liam. He was sitting in a strange woman's kitchen while his daughter slept upstairs. Meanwhile his wife was shacked up with this strange woman's husband and the pair of them were taking care of her children. Three other women were laughing like hyenas in the living room and breaking into frequent renditions of *the A-Team* theme while this particular strange woman looked like she might faint at any moment.

She had explained to him what had just been revealed in the bathroom – and how Niamh and Seán's marriage had not been the happy dream everyone thought it was.

She was now slowly explaining to him how they had decided they were all slightly disturbed in the head and that they might as well live up to their name and go on a rampage against those who had wronged them. She was joking, he thought. Or, at least, he hoped she was joking. He never quite knew where to place himself with Ruth Byrne. They had certain shared interests, of course. They had both been wronged in exactly the same way and both of them were left holding the babies. He figured, out of all the women at the Lone Parents Group, she should have been the one he connected with most of all, and yet there was something closed off about Ruth that he couldn't get past.

And he wasn't one to try. Laura had often completely lost the rag with him when he clammed up each time she wanted a nice chat.

"Let's turn the telly off," she would say, curling up beside him.

He would of course think his luck was in and would have to fight with the growing erection in his trousers at the thought of some quiet time with his wife.

The erection would however fade as soon as she followed that suggestion with: "Why don't we just have a nice chat?"

"What about?" he would ask, hiding the frustration from his voice.

"I don't know. Just a chat. We rarely get time to chat any more. Remember when we were first going out and we would sit up all night just talking?"

Of course Liam remembered those nights, but to his recollection there was a lot more going on than "just talking". But he knew to make such a suggestion when Laura was in talking mode would end in disaster. She would storm off saying he was a typical man while he seethed on the sofa that she was a typical woman.

So he would sit and say "Okay then," and she would gaze at him expecting him to start some life-altering chat about the state of their marriage, the town, the universe, anything.

"Poppy's a star, isn't she?" he would offer and they would have their one safe chat, the one thing they agreed on: how wonderful their daughter was. Liam often wondered what they used to talk about before Poppy, but as they laughed and joked about their daughter's latest misadventures he put any concerns about their marriage to the back of his head. They couldn't be unhappy if they were laughing like this, could they?

So now, he sat nodding as Ruth spoke and laughing at the appropriate moments. At least now the renditions of the *A-Team* made sense.

As the cooker pinged, he tipped the sausages onto a plate and carried them through to the living room.

"Would you Loonies like some tomato sauce with these?" he asked with a smile as they descended on the food as if they hadn't eaten in a week.

"I take it Ruth has filled you in on our dastardly plans?" Detta asked with a smile.

"Oh yes, I'm practising my Mr T impressions as we speak," Liam said.

"You know it would be some *craic* if we could take on the world one bad shite at a time," Detta said, sitting back.

"I'd be happy enough to sort out our own problems," Niamh replied, sitting down.

"Well, I don't see why we can't," Liam replied. "What is it we all want most in the world? Can we not support each other to get through this?"

"Any of you good at resurrections then? Because I would love Seán back just so I could cut his cheating nuts off," Niamh said.

"And I'd like Ben Quinn and everyone else to know I'm not the village tart," Ciara added.

"I'd like you all to be happy," Detta said magnanimously from her chair while Ruth said she would just like her children to be content.

What would Liam want most in the whole wide world? Well, he didn't have to think about that at all. "I just wish Laura still loved me," he said, sitting down. "Or failing that, and forgive me for saying this, Ruth, I'd just like to batter seven shades of shit out of your husband."

"Amen to that," Ruth replied with vigour.

"Well, let's do it then," Ciara said.

Liam was shocked. "What? Seriously? Kick seven shades of shite out of James?"

Ciara laughed. "No, but do what we want. Get what we want. We deserve to be happy. None of us are bad people. None of us have done anything wrong to anyone in our lives so how come we are sat here like the black sheep of the village? I think we need to take control."

Liam was impressed. Ciara was only seventeen and yet she was kicking the arse of the entire group as she spoke. She had a wise head on her shoulders. He couldn't imagine Poppy being like that in just seven years' time, but then hopefully she wouldn't have a baby to deal with. Christ, when Liam thought about it, he could be granda in a couple of years. That was too scary a thought to consider – not now when he had still been hoping that he could have another child of his own. But he couldn't deny it. He admired Ciara greatly for her guts. He would have stood up and applauded her if this night hadn't been surreal enough already. He was pretty sure when he woke up tomorrow he would wonder if they had really agreed to do whatever they could to help each other when just a few weeks ago they had been virtual strangers.

"Feck it," he found himself saying. "In for a penny, in for a pound. Why not? Why not work together to get what we want?"

"As long as we are realistic about what we want and what we can achieve," Detta sounded a warning note. "Sorry to be a party pooper but we need to really think what we are after because, clichéd as it sounds, you really do have to be careful what you wish for."

They talked for another while, formulating plans, discussing dreams before Liam had felt his eyes start to droop. It was now almost one o'clock and he knew he would want to be awake again as early as possible so that Ruth wasn't left with all the kids to look after.

"I'd better make a move," he said reluctantly – reluctantly because, let's face it, staying where he was enjoying the company was a better option than going home to an empty house, but he had to be sensible.

"Right then," Detta said. "Well, I'd better move then too, if you are to walk me home."

They stood up and said goodbye to the group. Liam did

wonder for a moment should he hug them – it just felt like a night where hugging might be appropriate. He decided however that was a step too far for his gruff Donegal exterior and instead he nodded his goodbyes and walked out into the cold air, holding the door open for Detta as he went.

The streets of Rathinch were deserted, but then they always were at this time. It was hardly a hotspot of pubbing and clubbing. On the average night everyone would be tucked up and in bed by eleven – with the stragglers only managing to make it past one. In many ways Rathinch was the Sleepy Hollow of Donegal, but without the headless horseman.

"That was a strange night," Detta said as they walked along the Main Street.

"Good strange, though?" he asked.

"I think so," she replied, digging her hands into her pockets.

Liam had to admit it had got cold and he wondered what the corrected etiquette was. With Laura it would have been simple. He would have offered her his scarf or his coat or put his arm around her to generate some body heat, but he wasn't sure any of that would be appropriate.

"Are you okay?" he offered. "I've a scarf here you can have." He hoped she wouldn't read it as a sign that he wanted to jump her bones but she shrugged.

"I'll be grand once I'm walking a bit," she said. "It's the tiredness that has me shivering more than anything."

"I know, I can't believe how late it is."

"At least I don't have a wee one to get up with in the morning," she said, with a half smile.

"Did you never want a family yourself?" Liam asked, recalling the conversation they'd had in the Country Kitchen.

"Yes, well, yes," she replied. "It's not much further now. I'm only down here and round the corner. I can walk on if you want and you can head on home. I know you have to pick Poppy up right and early."

Liam knew he was a man and as such not known for his intuition and empathy but he was sensitive enough to know that Detta clearly didn't want to talk about her family life any more and he wasn't about to push her.

"I'll see you to your door," he said. "It's only good manners. And, besides, if I'm to become a feckwit fighting Action Man I could do with a little more exercise."

"You're just fine the way you are, Liam," Detta replied, linking her arm in his. "And I don't think we really are going to become the village vigilantes but maybe we are all a little more focussed on getting what we want."

* * *

Liam let himself into his house and climbed the stairs. He didn't have to put his head into Poppy's room to wish her sweet dreams and he didn't have to share the minutiae of his day with Laura. He was alone with his thoughts and he sat down on the side of the bed and peeled off his socks. Detta had said they should be careful what they wished for and that, along with everything else that night, made him wonder if he was wishing for the right things.

If Laura walked back in now, what would he do? If she fell to her knees and begged his forgiveness, would he offer it? He always, until tonight, thought that he would. But then his wish wasn't to have Laura back. No, it was to have her love him again – the way she had done when they first got together. He wasn't sure that was possible and, he realised with a start, he wasn't sure he wanted it anyway.

She had hurt him, and their daughter deeply and no amount of love could erase the last few months. It didn't matter that she still saw Poppy several times a week. It didn't matter that most of the time she was civil, and dare he say it, nice to her. The hurt was there, and that was for sure. Completely confused and utterly wrecked, he lay down and drifted off into a dreamless sleep.

28

Ciara curled up in the bed and pulled Ella towards her. Her daughter was sleeping soundly – her curls damp with sweat, her dummy going nineteen to the dozen with whatever little dream was going through her head. Staring around the room – that of a girl just a year younger than her – Ciara felt as if she was in some sort of weird alternate universe. There, amid the posters for Girls Aloud and Rhianna were pictures of teenagers laughing together, huddled in groups. The trained eye could spot the bottles of WKD and tins of cider on the ground beside them. They wore clothes that were too tight and too short. They were exactly the kind of clothes that Ciara would wear if she could get away with it, she thought enviously, breathing in and putting a hand to her now flabby tummy.

Not that it really mattered if her tummy was flabby or not, given the not-so-stylish uniform Mrs Quinn made her wear. She couldn't help but smile to herself. If Mrs Quinn knew the truth about her precious grandson she would no doubt have Ciara dressed in sackcloth and ashes. He was her blue-eyed boy and make no mistake. Ciara often wondered how, on the few occasions she brought Ella into the shop, the old bag didn't notice those exact same blue eyes staring back at her? But then, she supposed, the heart only sees what it wants to see which is why she herself fell for that ignorant self-obsessed twat in the first place.

Ella let out a gentle baby snore and lifted her tiny hand to her face to rub at her cheek. Her dummy slipped out onto the pillow and for a second it looked as though she might wake, but instead she rolled over closer into her mum and slipped back into her dream. Ciara could only imagine what was going through her head – probably dreams of fairies and fireworks and bus trips to strange cities. Ciara almost envied her sense of innocence, but then looking around Eimear's room she kind of envied Eimear's sense of innocence too. She was leading the life Ciara should have been but then, Ciara remembered, if she wasn't very careful she would be living the life Ciara was living now. Only perhaps then Ben Quinn would have to take responsibility for something.

Ciara closed her eyes and fell back to sleep – slipping off into the same strange dreams as her daughter no doubt.

When she woke the house was already buzzing with noise. The Quigley twins were obviously awake and she could hear Poppy singing to them. Ella was playing with her hands and feet on the bed and a broad smile broke across her face when she noticed her mammy was awake.

"Morning, princess," Ciara said, sitting up and lifting her daughter to her. Ella gurgled and clapped her hands with excitement, her eyes wide at the sound of the racket downstairs. "Eight o'clock, Ells. That's a world record for you," Ciara grinned. "Now if only you could do that every morning because it would make both me and your Granny Lorraine much, much happier and maybe I wouldn't almost fall asleep over the buns every morning at work."

Ella gurgled contentedly, not one bit bothered at Ciara's plea for a more acceptable morning routine.

She probably likes the distraction of MTV in the background while I burn my toast through exhaustion, Ciara thought with a smile.

She changed her daughter's nappy and made her way downstairs to where Niamh was cooking bacon for the assembled masses while Ruth sat on the floor doing jigsaw puzzles with the twins.

"Morning, sleepy head!" Ruth called.

Ciara smiled. "How do you have the energy?"

"What do you mean how do I have the energy? You're the young whippersnapper, you should be bounding around here full of the joys of spring!"

Ciara bit back the urge to grunt. It wouldn't be very well mannered and she knew deep down that Ruth didn't mean any harm. Her comments weren't laced with arsenic like Mrs Quinn's.

"It's autumn," she muttered with a half smile and sat down on the floor beside her friend.

"Here, give that wee woman to me," Ruth said. "You look beat out and believe me, Ciara, I know how exhausting they are at this age. Go back to bed. Close that living room door as you go and you shouldn't hear much."

"I couldn't . . ." Ciara replied, taken aback by the kindness. She couldn't remember the last time she got a lie-in. It was probably the night after Ella was born in the hospital.

"'Course you could. Get up them stairs and don't come down until you are properly awake. I've enough experience of this carry-on to keep madam entertained and, besides, young Poppy here is dying to get pushing this one down the street in her pram so we are going to head out in a bit."

"Are you sure?"

Ruth raised an eyebrow. It was a very mammy eyebrow, one that Ciara knew better than to argue with, so she muttered a quick thank you and climbed the stairs, almost giddy with excitement at the thought of getting another hour or two in bed. This was her teenage rebellion and she was going to enjoy every moment of it.

She kicked off her shoes and climbed under the duvet, feeling the cool sheets around her toes. Plumping the pillow, she lay down and could barely keep the smile from her face.

It was hard to put her finger on what had changed but something had. Her secret was out and she knew that Ben could say whatever he wanted, to whoever he wanted, and there would be people out there who would believe her. And those were the people she cared about – not some big gaggle of teenage girls who she had little in common with any more, apart from her age and her mild obsession with Justin Timberlake. He could bring sexy back any time he wanted. She would gladly give up her self-imposed chastity for a bit of Justin.

The future, Ciara felt, was just that little bit brighter and she didn't feel so completely alone. She knew – sensed from deep within her – that something was going to change and not necessarily in the usual "all gone a bit shit" way.

Of course, come Monday morning she would still be going to work in the shop and outside of today she was unlikely to see a lie-in this side of 2015, but she didn't feel completely fecked off with her lot for a change. Even this room and all the paraphernalia of teenagedom didn't depress her (apart from the skinny clothes). None of them had what she had.

She made a promise to herself, as she drifted off into a gorgeous sleep, that she would try and be a little more grateful for everything. And she would continue to work at making things better with Lorraine. And if she got the chance she would, with the help of the Rathinch A-Team, come up with some way to put Ben in his place and keep Eimear safe from harm.

* * *

Something had shifted in Niamh. She left Ruth's house and walked back to her own home singing "Follow the Yellow Brick Road" with the twins trailing behind her, skipping and laughing. They clearly liked their new mammy – even if she was slightly manic with a determined look on her face which was kind of like a smile, only with a healthy dose of crazy added for effect.

Opening the huge oak door to their marble-covered hallway, Niamh told the children they could have Smarties and fruit juice and they could eat their treats on the cream living-room carpet. Seán would have turned over in his grave at the very thought but Niamh didn't give a damn. She was almost tempted to let them run riot with a jar of Nutella and to hell with the shag pile. Putting on a DVD to amuse them, she kicked off her boots and walked into the kitchen where she switched the percolator on and lifted the phone.

"Mum," she said, almost before her mother had time to answer.

"Yes, darling, are you okay?"

"I am, Mum. I'm doing great. Can you come down today?"

"Are you sure you're all right?" Try as she might, Mary could not keep the concern from her voice.

"Honestly," Niamh replied. "I just have something to do and I don't want the kids to come with me and besides I had a few drinks last night. I'm hung-over and I could really do with your help to mind them while I sleep for the afternoon."

She knew her mother might be mildly concerned at her confession of a hangover, but she hoped that Mary would be happy enough that her daughter was, on this occasion, drinking with other people rather than wailing over her well-worn copy of *Ghost* on DVD while sinking a bottle of wine.

"Of course, darling," she replied and Niamh thanked her before walking into the utility room and lifting a roll of black bin bags from the cleaning cupboard.

She poured her coffee and, sticking her head round the door to make sure the children were fine, she shouted to them that Mammy was just going upstairs and they should call her if they needed her.

She went to her bedroom and pulled her hair back under a scarf, before changing into her oldest and comfiest non-designer jeans and an old white T-shirt. Sitting down on the bed, she contemplated what she was about to do next.

There was an energy in her that hadn't been there before – a fire in her belly. She rolled out bag after bag and sipped from her coffee cup. She wouldn't pack everything up. She wasn't that brave. But by God she was going to start.

Pulling suits and ties, shirts and jumpers from his wardrobe, where they were pressed and hung neatly row on row, she bundled them into the bags. Some came easily off their hangers and some of the hangers decided they wanted a new life in the bin bags as well and she didn't care. This was the not the precision packing she was used to – this was a life detox.

The shoes were next and then the socks. He had so many socks and one of those anally retentive sock-sorter thingies in his drawer because God forbid there would ever be an unmatched sock in their perfect boudoir. His aftershaves came next. He had more scents than she had. Perhaps that should have given her a clue he was a useless cheating bastard.

Next came his books – reams and reams of really annoyingly boring law tomes and John Grisham-style thrillers.

The man, she thought as she piled more books into another bag, was a walking cliché. Lawyer in the city, wifey in the country, mistress in the riverside flat.

She felt some rage bubble up then but she bit it back. This was the new her – the one where her friends in Rathinch were going to help her find herself again and she wasn't going to be the quiet, well-behaved trophy wife any more.

Hauling five bin bags into the landing, she heard the children call that their granny was arriving.

"Niamh, sweetheart, are you okay?" Mary's voice called from the hall.

"Just fine," Niamh replied, walking down the curved staircase to where her mother stood, armed with a bag of chocolates, wine and tissues.

"I'm fine, honest," Niamh repeated, looking into her mother's eyes. "But there is something I have to do, so could you watch the children for half an hour or so? I won't be longer."

Mary nodded, but she didn't talk. Niamh would have tried to explain to her what she was about to do, but she doubted her mother would really understand. She would most likely just think her daughter had lost the plot altogether and send for the doctor, or Robyn, or the men in the white coats.

She would explain to her later, Niamh thought as she lifted her coat from the cloakroom and wrapped her scarf around her neck.

"I won't be long," she said, waving to the children and heading out down the gravel driveway towards the shore.

* * *

The cemetery in Rathinch sat, as all good Irish cemeteries do, on a hill. It was shielded from the wind coming off the sea by a row of tall and sad-looking trees which were shedding their leaves all over the gaudy floral displays and stony paths.

Niamh was pretty sure that if she tried she could walk to Seán's grave with her eyes closed. She had been there often since he died just to make sure the flowers were fresh and the stone kept clean. Seán would not have liked a dirty headstone – nor would he have liked wilting flowers. It would have tarnished his image and he was all about the image.

Standing at his grave she thought of all the times she had cried there and all the times she had hidden her tears because the children were there to leave pictures and presents for their daddy. Still there, on the foundation for his headstone, was a little yellow tipper truck Connor had left the last time they had visited. Normally the sight of one of her son's toys on her husband's grave would have made Niamh weep wild and hysterical tears, but today it just made her angry.

"They didn't deserve a daddy like you," she muttered, snatching it and putting it in her bag. "And I didn't deserve a husband like you. All I ever did was love you."

She sat down on the damp grass.

"How could you hurt me?" she asked. "How could you deceive us? Why was I not enough? I did everything you wanted! I was the perfect wife. I cooked. I cleaned. I gave you as many blowjobs as you wanted. I polished your shoes. I never showed you up in front of any one. I never told Kevin to fuck off, even though I wanted to on many, many occasions. I loved you!" She realised that with every word she had been tearing flowers from his grave.

He loves me. He loves me not.

Standing up, she dusted herself off and looked at the gold lettering again: *Beloved husband and father.* She wondered how much it would cost to alter and then, knowing she would only ever come back when her children asked her to, she walked through the weeping willow trees and onto the beach.

She didn't feel sad – disappointed maybe, but not sad.

She had loved him. She knew that. She loved him from the moment their eyes had locked over the daily post delivery in his solicitor's firm on her first day as his PA. It wasn't the most romantic meeting in the world but she noticed almost straight away how he sat that little bit taller and smiled that little bit broader when she came into his office.

It had taken him three weeks to ask her out. Well, to be honest, he hadn't really asked her out – more told her that they would be going out and she should wear something nice. Something just like the black pencil-skirt and satin blouse she had worn with her killer heels the day before.

She had been flattered. He was gorgeous – tall, dark, handsome, perfectly groomed with an ass that fitted snugly in his tailored suits and hands that were tanned and worn and perhaps the sexiest things she had ever seen.

He had taken her out to the Exchange for dinner and plied her with champagne and it was all she could do at the end of the night to resist the urge to pull him into her apartment and ravish him.

He, however, was a gentleman. He kissed her softly on the cheek – just long enough for her to breathe in the smell of his aftershave and be told he couldn't wait to see her at work that Monday.

Thence followed a grand wooing. Before she met Seán, Niamh was pretty sure no one was ever wooed any more. It was old-fashioned and everyone she knew fell in love in the bog-standard, snog-outside-the-pub kind of a way. But, as with everything else in life, Seán even did romance perfectly.

He sent flowers, lots of them, and bought chocolate (but not enough to increase her waist size). He planned weekend trips to country-house hotels and overnight stays in plush five-star retreats. He bought jewellery – bespoke from Thomas the Goldsmith – and delicate slips of satin and lace which made her feel feminine and horny.

And, to top it all off, he told her he loved her and proposed in the poshest hotel she had ever set her eyes on. Her stiletto heels had sunk into the plush carpet as she walked across the restaurant floor. Their table had been waiting – stuffed to the gills with more cutlery than she could ever use and an ostentatious display of candles and flowers that almost blocked their view of each other.

He had ordered the most expensive bottle of champagne on the menu and insisted on having oysters for starters. She declined. She was about as much a fan of oyster as she was of pea and ham soup. All snotty-looking foods turned her off – but he had gulped them back and washed them down with champagne before telling her they had aphrodisiac properties.

She would have found it endearing and funny if three slightly bored-looking waiters hadn't been hovering around them, topping her glass up as soon as she took so much as a sip from it. However, she brushed her concerns aside and screamed with delight when he told her loved her and presented her with a rock the size of an island.

She looked at it now, glinting in the autumn twilight, and she looked at the band of platinum and diamonds behind it. She wondered should she be melodramatic and toss them into the sea. She had contemplated that as she stormed across the dunes. It would be so very Scarlet O'Hara of her to toss the rings into the foamy water and shout that she was free of him now. It would make a great story to tell her friends over a glass or ten of wine, but she was a realist.

And she liked diamonds.

So she blew a kiss to the sea, smiled, and walked home.

* * *

When she got home Mary was cuddling the children on the sofa, with a distinct look of confusion on her face.

Niamh sat down beside her and rested her head on her mother's shoulder.

"Please tell me what is happening, Niamh, because I'm really worried about you."

"Mum, you have no need to worry."

"But you've been through so much, especially this last week," Mary was whispering now, her eyes darting between the children and Niamh, afraid of upsetting anyone.

"I've been through a lot these last five years," Niamh said stoically. "And I'm going to change. I'm going to make this all work, Mum, for me and for the children."

"I see you have bin bags at the top of the stairs?"

"Charity shop," Niamh said. "All of it. And tomorrow I'll be starting on his office. You can help if you want, or you can just keep the kids out of my hair while I do it. Now, who's for dinner? I fancy chips."

29

Ruth's house was quiet too – much too bloody quiet. Her last guest had left just after lunch and she had spent a couple of hours tidying up and cleaning. Then she had sat down, cup of tea and chocolate biscuit in hand, alone with her uneasy thoughts and an increasingly guilty conscience.

Everyone had left her house in great form. She'd had a lovely morning with Niamh, the twins, Ella and Poppy. Ciara had looked like a new woman – or new teenager – after her extended lie-in and Ruth was delighted to see someone walk down her stairs with a smile on her face as opposed to the usual sour grimace her daughter wore these days.

They had all gone, en masse, to the Country Kitchen where Ruth and the rest of the mammies had tea and scones while the children had ice cream. It should have all made her happy – especially the scones. They were light and fluffy and covered in a rich cream and deliciously sweet strawberry jam but she had felt the disquiet growing.

Poppy had sat on her knee. It was clear she was tired out from the previous night's excitement. Ruth had hugged her close and enjoyed chattering with her and sharing a bit of *craic* but at the same time she was aware that by keeping quiet she could be exposing Poppy to the same things her children had been exposed to.

Not that she thought they had seen too much. She had done her best to keep James's temper under control when the children were around and, for all his faults, he had been oddly obsessive about not hitting out in front of anyone. Strange, how she had seen the good in that.

Sure, he was a grumpy beggar with them – and he was strict. There was no way Eimear would have got away with her shenanigans with her dad still in the house. There would have been no late nights and definitely no drinking. And as for Ben Quinn, should he have so much as held her daughter's hand James would have been out to threaten him with castration should things go further.

He ruled their house with an iron fist – mostly aimed in her direction.

She shuddered as she recalled the time he had held her over the stairs and threatened to throw her down. She sort of knew he wouldn't do it – a lot of the time the threat was enough – but for a split second she had imagined crashing down the stairs and landing in a crumpled heap at the bottom where her children would find her.

Much as she hated Laura – and much as Poppy was not hers to be concerned about – she felt a wave of guilt and worry wash over her. The scone didn't look so appealing any more and she pushed it away.

"Are you not hungry?" Niamh asked, pushing her blonde hair back from her face.

"Must have had too much to drink," Ruth replied.

"Well, once we're out of your hair, why not have a lie down or go for a walk along the beach and clear your head? It's a lovely day."

Ruth had nodded. Crawling back into bed, after she had cleaned, of course, seemed like a good idea. When she was sleeping she couldn't be thinking about the mess she was in.

* * *

When she was a teenager, Ruth had been obsessed with romance and wild romantic novels like *Wuthering Heights*. She would tie her dark permed hair on top of her head, wear her longest most flowing skirt and go for a walk along the coast where the wind would whip around her and she would feel like Cathy. She was always looking for Heathcliff.

James wasn't exactly dark and brooding, but he was mad about her in that same all-encompassing way Heathcliff was obsessed with the fair Cathy. It was almost obsessive and she was flattered by it. He wanted to have her all to himself and she didn't mind. It was nice to be wanted and, being young and foolish, when he made arrangements so that she rarely spent time with her family and friends, she lapped it up.

She didn't feel suffocated back then. She liked that she was so deliriously in love that they could spend all their waking and sleeping hours together, and by the time the children came along she was too busy to chase up her old friends anyway. She raised her family, got her part-time job and chatted to everyone nineteen to the dozen.

To the outside observer she was a lucky wife and he was the perfect husband and their children were just gorgeous. But Heathcliff, as every Brontë reader knows, was a couple of sandwiches short of a picnic and now Ruth could see that James always had been too.

* * *

Laura waited in the car when James dropped the children off. She didn't wave, or look in Ruth's direction. She didn't look downtrodden and beaten though. Her hair was perfect and she had the glow of someone whose top layer of skin had been scrubbed off with a fancy rock-salt concoction.

Eimear had a similar glow, and eyebrows that were at least half as thin as they had been when she left. Her nails were painted a pale pink and tiny gems were studded on her thumbs. Her hair was swept back in a new pair of distinctly designer-looking oversized sunglasses and she walked past her mother as if Ruth were a desperate groupie looking for an autograph.

Thomas looked at her and smiled and walked in while Matthew ran into her arms, squealing with delight.

"Mammy, Mammy, it was brilliant! And I got new toys! *Ben 10* toys. I love them. Do you want to see them? Daddy says I'm a great boy. Can we have pizza for tea? I'm hungry!"

Ruth couldn't help but smile. She said a silent prayer of thanks that things had at least gone well and that James had obviously kept his temper. Of course it would be a complete pain in the arse to compete with his super-daddy powers now – but maybe this was nothing more sinister than a sign that he was changing.

Maybe away from her he wasn't the violent monster she knew him to be. Maybe it was just her that brought out the worst in him. Maybe she was the useless creature he told her she was, but then again, if she were, would she be coping so well on her own? Maybe they were just wrong for each other and just better off on their own.

"Thanks," she said to him, and she meant it. "It looks like they had a great time altogether."

"They did," he replied, a hint of a smile on his face.

"It's nice that they got to spend some time with you."

"I spend plenty of time with them," he said, his voice edgy.

"That's not what I meant. I just meant, it was nice for you to take them away and all. You and Laura – you know."

"They're my children. Why wouldn't I take them away?"

Ruth didn't like where this conversation was going. If this were a cartoon, huge warning signs surrounded by bright lights would burst into life just above her head and some weird bird-like creature would sound a huge warning klaxon: "*Turn back now. Do not pass go. Do not collect £200. Do not get involved in mind games with a man who has a limited ability to use his brain instead of his hands.*"

Then again, he wasn't likely to completely throw the head in front of Laura. Still, she wasn't sure she wanted to take the risk.

"No reason, none at all," she said, realising any confrontation would take the sheen off the weekend for everyone and from the corner of her eye she could see Matthew watching with a worried look on his face.

And she realised James didn't actually have to hit her to hurt her any more.

30

Liam woke at ten. He blinked, a feeling that something just wasn't quite right washing over him. He ran his fingers through his hair and stretched in the bed. It was quiet. Too quiet. His brain felt fuzzy and he was almost tempted to roll over and fall back to sleep. He had been drinking – he knew that from the fact his mouth felt like the inside of one of his socks after a long day on the site.

Poppy. She wasn't here. It came into focus, as did the memory of walking Detta home the night before, and singing the theme to the *A-Team* over in Ruth's house.

He hoped, with every fibre of his heart, that he hadn't made a complete eejit of himself. The combination of the fireworks, the beer and the bit of *craic* had made him act just that little bit less reserved than he was used to.

In fairness he couldn't remember the last time he had been out for the night. Laura hadn't really liked him going out with the lads on their Friday evening sessions so he tended only to spend time in the pub with them when it was absolutely necessary. He always took them out for a good drinking session for Christmas and St Patrick's – the rest of the time he had waved them off sorrowfully from his desk on Friday afternoons as he trudged home to Laura and Poppy.

But he'd loved going home to Laura, he reminded himself. He put his head in his hands, trying to get his brain to catch up with the rest of his body and wake up. Of course he loved coming home to Laura, how could he think it had been any other way?

It would have been nice, though, to have joined the boys in the pub. He wasn't a party animal – a couple of beers in one of Rathinch's cosier pubs would have finished off the week just nicely. God knows he worked hard enough and at the weekend he always made sure he was available to take Laura where she wanted to go or run his mother up to Letterkenny for her shopping, or take Poppy to her riding classes at the Equestrian Centre.

Yes, by week he was a rugged builder commanding a team of weatherworn and testosterone-filled men in proper manly man's work and at the weekend he might as well have cut off his dangly bits and handed them to the three women in his life on a plate.

Detta would let him go to the pub for a drink, he thought. Damn it, Detta would probably meet him there and drink pints with him and the boys and not once scold him for swearing or roll her eyes when he suggested stopping off at the chipper for a fish supper on the way home.

And he knew Detta wouldn't run off and leave him and his daughter in the lurch.

Walking downstairs he switched on the kettle and opened the curtains to let the bright autumn sunshine flood in. Very quickly, he closed them again. His eyes were not ready for bright autumn sunshine – they were not even ready for murky autumn sunshine or light of any description.

Lifting a mug from the cupboard he knocked a plate to the

floor and it crashed at his feet, splinters of porcelain bouncing off his toes.

"Oh for fuck's sake," he swore, slamming the cupboard door so that all the other plates and cups wobbled precariously.

Leaving the broken plate on the floor, he walked around the breakfast bar and sat down on the sofa. He felt unsettled and grouchy and hung-over to hell but most of all he felt as if a big cloud was lifting from in front of his eyes and he felt angry. He felt like punching a hole in a wall, or a door, or James's face, but then, he acknowledged, his anger wasn't with James. It was Laura who had left him and it was Laura who had made him feel like it was all his fault when, he realised with a start, that couldn't have been further from the truth.

Agnes would say Laura was the kind of person who had ideas above her station. "Fur coat and no knickers," Agnes would say, whispering the word "knickers" of course because, as we all know, God does not like references to pants.

It hadn't surprised Liam that Agnes and his wife had never become best friends. His mother had taken against almost every woman he had ever brought through her front door – not that there had been many. But Agnes's dislike of Laura seemed to go deeper than a mother's protective instinct for her son. It could almost be described as hate, except of course, God didn't like the word hate either so Agnes never used it.

They had bristled off each other from the first time they met. Liam had brought her over for tea, and they had stopped off at Mrs Quinn's shop first for some French Fancies, even though he hated French Fancies. They looked as if they tasted nice but they made his teeth shudder with their sweetness. Agnes, however, liked them so he bought the packet and gave it to Laura, telling her she should hand them over when they arrived.

He so wanted this meeting to go well. He wanted the two

of them to hit it off because he knew he loved her already, even though they'd only been going out for a month. But then he had loved her from the first time saw her – or more accurately from the first time she smiled back at him and acknowledged his existence. She had asked him out – and he liked her ballsy attitude. She knew what she wanted and how she was going to get it and Liam was delighted that she wanted him and knew just how to get him. That plan, of course, involved lots of passionate sex, home-cooked dinners and her parading around his house in his football shirt with her hair hanging loosely around her shoulders and her legs bare, tanned and lovely.

He couldn't resist her and while he knew, or sincerely hoped, that Agnes wouldn't be interested in her long legs and silken hair, he wanted his mother to see her for the amazing person she was – with or without the help of French Fancies.

Laura had sighed when Liam handed her the box of buns. "I'm sure I don't need these to impress your mother," she said, with more confidence than she felt.

"My mother is like Tesco," Liam laughed. "Every Little Helps."

"I'll do my best and she can like me or lump me."

"But I like you and I'd really like to lump you too," he replied with a waggle of his eyebrows.

Laura laughed – her gorgeous full-bodied giggle that made him weak at the knees and hard at the crotch. She threw her hair back and the sunlight glinted through it. It was just like one of the slow-motion moments in films where the leading man falls even more in love with the leading woman as the sun catches her at just the right angle. This was the kind of thing The Carpenters sang about in "Close to You".

"I promise you can lump me later, but preferably far away

from your mother's house. I don't think any amount of French Fancies would endear her to me if she knew we were at it."

Liam nodded, because Agnes would have a hissy fit if she knew about the way Laura walked around his house so brazenly in the football shirt. And she would be for the coronary ward had she known what exactly they'd got up to on his kitchen table that morning. She'd have been round like a whippet with a lethal combination of Holy Water and Domestos to give the place a thorough cleansing.

When they arrived at Agnes's house – a place which felt as much like a shrine as it did a home – Laura had clutched her box of French Fancies to her and smiled politely.

Agnes had regarded her with a look that left little to the imagination. It was the same kind of a look you reserved for those blasted chuggers who try to make you as enthusiastic about their charities as they are paid to be, or small yappy dogs that try and pee up against your leg.

"It's lovely to meet you," Laura offered, reaching out her hand.

"Yes, indeed. Come in. Liam, take her coat and let's have some tea."

They had walked through to the good front room and Liam had instantly noticed his mother had her best wedding-present china out, complete with her favourite little cake stand adorned with enough French Fancies to sink a small ship.

"Why don't I be mother?" Laura offered, lifting the teapot to pour for them all.

And it was at that exact moment that Agnes determined that the pair of them would never be friends.

They had clashed at almost every meeting since. When it came to the wedding Laura had very definite ideas about what she wanted: a quiet affair with immediate family only. Agnes had been almost apoplectic with anger. "But what about my sisters and Liam's cousins? And his great-aunt? She won't be happy about this, no way. Are you shunning my family?" she had raged.

Laura had stood firm and when Liam tried to act as a go-between, begging her to sneak a few extra people onto the guest list, his wife to be had been able to wrap him around her little finger – much to Agnes's chagrin.

"It's our day," Laura said, "And this is what I want. I don't care about your aunts, or cousins, or my aunts or cousins for that matter. I only care about us."

She had batted her eyelids and Liam had eventually agreed to her requests. Agnes hadn't spoken to him for a week after that and when she cried through the ceremony he knew they weren't tears of joy.

The next major clash came with Poppy's arrival.

"Sure, that's not an Irish name," Agnes had sniffed as she cradled her newborn granddaughter.

"No, but we like it," Laura had smiled.

"Is it even a saint's name?"

"Not sure. Haven't really thought about it."

"But babies have to have a saint's name," Agnes has said, her voice rising an octave.

"Not these days, they don't. Anyway she suits the name Poppy, so Poppy she is."

"Would you even give her a middle saint's name?"

"Actually we were thinking of Lola."

Agnes blessed herself and her new granddaughter. "But, that's a – a – stripper's name!" she blurted out eventually.

"Nonsense. We think it suits her," Laura had answered while Liam just sat there thanking his lucky stars that should blood be shed they were at least already in the hospital. Not even a king-size box of French Fancies from the cash and carry would get him out of this one.

If Liam was honest with himself he had spent the last eleven years of his life living in his very own no-man's land between the two of them, waving his flag every now and again to call a truce.

If he was even more honest with himself he had enjoyed not refereeing their battles over the last couple of months. Sure he listened to them individually tear shreds off each other, but it was much preferable to sitting with them over the dinner table worried about the very real possibility that someone could get stabbed with a fork at a moment's notice.

Life with Laura, he realised, had perhaps not been the bed of roses that he had thought it was. His rose-tinted glasses were developing a distinct crack.

31

"You look happy," Lorraine said, looking up from her magazine as Ciara pushed Ella and her pram through the front door.

"I had a good night, Mum."

"I hope you weren't drinking?" Lorraine asked, raising her eyebrow.

Ciara blushed.

"Well, not too much anyway," Lorraine added, putting her magazine down and lifting her granddaughter from the pram. "You did have this one to mind."

"I was sensible, Mum," Ciara said, sitting down. "Besides, the rest of them were there to help me. They are nice people, Mum. You would like them."

"I've spoken to Ruth a few times at the doctor's. She seems a nice woman – a bit quiet maybe."

Ciara thought back to the previous night and how Ruth had been twirling around dressed as the Wicked Witch singing to the children and couldn't think how any one could ever describe her as quiet.

"She's lovely when you get to know her," Ciara said,

wondering if this would be the perfect time to invite her mother along to the group. Then again, did she really want her mother cramping her style? Perhaps they would all start treating her like a young cub if her mum was sitting alongside them.

Sitting forward and tickling Ella's tummy while she was bounced up and down on her granny's knee, Ciara decided to keep quiet. But she did tell her mum one important thing.

"I told them about Ben," she said.

Lorraine paused for the shortest of moments and carried on. "And what did they say?"

"Well, they were shocked too. They thought the sun shone out of him as well, and Ruth is obviously worried now about Eimear but they were lovely, Mum. I can't believe I ever believed Ben when he said that everyone would think I was some kind of lying tramp."

"That young fella deserves a sound talking-to," Lorraine raged. Looking into Ella's eyes, she turned to look at Ciara and dropped her voice to a whisper. "How could he deny her? How on earth could he deny this little one?"

Ciara bit back the response that he could deny his daughter because the only person he ever really cared about was himself.

"And your friends," Lorraine continued, "do they think you are right not to confront him now? Or do they think like me that he could do with a swift kick up the ass?"

"They understand that she is better with no daddy than a daddy who doesn't want to know," Ciara said defiantly. Surely her mother would understand that more than most. Ciara's own father had left when she was a baby and, while he had visited on a very occasional basis during her early years, he had soon left Rathinch for Belfast and she hadn't heard as much as two words from him since.

When she was younger she used to dream of him coming

back. In her very melodramatic early teenage years she used to sit on her windowsill and sing songs from *Annie* wondering if he would come back to her.

She was fifteen, and pregnant, when it dawned on her that he wasn't coming back and that he was an awful gobshite anyway.

"I suppose you're right there," Lorraine said sadly, cutting through her thoughts. "I'm sorry I didn't give you the best example in life."

"Look, Mum, when you and Dad were together you thought he was a decent man. He only turned out to be a good-for-nothing pig after I was born." Then she added with a wink, "We've got a lot in common."

"With God's grace you'll grow out of it. Now here, have this wee woman because I'm dying for a smoke and to freshen up this cuppa. Can I get you anything?"

"I'm grand, Mum. I'll put madam here in her playpen and then get started on the washing. I'll have to make sure my uniform is clean for tomorrow's shift or Mrs Quinn will have a stroke."

"Will serve her right if she does, the stupid old cow!"

Lorraine walked out of the room and Ciara smiled. What she wouldn't give to let her mother let rip at Mrs Quinn one of these days! If only she didn't need her job so much and the money it brought in, she would enjoy watching the fallout from that one very much indeed.

As she sat Ella in her playpen, with some cuddly toys, her phone peeped to life.

"Did u have a gd nite?" Abby texted.

"Gr8. Was a laff."

"Can I call rnd?"

"Mt u on the beach 4 a walk?"

"C u in 10."

"Okay, missy. Change of plan," Ciara told her daughter. "Let's get you back in your buggy and go for a walk."

Calling to Lorraine that she was off to meet Abby for a quick natter, she wrapped her coat around her and headed out with the buggy into the cool evening.

Rathinch was quiet for a Saturday teatime. The shops – not that there were many of them – were closing. The pubs, corner shop and chippy were the only places that stayed open and even then Mrs Quinn always closed the shop between seven and nine out of season so that she was seen to be holier than thou as she traipsed off to Mass. In season, though, when the town was thronged with tourists, there wasn't a chance in hell she would close and miss the chance of making a quick buck.

It was still too early for the teenagers who hung around the play park at the edge of the beach to be out and about and Ciara was grateful for that. Although she felt buoyed up by the experiences of the last few days, she didn't fancy a full-on confrontation with Ben and his cronies – not until she had made a firm decision what to do about the whole situation anyway.

Abby was waiting in the park on a swing, kicking her legs out in front of her and throwing her hair back. For just a second, Ciara looked at her and thought she looked young – much younger than her anyway even though there were only five months between them.

"Hey there!" she called and Ella started wriggling excitedly in her buggy at the sight of Abby who always seemed to have a packet of chocolate buttons secreted somewhere on her person.

"Hey there, yourself," Abby answered, jumping off the swing with one smooth movement.

"How are you? And how's wee Ella here?" Abby crouched down in front of the buggy and tickled Ella's tummy. "Can I lift her out? Can she have a go on the baby swing?"

Ciara nodded and walked over to the swings where she took the one Abby had been on while her friend strapped the baby into the next swing along.

"So, are you dumping me now entirely for your new mates?" Abby asked as she pushed Ella gently.

"Don't be so daft," Ciara laughed. "But they are nice people."

"Yeah, I'm sure the *craic* is mighty," Abby said with a raised eyebrow.

"Hey, don't knock it! We can't all be living the high life, you know."

"High life?" Abby choked back. "No such thing. I'm lucky to be allowed out the door at the minute. It's all study and putting my head down and trying to decide what the hell I want to do with the rest of my life."

"At least you have choices. I'm stuck in the flipping shop selling baps and firelighters and fecking sausage rolls."

"God, I'd love a sausage roll," Abby said wistfully. "Besides, Missus, you do have choices. There is nothing to say you couldn't go to college and do the things you want to do."

"There *is* something to say that and you're pushing her in that swing," Ciara answered, nodding in the direction of her daughter.

"And there wouldn't be any parents who ever went to college then, would there?"

"Well, maybe they had a mammy who could watch their children or money in the bank?"

Abby sighed. "Most colleges have crèches now – I've been looking at the brochures – for day classes or evening classes. Surely your mum would mind her a couple of nights a week for you to allow you to go to college."

Ciara shrugged, despite the bubble of excitement building

inside her. Would she dare ask Lorraine to mind Ella so she could go to college? Before she had got pregnant there were so many things she wanted to do. She always fancied her chances at journalism. English was her favourite subject and, while at the moment she wasn't sure she could string together a written sentence without text-speak or getting baby-sick on her notebook, she was sure with a bit of practice she could manage it.

It was almost too much to hope for. She could just hear Lorraine telling her to keep living in the real world and leave behind her fancy notions – but then she had misjudged her mother before now.

"You know Abby, I think I love you."

"Of course you do," her friend answered. "Now, do you fancy walking over to the chippy and we'll share a bag of chips here on the beach."

"Only if we overdose on salt and vinegar?"

"No other way," Abby answered, lifting a thrilled Ella from her swing and strapping her back in her buggy. She then proudly took the handles of the buggy and all three set off towards the Main Street.

32

Niamh woke at six thirty – amazingly without the aid of a small child jumping on her head. The house was in darkness – the kind of darkness you only get in the country – no haze of street lights, just absolute pitch black.

She looked at the clock to get her bearings and thought about falling back to sleep but her brain was already ticking over. A list – she needed to make a list, so she switched on her beside light and fumbled in her drawer for a pen and a pad of paper.

God. Detta would be so proud of her, she thought with a smile as she opened a fresh page and started writing.

THINGS TO DO:
She was going to write, "THINGS TO DO TO GET MY LIFE BACK ON TRACK AND FORGET MY CHEATING DEAD BASTARD OF A HUSBAND" but decided less was more.

* Convince my mother she *will* take everything in the black bags to the charity shop and that no, I won't regret it down the line when I've calmed down. I am perfectly calm.

* Sort out the office. It has great light. Price dark-room equipment and/or good photo-editing computer equipment.

* Buy myself a damn nice camera and take photos like I've always wanted. Do it because "I want to" even though I don't need to.

* Book a holiday for the children – somewhere Seán would have considered tacky like Disneyland. Feck him and his gites in France. I think gites should be called shites.

* Swear more. Like at least once a fucking day. (Not in front of the children, mind.)

* Fill in the swimming pool. We don't use it, it's too cold. Or at least build an extension to cover the damn thing up. Phone Liam for a quote.

* Confront Caitlin.

Some things, she conceded, would be easier than others. She imagined she would be able to swan into PC World and Jessops or somewhere of that nature and pick up a decent camera without too much fuss. Picking up the ability to take pictures more complex than snapshots of the twins pulling crazy faces might be more difficult, but she was willing to start learning. There were probably dozens of books on the subject, or night classes or DVDs.

Similarly, thanks to the power of the internet her holiday would be easy to pull together. She would just need to convince her mother or Robyn to come and help with babysitting duties. She was brave, but not brave enough to take on two toddlers *and* Mickey Mouse all at the one time.

Swearing – well, that would be a piece of piss and sorting out the office would be easy. She was unlikely to find anything that would turn her life upside down again. She would actually enjoy the task. She hated the office – its austere feel had been out of keeping with the rest of the house. She had begged Seán to furnish it with light woods and neutral colours but he'd opted for mahogany and bottle green. The room was suffocating and stuffy even on the coldest of days and she would take great pleasure into making it an altogether more welcoming sanctuary for her blossoming hobby.

The only thing that gave her collywobbles – the major collywobbles – was confronting Caitlin, but she knew that for closure she had to do it. Still she wasn't sure how. It wasn't as easy as walking into a shop, or going on online or calling the local builder.

Niamh wanted to do it, but she didn't want to make a complete eejit of herself in the process. She was worried she would lose her cool and start to cry, or worse still lose her cool and slap the silly cow square around the face.

After all, she couldn't confront Seán – not properly. All she had of him was a gravestone, but Caitlin, she was very much alive and if all reports from Derry were to be believed very much getting on with her life as if she hadn't been responsible for tearing the heart out of her friend's life.

Niamh cringed as she remembered Caitlin's tearstained face as she arrived at the house in Rathinch the morning after Seán died. She had pulled her into a hug and sobbed while Niamh had held on to her, unable to break through her shock to cry herself.

"I can't believe it," Caitlin had sniffed. "I just can't believe he is gone. How can he be gone?" she had wailed, pouring herself a large glass of brandy and knocking it back.

"I don't know," Niamh had mumbled, sitting down and holding her head in her hands. "Oh Cait, what am I going to do? I can't do this on my own. I'm not supposed to do this on my own."

"I don't know, darling. I don't know what any of us is going to do."

* * *

It was obvious in hindsight – annoyingly, stupidly obvious. When Caitlin had held on to her sobbing that day it was because of her own grief – not any concern for Niamh or Connor or Rachel. She had come to the funeral in black, complete with a too-big hat and a red rose to drop onto the coffin. Niamh hadn't thought much of it at the time – she had been too busy trying not to throw herself into the grave after Seán – but now she saw Caitlin for what she was – a shameless bitch of a tart who didn't care who she hurt.

Now that the rage was coursing through her veins, Niamh got up and jumped in the shower. There was no better time than the present to start on that office. She pulled on her tracksuit bottoms and T-shirt and lifted the roll of bin bags from the top of her dressing table and set to work.

Opening the door and switching on the light she saw his blasted Post-its flutter with the draft. Some fell to the floor and she simply lifted them and shoved them in the bin. She didn't bother to read them – feck knows what they might have said.

She looked at his shelves of law tomes – books he liked to have just to look important. Sure he used some of them but many were there for show. Still, she thought, they were worth a lot of money and some law student somewhere would be grateful for them. Stacking them up at the door she resolved to drop them into the university the next time she was in Derry – she would get Mary to stick a notice up in the library advertising the books as free to a good home.

The drawers of his desk were anally tidy – a complete opposite to his office life – but then everything had to be just so in Rathinch. Mess was not allowed. Still it made her job easier as she tipped the contents into bags.

When that was done she walked to the windows – the musty dark-wood blinds gave the room a glum look so she pulled them down and opened the windows wide allowing the biting cold November air to sweep in. The coolness caught her by surprise but she breathed the fresh air deep into her lungs and thought of just how her life had turned around.

She was still standing there, staring, when Mary walked into the room. Walking up behind her daughter, she put her arms around her.

"I'm worried about you, darling," she said.

"There's no need," Niamh replied, closing the window and turning around to face her mother.

"You've had an awful time. You must still be in shock. Darling, you need to take it easy. Doing this," Mary said, gesturing to the bin bags and the empty desk "might seem like the right thing to do now, but you are grieving. I don't want you to wake up in two weeks, two months or two years and regret erasing every trace of him."

"But 'him', Mum, I don't know who 'him' was any more. He wasn't the man I thought he was and this – all this – was just an act."

"You can't say that! He loved you." Mary looked stricken. It was as if she believed in Seán more than she believed in Niamh.

"He might have done, Mum. But he didn't love me, or this, or anything enough. And while all this stuff is nice – and all of it is a part of him – it's not what I thought it was and what I want now is reality. I don't want to live a lie any more."

Niamh was impressed with herself. She was impressed that she remained calm while talking. She was impressed she didn't weep and wail and generally make a show of herself. She would like to say she felt numb, but it was not numbness that was getting her through this now. It was anger.

Mary just nodded. "Just think about it," she said. "Think about what you are doing."

"Do you think," Niamh asked, the calmness remaining, "that I've thought of anything else this past week? It's there wherever I am. When I look at the twins, it's there. When I look at this blasted house, it's there. From the white fecking sofa to the marble floors to the poncy claw-footed bath that's not even long enough to get a good fecking soak in."

Mary looked horrified and Niamh could not help but wonder if she was simply shocked that Niamh could dare criticise the house – this thing of absolute beauty.

She knew her mother loved her, but she sometimes wondered if she loved the fecking claw-footed bath more.

And it dawned on her that her mother was embarrassed by all this. She was supportive, of course she was, but there had been a certain kudos in being the mother-in-law of a dead highly successful solicitor. That kudos would fade away when everyone found out what a dirty-balled bastard he really was.

Mary loved her and her intentions were good, but she wanted to keep this under wraps. She wanted this – this perfect everything – to remain perfect.

She would be in for some shock, Niamh realised , when she realised the holy row her daughter was planning on kicking up when she confronted Caitlin head on.

"I love you, Mum," she said, hugging her mother tightly. "But I have to deal with this my way and you might not understand it, and I might not even understand, but I have to do it all the same."

Mary nodded, hugged her daughter back and gave a small smile.

"The children will be up soon," she said. "I was thinking of making scrambled eggs if you fancy some."

"That would be nice, Mum. And then, this afternoon I thought we could call up to Letterkenny. I want to buy a new camera."

33

Eimear walked into the living room, dressed to all intents and purposes as if it was a balmy summer's evening and not the start of November.

"I'm just off out, Mum," she said, lifting her bag and turning on her heels.

"Hang on just one minute," Ruth said, her heart already sinking at the thought of the row that was sure to follow.

"Mum, I'm going to be late."

The whining in Eimear's voice made Ruth cringe.

"Late for what? It's a Sunday night and you have school in the morning. Not to mention it's freezing out there and you've no coat."

And besides I need to tell you what a bollocks Ben is, Ruth added silently. She knew, just as mammies always knew, that now was not the time to trample all over love's young dream. She would have a battle enough dealing with tonight. After a weekend being spoiled by Daddy Dearest, Eimear was in full-on spoiled diva mode.

"So if I put a jacket on, can I go?" Eimear asked, rolling her eyes to heaven.

For a second, just the briefest of moments, Ruth was tempted to let her go on out without one and live with the consequences of getting the inevitable dose after. Except Ruth knew that Eimear wouldn't keep her illness to herself. She would do the full wilting-flower routine on the sofa while her mother ran rings around her – dosing her with paracetamol, Lucozade and ice pops for her sore throat.

"Put your coat on and be back by ten. You have school tomorrow."

"But everyone else will be out till eleven!"

She tried not to say it. She felt it bubble up and she tried to push it back down, knowing that once the words were past her lips she would have officially become the boring old fart of a mum she dreaded being. And yet, it was almost as if the words had a power of their own. Many had said them before and many would say them again. Perhaps it was simply her destiny as one who had pushed a child from her fandango.

"If the rest of the world put their hand in the fire, would you do it too?"

"Mum," Eimear said with an even more exaggerated roll of the eyes.

"Don't 'mum' me. I said be back by ten, so be back by ten."

"But, Mum!"

"But nothing. Do as you are told."

Eimear stormed out without taking her jacket from the hatstand and Ruth swore at the front door.

"Mammy, that's a bad word," Matthew said, looking up from his Lego.

"I know," Ruth said dejectedly and walked into the kitchen to switch on the kettle, kicking the table leg as she walked past and yelping in pain.

"Fuck, fuck, fuck, fuckity, fuckity, fuck," she said under her breath, before sitting down. "And double fuck!"

She had known it wouldn't have taken long for the calm to lift once the children were back, but she thought she could have at least lasted till morning without letting rip a string of expletives. There was no doubt she was losing her ability to think about things calmly and rationally.

If she didn't keep her cool there was no way at all she would be able to talk to Eimear about anything. Long gone were the days when they used to be best friends – a real "me and my shadow" of mother and daughter, baking together, laughing together, walking everywhere hand in hand. Taking a deep breath, she poured her tea and sipped from it while staring out the window. It had started to rain and she was all too aware of the jacket still hanging at the bottom of the stairs.

Lifting it and putting on her own coat, she called to Matthew and Thomas that she wouldn't be long and set out into the evening.

It was biting cold. She wondered if Eimear just did not feel the chill. Maybe she had been the same at seventeen – she couldn't really remember – but now she loved the feel of her coat around her and the softness of her trusty gloves. Then again, she knew she was getting older. At thirty-seven she felt more like sixty-seven. She baulked at the thought that women at her age were just getting married now, just having babies, still going out clubbing and wearing short shorts and low-cut tops. She couldn't imagine doing that. Then again, she couldn't remember ever wearing short shorts. Such things were not allowed.

Even compared with Detta, and her funky out-there hippy style she felt fat and frumpy. Detta was like Ruth without the worry lines and cellulite.

Ruth knew where the young people usually met – at the old shelter near the beach car park – and headed straight there. She knew she would have to cover up her actions in some way. Eimear would rather die than her mother hand her a coat in front of her friends, so decided to offer her a further peace offering of some cash for chips for her and her friends. She fished about in Eimear's jacket for her wallet and slipped a ten-euro note in it. It wasn't really something she could afford but she was tired of the constant fighting between them now and wanted to start making amends.

Maybe, she thought, it would go some way to healing the rift between them so they could actually talk about things – like they used to. She could hear the laughing before she got there. Sensing she would look like an old fogy to their young eyes, she pulled her tummy in and stood tall. She could do the funky, young and trendy mamma thing if needed. She could be down with the kids. God knows she was even semi-competent at texting these days although she never quite got it why people seemed to hate vowels so much.

Painting a smile on her face, she walked towards the chattering voices and called out to her daughter who was sitting on a bench, her arms wrapped around Ben Quinn's waist – laughing and joking and throwing her hair back in a distinctly flirtatious manner.

At first she felt sick at the sight – and she resolved that she really had to talk to Eimear about Ben and just exactly what he had been up to with Ciara and how badly he had treated her. But she knew she had to pick her moment. There was no point at the moment in trying to explain it to her. Eimear wasn't in the frame of mind for listening and Ruth certainly was not in the frame of mind for yet another battle. No, she would tell her when things were calmer. For now, even though it galled her, she would have to grin and bear it and let her daughter wrap her arms around the most fertile boy in the village.

"Eimear!" she called. She had wanted it to sound light-hearted. She had wanted to sound like a cool mum, but she could not deny there was a hint of fishwife to her tone.

It seemed as if fifteen pairs of teenage eyes turned to stare at her all at the one time – and each and every one of them looked mildly disgusted that their *craic* had been disturbed by a grown-up.

Eimear, however, was clearly the most disgusted. She quickly unwrapped herself from Ben and stormed over to her mother. There was a glower in her eyes that reminded Ruth so much of James she had to take a deep breath and remind herself that it was she who had the control in this situation, even if it didn't feel like it.

"Mu-um," Eimear hissed. "What are you *doing* here?"

"I brought your wallet. You forgot it," she said, gesturing to Eimear to follow her away from the crowd. "I brought your coat too," she whispered. "It's freezing, Eimear. I thought you would need it."

"Oh Mum, you are so embarrassing," Eimear hissed, grabbing the jacket, and turning on her heel she walked towards her laughing friends.

Standing at the edge of the beach, like a cold snotter, Ruth knew she had no options. No matter how she wanted to shout at her daughter to get her skinny little too-big-for-her-boots ass back over to her right there and then, she knew she had to just walk away. She had been naïve – downright stupid even – to think landing up near the beach was going to make things better.

If anything, she had just made it all worse. Biting back tears she turned and walked away and yet she wasn't ready to go home. She didn't want Matthew and Thomas seeing her in a state. They would only either get annoyed with her for being so soft on Eimear or annoyed with Eimear for being a bitch and either way there would be a row she just didn't feel up to at that moment.

So she walked on and decided to drop in on the one person she knew was having an even shittier time than she was.

* * *

As she walked through the iron gates she couldn't help but feel a little like Maria in *The Sound of Music* when she first visits the Von Trapps. Of course she had been here before but then she was there to check on Niamh and totally in control. She had been going to offer a listening ear with no other motive than to try and help her friend. Ringing the doorbell she stood back and waited for Niamh to answer. She contemplated the fact that she was probably an awful bitch for wanting to make herself feel better by losing herself in Niamh's problems but then she did genuinely care for the girl.

The pair of them had so much in common, when she thought about it. They were a similar age and had both been treated horrendously by the men they loved. Although, looking at the manicured lawn and gorgeous stonework façade of the Quigley house, Ruth thought that Niamh had definitely got the best deal out of the two of them.

The door opened and Ruth was shocked to see Niamh stand before her – a dishevelled mess compared to her usual carefully groomed self. She was dressed in faded jeans, with a pair of Crocs on her feet. Ruth would never have thought Niamh would have been a Croc-wearing kind of a gal. She couldn't see her ever wearing anything that wasn't Jimmy Choo or Manolo Blahnik or some other deliciously decadent designer brand. Niamh wiped her hands on her already stained T-shirt and ushered Ruth in. As she turned to lead her towards the kitchen, Ruth was sure she saw at least ten hairs out of place. No, no, this was not like Niamh at all.

She followed her into the kitchen where Niamh was already opening a bottle of wine.

"You look like you need it," her friend said, turning round and setting a glass in front of her. "And it's a good one. From Seán's wine cellar. He would turn in his grave if he knew we were drinking it – he was so precious about the bloody stuff. I'm happy with Jacob's Creek."

"You look different," Ruth said, eyebrow raised. There was an energy to Niamh she hadn't seen before and she wasn't quite sure if it was a good one or not.

"I've been cleaning all day. Sorting things out. Getting rid of some of the old shite from my life."

Ruth was pretty sure if she raised her eyebrow any further it would float clean over her head and dance about like some fuzzy halo.

At that the phone rang and Niamh excused herself to answer it. Ruth took a slug of wine, allowing the ice-cold, crisp liquid to slide down her throat. She realised her heart had stopped thumping with the mixture of anger and embarrassment that had caused her to stomp into the middle of Niamh's kitchen at gone nine at night.

Jesus, Niamh must think she was totally cracked. Ruth pushed her hair back from her face and looked around her.

The Bible says it is a sin to covet your neighbour's ass, Ruth thought, wondering what he would think of her coveting a kitchen island instead. This was a room that looked as if it had come straight out of an *Interior Design* magazine. With its smooth lines, and granite worktops – complete with the Belfast sink Ruth had always dreamed of – it made her realise this truly was how the other half lived. For the love of God, the fridge even had a wee button you could press to get ice dispensed without even having to open the door. Ruth relied on a bargain set of ice-cube trays from Mrs Quinn's, and of course she was the only person who ever remembered to fill them.

Ruth could only dream of such things. She threw back another slug of wine and pulled her coat off, noticing that her top looked misshapen and faded under the glorious spotlights of the designer kitchen.

Niamh walked back in, lifting her glass and clinking it against Ruth's.

"That was my mother on the phone – she wants to know if I'm okay," she said, sitting down and reaching for the box of Green and Black's chocolates on the island. Stuffing a sweet into her mouth, she said: "Why won't she believe that I'm perfectly fine? I feel as if a cloud has lifted – as if I'm seeing things properly for the first time in a long time."

"You are acting a little bit, well, unlike yourself?" Ruth offered.

"No, you know, I think I'm acting exactly like myself – the real myself."

Ruth looked behind her friend and saw a big pile of bin bags stacked up in the utility room.

"Is that the stuff you're getting rid of?" she asked, nodding her head in the direction of the bin-bag mountain.

"All his stuff. Well, to be honest, most of his stuff."

Ruth could see why Niamh's mother was concerned. Sure she'd had a shock, but to clear everything out without fully coming to terms with his death? Ruth couldn't help but feel her friend would live to regret it.

"Oh don't tell me you're concerned about me as well?" Niamh said with a hint of annoyance in her voice.

"It does seem a little sudden," Ruth offered, trying not to aggravate the situation further.

"He's dead almost four months. Am I to keep looking at this stuff? He has no need for it now, and neither do I." Niamh's eyes blazed. She seemed utterly determined that what she was doing was exactly the right thing.

Ruth was unsure whether to say anything more. She had enough of bearing the brunt of other people's aggression today, so she just sipped her wine.

"Look," Niamh offered, after a short pause, "I know that this looks a bit strange but, Ruth, I know what I'm doing. And I haven't known what I'm doing for a very, very long time. This is my way of getting control – you know. Just sorting through his stuff, sorting out this house, doing what I can to feel less helpless than I have done."

"Well then," Ruth said, breathing out, "fair play to you."

"Thanks. Now what can I do for you? Because trust me no one comes out here at night-time without a good reason. Come to think of it, no one tends to come out here at all. Except for the wake, they all crowded in for the wake. Secretly I think they wanted a good nosy."

"Can't say as I blame them," Ruth said. "You have a lovely house."

"It's a great showhouse," Niamh sniffed, "but it's never really felt like home, if you know what I mean. That's why this is so important to me. I want to make it the way I want. But anyway, it's not about me now – how are you, Ruth?"

This was her chance, Ruth thought, to come clean and spill out her secrets. She could just tell Niamh and have it out in the open. Surely Niamh would be okay with it all – with the fact that her husband was an abusive twat and his daughter seemed to following in his footsteps.

She could easily tell Niamh that she had just been humiliated in front of a group of teenagers on the shorefront and that while everyone else in the Loonies seemed to be getting their lives together, hers seemed to be falling apart.

"Ach I was just out on a walk and decided to call in," she said, knowing in her heart that she was bottling it but afraid of what might happen if she finally started letting out all the hurt. "I wanted to make sure you were okay."

"Are you sure that's it?"

"Absolutely," Ruth lied, drinking back more wine. "Now tell me this, when you say you want to make the house the way you want it – you're keeping the kitchen island? Aren't you?"

Niamh laughed. "It is nice, isn't it? Would you believe Seán flew to Italy for the granite? I told him there was plenty in Ireland, but oh no, Italian granite had to be the thing."

"You know, I could believe that of him all right," Ruth said.

34

Liam was lost in his thoughts. He was sitting, feet on his desk, tapping a pencil against his notepad. He was supposed to be doing the rota for the following two weeks, but he found himself staring out the window at the battering rain instead.

Poppy had skipped into school that morning and the morning before – filled with excitement about her trip to Derry, eager to tell her friends how Ruth and Detta had dressed up and they had the best *craic* ever. Liam was almost sick of listening to her going on about it, but the smile on her face each time she recalled the dazzling colour of a fireworks display or the way her Dorothy dress had swished when she twirled around made him bite his tongue.

Besides he had a warm fuzzy feeling about it all himself. Much as he had tried, and he *had* tried, he could not get Detta out of his mind. And part of him felt guilty because when he was thinking about Detta he was not thinking about Laura and just one week ago he would have given his left arm to have her back in his life.

Now though, well, now he wasn't so sure. If she walked into his office now, got down on her knees and begged him to take her back he would actually have to think about it, and that empowered him. (Although he quite liked the thought of her on her knees in front of him.)

Christ, he thought, taking his feet off the desk and running his hands through his dark hair, here he was thinking about empowerment. Detta with all her new-age mumbo-jumbo, not to mention her gorgeous curly hair, was really getting under his skin.

Thankfully the phone rang at that moment and he answered it in his usual cheery style.

"Liam Dougherty, good morning, and how can I help you?"

"Liam, hiya, it's Niamh. I was wondering if you could come round and do a few jobs for me."

Liam was surprised to hear her voice. The big house on the hill had been the talk of the village since it was built only two years ago. What could she need doing to it now?

"Sure, what do you have in mind?"

"I want the pool filled in. I'm always terrified one of the twins will take a dive in it and we never use it anyway. And then I was wondering if it would be possible to change the windows in my new studio. Do you think we could make them bigger? There's a lovely view from there and I would love to let more light in."

"Well, I'll certainly have a look," Liam said, opening his diary. "I can call up tomorrow and sure we can talk about it more tonight at the group. I'll get you all the figures by the end of the week and you can make your decision then."

"Money isn't a problem," Niamh said, "and I've heard you're good. So whatever you say is a fair price I'll pay, but I'd like it done as soon as possible."

"We'll do our best, Niamh. Look, I'll see you tonight and we'll get the ball rolling."

"I look forward to it."

She hung up and Liam admitted to himself that he was impressed with the determined tone in her voice. She seemed a lot stronger than the wallflower who had walked into the community centre a few weeks ago snivelling everywhere. It was nice to see – and of course the work would be great too. While they were kept busy enough at the yard, November didn't usually bring in a raft of new work and he was grateful for anything they could get.

Things might in fact be looking up for everyone.

* * *

Agnes arrived shortly after six so that Liam could get out to the group. Why she needed to arrive a full hour before he was due at the community centre was beyond him, but she always had been on the compulsive side about being punctual.

"Granny, Granny!" Poppy cheered. "Let me tell you all about Derry and the fireworks!"

Agnes raised an eyebrow. "Oh pet, did you go somewhere nice? I'd love to go somewhere nice. I can't remember the last time anyone took me out for a night."

The dig was not lost on Liam, but he simply rolled his eyes (out of her sight, of course) and went about getting ready while Poppy babbled on excitedly in the background.

Usually he'd throw a jumper on over his jeans and maybe brush his hair but tonight he felt like making a bit of an effort – not so much of an effort that it looked too obvious, but an effort all the same. He shaved, sprayed on some Calvin Klein aftershave, put on his best sweatshirt and looked in the mirror. He had to admit he was impressed with what he saw.

Poppy had changed into her Dorothy dress and was twirling around in front of her granny. As Liam walked back into the room they stopped to look at him.

"You smell nice, Daddy," Poppy said, running to give him a cuddle. "And your face isn't all spikey."

Agnes looked at him and looked for all intents and purposes as if she was about to open her mouth and let rip a litany of questions, but just as he was preparing to tell her that it was none of her business, she swallowed her words back down and said nothing. She did, however, seem to have the slightest hint of a smile on her face as she called Poppy over to show her the ruby slippers once more.

"Don't you worry about hurrying home," she said to Liam. "I'll put madam here to bed."

Liam nodded, kissed them both goodbye and left.

He had a smile on his face and a spring in his step when he arrived at the community centre. He had purposely left home in time to make it to the centre that little bit early to help Detta with the setting up, but when he reached it Ciara was already setting out the chairs.

"Liam, how are you?" she grinned as he walked in the door.

"Just grand," he smiled back. "Do you need a hand?"

"Naw, I think I can manage putting four chairs out," she laughed, "but Detta was sticking on a pot of tea in the kitchen. I'd burn water so I'm not the best person to help. Maybe you could?"

He blushed and then swore at himself under his breath for acting like a teenager. He was a grown man, for the love of God, and a grown married man at that.

"You okay?" Ciara asked.

"Fine, fine," he muttered walking into the kitchen.

Detta had her back to him. She was wearing a long cardigan over a long denim skirt and her hair was hanging loosely down her back. Laura would never have let her hair grow that long – anything beyond shoulder length was too messy for her. She liked things to be organised – although Liam had loved it when her hair grew that bit longer. He loved when the wind whipped it around her face as they walked along the beach and he loved pushing it back from her face so that he could kiss her.

Feeling a pang of foolishness for believing Laura was firmly in his past, he turned and walked back into the main hall.

"She has everything under control," he said and sat down, chiding himself for being so childish. Imagine taking notions on another woman!

Niamh was next to arrive and, to be honest, Liam was glad of the distraction.

"Liam, how are you? Do you think you'll be able to fit me in then?" she asked, sitting down beside him.

"Christ, you pair are fast movers," Ciara laughed, before blushing. "Not that I want to be insensitive or anything. God, sorry."

"Don't worry about it," Niamh said with a smile. "Liam here is going to do some building work for me. So Liam, tell me, can you fix it?"

"Yes, I can," he replied with a smile. "We can start work the week after next – as long as everything is in place. I'll be out at ten tomorrow to measure up, if you'll be about."

"I'm always about," Niamh said. "And I've no plans to go anywhere soon, unless you count my plans to drive up to Derry and have it out with Caitlin."

"Are you really going to do that?" Detta asked, walking into the room.

"I have to," Niamh replied, "But look, this meeting isn't about me. If we get time later we'll talk about it."

"But this is about all of us, and what we all want to do," Ciara said, pulling her chair up closer.

"Yes," Detta said. "If you want to talk it out, we'll talk about it."

"And miss out on writing a list or something? Look, I know everyone means well but this is something I have to do and I don't really want people trying to talk me out of it."

Liam looked at her face. She had a determined look about her and he knew better than to argue with a woman with that particular facial expression. No good could come of it. It was like the time he asked Laura if he could go away on a lads' week with the boys from work, or the time she set her heart on a new car even though her own was perfectly fine and money was a bit tight.

"Well, then, we'll just get started," he said.

"But Ruth isn't here?" Ciara piped up.

"No, no, she's not. This isn't like her," Detta said.

"And I'd brought her a box of chocolates from the shop to thank her for Friday night," Ciara said. "They aren't anything fancy, just some Celebrations, but I know she is a fan of the Malteser ones."

"Isn't everyone a fan of the Malteser ones?" Detta laughed.

Christ, thought Liam, now they're talking about chocolate. He wondered how easy it would be to turn the subject matter back to things more important – like Niamh's building work, or football or anything that wasn't contributing to his transformation into a bloody woman. It was all well and good feeling empowered but he didn't want to start craving chocolate and a nice glass of wine more than a good rare steak and a pint of beer.

"Right, well, maybe we should give her a wee ring and see what's happening?" he said.

"You know, I'm worried about her," Niamh offered. "She called out to see me on Sunday night and while she said she was just passing, it's very rare that anyone is just passing my house. It's not exactly on the Main Street on the road to anywhere It's just a house in the middle of nowhere."

257

"But did she seem okay when she was there?" Liam asked. He knew that Sunday was the day the children were due to have returned from their time away with James and Laura. He couldn't help but wonder if there was some news he should know about.

"A little bit jumpy," Niamh replied. "When I asked her she said she was fine, but you know the way you just know sometimes? I'm the bloody queen at hiding things so I can read the signs."

Liam started to feel very nervous. Whatever it was that Ruth was hiding, he knew it was unlikely to be good news. It was highly doubtful she had won the Lotto or secured a blind date with George Clooney. Those kind of secrets didn't keep you from your friends but bad secrets, secrets about ex-husbands and their new partners, were exactly the kind of things that made you stay away from your support group and walk miles at night on your own.

"Are you okay, Liam?" Detta asked, her eyes full of concern.

He shook his head. "I'm fine," he lied. All he really wanted to do was lift his coat and head right over Ruth's and have it out with her. He felt an anger build up inside him – why was he always the last to know about everything? No doubt James and Laura were talking marriage or something like that and of course Laura wouldn't have thought it appropriate to tell him. He was not of importance. He probably never had been to her. How could he even equate this selfish woman with the same one who had cried on the night he proposed? Although, come to think of it, the tears were probably because the diamond wasn't big enough or the band wide enough.

"I've just remembered something," he said, standing up. "I have to go."

He knew he was looking like a bit of a melodramatic gobshite for walking out but he didn't really care.

"Liam," Detta called as he walked out the door and while he should have turned back, he wasn't in the form.

He was now confused and he didn't want to look back and see her face and feel even more confused.

* * *

When Laura had first left he had spent many nights drinking a few beers and plotting a way to get her back. He was going to get rid of dead things. He would join the gym and nip out in his lunch breaks. And he would eat porridge, every morning. He would even go for those bloody facial things so that his skin lost that weathered look if necessary. And then he was going to get himself new clothes, get a hair cut and march up to her workplace, like Richard Gere in *An Officer and a Gentleman* and whisk her off her feet and give her no choice whatsoever about coming back to him. If necessary he would even learn to dance, or take singing lessons and sing "That Loving Feeling" to her in the bloody pub in front of all his workmates.

He was determined he would do whatever it took to get her back, to make her his wife again and Poppy's mammy again.

Now, as he walked up to her front door, he thought of how far he had come since then but there was no doubt in his mind he still had a long way to go. While she still made him angry and provoked a reaction from him he realised he hadn't moved on as much he had wanted, or hoped.

He rapped on the door, with more force than he intended.

Laura answered. She was wearing her pyjamas and her hair was swept back from her face. She carried a glass of wine in her hand and he could see she had been laughing.

"Liam! What are you doing here?"

"Is there something you want to tell me?" he asked.

"What do you mean?" Laura asked and he blushed as she looked genuinely confused.

"Is there something you should have told me but haven't had the good grace to?"

"Liam, I think you should go home," she said sadly.

"Laura, I have a right to know what is going on with you. You might not like it, but you are still my wife."

James walked into the hall and looked at Liam with a mixture of pity and, if Liam was right, amusement.

"Are you okay, big lad?" he asked.

"I just wanted to know what is going on."

"Nothing is going on." Laura answered. "Now if you don't mind –"

"Well, I do mind actually. I have it on good authority something is going on," he lied. He knew he hadn't actually spoken to Ruth yet but, it was obvious, wasn't it? What else would make her embarrassed to come to the group and to see him?

"Well, your good authority is talking through their arse," James said.

"Liam, go home," said Laura. "There's nothing to tell you and, even if there were, I'm not really sure it is any of your business."

"How can you say it's none of my business?"

"This is ridiculous," she replied. "We're arguing over nothing."

"Well then, tell me, if this is nothing," Liam said, his temper flaring, "why is Ruth acting oddly? Don't tell me it has nothing to do with you two because I won't believe it."

"Believe what you want," Laura said.

"Just go," James added and slammed the door in his face.

* * *

When he got home, Agnes was making a cup of tea and singing to herself. She had more of a spring in her step than in recent weeks but he was in no humour for her.

"Ah, son. How are you? How was the group?"

He grunted that it had been just fine.

"Can I make you a cup?"

"I'm going to have a beer, Mum," he said.

"But it's a work night!" She looked horrified.

"And I'm a grown man," he snapped.

She looked instantly wounded and he apologised before sitting down and drinking the token cup of tea with her before she went home.

As he climbed the stairs to bed, the only thought that crossed his mind was that he was sick to the very back teeth of women and all their ways.

35

"Well, love, how did it go?" Lorraine asked as Ciara walked through the door.

"It was a strange one, Mum. Ruth didn't arrive at all and then Liam left early."

"You don't think those two are, you know, together?" Lorraine asked with a sly smile.

"God no. Not at all."

"Shame, they would make a nice couple. Look, pet, I'm off out now but I shouldn't be too late. Madam went down with no fuss you'll be delighted to hear. I've put the washing machine on for you – could you stuff the towels in the tumble drier before you go to bed?"

"Yes, Mum," Ciara said, flopping down on the sofa.

"Okay, love, take care."

Lorraine left and Ciara stared at the flickering TV screen for a few minutes before going up to her room to leaf through the college prospectus Abby had given her earlier.

It was a good thick book, with a hundred and one different courses and she wasn't sure where to start. She supposed the night classes would be as good as any, but before that she decided to read the section on "Student Life".

The slightly dated pictures showed posed shots of students enjoying a few drinks and a game of pool in the Students' Union. There was another of a group of people laughing in the library as they pored over books. She had an urge to tell them to shush, but she couldn't deny the flutter of excitement as she read on about all the facilities on offer.

The crèche looked great – newer than the one Ella went to now anyway – and while she wouldn't need to use it while she was at her night classes it was good to know that if she did go on to do the journalism course after she would have childcare sorted. Or at least she would if she could afford to pay for it.

"You're being an eejit," she muttered to herself as she traipsed back downstairs. It was intimidating to consider balancing a full-time course with minding Ella and making a bit of money on the side.

Cross that bridge when you get to it, she told herself. For now she wasn't sure she would be able to get through a few classes a couple of nights a week never mind whatever might come next.

But having a new focus – her secret escape plan from Rathinch – had given her a whole new perspective on life. She had gone to work that morning, on time and in full uniform. She had sung along heartily to the cheesy country tunes on the radio and Mrs Quinn had looked most unsettled. She had enjoyed making the old doll feel slightly freaked out. Whenever she had barked her orders at Ciara, she had just smiled and got on with her job even when that meant cleaning out the dairy cabinet of congealed yoghurt and moulding cheese.

"You've a spring in your step today," Mrs Quinn had said,

her voice laden with suspicion. Most people would have been delighted to see a young person enthusiastic in their work, but Mrs Quinn wasn't happy at all. Her statement was more of an accusation than an observation.

"Aren't I allowed to be happy?" Ciara smiled.

"Of course you are. It's just not often we see it."

Ciara had wanted to bark back that Mrs Quinn, who had a permanent look of one chewing a wasp, was one to talk but she just smiled instead. It was strange how a change of focus in her life made the most mundane of tasks that little bit more enjoyable.

Shortly after three the crowds of school kids began to pour into the shop, eager for a bar of chocolate or a can of Coke to enjoy as they walked home. Usually this caused one of two reactions in Ciara. She would either think they looked pathetically childish as they counted their cents out for whatever they were buying, or she would be swallowed by a sense of jealousy that they were young and free while she was babied up and smelling vaguely of Calpol and dirty nappies. (No matter how often she showered she was sure there was always a vague smell of runny nappy about her.)

At the beginning she wouldn't really talk to any of her old school friends when they came into the shop. And then she went through a really quite aggressive phase – of which she wasn't proud – where she would just grunt at them and practically throw their Star Bars across the counter.

That particular behaviour didn't make her too popular with her boss, which was ironic really given that Mrs Quinn could have won the Olympic Gold Medal for Star-Bar-throwing herself.

That day, however, when the students arrived in, full of chatter and gossip Ciara smiled. Either she was growing up or going mad, but she was fully looking forward to student life again.

* * *

The following morning she was woken by Ella having a good cry in her cot. Hauling herself from her bed – where she had been enjoying a lovely dream about Justin Timberlake – she poked her head over the side of the cot.

"Hey, baby girl, shush now," she said, lifting her daughter in her arms. She noticed immediately that she was flushed and her cheeks were burning. "Oh baby, what's wrong? Are your teeth annoying you, wee woman?" she soothed as she jiggled her up and down. But the jiggling only caused Ella to scream all the louder.

Lorraine looked distinctly unimpressed as she poked her head around the door. "Are you pinching her or something?" she asked as she wrapped her dressing gown around her.

"I think she's sick, Mum," Ciara said, feeling panicked by her daughter's temperature.

"I'm sure she's fine. She was grand last night but, here, let me have a wee look. There's nothing up with her that her granny can't make better."

Ella handed her daughter over to Lorraine and almost instantly her daughter quietened – but she didn't start cooing or chattering as she usually did. She just snuggled her head into her granny's shoulder and whimpered.

"She's burning up, love," Lorraine said. "Get some Calpol and I'll strip her off."

Ciara ran down the stairs, pulling cupboard after cupboard open looking for the pink sticky medicine that made everything better. As she clattered around looking for the medicine syringe, Lorraine called that she would need to bring a basin as well just as Ella started to squeal all the louder.

Taking two stairs at a time, Ciara walked into her room just in time for her daughter to projectile vomit everywhere.

"Jesus and the wee donkey," she swore, before rushing to comfort her child.

"Don't worry," Lorraine said calmly. "You did worse when you were little."

"But, Mum," Ciara said, feeling tears prick at her eyes as Ella looked at her mournfully.

"Now, it will be fine, sweetheart. Let's see if we can get some Calpol into her – but she might not keep it down. Then I'll phone Mrs Quinn and tell her you won't be in today, and ring my work too and then we'll get her to the doctor's. Stay calm, pet, it will do her no good to see you in a state."

Ciara nodded and reached out for her daughter, who was still burning hot. Stripping her down to her nappy, she rocked her in her arms as her mother gave her Calpol and sang "Horsey Horsey" gently to her.

She was transported back to when she was little and sick and Lorraine sat with her all night, mopping her brow and kissing away her tears, singing gently. She must have been terrified at times – alone with a young sick child. Ciara had no doubt she would have had a complete fit if her mother hadn't been with her that morning, and she realised, once again, just how much she undervalued and underestimated Lorraine.

"Mum," she said, as Ella settled into her arms.

"Yes?"

"Thank you."

* * *

If Mrs Quinn had been her usual apoplectic with rage at hearing Ciara wouldn't be in, Lorraine had the good grace to keep that information to herself. She had simply come up and taken over the care of Ella while Ciara got herself dressed and set about clearing up some of the puke. By God that stuff could get everywhere. It was quite impressive when you thought about it. There was even a smattering on the ceiling.

When the cleaning was done, Lorraine said she had been able to get them an appointment at the doctor's and that she had called them a taxi to take them down. "I don't want her getting a wee chill if we walk down," she had said, her face filled with concern.

Dressing her granddaughter in clean pyjamas and wrapping her in a blanket, she carried her out to the waiting car and got in.

Although Ella had calmed down since the major vomit incident, Ciara couldn't help but worry that something was seriously wrong – like meningitis or the like. She had seen a brochure about it in the doctor's the last time she was in but she hadn't really paid attention. She was raging at herself now for not reading it more closely.

"She'll be fine," Lorraine said, rubbing her daughter's hand. "Babies just like to give you a big scare every now and then. They can be right wee feckers."

Ordinarily Ciara would have bristled at any description of her daughter as a wee fecker, even though at times she definitely suited that description – but Lorraine said it with such affection that she didn't mind this time. Not one bit. And she hoped against hope that Ella really was just being a wee fecker and had not contracted some killer illness.

God, there were times when she wondered if there was ever a time when being a parent became easy? There always seemed to be something to worry about. First of all it was that Ella wouldn't feed well, and then she got colic and then she had awful bother teething and would scream herself silly. Then, when she started crawling there was the mission to baby-proof the house, not realising that to make a house truly safe from the evil clutches of a mobile baby you really just have to wrap everything (baby included) in cotton wool.

They arrived at the doctor's and she had to restrain herself from running in like an extra from *ER* shouting for medical attention, 'stat'.

By now of course, her daughter, although still pale and mildly lethargic, was smiling and even cooing gently.

"Ah, Ciara. You're here with the patient," Ruth said kindly, stepping out from behind her desk and smiling at her. "How is the wee pet?"

"Well, she looks better now, but God, I was so scared," Ciara said, starting to cry.

"Come on, I'll take you through to Dr Donnelly. You know, we've all been there. They like to scare you, you know."

"That's what I told her," Lorraine piped up apologetically from the background.

Ciara looked at her and saw that her mother's confidence seemed to have deserted her.

"Of course you did," Ruth said, with a smile, and led all three through to the doctor's surgery.

* * *

"Well, what's the verdict?" Ruth asked as they walked back out.

"She's fine, a virus. We're to dose her on Calpol, or give suppositories if she won't keep that down and see how she goes."

"That's a relief," Ruth said.

"Too right it is," Ciara said.

"Right, well, can I call you a taxi or run you back up the road? We're quiet this morning and Dr Donnelly won't mind if I nip out for five minutes."

"That would be lovely," Ciara smiled.

"I'm sure a taxi will be fine," Lorraine said.

"It's no trouble."

"Come on, Mum. We'll just go now and get Ella home rather than hanging around here waiting for a taxi."

Lorraine nodded, "Well, if you're sure?" she said to Ruth.

"Of course I am."

On the drive back to the house Ciara wondered why her mother, who was such a strong and vocal character so much of the time, became this quiet shadow of herself with other people? As they drove Lorraine sat in the front, her hands on her knees and her gaze fixed strictly ahead. Ruth's attempts at small talk were met with nods, smiles and the occasional verbal (one-word) response.

Ciara almost felt tempted to tell her to "talk to the nice lady properly" but she bit her tongue. Still, the silence was getting increasingly awkward.

"So, Ruth, how come you didn't come to the group last night?" Ciara asked.

"Erm, well, I was busy," Ruth answered awkwardly, adopting the same gaze-firmly-forward pose Lorraine had.

They looked like a pair of petulant children and Ciara wanted to bang their heads together. They were supposed to be the adults – the ones she looked up to and who took responsibility for their lives and were confident. Christ, she had even read in one of her mother's magazines that your thirties were supposed to be the best decade of your life, that you no longer have spots on your face or care about the size of your boobs – fair enough, you might care about which direction they point, but the size, well, you accept that. In your thirties, according to the magazines, you accept yourself for who you are and you aren't afraid to speak your mind. You don't purposely set out to hurt people but you don't hold back if someone really gets on your goat either. And here she was looking at these two grown women doing everything to avoid having any level of conversation with anyone apart from on the latest offers in the supermarket or the state of the weather.

She would have questioned them about it if she wasn't worried they would both turn on her and if she wasn't so swamped with emotion after everything that morning.

But she vowed that she would get the pair of them together – sooner rather than later – and get them chatting.

If she could find a new her then they sure as hell were going to come out of their shells too.

36

"These are my ass-kicking boots," Niamh said as she stretched her legs out in front of her in the shoe shop and admired the knee-length, real leather, three-inch-heeled boots she had just tried on.

"They are things of beauty," Robyn said. "But do I have to worry that my ass is in for a kicking?"

"You know full well whose ass I'm going to kick."

An elderly lady, trying on a pair of beige sandals beside Niamh, looked at her oddly before shuffling along the bench nervously.

Niamh bit back a smile. "Of course, the ass-kicking is purely metaphorical. I don't really believe in violence," she said loudly, before turning to Robyn and adding with a wink, "in most cases, anyway."

"Are you sure this is a good idea?" Robyn asked.

"Well, no, they're not practical when it comes to trying not to slide on my ass on our berluddy marble floors, but fashion knows no pain."

"You know that's not what I meant," Robyn said.

"And you know that this is something I have to do. And

when I do it, I want to look as good as possible. And I want to stand taller than her – if that means crippling myself in admittedly gorgeous, high-heeled boots then so be it."

"I'm not going to be able to talk you out of it, am I?"

"No, and to be honest, I don't see why you want to."

Niamh took off the boots and slipped her feet into her more comfortable (and marble-floor-friendly) Uggs and went to the paydesk.

She couldn't understand why everyone seemed so against her having it out with Caitlin. Sure, it wouldn't change anything. It wouldn't undo the past, or bring Seán back but it would make her feel more in control.

And of course she didn't really want to kick Caitlin's ass – not really anyway. But she did want answers and she sure as hell couldn't get them from Seán and she had tried. She had sat the previous night in the newly gutted office, where she was boxing up the last of his law books and bulk supply of Post-its, and asked him loudly to let her know why.

"Give me a sign. Something. Tell me why you did this?" she had said but got no reply.

Until she knew why – and when, and where and how often – she couldn't let it go.

"C'mon," she said to Robyn, "let's go and get some coffee and then we'll go and get some ass-kicking new jeans and some blingy jewellery too."

"Okay," Robyn said reluctantly.

Niamh took a deep breath. "Look, Robyn, I don't expect you to understand why I need to do all this, but I'm asking you to support me. If you are my friend you will help me through this because that's what friends do – unless of course they are sleeping with your husband, but I'm thinking you never did that. I might be prancing around buying perhaps the most fabulous boots in the world ever, and I might be filling in the swimming pool and redecorating his office and I might seem as if I'm completely in control but this," she said, gesturing to her shopping bags, "is the only thing keeping me any way sane."

"Fair enough," Robyn said, looping her arm in Niamh's. "I'm only concerned because I care."

"I know, but I'm a big girl and it might not seem like it but I do know what I'm doing. Now, how about we forget the coffees and go for a Cosmopolitan instead, with double the vodka?"

* * *

"I could talk to her for you," Robyn said, sipping on her drink.

"I know you could, but do you think she would tell you? She hasn't told you anything so far. Seems she likes her secrets, that one."

"I still can barely believe it."

Niamh took a deep breath. Could she believe it herself? Well now, if she was honest, she kind of did. She had spent the last two weeks searching her memory for clues. Of course there had been Caitlin's "performance" at the wake and funeral and the dinner dance where Seán had held her close while Niamh looked on. She had also remembered their squash phase. When she was pregnant and struggling to get off the sofa never mind exert herself, the pair of them would meet up for a quick game. She thought nothing of it at the time – sure Seán came back sweaty and tired, but she thought that was down to a whole different sort of ball game to the one he was actually playing. And, of course, there was that time at the twins' christening when the pair of them had cleared off to buy some champagne and had taken just that little bit too long about it.

So, now that she thought about it, even though Seán had never seemed to waver in his affection for her, she could believe he had been unfaithful. After all, what Seán wanted, Seán got – and the cost was never important.

* * *

"Can we get a play park instead of the silly pool?" Connor asked wide-eyed that night over dinner.

"Well, I'm sure we can get some slides, and I'll ask Mr Dougherty to build a play house. Does that sound good?"

"That sounds brilliant, Mammy. I don't like the pool. S'too cold and wet," he replied solemnly.

"Can we have pink curtains in the house?" Rachel asked.

"'Course you can," Niamh said, spearing her fork into a crunchy potato waffle and dipping it in tomato sauce. Of course once again Seán would have duck disease to see his family eating processed food but for all their years together Niamh had missed the basics of potato waffles and fishfingers. While other mums had complained about the solid diet of Captain Birdseye's finest fingers, Niamh had blushed. If it wasn't organic, it wasn't allowed past their front door. Seán was more than a little anal about it. He had been almost apoplectic with rage one night when she told him how her parents had taken the twins for a Happy Meal as a treat.

"And can we have tea parties in there?" her daughter asked. "With Poppy and baby Ella?"

"Yes, darling."

"And I can play Power Rangers there too and make it my magic fort?"

"'Course you can!"

"Yay!" the twins chirped in unison, spooning (tinned) peas into their mouths with gusto.

Once the twins were gone to bed and Niamh took up her

seat in the den – on the pristine leather sofas Seán had imported from Italy – she pulled her feet up to her and stared into the fire.

For the first time in a long time, she didn't feel heartbreakingly lonely but she did wonder why it was that her family and Robyn seemed much more comfortable with her when she was bursting into tears every three seconds and walking about doing her best Mother of Sorrows impression?

When she had told Robyn earlier that she was just about holding it together, she had exaggerated. Of course the pain of losing Seán hadn't gone away. Just that night she had to fight back tears when Connor asked was Daddy "really, really never coming back?". But that sadness now was because her children were suffering. She couldn't allow herself to miss Seán any more when he wasn't the person she had thought he was.

She sipped from her mug of hot chocolate and thought about how it had just been easier to pretend she was still lost in a fug of grief than to tell her family that she actually felt okay in herself. No, she wasn't ready to start singing "I Will Survive" at the top of her lungs but she, and her new boots, were doing just fine and dandy.

And for all her posturing she hadn't decided exactly when or where she would talk to Caitlin. She wanted her roots done first, that was for sure. She didn't want to look like a snivelling wreck when she showed up at her friend's door.

Liam would be round the following morning to start work on the pool. She would speak to him then about getting some of that soft padding they used in parks laid down so the children could play happily without fear of serious injury. Maybe when that was done she could invite Poppy and Ella round, and young Matthew come to think of it. Connor could do with a decent male influence.

That made her think of Ruth and chide herself that, despite her best intentions, she still hadn't phoned her to make sure she was okay. After all it was Ruth who had beaten a path to her doorway when she had given the group a miss so Niamh knew she should have returned the favour.

If she'd had her number she would have given her a call but she didn't, so she promised that tomorrow she would make that effort and then maybe she would talk to Ruth, who seemed to understand her more than most, and maybe even talk her into coming along for the big showdown.

The A-Team could live to fight another day. Maybe they could even talk Liam or Detta into driving the big bus up to Derry for the *craic*.

Niamh smiled to herself, curled up on the sofa, closed her eyes and began to dream about boots and swimming pools and potato waffles.

37

The silence in the car on the journey back to Ciara's house had been odd. Ruth always thought of herself as a fairly sociable person but perhaps sometimes she really had to admit she was just an old fart in pleasant woman's clothing.

It was a bit mad really. She knew Lorraine from out and about in the village. But let's face it, she knew everyone in the village. In a town the size of Rathinch everyone knew everyone, their business, what they were having for their tea and the size of the clothes flapping on the washing line. So she was annoyed at herself for not being more sociable. Jesus, usually she could talk the back legs off a donkey but that morning she had sat like some grinning eejit driving the car. Demented Dora, that should be her new name she thought. Perhaps if she felt more confident in how she looked that would translate into how she was around other people. They were always saying that on those makeover programmes on Channel 4.

She was determined she was going to make more of an effort. She had been doing so well with her long walks along the beach. She was sure she would feel her waistbands loosening – and that made her happy. A month ago she had been disgusted with herself while she stood staring at a pair of jeans with an elasticated waist, thinking they might just be the comfiest-looking creations she had ever seen. Shuddering at the thought, she smiled to herself.

She would get back on track. She would sort things out with Eimear and she would invite Lorraine around for coffee. It was about time she became a social butterfly. She might even make it back to the group the next week – after all, she had nothing to hide. Feeling a little brighter she got up and started to clear away the dinner dishes. She was just wondering if Fairy really did give you softer hands when the front door opened. As all the children were sitting glued to *The Simpsons* she knew it had to be James. No doubt Matthew had left something in his car or Eimear had called begging some money and he was calling over to oblige. She would have shouted at him about him not actually living there any more, but what would be the point? She didn't have the strength to argue with him any more – he was out of her life and that was all that mattered.

Turning to face him she was shocked to see his face was contorted with anger.

"James, what's wrong?" she said, folding the tea towel in front of her.

"Why don't *you* tell *me*?" he said, walking close to her – standing perilously close. She remembered the line from *Dirty Dancing* about dance space. He was definitely in hers. But he didn't seem quite in the mood for her to quote it to him.

She took a deep breath.

"I don't know, James," she said, her heart starting to thump.

He raised his hand, slowly, almost gently, to the side of her face and stood so that his nose was almost touching hers. He moved his hand around, again slowly and gently, to the back of her head and then pulled her towards him, his hands wrapped in her hair, pulling it tight.

"The children," she said, knowing in her heart what was coming. This was a well-rehearsed dance in the Byrne household.

"What have you told him?" he sneered, his breath rank on her face.

Every way she turned her head sent a shock of pain through her neck as her hair pulled tighter.

"Who? I don't know what you mean," she said, almost pleading.

"Don't lie to me, Ruth. Why are you such a liar?"

"I'm not," she said, starting to cry, her eyes darting to the doorway hoping the children wouldn't hear what was going on.

"Yes, yes, you are," he said calmly before releasing his grasp and turning from her. She sagged with relief.

"Liam has been round," he said. "He wants to know what is going on. Have you told him? If you have then I'm damn sure you only told him your side of this sorry story."

"I've not told him anything," Ruth said, feeling like she was caught in some sick version of *Groundhog Day*. "I've not seen him. I've not even been to our group."

"Liar!" he shouted, turning towards her, his hand raised this time with no hint of gentleness, no quiet introduction to what was to come.

She saw it move towards her. She tried to move out of the way, but he always knew where she would go. James always could second-guess her every move. She bit down hard on her lip as his heavy hand connected with the side of her face, sending her hurtling towards the ground.

"You have to ruin everything!" he shouted.

"James, the children!" she sobbed.

"You can't let anyone be happy. You can't bear to let anything good happen. You are a useless, evil bitch of a woman and I regret the day I ever set eyes on you, let alone set my hands on you," he shouted, his eyes darkened with rage. "And I'll not forgive you for this, Ruth. And I'll sure as hell never let you forget it."

He advanced once more and drew his leg back to kick her. She braced herself for it. She knew what it would feel like. She had felt it so many times before. There was no mystery to this. Closing her eyes she waited for the impact, her heart thumping in her ears, tears falling.

"NO!" the shout rang out. "No. Leave her alone. Leave her alone now or I'll call the Guards!"

James stopped, frozen to the spot and Ruth opened her eyes. Thomas was standing there, his puny fourteen-year-old frame standing tall to his father. Eimear stood behind, her face frozen in fear, while Ruth became aware that she could hear Matthew sobbing.

James turned, slowly, towards his children as Ruth made to right herself. She was suddenly aware her clothes were dishevelled, her hair over the side of her face.

"Kids," he said, his voice weakening, "this is between me and your mum – go back to your TV."

"No," Thomas said resolutely as Eimear started to cry. "Get out, Dad! Get out now!" he shouted, his voice breaking.

"Look here, Thomas, you don't talk to me like that!" James roared.

"No, you're wrong. This *is* how I talk to you and I'm telling you to get out."

Ruth watched, her heart still thumping as her husband walked towards her son, his hand clenching again. She stood up. She may not ever have been able to do it for herself but by Christ she could do it for her children.

"No, James! You don't!" she said, throwing herself at him and pummelling his chest with her first. Years of built-up rage and hurt poured out of her. "You don't hurt our children. You don't do that. You get the hell out of my house and you don't come back!"

With Thomas and Eimear behind her, she was ashamed to say, she felt stronger and as she and her strong, brave son pushed him out the door, slamming and locking it behind him, she felt something in her change.

Yes, she was bruised and battered and she had a family of children – stunned into silence – to deal with but her eyes were open at last. (Which given the fact that one was swelling was quite an achievement.) It hadn't been her fault. She hadn't asked for it. What a fecking daft notion. Who asks for it? Who wants someone to thump them, hit them and kick them? She wasn't useless. Here she was, having protected her children up until tonight from any sign of what she had been going through. And she had kept a roof over their heads and yes, Eimear was like the anti-Christ on speed at times, but she was a good girl at heart and that was down to Ruth. It wasn't anything to do with the useless big fecker of a man who had just been pushed out the door.

"I'm sorry," she said, her voice shaking, and she pulled her children into her arms. "I'm so sorry, babies, but that isn't going to happen again. It's never going to happen again. I promise."

They stood there, in the hall, for a long time, hugging each other and reassuring each other until Ruth moved, stiff and sore, and got some ice for her face.

"It looks bad, Mum," Eimear said gently, taking a clean tea towel from the drawer and wrapping some ice in it.

"I'll be okay."

"I'm so sorry, Mum," Eimear said, breaking down.

"You've nothing to be sorry for."

"But, Mum, he's my daddy and I love him. But I hate him and you've been dealing with this and I've been a cow."

"Now, pet, enough please," Ruth said, grimacing as the ice soothed her face. "We've all made mistakes but we won't make them any more. Things are going to be different. Can you get me the phone?"

38

Liam was just sitting down to read the latest *Hannah Montana* book to Poppy when the phone rang.

"I'll get it, I'll get it," Poppy shouted and ran for the kitchen.

He wondered if she would be gone long enough to either forget all about the *Hannah Montana* book, or at least to give him the time to shred it and dispose of the evidence. He had lived through *Angelina Ballerina*. He had survived the *High School Musical* years relatively unscathed, but *Hannah Montana* with her grinning face and cheery outlook was almost enough to drive him to distraction.

"Daddy, it's for you," Poppy called as she ran back to him.

"Thanks, pet, let me take this and then we'll read the book."

Poppy pulled a face which let him know that she wasn't one bit impressed at being second-best to a phone call.

Laim strode into the kitchen and picked up the phone. "Hello?"

"Liam, thank God you're in. I need your help."

It took a few seconds for him to place the voice and when

he did he had to try and hide the smile in his voice. It was unlikely when Detta said she needed his help that she actually meant "Hey there, big guy. Why don't you come over and let me help you forget all about that Laura one?", but still he liked it that she needed him.

"What can I do for you?" he asked.

"Well, it's for Ruth really. But, Liam, I need you to stay calm over this and I need you to come now to her house. Could you leave Poppy with your mum and bring your tool kit?"

His mind began to whirr. Why did Ruth need him? Why did he need to stay calm and why on earth did he have to bring his toolkit with him?

"Liam?" Detta repeated, her voice softening. "Sorry to be so cryptic, but we really could do with your help."

"Okay," he replied. "I'll be over as soon as I've left Poppy off."

Of course Poppy wasn't one bit happy to be left off at her granny's. He had to bribe her with the promise of a new *Hannah* fecking *Montana* DVD to get her to agree to it.

Agnes looked at him oddly when he arrived on her doorstep.

"Detta wants to see him," Poppy said with a roll of her eyes and a small smile crept over Agnes's face.

"Oh, does she now?"

"It's not what you think, mother," Liam replied with a roll of his eyes.

"And how would you know what I'm thinking?" Agnes said with a sniff before ushering Poppy inside.

When he arrived at Ruth's house, every light was lit. Detta's car was outside, as was Niamh's people carrier. Whatever was going on, it had to be some big shakes. Christ, he realised, there was even a Garda car parked two doors up.

He lifted his toolbag from the seat beside him and walked up the pathway. The door was already open and he saw Eimear sitting on the stairs, the colour of a ghost, being comforted by Ciara.

"They're in the front room," Ciara said, nodding towards the door, and he walked in – not quite sure what would greet him. Christ, he hoped Ruth hadn't taken it on herself to beat seven shades of the proverbial out of James and Laura. Although he couldn't see Ruth as the violent type.

"Liam, you're here. Thank goodness," Detta said, standing up and ushering him back out of the room and into the kitchen.

"What's going on?" he asked.

"Look, Liam, sit down."

"I won't sit down. I'll have you tell me now what's happening." He tried to keep his voice as measured as possible but he was worried now. You don't tell someone to sit down unless you have bad news for them.

"Right, first of all then, Laura is fine. This isn't about Laura. Not really. I think you need to hear that."

He breathed out. "So what is it about?"

"Liam, really, come on, sit down with me, please."

She reached out and took his hand and the softness of her touch had a calming effect on him. He sat down and looked into her eyes. They were the softest of blues and he knew instantly he could trust her.

"Ruth's been keeping a secret from us. It's James. He's good with his hands. He likes to lash out. Now we don't think he has hit out at Laura, but you need to know – especially if Poppy is about to spend any time with him."

"Has he hit his own children?" Liam asked incredulously, thinking if that fecker dared lay a hand on his precious daughter he would do time for him. No question about it. In fact there was no way he was ever going to take the chance that James fecking Byrne could ever get close enough to hurt his daughter. No way.

Detta shook her head sadly. "No, seems he saved it all for Ruth. He came back tonight and he hit her again. Only for wee Thomas standing up to him she'd be worse off."

"How bad is she?"

"She's sore-looking all right. I wanted to warn you before you saw her."

"Christ," Liam said, putting his head in his hands. He remembered with sickening clarity how the night before he had marched up to James and Laura's house like a bull with a sore head and now he wondered if he was responsible?

"Detta, oh God. This is my fault. I saw James last night. I thought this secret Ruth has been keeping was that they were getting married or something. Jesus . . ."

"Now, Liam," Detta said, reaching out to his hands once more, "look at me." She touched his cheek softly. "This is nothing to do with you. By all accounts it has been going on for years. It's just the sort of man he is. Now we need you to help. We need you to change the locks for Ruth, and add a few deadbolts – that kind of thing. The guards are here taking a statement and we'll take it from there, but we want to make sure he doesn't get back into this house."

"Anything. I'll do anything."

"Great. I knew we could count on you. And as for Laura, well, she'll know about this soon enough so you better prepare yourself for some flack."

He nodded. "God, she left me for him? I must be some right catch."

"You are, you know. You're a great catch altogether."

If he hadn't been standing in Ruth Byrne's kitchen, knowing that the man his wife had left him for had just battered the life out of the poor woman, he would have found the moment very romantic.

And there it was, dawning on him, finally that his main concern now was Detta and Ruth and his new friends and while, yes, he was concerned about Laura and he would have to talk to her she was no longer the centre of his universe.

"Right, well, I'll have to go to the yard to pick up some new locks, but I'll get straight onto it."

Detta nodded, and gave him a soft smile.

"Can I see Ruth now?"

"Come on," Detta said, taking his hand. "I'm sure the guards are nearly done."

He walked through and he had to admit he felt a little like an intruder. There was Ciara on the stairs with Eimear. He could hear Niamh's Derry accent as a female guard left the room. He'd never laid his hand on anyone in his entire life, but he felt somehow like the enemy. It was as if James's actions had tainted all men. He felt sick to his stomach as he looked at Ruth and her blackened eye. There was a small cut to her cheek and her face was pale in stark contrast to the vivid colours of the bruising. She looked old – a lot older than her thirty-seven years – and he wanted to turn in that instant and go and hit James, or kick him in the balls. And not because he had stolen Laura, or that he was a feckwit, but because he had taken the shine out of this most wonderful of women who had become such a friend to him over the last few weeks.

"I'm so sorry," Ruth sobbed as he sat down beside her.

"What on earth do you have to be sorry for?"

"I should have told you. I'm sorry, Liam. It wasn't fair of me – not with Laura there. But he's not hit her. I'm sure of it. But still, I should have told you. Poppy could have seen something." With that she started to sob.

"The kids saw it all," Detta said. "Thomas is in his room and Matthew cried himself to sleep."

Liam shook his head. "Ruth, you are not to apologise to me ever again. I understand. And sure, I know now. We all know now so don't even let it worry you at all – not even for five minutes."

She nodded and he wanted to hug her, but he was afraid he would hurt her, so he rubbed her hand gently instead and pretended not to notice her flinch slightly.

As soon as he could, he excused himself. He had locks to change, bolts to retrieve, work to be done, so he got into his van and drove to the yard. It was only when he got there he realised he was shaking. It might have been shock, or it might have been anger or a combination of the two but he took several deep breaths and tried to shake off the feeling. He prided himself on keeping his cool in almost every situation – should a house literally (as had happened at least once) fall down around him he would usually just brush himself off, take a deep breath and get on with things.

He couldn't imagine ever lifting his hand to a woman. And he had been tried all these years, between Agnes and Laura and their increasingly demanding ways. They had made him angry – of course they had – but he would generally stomp off and swear a bit before calming down. If it was a real doozy of a fight he would maybe decide to have a two-day huff – which would drive Laura to absolute distraction. But most of the time Liam was a two-minute-rage kind of a guy and he could never imagine willingly inflicting pain on someone he was supposed to love just to exert control.

He set to work collecting locks and bolts, rattling about in the yard giving things a good kick to vent his frustration.

"Damn it," he swore, realising the steel toolbox had won the fight between it and his toe and sat down and put his head in his hands. His gut instinct told him to go round to Laura now and warn her – but not because he wanted her back, he realised once again, but because no matter what she had done to him she did not deserve to live with such a bastard of a man.

He would go and see her in the morning, at work, when James wouldn't be about. Maybe Ruth was right that he hadn't hit Laura yet, but he was pretty sure he wouldn't get a straight answer from her while yer man was knocking about.

He didn't understand it, not one bit. He took a deep breath, closed his eyes and tried to steady his thumping heart. He thought of Poppy and reading her a story, he thought of drinking a cold beer and putting his feet up and then he found himself thinking of Detta and her blue eyes and the way she had tried to reassure him – which of course led him back to thinking about getting a cold drink – and soon. Things were definitely getting more complicated.

39

That had to have been the most surreal night Ciara had ever experienced. She had thought her strange night in Derry was off the wall enough – her at seventeen enjoying the company of those twice as old – but this beat that hands down.

She had just been putting Ella, who was now feeling much better, to bed when her mobile had burst into life. At first she hadn't recognised the number and had been tempted just to ignore the call. When she had first got pregnant she got all manner of anonymous calls from Ben Quinn and his cronies calling her all sorts of names until she had taken to ignoring them altogether, but it had been months since anything like that had happened so she figured she was safe enough.

When she answered Detta had breathlessly asked her to come to Ruth's, as quickly as she could, as there was a bit of an emergency. It had unnerved Ciara that Detta sounded less than calm and collected. She wasn't the type to get in a flap. Ciara had been sure she had never been in a flap her entire life. No one who smelled so strongly of essential oils could be flappable, surely?

"What's wrong?" she had asked.

"Best I tell you when you get here. Your mum won't mind, will she?"

Lorraine had just sat down with a cup of tea and *Corrie* so Ciara was sure she could wangle an hour's baby-sitting. "It should be fine."

"Great, great. We'll see you soon," Detta said, hanging up before Ciara could say her goodbyes.

Pulling on a cardigan over her T-shirt and jeans, Ciara had run downstairs and popped her head round the door to Lorraine. "I need to go out, Mum. Some crisis with Ruth. I shouldn't be long."

"What kind of crisis?" Lorraine asked.

"I don't know, Mum. Detta just phoned and asked me to get there as soon as possible. You don't mind keeping an ear out for Ella, do you?"

"This isn't anything dodgy, is it?" Her mother's eyebrow was raised. Lorraine was trying to be more understanding these days but it was never going to be easy for her to let go of her suspicious mind.

"Mum, it's Detta and Ruth, not Thelma and Louise."

Lorraine didn't seem to appreciate the humour.

"Look, Mum, I'll phone you when I get there and let you know what's going on. I don't imagine I'll be long. Please, Mum, it sounded important."

"Okay," Lorraine replied, "But yes, make sure you phone me."

Ciara had nodded and headed out down the road towards Ruth's.

She was shocked to see a Garda car outside, and the door ajar.

Gingerly she pushed at the door and opened it to come face to face with Eimear. It was odd to walk into her house looking for her mother. In any other circumstance it should have been

Ciara and Eimear who were friends. They were more or less the same age and they had enough in common – the mutual Ben Quinn obsession – and yet Ciara couldn't help but see her as just a child.

"Is your mum in?" she asked.

Eimear nodded in the direction of the living room door before bursting into dirty big snottery sobs. Ciara suddenly felt a panic descend on her – the Garda car, the open door, the daughter sobbing on the stairs. It didn't sound good, did it? Jesus, what if Ruth was hurt or dead or something?

"What's wrong?" she asked, sitting down beside Eimear and taking her hand in hers. She felt sort of as if she should be hugging her – but she didn't want Eimear to think she was some mad kissy huggy loony. She wanted to at least maintain some air of coolness about her. She was seventeen not thirty-seven.

Eimear sniffed at the touch of her hand. Ciara almost thought she was going to pull it away, but she obviously changed her mind and held on a little tighter.

"My daddy, he hit Mum," she sniffed and Ciara felt as if she, in a way, had been hit herself.

"Is she okay? Are you okay?" The words were coming out jumbled and rushed. She was trying to remain cool while at the same time trying to show enough maturity so that Eimear felt she could confide in her. She obviously needed to sound off to someone and there wasn't a chance that Ben and his cronies would offer a supportive listening ear. The Samaritans would never coming knocking at his door looking for his services as a volunteer.

"She's hurt, but she's okay. She called the guards. Thomas helped her chase him off."

Eimear looked upstairs towards a closed door. Thomas was no more than fourteen or fifteen. Ciara could only imagine how scared he must have been.

"And you?" she added gently.

"I saw it. I saw him hurting her. It's my fault, Ciara. It's all my fault!"

Ciara shook her head. "Now why would you think that?" She wanted to add that James was obviously just an awful bollocks of a man and that was no one's fault but his own, but she figured Eimear had seen her daddy fall far enough off his pedestal for one night.

"Because I knew. I knew and I did nothing."

"You knew?"

"That he hit her before. That he called her names. I knew but I said nothing and then when he moved out I thought it was all in the past, and I've been such a cow to her lately and I've been nice to him and it's all my fault."

Ciara felt herself blush. Yes, she was mature but she wasn't sure what to say. She'd never dealt with anything like this before. She didn't have a daddy she adored, or a mammy who was knocked about. Lorraine had her faults but she didn't take abuse from anyone – not that Ruth had been asking for this, obviously. Her thoughts became as jumbled as her words – she was struggling to process all this. A part of her wanted to go into reverse, get back out of that house and back to her own home where things, if not perfect, were at least a little less scary. If she left now she could easily make it back in time for the second episode of *Corrie*.

But then she felt Eimear's hand holding tight to her own and she looked at her. She was far from the confident, overly smug, sixteen-year-old Ruth often spoke about. In fact she looked like a scared child.

"I don't know much," Ciara said, as Liam blundered through the door looking equally as flustered as she felt, "but I know that, horrible as this is – and I know it is really horrible – it isn't, and wasn't, your fault."

Eimear nodded – not quite believing what she was being told but all Ciara could do was reassure her.

"Look, the police are gone now. Let's go in and see your mum." Ciara said the words but she didn't feel half as brave as she sounded. She really, really liked Ruth. Of all the people in the group, Ruth had been kindest to her and she didn't know what she would feel like when she saw her. When Detta had said she was in a bad way, Ciara's imagination had run away with her and being a teenager she had quite the imagination.

She took a deep breath and held Eimear's hand as they walked in together. Ruth was sitting there, hand to her swollen face.

"It only hurts when I laugh," she said with a watery smile and Ciara sat down beside her.

"I don't know what to say," she said honestly.

"It's okay, neither do I. But thanks for being here."

"Least I could do," Ciara replied, rubbing her hand and feeling very much out of her depth.

* * *

Walking home later, after the guards had gone and Liam had come back with enough locks to secure almost every house in the village, Ciara shivered. It's funny, she thought, the things that go on behind closed doors and you never even know about it. She would never have thought Ruth – motherly, funny and confident Ruth who had encouraged her to follow her dreams – could have been the victim of domestic violence. She shuddered thinking of the life she must have had, and yet she wondered why it was Ruth had still managed to look devastated when James left her?

Eimear had really been quite a pathetic-looking creature too and Thomas hadn't come out of his room all evening.

Matthew came downstairs at one stage and Ciara had felt physically sick when she saw his tearstained face. In a lot of ways it was harder to see than the cut on Ruth's face.

She opened her front door and walked in, and when Lorraine looked at her she burst into tears and buried her head in her mother's shoulder and sobbed until she could cry no more.

Lorraine and Ciara never really been the huggy types. Yes, they got on reasonably well and when she was a child, Ciara remembered curling up on her mother's knee for countless stories. But they didn't do public, or private, displays of affection any more. Since Ella arrived on the scene it felt as if they channelled all that affection into the baby and the most they managed for each other was a cursory kiss on the cheek or a friendly rub of an arm.

It should, therefore, have felt alien to hug now – especially with tears and snotters included. The last time Lorraine had seen Ciara cry had been when she was in labour and was sobbing buckets at the thought of having to actually push a baby out of her fandango when all she wanted to do was go to sleep and wake up with it all over and done with. She had begged her mother to make it stop and Lorraine had simply taken her face in her hands and told her that she would have to be a brave girl and get on with it. There she was, just emerging into motherhood – the most grown-up responsibility in the world – and her mother was referring to her as a girl. She cried harder then, and Lorraine had mopped her brow and assured her that she wasn't going to die from the pain. At least, Ciara had consoled herself, as she felt her tummy tighten again, her mother was no longer telling her how disappointed she was or that she going to kill her. Although, at that moment she would have been quite happy to be a murder victim.

Now though, she allowed Lorraine to hug her – she didn't

care if it felt awkward or if they didn't normally do hugs. She loved her mother. She needed her mum. She wanted her mum to know she loved her back and that she was grateful her mother wasn't an evil baggage who knocked her about.

"What is it, love?" Lorraine asked as she shushed her appropriately and stroked her hair.

"Oh Mum, I know we don't think it often, but we're lucky, aren't we? Me and you? We get on okay and we're happy?"

"Ciara, you're scaring me now? What has happened that has you so upset?"

Ciara spilled out the details while Lorraine listened, horrified.

"That poor, poor woman," she said, shaking her head. "I would never have known."

"I don't think anyone did."

"And those poor children!" She shook her head and pulled her daughter close to her and they sat there, for a long time.

"I'm going to go see Ruth tomorrow," Lorraine said determinedly. Ciara looked up.

"Don't look at me as if I'm cracked in the head. Sounds to me like she could do with a friend at the moment and, yes, I know she has all you Loonies. But I'm a 'lone parent' too." She pulled a face and used finger quotation marks at the phrase "lone parent".

"I think that's a brilliant idea, Mum."

"Good, because I'm going to do it."

It almost sounded to Ciara as if her mother was trying to convince herself of that, but she decided to say nothing.

They sat in silence for a bit, still cuddled on the sofa, before Lorraine spoke again. "Did I see you had a prospectus for the college?"

"Yes, Mum. I was thinking of taking a night class. Just thinking, mind," she said almost apologetically.

"Well, I think that would be a great idea. I might have a look at it myself."

40

Niamh stood under the power shower and let the hot water wash over her. This was her third attempt at a decent, relaxing, massaging and reviving shower. First of all Connor had decided he needed a poo and could absolutely not use any of the other bathrooms in the house, and then when he was done and she had just stepped back under the soothing jets, Rachel had decided it was her turn for the toilet.

Niamh had given up then, wrapped herself in her robe and waited till the children had gone to bed. She wanted to enjoy herself – luxuriate under the bubbles and release the knot of tension in her neck and shoulders.

If she was honest with herself she felt pretty useless. She had offered, last night, to let Ruth and her brood come and stay with her for a while. Lord knows she had enough room and thought it might have been good to have some company for a bit. Ruth had, however, politely declined. "If I take us out of this house now, then he has won, and I'm not going to let him win," she said. Niamh had to admire that.

When she had got home she was utterly beat. Robyn, who had been minding the children, had gently asked what had happened and all Niamh could think to say was that all men were bastards. It was clichéd and she didn't really mean it. Her daddy was as lovely as they came and Liam seemed like a decent sort – but as for the rest of them? They could go hang.

Robyn had looked a little dejected, so Niamh opened another bottle of Seán's good wine and sat down to fill her in on all the gory details.

When she was done, and Robyn was thoroughly shocked at the goings-on in what seemed like such an idyllic village, Niamh raised her glass and said: "Let's just be merry. We never know what's around the corner."

At that she thought of her husband, his car careering down a bank and she realised that she was right and the only way to survive was to take things slowly and hope for the best.

"Good idea," Robyn said, clinking her glass against Niamh's and settling back into her chair. "God, there's a lot of drama around this here village," she said in a fake American accent.

"There sure is," Niamh replied. "It's like *The Waltons* meets *Dynasty* – never a dull moment."

"And I thought Derry was a centre of scandal and intrigue," Robyn laughed.

"Oh, but it is," Niamh replied, her mind once again turning to Caitlin. It was actually starting to annoy her now – how much she was thinking about it. She would have to tackle it – there was no reason now to put it off apart from her roots still needing doing but she could have them done en route. She would have to go to Derry to get them sorted anyway – there was no way she was letting the purple-rinse brigade at Curl Up and Dye (no, they hadn't quite got the pun) on the Main Street have a go at her hair.

She decided then that on Friday, when her parents usually kept the children, she would get her hair done, book into

Natural Touch for a last-minute manicure and then put this whole sorry mess behind her once and for all.

You never knew what was around the next corner, she reminded herself again, and she wasn't going to spend the rest of her days wondering. Caitlin would have to give her answers – whether she wanted to or not.

Climbing out of the shower, she wrapped herself in her warmest, fluffiest bathrobe and lay down on the bed. The real-flame, natural-gas, uber-designer fireplace was glowing softly across the room and she had a glass of wine (just Jacob's Creek this time – fancy wine not being as fabulous as Seán would have had her believe) on the bedside table alongside a king-size box of Lily O'Brien's chocolates.

She revelled in the decadence as she applied a rich facemask before popping a chocolate in her mouth and allowing it to melt slowly.

"Aaaaah," she exhaled blissfully as the sweet chocolate dissolved. Had Seán been there he would have given out buckets about her eating in bed, and risking melted chocolate on the Egyptian cotton sheets.

Funny, she thought to herself, he never had any concern with melted chocolate on the bedsheets when she brought out the chocolate body paint and covered his doodah in it. She flushed as she remembered their long, slow nights of lovemaking, how they had explored every inch of each other's bodies, how they loved experimenting. It was just a shame he liked experimenting outside of the bedroom, and outside of their marriage, as well.

She shook away any negative thoughts and took a deep breath, reminding herself she was a strong, confident woman. She had survived the worst that could happen to her (chocolate doodahs aside) and the following day she would put her remaining demons to rest. Her kick-ass boots were sitting ready for action, her jeans and her figure-hugging top were primed as well. Appointments were made for her hair and make-up and the children would be with her parents.

It was unfortunate that Robyn hadn't agreed to meet her for a pre-confrontation drink. She didn't relish facing it all alone, and she knew that she would need a touch of Dutch courage before she would do what she had to. Still, if Robyn wasn't there she wouldn't at least try to talk her out of it for the 156th time. That had to be a bonus.

She sipped from her wine, selected the most delicious-looking chocolate from the box, lay back and breathed in and out – slowly.

This would be fine. This would all be fine and she was doing the right thing. She was convinced of it.

* * *

"You'll love him. He's perfect for you. Gorgeous too. And, best of all, rich!" Caitlin had been buzzing as she sipped from a glass of champagne while she toasted at securing the interview.

"It's a job interview, not a date!" Niamh had groaned.

"But he is very single and you know that a 'man in possession of a fortune must be desperate for a wife to spend it for him' or whatever that Austen woman said."

"Yes, but *I'm* more in need of a job than a man at the moment."

"Well, you are only saying that because you haven't seen him yet – you will change your mind. I'm sure of it."

"If he's so perfect, why haven't you pursued him yourself?" Niamh had asked, biting into a strawberry.

"Because I've heard he's the settling-down kind, Niamh, and you know me – the oldest swinger in town."

"You're still young!"

"And with no intention of settling down and becoming a frumpy wife."

"And you want me to settle down to frumpy wife-dom instead then?"

Caitlin had laughed. "Niamh, my darling, you've always been a wife in waiting. But I doubt you will ever be frumpy, I just want you to be happy. And to get some regular, decent, sex and by all accounts Seán Quigley is the very man to fill the gaps."

"My gap is just fine, thank you very much," Niamh had laughed loudly.

Still, once she had seen Seán in the flesh, and he had flirted with her on her first day in the office, she had started to warm to the idea of life with her boss in a strictly unprofessional capacity.

She was aware, the whole time, she was living out the biggest cliché in the book – dashing young PA falls for boss and humps on his desk after hours. But she hadn't cared because in all those pastel-coloured books telling of office romances the heroine always got her happy ending and she was convinced she was going to get hers too.

Their wedding day had certainly been fairytale. Although she had shunned the acres of tulle in favour of a slip of figure-hugging satin which showed off her curves almost indecently, the day had been fairytale all the same. Caitlin had been her bridesmaid – dressed in even more figure-hugging cerise pink. Her mother had joked that they were more suited to *Sex and the City* than a wedding ceremony in St Eugene's Cathedral and they had laughed. Mary would have had a minor stroke if she realised the cost of Niamh's coveted Jimmy Choo wedding sandals. Her mother knew they had been expensive, just not quite how expensive they were. And of course she had treated Caitlin to an equally gorgeous pair which they had bought on her hen weekend in New York. Seán had insisted on paying for it all – treating his best girls – and she had lapped it up.

*   *   *

She woke up: 3.34 a.m. The house was in silence apart from the gentle buzz of the baby-monitor from the twins' room. It was pitch dark, only the red glow of the alarm clock let her know the time. *Treating his best girls*. Seán was always treating his best girls. No expense spared. Nothing was too good.

She felt like doing a Homer Simpson – smacking her hand to her forehead and giving out about her own stupidity – but then she had wanted to believe it all along and she had been prepared to overlook some of the more obvious flaws in their relationship.

Because when it was good, it was very, very good but when it was bad . . .

She shook the thoughts away as she stepped out of bed and walked to her designer walk-in wardrobe. She knew they were there somewhere – among the boxes and the bags of gorgeous clothes that he had lavished on her. She pulled them out, one by one, box after box all carefully labelled, until she found what it was she wanted. Sitting down on the floor, in her pyjamas and with her hair like a scarecrow from tossing and turning in bed, she opened the box and slipped on the two dainty Jimmy Choo sandals, in delicate satin with jewelled detailing and heels so high it was a wonder she could ever walk in them without tipping over. And she clacked her way down to the kitchen, made a hot chocolate and contemplated the last five years of her life.

41

Ruth had made a conscious effort that night to go back into the kitchen, to invite all the children down to sit round the table so that the room, and what had happened there, didn't become like some big horror floating over them.

She had made them all hot chocolate and opened a packet of fancy chocolate biscuits – the ones usually reserved for guests – and they had started talking.

Of course it had been stilted at first. Thomas didn't want to meet her eyes while Matthew had wanted to sit on her knee. Eimear had stopped sobbing, just, but was dabbing her red eyes much too frequently with a battered tissue.

"Okay, you lot, well, we know what happened. And I'm so sorry you had to hear that and see that, but I promise you now you will never have to again."

"How do you know?" Thomas had asked, and while there was a defiance about him Ruth could see something in him that looked just as young and innocent as his baby brother.

"Because it won't. You know the Guards were here and they've taken a statement and they'll warn Daddy not to do that any more."

"Will my daddy go to jail?" Matthew asked, his eyes wide.

Ruth didn't know. Maybe? Probably not. Did she want him to go to jail? Maybe? Probably not. She just wanted him to stop – to never hurt her or anyone again.

"I don't know, pet. I'm not sure."

"But if he did something bad he should go to jail," Matthew said softly.

That started Eimear off sobbing again.

"I know this is a very confusing time," Ruth said, taking a deep breath, "but we'll get through it if we stick together. We're a family now and your daddy, well, what he did was wrong, very wrong. But he is your daddy and, if you want to still have contact with him, we'll try and sort something out. But you know it will have to be different now, don't you?"

It would have been easier for her if they could have broken all contact, of course. She wanted to keep them from him forever, but she had to be realistic. They had to make their own choices, even if the thought of them with him made her skin crawl.

"I never want to see him again," Eimear said. "I hate him."

"Hate is a very strong word."

"How can you defend him, Mum?" Thomas asked. "Admit it. You've always protected him!"

"I haven't, darling," Ruth said, tears springing to her eyes, knowing that what Thomas said was partly true.

This was so hard to talk about. It was hard to explain to her children how she could have safeguarded James's secret all these years.

Once upon a time she used to think, like most people, that it was black and white. Man hits you, you walk away. Simple as that. But what if man hits you, and you have a baby together, and you are both tired and then he apologises. And you forgive him. But he hits you again, and you tell him – again and again – that this is the absolute last time he can act like that until he starts to make you feel like you deserve it. If you don't do things the wrong way then you won't get hit, so there is something inside you that is making this happen and as much as you want to blame the man – because the books tell you that you should – you believe that you are at fault too.

Or so you think.

And then you find yourself trying to help your three children make sense of it all when you don't understand it yourself.

"Whatever I did in the past, I'm not defending him now," she went on. "I know what your daddy did was wrong. God knows, I do. And I don't ever want him to do it again. But you have to think about this now, yourselves, and decide what you want. I promise I'll support you, I promise that with all my heart."

The following day the children had been allowed to stay off school and had been delighted with their sneaky day off. Eimear and Thomas had remained quieter than usual, while Matthew was that little bit clingier but they also milked it in their own way too – getting treats of sweets and chocolates.

Dr Donnelly had visited, telling her to take as much time off work as she needed and pressing a leaflet for Women's Aid into her hands. "Hopefully now you'll get the help you need," she said and Ruth felt suitably embarrassed.

In fact the flush had only been starting to leave her cheeks when the doorbell rang again. Matthew lifted himself from the floor where he was drawing a hundred and one pictures – which Ruth feared a child psychologist would have a field day with – to answer it, but she jumped ahead of him. Her heart was in her mouth now – every time the phone rang or the door went just in case James had the balls to come back.

Feeling a little like Quasimodo or the Phantom of the Opera revealing herself to the world for the first time she opened the door to find Lorraine standing there nervously.

"I brought some biscuits and some flowers," Lorraine said, awkwardly. "I thought you might need someone to talk to."

Ruth was touched, even though she was surrounded with people to talk to. She knew that apart from her nights out with the girls from work once a week Lorraine didn't really mix much. And she had sensed Lorraine had felt as awkward as she had earlier in the week when she had given her a lift.

"Thanks, come in. I'll boil the kettle. Although to be honest, it's probably close to blowing its fuse at this stage. It's been like a bloody wake house here."

Lorraine smiled faintly and followed Ruth through to the kitchen. Ruth could tell she was trying not to picture what had happened there the night before. The rest of her guests that day had almost sent themselves cross-eyed trying not to look around the room for traces of blood, or bone, or DNA. She blamed *CSI*. Everyone thought they were a crime-scene investigator these days.

"It must be strange all right," Lorraine said. "Now I'm not here to be nosy, and tell me to bog off, but you know I just thought you might need a friend and if I'm honest Ciara has been putting me to shame these last weeks. She's been out there making friends while I've been stuck in my wee status quo."

"She's a credit to you," Ruth said. "She's a fine young woman."

Lorraine began to laugh. "God, can you believe it? Us old enough to have young women for daughters? Seems like only yesterday we were at school!"

Ruth smiled and nodded. Although they hadn't been in the same class, or even the same year, she remembered Lorraine from back then – bolshy and full of life – a bit like Eimear if the truth be told.

"I appreciate you coming here," she said softly. "And yes, I could do with a few friends at the moment, so thanks."

She reached her hand gingerly across the table and held Lorraine's and for the first time since James had walked out – or been pushed out – of her house the night before she allowed herself to break down and cry.

* * *

And now Detta wanted her to put all those awkward conversations and bizarre memories behind her and get dressed up to go to some fancy waterfront bar in Derry and sip Cosmopolitans and champagne as if everything was just fine and dandy.

Then again she would be going there with the purpose of helping Niamh put her own demons to rest and so it wasn't going to be just your average night on the tiles.

Detta had come up with a grand plan altogether that they should all, as a group, head up to Derry to join Niamh for pre-confrontation drinks, and also, Detta had said, to make sure Niamh didn't get herself into any trouble. "Those arse-kicking boots look like lethal weapons," she had smiled and Ruth joined in – a smile spreading across her face for the first time in three days.

"I'm just not sure I'm up for it yet. And I'm not sure I want to leave the children."

"The children will be just fine," Detta soothed. "Eimear is a grand girl with a great head on her shoulders. I wouldn't worry about that one at all and besides James would have to have some brass neck on him to come near the house with the non-molestation order in place."

But that was the whole point, wasn't it? James did have

a brass neck. And brass fists and steel-capped boots to match.

"Besides, Ciara has even offered to come down for an hour or two and keep them company," Detta continued. "Shame we can't smuggle her into the bar but we'll only draw attention to ourselves drinking with an underager."

"Still . . ."

"Still nothing. Ruth, you can't mope about all your life."

But Ruth wasn't planning on moping about all her life. Moping about was not her style – but much as she tried to deny her vanity she was very aware of the large bruise on her cheek and she knew everyone else would be too. She swore if you looked close enough you could see the imprint of a hand.

"I'm not moping," she said, and she wanted to find the words to adequately explain that she felt vulnerable – as if she were leaving the house with no clothes or no shoes like in one of her nightmares.

And she was scared – funny that. She'd lived with it for sixteen years but it was only now, when he was gone and the police were preparing a file, that she felt scared.

"No," Detta said softly. "I know you aren't moping. Sorry. I just want to make sure you don't start to mope. It's too easy, you know – and you have nothing on earth to be ashamed of. You're not the nasty bully here. And I want this to be a mope-free zone."

"But I'm the walkover. Sure didn't I let him do it?" She touched her hand to her cheek tenderly.

"No. No, you didn't. I don't think he asked for permission."

The pair sat in silence for a bit, sipping tea over the rickety kitchen table. See, Ruth thought defiantly, I'm not moping. If she had been moping she wouldn't be sitting in the very corner of the room James had thrown her in.

"Have you any make-up I can borrow?" she asked and Detta smiled.

"Of course I do. Just call me a one-woman Clarins counter."

Ruth looked at Detta. She didn't seem the type to slather on make-up – in fact she didn't think she had ever seen her wear more than a slick of lipstick and the finest lick of mascara. Her skin didn't need it – it was perfectly porcelain as it was. There were no dirty big bruises to hide and no wrinkles either.

Then again maybe she was a Botox addict. No one really knew anything about her – she didn't let anything of herself out. She was all about helping other people – but that was kind of infectious.

"Okay then," Ruth said, "count me in."

42

As he dressed Liam made sure he looked his best. He even slapped on some hair gel – some that Laura had bought him a long time ago to try and encourage him to update his look. He put on his good shoes – which again Laura had bought – and his suit, the one he usually wore when he was trying to secure a big contract or the like. He was more a jeans, shirt and heavy boots type of guy.

He phoned one of the lads at the site and told them he would be late and then he set off down towards the Main Street to meet with Laura.

He realised some people might think he was out to impress Laura. She might think it herself, but there was nothing further from the truth. He just wanted to go in there not looking so much of a mess. He wanted to be taken seriously. Still, he thought, he didn't want to give her any reason to think he still held a candle for her – so he took off his tie and opened his shirt button. He even flattened his hair down a little too – even if it gave him a greasy-haired look that definitely was not attractive.

When he walked through the doors of the solicitor's office,

Clodagh eyed him suspiciously. It was clear she knew what was going on – it was a fair bet that everyone in Rathinch knew by now. For all Liam knew one of the solicitors upstairs could this very moment be preparing a defence for James the wife-beater.

"Hi there, Clodagh."

"Liam," Clodagh stated, her face slightly tinged with red.

She was probably terrified he was going to go nuts and start tearing the place up or something. But that wasn't like him. He was very tempted to say in a childish manner that his name was not James and he wasn't prone to violent outbursts but he doubted that would encourage Clodagh to lift the phone and buzz to let Laura know he was there.

"Is Laura in?"

"Yes," she said. She was clearly not in the mood for small talk or idle conversation and he was, he had to admit, not in the mood to try.

He sat down and lifted the same old copy of the *Ulster Tatler* as he had the last time he was in and started to read.

Clodagh lifted the phone and tapped in a short number. "He's here," she said, almost in a whisper – but not quite.

Nil points for subtlety.

So, he had been expected – well, he thought this should be interesting at least. Setting the magazine back down, before having the chance to discover who had married who, divorced who or started some poncy art show somewhere, he waited for the door to open.

He wasn't sure what to expect. Would Laura look exhausted, or beaten down, or defiant? He didn't know which he dreaded more – or which would be easier to deal with.

As it happened she looked okay. Her hair was tied up in a loose pony-tail and there were no obvious signs of sleepless nights and buckets of tears. Then again, Laura wasn't a buckets-of-tears kind of a girl. She was a foot-stomping, pouting, get-her-own-way type of a person. He used to like that. When she told him he was the one she wanted, and she was going to get him – he liked that a lot.

She nodded towards him. "Come through."

He stood up, nodded and followed her. She held the door open for him, as she would for a client and gestured towards a chair before sitting down opposite him. All they needed, he thought, was an uber-strong flashlight pointed directly in his eyes and it would feel like an interrogation.

Laura sat forward, resting her arms on the desk. She was wearing a crisp white short-sleeved shirt with a pencil skirt. It was November and it was freezing. Liam couldn't help but feel she was showing off her unbruised arms to make a point.

"Well, I guess we know why you are here," she said.

"Are you okay?"

"Of course I'm okay," Laura said sharply, sitting back in her chair. "Why wouldn't I be?"

He assumed she was looking for an answer less obvious than "Your partner is a wife-beating scumbag" but those were the only words racing through his head.

"Well . . . you know," he offered after a short pause.

"Well, if you're worried, James hasn't hit me. I'm fine."

"You are fine? With what he has done?"

"He hasn't done anything to me. But no, Liam. I'm not okay with what he has done. Not one bit."

"So it's over then?" He felt he might as well come out and ask it.

"Oh, don't be so overly dramatic, Liam. It's not all black and white. You're only hearing one side of the story. He's not a bad man – they just had a bad marriage. Bad marriages do happen, you know," she said, this time meeting his gaze.

The meaning wasn't lost on him and he just couldn't

believe it. Here she was, bold as brass, comparing what they had with what Ruth and James had.

"What he did was wrong and we will deal with that. Maybe I'll leave him. I don't know. I'm not sure what will happen at this stage. But," Laura said caustically, "whatever I decide it is none of your business. I'm sorry if that sounds harsh but you have to accept that regardless of what happens with me and James, we – you and me – are over."

Shaking his head, he made to stand up. "That man won't be near my daughter. And if you are sensible, Laura – which I'm seriously starting to doubt now – you'll be careful. You didn't see Ruth last night – her cuts and bruises. You didn't see her children – his children – crying their eyes out. If that is the kind of man you want to be with then I wish you all the luck in the world."

Laura stood up and pushed her chair in. "If you don't mind, I do have work to do."

"Yes, I hear there are a few wife-beaters needing a defence round these parts this morning."

It was a cheap shot – not one he was proud of, but he couldn't help himself. He just could not believe that she was standing by James. When Tammy Wynette sang her song encouraging all women to stand by their men surely that didn't extend to violent, manipulative bullies? How could Laura, perhaps one of the most determined and bolshy women he had ever met in his life, be taken in by this man?

He was shaking his head as he left the office, not even bothering to say his goodbyes to Clodagh.

There was no way though, and he promised that to himself now, that his daughter was going anywhere near James and his heavy fistedness.

He dug his hands into his pocket and headed straight for the Country Kitchen where he was going to treat himself to a cooked breakfast and mug of over-stewed tea while he tried to calm himself down.

Pushing the door open, the chatter of his neighbours faded slightly when they saw him. It didn't take a genius to work out what they had been talking about.

He felt as if he was walking into the scene of an old Western film. The Country Kitchen was the saloon bar and the townsfolk were eyeing him up suspiciously. He would not have been in the least bit surprised if someone piped up with a quick "You're not from round these parts now, are you, boy?"

As it happened they just stared at him for the briefest of moments before returning to their chatter. But he was sure as he walked up to order his full Irish he heard someone whisper "Aye him, that's yer man. His wife ran off with that fecker."

He felt his face blaze. The shame of it, he thought, being left for a wife-beater but worse than that was the fact that even though Laura knew the full sorry story she seemed to prefer James anyway. She had to question whether or not she would leave him. How was that right?

"Liam!" he heard a voice call out and he looked round to see Detta by the fire, smiling warmly. She called him over, a little more loudly than she needed to and gestured to him to come and sit beside her. "Here! I've a seat by the fire. C'mon over!"

As he walked towards her she stood up and when he got to the table she reached across and kissed him square on the lips, rubbing her hand gently along his cheek before pulling him into a tight embrace.

"Let's give them something else to gossip about," she whispered as he stared dazed into her curls.

It wasn't gossiping he was in the mood for now.

Sitting down he stared at her – trying to read from her face if it was just a kiss to distract the jungle drums of Rathinch, or if it meant something more.

It wasn't something you could really ask, was it? Especially not in a cafe were the customers had ears like bats and all appeared to have their mobile phones at the ready, set to text the latest news as it broke. Who needed reality TV when you have live action in the Country Kitchen?

And it wasn't something you could easily move on from and fall into a safe and easy conversation. But he should have known none of this would phase Detta. Nothing ever phased her. He admired her for that.

"Right, the full Irish, is it?" she asked. "Can't beat a full Irish on a cold morning."

He nodded, stupidly. Like a nodding dog. He had to put his hand to his jaw line in a cool "thinking man" pose to stop looking like a complete eejit.

"I've ordered scrambled eggs and toast. I'm watching my figure," she said, sitting back and patting her almost flat stomach.

"You're lovely the way you are," he answered, realising that sounded weak and geeky. But what was he supposed to say? Let me do the watching, baby, I like the view? He cringed at the thought. It had been a long time since he had to chat any one up – seven years since he had wooed Laura and she had done most of the running.

It was strange, when he was at work sorting out deals and making orders he could charm the birds from the trees but put him in a room with a woman he found attractive – never mind a woman he found very attractive – and he lost the ability to form any sort of coherent sentence. He would just mumble like some stereotype of an Irish thicko.

"Ach thanks, but sure I've got to keep watching anyway. Especially with the way I like my chocolate biscuits. I swear if there was a twelve-step programme I would join up."

He smiled. He was partial to chocolate biscuits himself.

Laura used to ration him to one each evening with his cup of tea. He stuck to that habit even after she left but feck it, tonight he was going to eat half a packet if he damned wanted and if he was lucky Detta would eat the other half. He smiled at the thought.

"How are you anyway?" Detta asked, leaning close to Liam and taking his hand.

To give the gossips something else to talk about apart from the James/Ruth scandal? He didn't know – but he let her hold his hand and he liked it. Her hand was soft and warm and when she squeezed his he felt a shiver of excitement run through him.

"I'm okay. I've just seen her – Laura. She's considering staying with him. She's okay with him."

Most people would have looked shocked, or gone into a disgusted rant. Detta just shrugged her shoulders.

"What do you want her to do, Liam? Did you want her to leave him and come back to you?"

"No. But I don't want her to get hurt. I might not be in love with her any more but I don't want her to get hurt."

Detta raised an eyebrow. "You're not in love with her any more?"

Liam sat back, still holding her hand and thought for the briefest of moments.

"No, Detta," he said, looking into her eyes. "I'm not in love with her any more."

"That's good to know," Detta said with a smile as the young waitress placed their meals in front of them and they let go of each other's hands – as the beeps from incoming text messages from the other diners reached fever pitch.

* * *

He had gone back to work like a man possessed. One minute he was dragging his heels worrying about Laura and Poppy and the next he had a distinct spring in his step at the memory of Detta's kiss.

And when he was in neither of those moods he was wondering how on earth he had managed to get roped into driving himself, Ruth and Detta up to Derry the following night to make sure Niamh didn't end up locked in a police cell or lying drunken in a gutter somewhere, which – according to Detta – was a distinct possibility.

Of course he would have to ask his mother to baby-sit again, and she would assume he was out wooing Detta and he couldn't tell her that he wasn't – or that he was for that matter.

He switched his computer off and put his coat on. Calling down to the lads in the yard that he was taking a half day he went home, buried his head under his pillow and decided he wasn't going to shift it until he had to pick Poppy up from after-school club.

43

Lorraine had a smile on her face when she came back from Ruth's house. Ciara had been feeding Ella and watching *Hollyoaks* when her mother walked into the house.

Ciara found it a little strange – after all, she had just been with a woman going through the wringer and yet she seemed almost chipper.

"Hello, pet," her mother said poking her head into the kitchen, "and hello, wee princess. How are you?" she added, cooing at her granddaughter.

"I'm fine and she's fine," Ciara replied, handing her daughter a sippy cup which would start their nightly game of throw the cup, pick up the cup, and throw the cup again. "How are you?"

"I'm fine too," Lorraine said, switching on the kettle.

"And Ruth?"

"Fine."

"Do you think we can maybe move past fine?" Ciara asked with a smile.

"Sorry, pet, lost in my thoughts. We had a nice chat. She's a nice woman – we've lots in common though you wouldn't believe it. We're going to try meeting up a bit more. But don't you worry. The support group is still your own! We're going to do something even more exciting instead," she said with a smile.

In that moment, Ciara felt her heart swell with love for her mother. She knew then that they were both over the rocky times of the last year or two and that things could only get better from then on in.

"I love you, Mum," she said. "You do my head in at times – I'm not denying it – but I think you've done pretty damn well over the years. I've turned out pretty okay – aside from the whole teenage-pregnancy thing." She glanced at her daughter, feeling a little guilty for talking about her like she was some sort of mistake. Of course, Ella was a mistake or, as she preferred to think of it these days, some sort of "happy accident" – although in her mind the words happy and accident didn't really belong together. If she could have gone back in time she would have – through some magical force – arranged to have her daughter when she was older and wiser and not quite so marked out as a social leper for being a teen mum. Or she would move them all to a big city where no one would have noticed let alone cared.

"What's done is done," Lorraine said. "And we wouldn't be without her for the world."

"Except at three in the morning," Ciara said with a smile.

"Well, that goes without saying. But even then there are worse things you can be dealing with at three in the morning than Gummy the Wonder Baby over there."

Lorraine poured her drink and sat down at the table. "Oh yes, and I meant to tell you. Ruth and I are going to go shopping – just as soon as she feels up to it. We're going to buy some gorgeous new clothes and a pair of high heels the like of which have never been seen in this neck of the woods. We're going to help each other get back out and stop living like sad old baggages."

"You don't live like a sad old baggage – neither of you!"

"Aye, but if we keep on the way we're going it's only a matter of time. Have you not noticed the serious lack of glamorous grannies round these parts? Before you know it we'll be wearing cardigans and slippers out to do the weekly shop and we'll have developed moustaches and everything."

Ciara laughed out loud. "Mum, I don't think that's quite you or Ruth somehow."

"Well, we're going to make sure of that, and that's for sure." Lorraine said, sipping from her cup of tea. "Why don't you put madam down to bed? I'll nip out and get us a DVD and we can watch it together. Something girlie with Brad Pitt in it?"

"I'm more of a Johnny Depp woman myself," Ciara replied, "but either suits me. Get some sweeties too?"

"And crisps!" Lorraine said with a grin. "I'm supposed to be watching my figure but might as well be hung for a sheep as a lamb, eh? Life is too short to say no to Pringles."

* * *

Ella's eyelids were drooping heavily. She had just finished her bedtime bottle and Ciara was rocking her gently on her lap watching her face for signs that she had finally given in to sleep. She may only have been a baby but she could mess with her mother's head like you wouldn't believe. She would close her eyes and Ciara would dare to breathe out, convinced her daughter was finally in the Land of Nod, only to open them wide again and let out a gurgle of laughter. This would happen at least three more times before they would droop in one last effort – the poor child nearly going cross-eyed with the effort of trying to stay awake for just one more minute.

Lorraine had left for the DVD shop shortly before and Ciara was planning to light the fire for her return. They used to enjoy curling up in front of the fire when she was smaller, watching *Annie* over and over again until she knew the words to all the songs, and the dialogue and most of the dance routines.

Kissing Ella goodnight one last time she crept down the stairs and set about making the room as cosy as it could be. She even lifted the cream fleece blanket from her bedroom and brought it down so they could curl up properly.

Lorraine arrived home with a handful of goodies and a smile on her face. "I got *Pirates of the Caribbean* and *Thelma and Louise*, so everyone's a winner!"

"I've only one thing to ask," Ciara replied. "Which one of you and Ruth is Thelma and which one is Louise?"

"Which one gets to bonk Brad Pitt? I'll be that one," Lorraine laughed.

* * *

Ciara woke to Ella's chatter at just gone seven. She was quite impressed – seven was quite a lie-in these days. She was grateful for it too. Today was going to be a long day. First of all she had to go to work and deal with the weekly delivery of household goods. So for the majority of the day she would be up to her eyes in pricing toilet rolls, kitchen rolls and a variety of soaps and washing-up liquids. Mrs Quinn was still resisting a modern till system – shunning a fancy new scanner and barcode system for the old-fashioned pricing gun, stickers and push-button till. Ciara had long since given up on trying to explain to her that she would save time and money by moving with the times after Mrs Quinn accused her of being work shy. She now just got on with her work, wielding the pricing gun as if it were an AK 47. How she dreamed of sticking one of the lurid orange stickers square on Mrs Quinn's forehead! That thought got her through many a long morning.

But that aside, she had promised Ruth she would call past her house when she was finished work and check on Eimear, Thomas and Matthew. Ruth had, despite her better judgement it would appear, been talked into going to Derry to act as one of the minders for Niamh who was going to confront her husband's mistress. They had explained to Ciara that they might draw unwelcome attention to themselves if they invited an underage drinker along. She was fine with that. She wasn't quite up for a night in a stuffy fancy bar which only sold fine wine and designer beers. She was happy to be friends with the Loonies, but it so wasn't her scene.

Still, she had made them promise that she could come along for the debriefing the following day when they had arranged to meet en masse at the Country Kitchen for breakfast. Even Lorraine was eager to come along to that. The scandal of the Loony Lone Parents was giving her a new lust for life, she said, and Ciara was delighted to see her more alive than she had been in years.

All that aside though, she still had to cope with calling over to Eimear and Co that evening without making it look like she was baby-sitting. She was almost the same age as Eimear after all and, while the pair of them had shared a good heart to heart after James's outburst, Ciara was still very much aware that they still had the potential to be sworn enemies. Ciara was Ben's ex and the mother of his child – even though he refused to admit it – and Eimear was his latest squeeze. If Eimear was anything at all like Ciara had been two years previously she would be unwilling to hear a word against the gorgeous Ben Quinn. But could Ciara really keep her mouth shut?

"C'mon, baby," she said, lifting Ella from her cot. "Whatever happens today I think it's going to be interesting. Whoever said life was boring in Rathinch?"

As Ella ate her breakfast a short time later Ciara filled in the remainder of her college application form. "Watch out, Lois Lane," she grinned, "there's a new gal in town and if she is in luck she might just find her Superman."

44

"James has been charged with assault."

"That's a good thing, isn't it?" Detta asked as she emptied her make-up bag on Ruth's dressing-table.

"I suppose so."

"You suppose so?"

"Well, yes, it is. But, you know, having him dragged through the courts will just bring this whole sorry mess to everyone's attention."

"But doesn't everyone know anyway? Isn't that what Rathinch – with all its good points – is about? Gossip spreading like wildfire?"

"Well, yes, but you know the courts make it more official." Ruth lifted a tube of pale foundation and examined it closely. "There'll be a reporter there from the local paper and everything. Can you imagine it? Me getting battered, in black and white, in a newspaper for anyone to read."

"Tomorrow's chip paper," Detta said, taking the tube of foundation from Ruth and handing her an altogether more suitable colour.

"They don't actually wrap chips in newspaper any

more," Ruth said. "Health and Safety or some other such bollocks."

"Well, tomorrow's firelighters then, or tomorrow's litter-tray filler. Whatever it is, it's in one ear today and out tomorrow. I don't mean to be flippant but everyone is too busy leading their own lives and worrying about their own sorry problems to focus too much on yours."

Ruth sniffed and sat down on the bed.

"Sorry," Detta said sitting down beside her. "That wasn't meant to sound as harsh as it did. It's just that, well, the main thing is he gets his comeuppance for being an awful gobshite."

"But what effect will it have on the children? To have a daddy before the court? They'll be mortified."

"No more mortified than they felt seeing him knock lumps out of you," Detta said matter of factly. "But there are places which can help. They can talk to the kids, talk over what has happened and help them keep it in perspective. I'll get you a number if you want."

"That would be just lovely," Ruth said, sagging with relief. She was getting truly fed up with these thoughts running around her mind. It was there morning, noon and night as if a light had just gone on. Even though she had known for the last umpteen years what a bastard James was, it was as if she was only really, truly accepting it now and it was there all the time. It had been there when Dr Donnelly had come and spoken to her and signed her off work for a week. It had been there when she had forged her new friendship with Lorraine over a packet of Coconut Creams and it had even bloody been there the night before when she went to the chippy. It was like a constant sing-song in her head "Battered wife, battered wife, battered wife!" When someone had ordered a battered sausage she had almost replied "You called?"

And at times she was okay with it all. She would smile even – get a surge of joy that it was finally done forever. Life was going to change for the better now and she was young enough to make her life work for her. Yet at other times she wanted to curl up in a ball and put her hands over her ears to block out the world.

But somehow, amid all this confusion, she had managed to get herself talked into a night on the town in Derry. Detta handed her a brush and told her to get to work.

"What's this for?" she asked, looking at it. It didn't look like a blusher brush and it was much too wide for eye-shadow – not that she ever wore eye-shadow.

"Your foundation!"

"With a brush? Are you mental? You don't use a brush – you use your fingers or a sponge!" Ruth laughed.

"No, my dear, these days we use brushes. We use them to sculpt and highlight and define. Now let's get you sorted. Trust me, once you try a brush you'll never go back."

It was strange, Ruth thought. Detta had never looked like a person obsessed with her appearance. That's not to say she looked like one of Wurzel Gummidge's spare heads, but she didn't seem high maintenance. She wasn't as obviously groomed, plucked and preened as Niamh, and Ruth very much doubted her clothes were of any designer variety, but nonetheless here she was tipping the entire contents of Debenhams' make-up hall all over her bedroom.

She had brushes, lotions, potions, powders, liners, creams, mascaras aplenty. Ruth thought of the crumbling case of pressed powder and stubby red lipstick languishing in her own make-up bag and blushed. She knew nothing about make-up. Eimear had tried to talk her into buying some decent products a while back but she had shrugged it off. She was, she was happy to admit, scared of the stuff and convinced that should

327

she even try and give it a go she would end up as a tangoed, streaky-faced painted doll.

Tonight though, she needed a little extra help and the look of sheer joy on Detta's face as she mixed together her moisturiser and foundation was a sight to behold.

"Let's glam you up," Detta said and set to work. "And let's forget about all this old nonsense and go out and have a great night for ourselves."

By the time she was transformed, Ruth was giggling like a schoolgirl. Detta had opened a bottle of sparkling wine and borrowed a CD player from Eimear and played some cheesy seventies tunes while they had got ready. They had just completed a resounding rendition of "Enough is Enough" and were wailing through a rendition of "I Will Survive" when Liam pulled up in his car outside. They stumbled out, the strains of the chorus echoing around the village as they went.

Eimear had laughed as she closed the door after them, shouting that she would be good for Ciara, her bad humour at being told someone would be popping in to check on them disappearing.

For once, as Ruth slipped into the back of the car and fastened her seatbelt, she felt happy to leave her house knowing it wouldn't be trashed by the time she returned.

"Wow," Liam breathed. "You two look fabulous."

"Are you trying to say we don't always look fabulous?" Detta asked with a wicked glint in her eye which sent Ruth into a further fit of giggles.

"Have you two been drinking?" Liam asked – with his best stern-daddy voice.

"Only a little bit – and come on, this is a night out. We are supposed to be enjoying ourselves!"

"I thought we were supposed to be making sure Niamh

doesn't make an eejit of herself?" he replied, looking in the rear-view mirror at them both.

Ruth focused on him and noticed the well-creased lines of a brand-new shirt and the not-so-faint-whiff of aftershave and smiled.

"So that's why you have your Sunday best on then?" she said.

"Nothing wrong with making an effort," Liam said gruffly.

"That's just exactly what we were thinking," Detta replied with a smile and Ruth looked from one to the other as it dawned on her that there might just be more to this night out than making sure Niamh was fine.

45

"Today is the first day of the rest of my life," Niamh told the cold marble gravestone in front of her. "I know you might not like what I'm going to do, Seán, but you would admire my ballsiness. You always liked that. You would hate it if I did nothing. You would hate it that we weren't both fighting it out over your memory, but whatever you and she had – well, it's not the same as what we had. I was your wife and I deserve that memory so wish me luck because today I'm sorting this out once and for all."

Niamh hadn't intended to go to the cemetery. Her day was going to be busy enough with her hair appointment and nail appointment – not to mention getting the children settled with her parents and dealing with the inevitable one hundred and five phone calls from Robyn asking her to reconsider her plan. She had decided that morning that she was going to switch her phone off. She was on a high now – she was ready to deal with this and whatever answers Caitlin was going to give her they had to be better than the answers she had running through her head.

So no one was more surprised than she was when she

found herself at Seán's grave in the biting cold. The twins were conked out in the car and she was glad of it – she couldn't imagine having this conversation with them there. His grave still looked tidy – the grass had barely grown in the two weeks since her last visit and there were no flowers there left to wilt. She hadn't left him flowers since she found out about Caitlin. Suddenly a chorus of "You Don't Bring Me Flowers" flooded through her head and she shushed away the image of Neil Diamond giving it lilty with Barbara Streisand.

"Right. Wish me luck. You would like what I'm going to wear tonight – sassy and stylish with a first-class pair of fuck-me boots. You would really like those," she said with a sad smile. "I'm so raging with you, Seán – raging that you didn't give me the chance to kick your sorry ass. Raging that you never had the chance to beg me not to leave and tell me you love me. I'll not forgive you for that."

Niamh stood up and dusted the dirt from her knees. She had to be going if she was to make her appointments. She was determined everything would run like clockwork today.

* * *

Her hair looked different – not telly-makeover different – but different enough. Instead of her sleek blonde bob she had choppy layers all over in a rock-chick style. Her hair wasn't so blonde either – it was now streaked with honey and caramel highlights which complimented the gorgeous make-up job Leigh at Natural Touch had done. Her hands felt smooth as silk thanks to the luxurious manicure she had enjoyed and now she enjoyed tapping her acrylic nails against the table in the bar, as she waited for the barman to bring her a vodka and cranberry. Normally she was a wine girl – or, to be honest, a champers girl – but she needed double Dutch courage tonight and vodka was the only drink that was going to cut the mustard.

Okay, so she had been calm and collected before. Her scene at Seán's graveside had been the epitome of a strong woman. All that was missing was her digging her hand in the soil and then standing up and declaring she would never go hungry again – or something. But now, despite the glorious make-over, her amazing boots and a delicious new bracelet purchased in Argento that very afternoon she felt a little out of control.

She hadn't seen Caitlin since the funeral. Who was to even know if Caitlin was in? She could be sitting here like a prize idiot waiting to drunkenly knock at a locked door while Caitlin, for all she knew, could have been on the other side of the world.

Suddenly she felt very foolish. Who had she been kidding coming up to Derry all lipstick, powder, paint and killer heels? Even the sexy new haircut couldn't hide the fact she was highly likely to be five minutes away from making a complete eejit of herself. As the barman sat the drink down in front of her she gave him a weak smile and knocked back as much of it as she could without choking on an ice cube. He gave her a strange smile back and she flushed. Tempted as she was to explain to him just why she needed a drink so badly, she refused to become one of those drunken middle-class women who spilled their guts out to barmen as they sat alone on a Friday night.

She felt a pang then for Robyn. Her phone had remained switched off all day and she was determined it would remain off – nonetheless, a little part of her wanted to phone Robyn and beg her to come and join her at the bar.

She sat back, took a deep breath and tried to regain her composure. She tried to find a focus in the room that would help her centre herself – but all she found was Seán's ex-partner Kevin, surrounded by a fair smattering of the great and the good of Derry. Of all the bars, in all the world, he had to be charming the pants off his clients in this one. "Shit," she muttered a little too loudly, just as he looked up and stared right back at her. Whether he was powered by an excess of wine and fine whiskey or whether he was just trying to act the big man in front of his guests, he called her name loudly across the bar. Then, like Moses parting the Red Sea, he stretched out his arms in an exaggerated hug and walked towards her declaring loudly: "Oh it's so nice to see you out and about again, you poor dear!"

Oh Christ, Niamh bit back. It was bad enough she was sitting drinking alone in a bar without Kevin, the wanker, drawing everyone's attention to it. She plastered on yet another fake smile and allowed him to hug her even though the smell of the body odour from his shirt made her gag.

"Oh my sweet Niamh," he continued.

Drunk, she decided. He was definitely and undoubtedly drunk. My sweet Niamh? What the hell was that about? He might even have been on drugs.

"We have missed you," he bellowed in her ear.

Why he needed to bellow was a mystery – everyone else in the bar had fallen into a hushed lull while they watched the scene unfold.

Glancing over Kevin's shoulder she saw elbows nudge elbows, hands try to cover up unsubtle whispers and a number of sympathetic glances in her direction.

"Here, come, say hello to everyone," Kevin continued, almost pushing her off her stool and in the direction of his crowd of cronies. Those who knew her – or knew Seán to be more exact – looked at her with sympathy. Those who didn't were clearly intrigued.

"This," Kevin said waving his hand in her general direction "is Niamh Quigley. You all know – knew, sorry, knew, Seán, our former partner at the firm? You know, he died in that awful, awful accident. Well this is his wife, sorry, widow. Doesn't she look lovely?"

Through his muddled introduction he glanced at her a few times, reddening with embarrassment and she would have saved him if she had been in a kind mood. But her kind mood had evaporated. Here she was, like a human exhibit in Show and Tell being humiliated by a drunken buffoon. She wondered should she give everyone a twirl – show off the post bereavement loss of weight – her rake-like bum in her designer skinny jeans?

Kevin's guests mumbled their hellos – a couple extended their hands and told her solemnly they were sorry for her troubles. Her chunky gold bangles jangled crudely as she shook their hands, aware of her choppy new hair cut bobbing up and down – like she'd just stepped out of a salon. Which she had, of course. She was hardly the advert for "destroyed young widow in a haze of grief". She had more of a look of a vampish man-eater about her. She could feel the women in the group stiffen up and begin to regard her as a threat. "Ha!" she thought. She wouldn't touch another man if her life depended on it.

"So," Kevin said looking over her shoulder, "Are you here on your own, or are you waiting for someone?"

His face had adopted a sympathetic look. He clearly thought she was on her own and she was taking to drink. The scandal would be mighty. He would have a great old time relaying her descent into alcoholism in the Magistrate's Court on Monday before proceedings started.

Of course, she thought blushing, he was half right. She was on her own. She wasn't a drunk though, not yet, but she could be tempted. That vodka and cranberry had tasted good and without it she was not sure she could have survived the last two minutes without decking Kevin right across his drunken face.

"Erm," she said, glancing back at the bar, "I'm just waiting for someone. They shouldn't be long."

"Well, why don't you join us until your friend arrives?" he winked, pulling a chair from a nearby table and sitting it close to his own.

Niamh's heart sank. She knew that if Kevin was going to be in this bar for as long as he normally sat in bars on Friday nights she would be sunk. But she could see no way out. She would slip away soon – sneak out via the toilet window if necessary. She might as well be the talk of the town for a really good reason.

"I'll get you another drink," Kevin bellowed, waving his hand towards the bar to call over the waiter in an arrogant manner. Niamh cringed at his gesture – thinking he could order anyone and everyone around. He really was an insufferable asshole, but then, when she thought about it, Seán would have done the same thing.

"What are you having?"

"Vodka and cranberry," she replied. The sooner oblivion came, the better.

Of course, being the black sheep of the group – or the black widow among the rich and wealthy men of the city – the conversation soon dried up. It was awkward and stilted. It was clear that the group was uneasy in her company and reluctant to boast about the week's achievements when her story was so utterly depressing.

"So how are things at the office?" she asked.

"Busy, you know. Thank God for the claim culture in this city. And the Magistrate's keeps us ticking over." Kevin was red-faced with pride, before he bumbled: "Of course it's not the same without Seán – but, you know, we cope."

She was tempted to laugh at his weak attempts to cover up just how quickly life had moved on for him and she probably would have laughed if she wasn't convinced everyone thought she was slightly deranged anyway. Here she was, dressed up like Samantha from *Sex and the City*'s understudy drinking alone in a bar miles from home alone on a Friday night. Worse than that she was listening to Kevin and company ramble on about their big houses and their bonuses when she would have been truly happy to trade in everything she had for a man who loved her, and only her, even if it meant living in a caravan by the sea.

Now, she thought, was just about the right time to make her hasty retreat to the ladies'.

"If you'll just excuse me," she said, standing up and making to turn on her designer heels.

"Of course, of course," Kevin said looking at his watch. "What time did you say your friends were coming at?"

She looked at her own watch – a reflex to buy some time. "I didn't," she answered, "but they shouldn't be long."

Offering up a silent prayer that she would get out of there in one piece she turned to leave and heard a clatter of friendly voices calling her name.

"Looks like they're here," Kevin replied, sagging visibly with relief.

Detta, Liam and Ruth looked mildly out of place in the city-centre bar but Niamh was delighted to see them. She had to stop herself from running over and hugging them. This was crazy, she thought as she bid a hasty goodbye to Kevin and his friends, and walked across the room. A year ago she would have thrived in the company of the group she was just leaving. She would have sat enthralled by Seán's witty banter, sipping fine wine and looking forward to getting him all to himself.

She knew they made a very attractive couple and she knew

that people were jealous of them. Shallow as it was to admit to, Niamh liked that. She liked that people would turn slightly green when she mentioned the interior-designed house in the country. She liked that when Seán talked, people listened.

She couldn't have imagined a year ago thinking that her previous life had all been false and fake. And it wasn't just that her relationship with Seán had been a lie – it was that these people weren't really her friends. They didn't really care about her – but Detta, Ruth and Liam did care. Her eyes welled up at their gesture and she had to clench her fists not to pull them into a hug.

"I can't believe you're here," she whispered.

"We figured you might need someone to hold your hand, and before you start worrying we're not here to talk you out of this," Detta said.

"I think I'm doing a fine job of that myself," Niamh sighed. "Come on, sit down. Let's have a drink – and whatever happens can we avoid that crowd over there? That's a blast from the past I have no desire to revisit." She nodded in the direction of Kevin and Co.

46

Liam couldn't remember the last time he had been in a bar like this. There certainly wasn't anything like it in Rathinch. It was all dark wood and big old prints on the walls. People in what looked like designer suits stood around drinking wine and laughing uproariously – and from what he could see, laughing at their own jokes. Smoking in pubs might well have been a thing of the past, but this place still felt stuffy. He shifted uncomfortably in his new shirt, while Niamh and Ruth ordered drinks from a harassed barman.

"So this was your local watering hole then?" he asked Niamh and she blushed.

"Well, once upon a time, in a galaxy far, far away," she said with a little laugh. "It's awful, isn't it? It's a bit OTT."

Liam nodded. To be honest, he found it hard to imagine the Niamh he knew amongst these people. Sure, she kind of looked the same – he was sure her clothes weren't from Dunnes Stores in Letterkenny – but she had more a more down-to-earth feel to her – big house and all.

"I think it looks great fun," Detta said with twinkle in her eye. "I couldn't handle it all the time but it's like a whole other world. Did you see the cocktail menu? The only 'cocktail' you get in Rathinch is a pint of snakebite!"

Liam looked at her, her eyes bright with laughter, and felt his heart soar a little. She was gorgeous tonight – her hair was soft and curled, pinned up on one side. She was wearing the most beautiful maxi dress, which he hadn't failed to notice showed off her breasts beautifully.

* * *

"Are you sure you want to do this?" Detta asked as they stood huddled for shelter outside a very swish apartment block.

Niamh nodded.

"We can just go home, you know," Liam said. "I'll get the car and we'll pile in and be home in Rathinch in an hour and we can forget all about it." Although Niamh sounded confident, she didn't really look it and he wanted to offer her this last chance at changing her mind.

"Let her do it," Ruth said. "She needs to."

Detta nodded. "And we'll be waiting here for you."

"With the engine running," Ruth said with a wicked wink.

Niamh laughed – a nervous giggle – and smiled at them.

"Thank you all, thank you so much for being here for me. It means a lot. Now wish me luck and if you hear screaming don't worry too much." She forced a weak smile and pushed open the large glass door of the foyer, leaving the other three standing in the cold.

"Come on," Liam said. "We can either wait in the car or go back into the bar. I'll buy you a drink if you like."

"I'd like that very much," Detta said, glancing to Ruth.

"Why not? After everything I've been through this week, a drink is the least I deserve."

Ruth linked her arm to Detta's and they walked to the neighbouring bar, each with their phones on, waiting for Niamh's call.

47

"Mum's a right laugh," Eimear said, opening the door and letting Ciara in. "Imagine sending somebody over to mind us."

"I'm not here to mind you," Ciara said, "Jesus, I can barely mind myself. I'm just here to check you are all fine."

"I know, sorry," Eimear said. "It's just sometimes Mum treats us like we're still babies. I'm nearly the same age as you!"

Ciara nodded. "Never mind. I'll not stay long."

"Stay as long as you want," Eimear said, softening. "Sorry I'm a bit touchy. It's been a tough week."

"I bet it has." Ciara followed Eimear through to the living room. Matthew was in his pyjamas watching cartoons on the TV.

"Thomas is upstairs." Eimear said. "I was just sitting here doing my nails. Do you want a drink? There's Coke in the fridge."

"That would be lovely."

"Right, well, sit down, I'll be through soon."

Ciara sat down beside Matthew who was engrossed in an episode of *Ben 10*. "Is this any good then?" she asked.

"It's the best. *Ben 10* turns into aliens. He has a cool watch."

"Sounds great to me."

"But I'm only allowed to watch one more episode," Matthew replied glumly – his dark-brown puppy-dog eyes staring right at her.

"Why's that?"

"Oh, Eimear has her friends coming round and I have to go to bed. If I'm good and don't make a fuss she's going to buy me a *Ben 10* watch tomorrow."

"Her friends?" Ciara felt a little uneasy.

"Yes, her friends and this part's extra secret." He moved closer to Ciara and whispered. "Her boyfriend's coming too. He's called Ben as well."

* * *

Ruth couldn't remember the last time she had been in a bar – never mind a fancy bar. She tried to remember the last time James had taken her out for an evening but she couldn't. They used to go out for dinner for their wedding anniversary each year, but a few years back they switched to getting takeaways in the house over a bottle of wine. Then they moved to having their dinner with the kids and then it moved on to him going out and her watching a soppy DVD on her own.

She had to admit that while she knew her make-up was covering bruises that ran deeper than the purple marks on her face, she kind of liked being dressed up for a change. Niamh had ordered a jug of Cosmopolitan when they arrived and Ruth thought she might have found a new addiction. Feck the weekly bottle of wine, she would be stocking up on cranberry juice, fresh lime and vodka and starting her very own cocktail bar in her kitchen every Friday at this rate.

After they had left Niamh off and they returned to the bar,

she hadn't hesitated in ordering another jug and delighted in how the barman mixed up the concoction in front of her.

So this was how the other half lived? This was life outside of Rathinch. Of course, some of the patrons of the bar looked like gobshites. That Kevin one Niamh had been talking to when they arrived looked like a Grade A asshole – all designer suit and fancy shoes. He obviously fancied himself as a big hitter but she had noticed people rolling their eyes as he babbled on about this and that.

There seemed to be a competitiveness here that she couldn't be coping with. Her second-hand kitchen table and chairs and 1998 Astra wouldn't go far in this company. She laughed – she imagined it would be hard to constantly have to live up to others' expectations. She'd rather just be her, and get on with it, and that was exactly what she was planning to do.

"Cheers," she called, clinking her glass against Detta's. "Here's to a new beginning!"

"I'm with you on that one," Liam said, and for the second time that evening Ruth noticed a little spark between him and Detta.

Oh, she loved happy endings, and this one – she thought – might just end up being very happy indeed.

*　*　*

As the lift ascended Niamh closed her eyes and rubbed her temples and there it was – a flash of what life must have been like for Seán and Caitlin. The doors of this very lift closing and them grabbing each other in a fit of passion. Seán always got horny in lifts. It was, as he would say with a wicked grin, the thought of something big and powerful rising up. Then he would add with a laugh "Of course, the lift goes up too," and they would fall into each other's arms. Niamh imagined he did the same with Caitlin, that he had pushed her up against the wall of this very lift and pushed his hand up her top, teasing her nipples the same way he had teased hers – pushing himself against her like he had with Niamh so many times.

She felt her resolve harden – this was about so much more than a friend's betrayal – this was about her friend stealing her memories. "Fecking bitch," Niamh muttered as the lift stopped at its destination and the doors pinged open.

She walked down the corridor as steady as she could be in four-inch heels after a jug of Cosmopolitan. She walked past the tables laden with delicate arrangements of fresh flowers, and shook off the images of Seán and Caitlin that filled her head. She could see them running hand in hand down the marble hallway, kissing, bumping carelessly into the tables and sending a vase crashing to the ground. She knocked her hand against one of the vases herself, just catching it in time before it smashed to the floor.

She could imagine Caitlin fumbling for her keys as Seán fumbled for her bra outside the dark wooden front door of her penthouse apartment.

She could imagine him kicking the front door closed with his foot, all the while kissing Caitlin passionately before leading her to the bedroom and ravishing her – probably without even bothering to close the blinds. He wouldn't have cared who saw.

She could imagine it because he had been like that with her.

It dawned on her, as she stood there ready to knock on the door, that she didn't quite know what to say. How do you greet someone who had made the worst year of your life worse than you could have ever imagined? She would have liked to smash the door in with an axe Jack Nicholson style and shout "Here's Ni – amh!" – instead she just took a deep breath and pressed the door bell.

"I'm coming!" she heard Caitlin call in a super-girly voice.

The door opened and Caitlin stood there, proud as punch in a satin dressing gown and a pair of god-awful marabou slippers and clutching a glass of champagne with a strawberry floating on top.

"Expecting someone else then?"

Caitlin's face was a picture, changing from excited anticipation to absolute horror in an instant.

"Niamh," she whispered.

"Still my name, yep," she said, pushing past her into her apartment. "So, whose husband are you expecting tonight?" She walked through the living room, a minimalist's dream home – all creams and stonework and fecking blasted marble. Seán would have loved it.

"It's not like that," Caitlin answered, her slippers clacking across the marble floors.

"No, I bet it's not. I bet his wife doesn't understand him, they don't even sleep together any more and you didn't mean for it to happen but it did anyway. You know, one minute you were all resolve, the next he was buck-naked in your bed and your clothes just happened to fall off too."

Caitlin blushed, just before she turned the most sickening shade of white and sat down on the impossibly uncomfortable designer sofa.

"Just so you know," Niamh continued, her voice rising. "I *did* understand Seán and we *were* still sleeping together. I think it's important you have all the facts."

"Look, Niamh, what's done is done and I can't change it." Caitlin sounded almost bolshy and Niamh fought the urge to physically knock the bolshiness out of her.

"So that makes it okay then? Don't you think you owe me an apology, not to mention an explanation?"

"It's not what you think."

Niamh gave a snort which turned into a belly laugh. She could read her friend like a book.

"Oh Caitlin, don't lie to me. I've known you forever and a day. I know when you're lying and to be honest I'd have expected more from you. I'd have expected you to come up with better that 'It's not what you think'. You were always more creative than that. I saw your little love-note to him. I saw that he had booked a weekend away, with you. I've realised how blind I was and God love me, I really was the stereotypical thick blonde, because in hindsight it was all so bloody obvious it scares me."

Caitlin lifted her glass and took a swig of her champagne, narrowly avoiding choking on a strawberry.

Niamh glanced around the apartment. Cold and sterile as it was, it was clearly set up for a night of romance. Candles were burning softly around the gas fireplace and soft jazz music was playing through the super-duper music system. The bottle of champagne was sitting on the work surface of the open-plan kitchen and a glass, already poured, sat beside it. Niamh lifted it and downed it in one, ignoring the bubbles that fizzed through her nose.

"You don't mind, do you?" Niamh asked, topping up her glass from the bottle. "After all, you kind of owe me. You sleep with my husband, I drink your champagne. Seems like a good start to me."

"I didn't know you would come here."

"Did you think I'd never find out? Is that it? Because one minute we're best friends and the next my husband is dead and you disappear, leaving me thinking I'd done something wrong. Did you think I'd never know – never find any hint of what you had done or that I'd just chalk it all down to experience? Do you think I would just let you disappear from my life without trying to find out why?"

"I don't know," Caitlin said. "I didn't know what to say to you."

"How about 'I'm sorry for being the biggest fucking slut in Derry' for starters?" Niamh spat, her temper flaring.

"There's no need –"

"There is every need. And here you are, dressed up like a slapper again and it takes not a wrinkle out of you. How do you sleep at night? How do you live with yourself?"

Caitlin sat her glass on the floor and stood up, her fancy fuck-me slippers clacking as she walked towards the hall of her apartment.

"I want you to go, Niamh," she said, in a shaky voice.

"Well, I want you not to have slept with my husband. Shit happens. Get over it."

"I can't undo it," Caitlin said, her eyes almost pleading.

"You've said that, but you *can* explain it. I've asked you before and I'm asking you now. If our friendship ever meant anything at all to you, tell me because I can't exactly ask him. Tell me why you did this to me."

"It was nothing to do with you," Caitlin said.

"How can you say that?" Niamh felt her blood start to boil.

"Because it's true. It was nothing to do with you or how he felt about you and how I felt about you. It just . . ."

"Happened?" Niamh snorted.

"Yes, actually. Yes, it just happened. He was working late and I was about and we met for a drink a few times. You weren't the same person you once were – you weren't up for nights out and the socialising you knew came with his career. Life wasn't what it once was and Seán and I just connected on some level."

"So that makes it okay then? I was a frumpy mummy and you were there waiting in the wings?"

347

"It wasn't like that. And you were never frumpy, but you know men like Seán . . . they have to have it all."

Niamh snorted again, a big sob bursting from her throat. "I thought we *did* have it all!"

"He never loved me," Caitlin offered sadly. "It was nothing more than a bit of fun to him."

"Did you love him?"

"Does it matter?"

"Yes, it matters. Of course it matters. How could it not matter?"

Caitlin shook her head and stood up. "I'm going to get changed into something less ridiculous and I have a phone call to make. Then we can keep talking."

She walked into the bedroom and Niamh sat down on the leather sofa in front of the glowing gas fire and shivered. She sipped from her glass of champagne but it sickened her now so she stood back up again and walked to the breakfast bar and set it down. She glanced around, at the sterile off-white walls, the few select arty prints hung here and there. There were no pictures of people on Caitlin's walls – no smiling faces, no grinning, drunken friends or messy, sticky children. There were no sticky fingerprints or doodles courtesy of overeager toddlers.

Everything was sterile, perfect, clean and controlled. Niamh wondered for a moment if Seán was more interested in having an affair with this apartment than with Caitlin. If there was one thing he liked, it was order. The one thing guaranteed to send him into a foul mood would be any sign that their perfect, gorgeous show home had actually been lived in. A trace of paint on the kitchen table, a glob of cookie dough on the kitchen tiles, a lump of Play Doh walked into the marble floor.

He wanted the perfect house, the perfect family and the

perfect life. He just wasn't so great coping with mess – except, of course, for his office which was a perfect breeding ground for experimentation in microbiology. She used to tease him that it was his dirty little secret – oh, how the absolute irony of it all stung now!

Caitlin walked back into the room, marabou slippers abandoned for a pair of fluffy socks, her body-skimming dressing gown for a pair of jeans and a jumper. Her face was still overly made-up, however. It made her look old, Niamh thought with some bitchy glee. Oh she knew it was wrong to be a cow, but in the circumstances she felt pretty justified. You sleep with my husband, I turn into a bitch. Seemed fair enough.

"Right," Caitlin said, sitting down across from Niamh. "You really want to know what happened?"

Niamh felt like banging her head off the wall. "No, I'm just here for the *craic*. Have you seen the new lip-glosses from Clarins? I thought we could chat about them," she said sarcastically.

"Yes, I loved him," Caitlin said sadly. "But he made it clear, Niamh, that he was never going to leave you. It wasn't one of those affairs where I was hanging on waiting for him to walk out on you and set up home with me. I knew the score. This was fun to him – stress relief – nothing more. I would imagine sometimes that it was more, but I knew it wasn't. You came first, Niamh, always."

"Clearly not," Niamh replied. "If I know Seán the way I know Seán, he would have come first most of the time. In and out of bed."

Caitlin gave a weak laugh and Niamh almost joined in. For a second it was like they were eighteen again and laughing over boyfriends – drunk on cheap Peach Schnapps with a sickening blend of pineapple juice. At any second she half-expected Caitlin to raise her hand and wiggle her little finger while raising one eyebrow. It would have been hilariously funny if it wasn't so tragic.

"I didn't mean to betray you. I can't explain it. I loved him. I knew it was wrong. I just got carried away."

"He wasn't yours to love."

They sat in silence for another while, Niamh gathering her thoughts. She knew that when she walked out the door she would not set foot here again. She needed all the answers now.

"So I know the why and the when and the where but what I don't get, Caitlin, is just how you could do this to me? How could you do it to us?"

"I dunno," Caitlin shrugged her shoulders. "What do you want me to say, Niamh? Does it matter now? He's gone and he's not coming back. Does *any* of it matter now?"

Caitlin looked stricken and Niamh felt a momentary pang of empathy pass between them. But she steadied herself. "Of course it matters. He was my husband. You were my friend."

"We just got close. We spent time together. It happened. It wasn't deliberate but we know we shouldn't have done it. I'll not patronise you."

It was very nice, Niamh thought, for Caitlin to have such consideration for her feelings as not to patronise her. It was only a shame she hadn't extended that consideration to not shagging the arse off her husband.

"But you were my friend. You visited my house. You chatted to me on the phone. We went to the spa together and all the time you were sleeping with my husband!"

Caitlin blushed.

"You really are a brazen slut, aren't you?" Niamh spat the words out, past caring any more.

"I'm sorry," Caitlin said, then paused. "Actually I'm not sorry. I loved him."

"What about me? What about our friendship? Did that mean nothing to you? You were my friend," she repeated sadly.

Niamh didn't understand – couldn't understand – how the one person she had trusted most in the whole world (apart from Seán, of course) could do this to her.

"And then you stopped," she said, looking into the fire. "You could be my friend when he was alive. You could sit across the dinner table from me and drink wine and share gossip and when he died, when he was gone, you stopped. You just walked away."

"I couldn't face you."

"You couldn't face me? You could swim in my pool and help yourself to the contents of my fridge (and my bed for that matter) two days before, but he dies and you couldn't even talk to me."

"It was too hard."

"You," Niamh said, her eyes blazing once again, "don't know the meaning of hard. Try telling two children their daddy is gone and not coming back. Try waking up to find out your life has been a lie. Try rebuilding it from nothing. *That* is hard."

"Try grieving for the man you loved in secret," Caitlin bit back. "Try wanting to tear your heart from your body because it hurts so much but not being able to tell anyone why."

Niamh ran her fingers through her hair and stifled what even she considered a cruel laugh. "Don't get all fecking dramatic-y *Wuthering Heights* on me. Tear your heart from your body? Caitlin, you don't know pain. You don't know hurt and you sure as hell don't know how to think of anyone else but yourself."

They sat in silence for a bit, each lost in her own thoughts. Niamh felt the anger drain from her. There wasn't much of a point any more. Her kick-arse boots would have to wait another day to fulfil their arse-kicking destiny.

"Do you miss him?" she asked, gingerly lifting the glass of champagne to her lips again.

"Do bears shit in the woods?" Caitlin said with a raised eyebrow – and then immediately apologised. "Sorry, I'm being crass. I'm guessing you're not ready for crass yet."

Niamh shook her head.

"Yes, I miss him. I miss picking up the phone and calling him, hearing his voice. Getting a text message, seeing him smile as he walks into the bar to buy me a drink. I miss him, everything about him."

The words cut through Niamh. But then again it would have been harder, she realised, to hear Caitlin say she didn't miss him – that him not being there hadn't touched her at all. That would have cut deeper – to know that he risked their marriage for someone who couldn't even miss him.

"I miss you too," Caitlin said, her eyes pooling with tears. "I'm so sorry, Niamh. Can you ever forgive me?"

Niamh nodded slowly. "I'll forgive you, Caitlin, but I don't think I'll ever forget. Thank you for explaining this all to me. Now, I think I'd better go."

She stood up, fighting back a crushing pain in her chest, and walked to the door. She didn't look back, or stop to say any further goodbyes. She just walked out, into the corridor and down the hall, her steps getting faster as she went.

No, she could never, ever forget.

48

"You can stay, if you want," Eimear said, sitting down beside Ciara. Ciara couldn't quite read the look on her face – was it a genuine offer or merely obligation? Sure, the pair of them had bonded on the stairs the other night but that didn't mean they were friends as such.

And even if they were, that didn't mean she wanted to stay and come face to face with the smug wee bastard that was Ben Quinn. Knee to bollocks with him, maybe, but face to face not so much.

"It's okay. I told my mum I wouldn't be long," Ciara lied and sat up straight.

"Well, if you're sure, but it might be a bit of *craic*. We're just going to watch a DVD or something. Ben's bringing some cider he smuggled from his granny's shop." Eimear immediately blushed. Ciara could almost see the lightbulb ping above Eimear's head as it dawned on her that gossiping about pilfered goods from the local shop might not be safe in the present company.

"It's okay. I won't tell," Ciara reassured her, falling short of adding that she doubted very much Mrs Quinn would believe any wrongdoing of her precious grandson anyway. That fecker could be caught out of his head on cheap booze, lying in a pool of his own puke and his granny would put it down to a bad cold or a touch of hay fever.

"Thanks," Eimear said.

"Don't worry about it."

"You used to hang about with Ben and his friends, didn't you?" Eimear asked.

"Aye, but not in ages."

"What happened? Did you fall out?"

"No, I just grew up."

Eimear bristled at the insinuation that she wasn't a grown-up. "Yeah, they said you were a bit snooty."

Ciara choked. She was as far from snooty as they came. For the love of God, she was seventeen, had a baby and worked in a corner shop. Where could anyone get the notion she had even an ounce of snootiness about her?

This wasn't going well at all. Ruth had entrusted her to check on Eimear and here they were on the brink of an all-out girly bitch fight.

"Look, I just wanted to warn you, be careful of Ben Quinn. He's not the big shakes you think he is."

"What do you mean by that?" Eimear asked, instantly enraged.

"I mean be careful."

Matthew looked at them, mildly alarmed, and Ciara took a deep breath. She wouldn't push this. The last thing she wanted to do was get Matthew caught up in the middle of this but she hadn't reckoned for Eimear's teenage brattishness and her determination to push things to the limit.

"If you have something to say, Ciara, then say it. And don't tell me it's nothing because you clearly think me and my friends aren't as good as you."

"Look, just leave it," Ciara replied, walking to the kitchen so that Matthew wouldn't be a witness to just how ugly this conversation could become.

If Eimear pushed her any further, she would tell her what a fecking gobshite Ben Quinn was and take the smug look off her face once and for all.

Eimear followed her. "I will not leave it," she raged, stamping her foot. "Don't you go telling me to be careful when you don't want to tell me why. That's just pathetic. You're just pathetic."

"You know what's pathetic?" Ciara replied, her temper flaring, "You running around after Ben Quinn like he is something special. He's nothing special at all."

"So you're jealous? He turned you down and you're jealous because he likes me now."

"You couldn't be more wrong if you tried. He didn't turn me down – and I have a baby to prove it."

"You're making that up," Eimear seethed.

"No, I'm not. Ella is very much real – not an ounce of her is made up. I have the dirty nappies to prove it."

"Ha ha, very funny."

"It's not meant to be funny, Eimear, but you wanted the truth and I'm telling it to you."

"You're lying!" Eimear's face had gone a strange shade of red.

Matthew was watching with a mixture of fear and amusement from the door.

"Why would I lie? What have I to gain from lying? There's only one person who has ever lied about this before and it's Ben Quinn."

"Well, he has nothing to gain from lying either," Eimear replied defiantly.

"Apart from remaining the golden balls of Rathinch, not

having his granny beat the head off him and not actually having to deal with the responsibility of a baby, you mean?"

Eimear's mouth opened and shut. Ciara could almost hear the cogs whirr as she tried to come up with a witty response. She obviously couldn't and closed her mouth, crossing her arms in a huff and blowing her fringe from her face.

"I'm not lying," Ciara replied, more softly this time. "And I'm not trying to be a bitch. I wish someone had warned me before I got involved with him."

"I'm not a little kid and I don't need warning."

"I didn't think I did either. I thought I knew everything," Ciara said, starting to feel sorry for Eimear. After all, she remembered all too well herself how it felt when Ben lost his shiny halo and turned out to be an utter prick. "Can we talk about it? Please. If you still don't believe me after, then fair enough. I'll go and we'll never mention it again."

"S'ppose," Eimear said opening a bottle of WKD.

In for a penny, Ciara thought as she lifted one herself and started to drink.

"We were kind of going out. I suppose everyone knew that, but Ben, well, he thinks he is one of the cool kids and he always toned it down around his friends. When we were together, just the two of us, things were different. We would go for walks along the beach and he would leave notes in my locker in school. I thought he was the perfect boy and he made me feel really special."

Ciara was aware that sounded really cheesy but she could think of no other way to describe it. At the time she had felt a little like Sandy from *Grease* and Ben had been her Danny. It was all she could do to stop telling Eimear he was dreamy and at the time her chills multiplied every time she set her eyes on him.

"I wouldn't have slept with him if I didn't think he loved

me," she went on. "I don't just sleep with anyone. He's the only person I ever slept with. And I didn't rush into it. I thought we had something special. He told me he loved me."

Eimear's face softened and Ciara could see traces of Ruth's compassion in her eyes.

Taking a deep breath, she continued: "When I found out I was pregnant I nearly died. I thought Mum was going to kill me, or throw me out of the house. She's a single parent and she always said she wanted more for me. I was disappointing her in the biggest way – but I thought, well, if Ben stands by me it won't be so bad. And honestly, I never even thought there was a chance he wouldn't stand by me."

"If youse were so in love, why didn't everyone know about it?"

Ciara could see that Eimear was grasping at straws in the same way she had grasped at straws when Ben had turned her away.

"I told you. In front of his friends it was all cool and casual. But when we were alone . . ."

"And he didn't want to know about the baby?"

Ciara shook her head. "Not a bit. He told me that if I tried to tell anyone the baby was his he would either deny ever having slept with me or tell everyone I'd slept around. That would have been worse."

"But how would it? He would have got what was coming to him eventually?"

"But not before me and Mum, and Ella too, had been dragged through the mud. I couldn't put my mum through that."

"You shouldn't have had to put yourself through it."

"I didn't think I had a choice."

Eimear gazed unseeingly at the clock on the wall. "Why now then? Why are you telling me now? If you wanted to keep this to yourself, why not just keep it to yourself?"

"Because why should I keep it to myself? I've kept it to myself for long enough. He made me think I had to. But Eimear, I don't want you going through the same thing. You don't deserve it, and neither does your mum."

Eimear sighed and put her head in her hands. "I don't know what to think," she muttered.

"Look, I'm telling you the truth. Think about it and be careful, that's all. You don't know what you're dealing with here."

* * *

Ruth decided to get some fresh air – and if she was honest with herself she wanted to allow Liam and Detta some alone time. It wasn't so much that she felt like a spare part, it was more that with the haze of several glasses of Cosmopolitan she was feeling a little bit like a fairy godmother. All she was missing was the big frilly frock and a wand. And maybe a tiara. She really fancied owning a tiara. When she married James all she wore was a single flower in her hair. And a dress, of course. She smiled to herself. A tiara would nice – one subtle and scattered with diamonds, and maybe pearls which would glitter when she turned her head. One day, maybe.

She walked out of the bar and stood by the river breathing in the night air. It was cold but the alcohol had warmed her bones so she didn't really care. Liam and Detta had been chatting nicely as she left. It was nice, she thought, there was no awkwardness between them at all. They were just like old, very dear, friends. Wouldn't it be a lovely success story for the group if they fell in love?

She would buy a hat to wear to the wedding, she resolved. She'd never had a hat before – well, not one that wasn't home-knitted or from the Aran shop in the village. She quite fancied something with feathers and beads.

Maybe she could be bridesmaid and wear a tiara? Ah, now that would be just perfect.

She was still smiling as she walked along the riverfront. She was glad that Detta had talked her into coming tonight. It would have been so easy to stay at home and hide. Admittedly the thick layer of make-up had helped, but she was starting to feel more confident now and if tonight was anything to go by, she had some chance of finally, finally starting to enjoy her life.

If she wasn't conscious of looking like a complete eejit she would have had a wee run and kicked her legs up with joy.

She looked up and saw a male walker and his dog approach. "All right?" he smiled and she grinned.

"I'm just fine," she said, "Absolutely, bloody fine."

* * *

"Do you think she'll be okay out there on her own?" Liam asked, gesturing his head towards the glass doors. He could see Ruth standing staring into the river and was mildly concerned she was going to throw herself in.

"She's fine," Detta said with a smile. "In fact, I'd go as far as to say she is more fine than we've seen her yet."

Liam looked out again. He had to admit she had been in good form that night. He wasn't sure what he had been expecting. If he was honest he was half expecting to see her sitting pale, wan and bruised, as she had been the last time he saw her.

He was quite impressed to see her dolled up to the nines, her hair primped and preened and her make-up done. He felt quite the ladies' man walking into the bar with both her and Detta, and to have Niamh waiting for him. Even though he hadn't been able to drink, he had been having a blast. And apart from worrying if Ruth was going to throw herself into the Foyle, he was very much enjoying having Detta all to himself. Perhaps, though, he should trust Detta's judgement. She hadn't been wrong about much, if anything, before. Sure she was a little different – a bit more out there than the usual residents of Rathinch – but that wasn't necessarily a bad thing. Being different from Laura was definitely a good thing, in his eyes.

"You've been a breath of fresh air, you know," he said looking at her.

"Don't be daft."

"I'm not being daft. It's no secret I didn't want anything to do with your single parents' group, but in hindsight I'm glad my mother forced me to go."

"I'm glad your mother forced you to go too," Detta said with a warm smile. "But you have to realise that the group is only what it is because of the members. It's nothing to do with me and my hand-drawn posters, and my silly little letter-writing. It's because you all came along and gave it a go."

"You made that easy," he said. God, he realised, now was his chance. He could say something and risk ruining the group dynamic but maybe be happy, or he could keep his feelings inside but regret it.

He looked at her, smiling at him.

"You know how I feel," he said, knowing in that instant that she did.

She nodded slowly.

"I don't expect you to feel the same. And I won't hold it against you if you don't, but I couldn't say nothing. You have to be stupid not to realise anyway, but you know, in case you needed any clarity . . ."

"I didn't."

Shit, he thought. Didn't was a negative word. It could mean no good. He felt his face start to blush. Who said women were the only ones who got themselves into a stupid old state by declaring their feelings? It wasn't like this with Laura. She had pursued him. Not that he was pursuing Detta as such – that sounded slightly sordid and maybe a little stalkerish. No, he just liked her and he hoped, really hoped, that she liked him back.

"I like you too," Detta said, reaching out and stroking his cheek. "I can't say I'm not torn because there should probably be some professional line here that I'm meant to stay behind, but you've given me a purpose again, Liam. And I don't just mean the group, and our meetings. I mean so much more." She leaned in, slightly woozy with drink and kissed Liam square on the lips, except this time he knew that she wasn't doing it to feed the gossipmongers of Rathinch. She was doing it just because she wanted to. So he kissed her back, just because he wanted to.

* * *

Niamh stood in the lift and got her breath back. Her heart was thumping. She couldn't help but wonder if she had chickened out and there was part of her – the arse-kicking shoes part of her – that was tempted to turn around, go back and clock Caitlin around the face just for good measure. But what good would it do? It wouldn't change anything except to get her a conviction for assault and besides, there was a high chance it would ruin her manicure.

More than that, however, was the fact that she simply didn't want to any more. It wasn't that she wasn't angry, or that she no longer felt betrayed. She had just seen Caitlin looking slightly pathetic and could tell that despite the scene being set for a night of high romance, Caitlin was still a pathetic creature who was pining for a man who was never really hers in the first place. In many ways, she had a lot in common with Niamh. There was no way Niamh could make her feel any more pain than she was already feeling and, she realised, she actually didn't want to. The lift stopped and the doors slid open. She straightened herself up and walked out, straight – once again – into Kevin.

He was standing with a smug grin on his face and a bunch of shabby garage flowers.

"Niamh," he blustered drunkenly. "Thank God you've finally left her. You know she called me and said to hold off for a bit but I thought you would be there all night."

"No," Niamh replied, shocked at just how low Caitlin had sunk. "She's all yours."

"Night, Niamh," Kevin replied with a smile and walked into the lift and Niamh walked out. Now, she felt even more sorry for Caitlin than ever as she walked away from the apartment block towards the riverfront.

"Niamh!"

Ruth called out to her and she looked up.

"Are you okay?"

"I'm fine, just fine. Are you okay? What are you doing out here? You'll catch your death!"

"I'm fine too, don't worry about me. Did it go okay?"

Niamh shrugged her shoulders. "Well, I know more now. Not sure if that's a good thing or a bad thing."

"So you didn't kill her then?" Ruth asked with a friendly smile.

"No, somehow the murderous urge left me when I saw her."

"Well, that's a good thing. You know, spending the rest of your years behind bars wouldn't be much fun. I mean, I know Rathinch isn't much better but at least you get the sea air." Ruth raised her eyebrows and smiled again.

"And the chips are nice," Niamh mused.

"And you know, there's always a steady supply of Aran jumpers for when it gets chilly."

"And the most impressive variety of spuds known to man in the corner shop."

"And you have that lovely house, with your gorgeous kitchen island of dreams."

Niamh laughed. "Actually, I'm getting rid of it. If you want it, it's yours."

"No," Ruth said with mock horror. "You can't get rid of it!"

"Oh I'll get another one. I just want to get rid of that fecking marble monstrosity. Can I let you into a secret?"

Ruth nodded.

"Well, it was only a month ago, when I was cleaning it, that I realised something."

"What? That it's a thing of beauty?"

"No. The marble – it's the same as Seán's gravestone."

Ruth's eyes widened. She was unsure how to respond.

Niamh looked at her and couldn't help but laugh.

"Oh don't worry. It gave me a shock at the time, but now I see the funny side. He would die – well, again anyway – if he knew he was laid beneath a slab of the finest kitchen marble." Niamh threw her head back and laughed.

Ruth paused for a second, not sure if the laugh was of genuine mirth or mild hysteria. She watched, looking for a hint that it was okay to laugh too.

"It *is* funny," Niamh laughed, "and I've discovered Flash kitchen cleaner is perfect for keeping both your worktops and your gravestones gleaming."

Ruth was gone then – she couldn't help but snort along.

"So if you want it, it's yours," Niamh reiterated.

"You know, I don't think I would have room for a kitchen in my kitchen if I had that in there, but I appreciate the offer. Just promise me you'll have a farewell party for it so I can come and pay my last respects?"

"I promise," Niamh said, linking arms with Ruth and walking back towards the bar.

* * *

The expression "bogging into each other" is often overused, Ruth thought, as she looked at Liam and Detta – for all intents and purposes bogging into each other.

The expression should be one of passion, lust and desire and it was very clear to her now that all those things were there in abundance.

It was oddly nice to watch and disturbing at the same time. Ruth thought it was a bit like walking in on your parents having sex – except of course Liam and Detta weren't having sex and they were very much in a public bar and not at all in the privacy of their own bedroom.

But they were clearly lost in the moment.

"Should we get a bucket of water?" Niamh asked, with a wicked glint in her eye.

"Ah, sure leave them to it. The only problem with me is jealousy," Ruth answered and then, realising how she could be misconstrued, added: "Not that I fancy Liam, or Detta for that matter – but I could just do with a bit of that passion for myself."

"God, I think I'm off men for life," Niamh said.

"Never say never," Ruth said, guiding her friend towards the bar. "Not all men are bastards, you know."

"I know. We've just been very, very unlucky."

"Ain't that the truth?" Ruth said, ordering two glasses of champagne from the handsome barman.

"Then again, without my bastard I wouldn't have the twins," Niamh said.

"And I suppose I wouldn't have my lot either – although sometimes with Eimear, well, I think I would be better off," Ruth smiled.

"You don't mean that?"

"Of course not – but let me tell you, missus, when your two reach the teenage years you will be grateful for that big house of yours. Take refuge in one end and lock yourself in till they are eighteen. It will save you a lot of trouble."

The barman – a handsome, gorgeously groomed man in his mid-twenties – put down the two glasses in front of the ladies and smiled warmly at them.

"You know," Niamh said, "I think a toast is in order."

Ruth lifted her glass.

"To our bastards –" Niamh started.

"And all who sailed in them!"

49

There are defining moments in your life, Liam thought, and defining kisses. His first kiss – an awkward fumbling affair when he was fourteen – was one. He felt so grown-up afterwards, but also mildly embarrassed and paranoid. He thought he had done it right, but he would never really know. His first kiss with Laura was another. It was as if it had been plucked from a Mills & Boon novel, as they stood under the pelting rain in the main street of Rathinch and he brushed the hair from her eyes before leaning in to kiss her.

This kiss – this moment now in the crowded, pretentious bar in Derry would be another. It reminded him what kisses should be like. It reminded him that they should be passionate and tender at the same time. It reminded him that a kiss could say more than words ever could and that a kiss was best when it was not a perfunctory peck on the lips or cheek at the end of a day. In their latter years, he realised, he and Laura both had perfected the art of the cat's-arse pout. A quick touch of the very tips of their lips without even the remotest chance breath would pass between the two or that a tongue could slip in. He had, he realised with shock, had more passionate kisses with his mother in the last four years. Pushing that thought to the back of his mind as quickly as it had made its way to the front, he sat back and smiled. This kiss, which had broken apart just a few seconds before, made him feel alive.

"That," Detta said, "was worth waiting for."

"Yes," he replied, lost for words but not worrying about it. He knew then that with Detta he could be quiet without worrying what was going on in her head, and without questioning how she felt for him.

All the years when he thought he had his perfect match were so glaringly flawed now. This, he thought, was what a perfect match felt like.

"Well," Detta said with a smile, "I'm thinking this is going to be the talk of Rathinch."

"Let them talk," Liam said. "Anyhow it beats them talking about Ruth and her fecker of a husband, or Niamh and her great tragedy, or even young Ciara and the father of her baby. This is a nice thing for them to talk about."

"You know what, you're right. Let them chat about us and give everyone else a break for a while."

"So this," Liam said, looking into her eyes, "is something more than just a kiss, isn't it?"

"I hope so," Detta said with a smile. "I really hope so." She locked eyes with him and they kissed again.

There weren't quite fireworks but there was a whoop of approval from both Ruth and Niamh who had raised a glass to their friends.

* * *

"So, we really should be getting back, shouldn't we?" Ruth said as the barman cleared up around them.

"Before they throw us out, you mean?" Detta laughed.

"I do think they want to go home." Ruth looked around at the almost empty bar and the look of exhaustion on the faces of the bar staff.

"I suppose we should be making a move," Liam said. "Niamh, can we drop you somewhere?"

"Actually, yes, could I cadge a lift with you? My mum will keep the twins here in Derry and there's something I need to take care of back home."

Detta raised her eyebrows. "Are you sure you're okay?" she asked for the twenty-fifth time.

"I'm fine. I just feel like having my own space tonight . . . and starting moving on with my life."

"Right, well, there's plenty of room in the car as long as you ladies promise not to get too rowdy on me."

"We promise we'll be good," Detta, Ruth and Niamh chorused and laughing they walked back to the car – each with a smile on her face for a very different reason.

* * *

"I'm a big enough girl to handle this," Eimear said as Ciara left.

"I know you are," Ciara said with false confidence. She was pretty sure as soon as Ben arrived with his big, dark eyes, his full lips and his floppy hair Eimear would be a lost cause. She knew she herself had been a lost cause on many occasions – hence her ending up the stick at fifteen.

"Look, I'm off now, I've Ella to deal with. But take care."

"I will," Eimear said, offering her an awkward hug before closing the door.

Ciara pulled her coat around her and headed home where Lorraine was waiting for her.

"Did you have a nice evening, love?" Lorraine asked, looking up from the TV.

"It was okay," Ciara said, flopping down on the sofa in

international teenage sign language for "No, actually, it was a bit rubbish and I want to talk."

"Really?" Lorraine asked.

"No. I told Eimear about Ben, and he's on his way there now and she'll either put her sensible head on and believe me and tell him to take a running jump or he'll convince her I'm the biggest slapper in town and I'll be a laughing stock."

"Pet," Lorraine said, hugging her daughter, "I know it's hard but we know the truth. The people who really matter know the truth – and those who don't believe you, don't matter. This is a small town. People like to talk and make up their own stories. It gets them through the day – after all, there is feck all else to do round these parts in the winter."

"That's not true. There's the cinema."

"That shows films that everyone went to see in Letterkenny three months ago? Look, pet, you can't control other people's actions, only your reaction to them. Hold your head high and hope that Eimear has the sense her mother gave her. Apart from that, there's not much you can do, love."

Ciara hugged her mum back. "I know. Thanks, Mum. Now I'm off to bed."

She climbed the stairs and looked into the cot where Ella was doing her best starfish impression. Her fists were clenched tightly and her lips pursed together as she was lost in a dream.

"Bugger them all," Ciara whispered in the dark. "You're worth it."

* * *

"Right, m'lady, you're home," Liam said as he pulled up outside Niamh's house.

"Thanking you kindly," she smiled, now tired and more than a little drunk.

"How about I come in and keep you company?" Detta asked gently.

"I'm fine," Niamh said, tripping as she climbed out of the car. "Damn kick-arse boots. I've only gone and managed to kick my own arse," she said as she collapsed in giggles.

Detta looked at Liam, who in turn looked at Ruth, who in turn looked back at Detta again. "Yes, I think you staying over would be a great idea," Ruth said and Detta nodded, smiling warmly at Liam and rubbing his hand gently.

"Right, well, thanks for a night to remember," she said adding, "although I'm not sure it's done just yet," with a wink before linking arms with Niamh and walking up through the front gardens.

Niamh noticed the wink, but said nothing. She was sure there would be more to this night yet. She had made yet another momentous decision on the way home. She couldn't describe it but seeing Caitlin – how pathetic she was – had helped. That probably made her a bad person – to take some ounce of joy from someone else's misery – but right now, hobbling up her driveway with her killer boots killing her feet, she didn't care.

"You don't need to stay, you know," she said again as she fumbled with her key at the door.

"I know, but I've been busting my arse to get a good nosy round this place for ages now so this is the perfect chance," Detta deadpanned.

"Really? You could have just called round any time – it's not that special. Or should I say, it is special but it's not really my taste."

She opened the door and wiped her feet on the rug to reduce the risk of sliding on her rear end along the marble hall.

"Not the most practical in Ireland, when it's always raining," she said to Detta.

"Yes, but it is a pretty."

"All about looking good," she said, keeping any hint of bitterness from her voice. She had liked it at the time – she realised. She had been just as caught up in Seán's show-house dream as he had been at the time. That was long before she realised there were more important things in life than Italian marble floors and SMEG fridge freezers.

"You know what," she said, walking through the house to the garden where Liam had left his tools, "feck looking good. I'm going to change a lot more about this house and make it the house I want."

"Good for you," Detta said with a smile.

"Wanna help?" Niamh said, a wicked thought forming in her mind.

"Sure."

"Here," she said handing her a hammer while she lifted a sledgehammer from the pile of tools. "Feck me, this is heavy."

"Niamh . . . are you sure?"

"As sure as eggs are eggs. You don't have room for a kitchen island in your house, do you?"

"I've barely room for a kitchen table."

"Grand job, follow me."

Niamh, still swaying slightly in her boots, walked back to the kitchen and lifted the sledgehammer as high as she could and swung it at the island.

She hoped it would split in half, in a dramatic gesture. Instead it barely registered a crack – but nonetheless there was one there which she could see if she looked close enough.

"Tomorrow," she said, sitting down, "fancy helping me choose the Shaker style kitchen I always wanted?"

"You're on," said Detta, almost too afraid to say no.

"Grand. Now for the grand tour."

* * *

Ruth's heart started to quicken as soon as they pulled up outside her house. Her front door was lying open – at two in the morning. Immediately she thought that James must be there – he must have finally flipped – and Liam had barely time to stop the car before she had jumped out and was running up the front path at full pelt.

"Ruth! Ruth! Calm down," Liam shouted after her.

But she didn't even register what he was saying. She just wanted to get inside and make sure her children were okay – she pleaded with God or whoever was listening to make them okay. The lights were blazing in the hall and in the living room – but there was no sign of the children. She called out – a strangled half-sob – and her heart almost stopped when the kitchen door creaked open.

Liam caught up with her, and rested his hands on her shoulders to try and soothe her. She shook him off and broke into the ugliest of sobs when Eimear – perfectly okay and utterly confused – looked at her stricken face and asked: "Jesus, Mum, what has happened?"

"The door . . ." Ruth stuttered, "the door was open. The lights were on. Was he here? Was your daddy here?"

"No. I had some friends round. That's all."

"Oh God," Ruth said, sagging with relief – almost swooning into Liam's arms.

"Your mother got a terrible fright," he said.

"Because the door was open?" Eimear seemed incredulous.

"Yes," Ruth said weakly.

"I'm sorry, Mum," Eimear said. "I didn't think."

"No, no, you didn't."

"But, Mum, I'm sorry. I've had a bad night too, you know," she said and burst into tears.

Liam stood, very bravely Ruth thought, looking bemused

but keeping his composure. She had to admire his uncanny knack of coping with hysterical women.

"Look, why don't you two have a wee chat? I'll head on and leave you to it and you can get in touch if you need anything."

"Thanks, Liam," Ruth said, embarrassed now that the shock had worn off.

"Any time," he offered.

Ruth followed Eimear into the kitchen and tried not to lose her cool at the sight of the empty alcopop bottles on the table or the fact that it seemed that every single one of her bowls had been taken from the cupboard and filled with crisps – which also seemed to be crushed into the floor.

"Mum," Eimear said, her eyes wet with tears, "I know I shouldn't have, but I had a few friends over tonight and it all went wrong. Ciara was over earlier and she told me about Ben so when he came I got him alone for a few minutes and thought, well, I'd just ask him outright. And then he called me every name under the sun and told everyone I was a liar. But I'm not a liar and I told them as much and then he left, telling me I'd regret it."

"Oh sweetheart," Ruth said, hugging her daughter, "no, you are not a liar and it's about time that wee fecker was exposed for the shite he is. Better you know now than stick with him for eighteen years and end up like me and your dad."

"But I did love him," Eimear said.

"I know, sweetheart. Sadly we can't always choose who we fall in love with but I promise you, with all my heart, you will look back on this one day and breathe a huge sigh of relief."

Eimear looked at her mother for a while, a thought obviously forming in her head.

"Are you glad Dad's gone?"

"Absolutely. I only wish he had gone sooner, before you and your brothers got hurt."

"I wish he'd gone before you got hurt, Mum."

"Well, we could wish all night but it won't change anything. The important thing is that he is gone now and he won't be hurting us again."

"I'm glad, Mum. He's my dad and I love him – but I don't like him. I don't like him one bit."

"I understand, sweetheart," Ruth said, her heart breaking a little to hear her little girl say she disliked her father so. Then again, he did kind of have it coming to him. She couldn't feel sorry for him – if she started to feel sorry for him then she would be starting to let him back in again and she was fecked if that fecker was getting anywhere near her emotions again.

She might not have given her daughter the best role model so far – but she bloody well was going to now – with one small exception.

"Open me one of those alcopops," she said and Eimear tried not to faint with shock. "And yes, go on and have one yourself."

Eimear did as she was told and Ruth lifted her bottle, clinking it against her daughter's.

"Onwards and upwards, Eimear! It's us against the world."

* * *

Liam could not help but smile as he opened the door and walked into his living room. He opened the fridge and took out his first beer of the night. As he sat down he replayed the evening – the whole gorgeous evening – over and over again. Things were finally on the up for him. And he went to bed for the first time in a long time without a gaping feeling of loneliness.

He woke to the smells and sounds of bacon sizzling. Sometimes he loved his mother and her insistence on a good breakfast more than anything on earth. Getting up, he slipped into jeans and T-shirt and padded down the stairs where he was met by two very inquisitive sets of eyes.

"Morning, you two," he said.

"Morning, yourself," Agnes replied, smiling and turning back to the frying pan. Poppy turned her attention back to her colouring-in but Liam could sense something was definitely up.

"Did you have a good night, Daddy?" Poppy asked and he wondered how it had reached the stage where he had to explain himself to his five-year-old daughter.

"It was fun, yes." He poured a cup of coffee and sat down.

"Was Detta there?" Poppy asked and Liam noticed his mother's shoulders start to shake.

"What on earth is going on with you two? Giggling like schoolgirls! Yes, Detta was there," he said, feeling the colour rise in his cheeks. It wasn't possible that they knew what had happened last night, he reminded himself, trying to keep his cool.

"She's a nice lady," Agnes said, turning to dish up the breakfast.

"Yes, she is," Liam replied coolly.

"And she's pretty, Daddy, isn't she?" Poppy smiled.

"Yes, she is."

"And you kind of love her, don't you, Daddy?"

"Poppy, eat your breakfast." But he couldn't hide his smile nor could he ignore the smiles on Agnes and Poppy's faces. Could it be he had just done the impossible and found a woman his mother actually approved of?

50

"I'll have some lunch ready for you at about one," Lorraine said as Ciara put on her coat and headed for the door.

"Thanks, Mum."

"It won't be anything fancy, mind, just a tin of soup or the like. Miss Ella here can have some too."

Ciara smiled and waved at her baby daughter and blew a kiss to her mum.

She was in great form. In her bag she had her application form for the night classes at the college, ready to go in the post. Niamh had also promised to pop into the shop at some stage in the morning to fill her in on the goings-on at the big confrontation in Derry. There was nothing like a bit of scandal to make the day go in quicker – maybe that is why Mrs Quinn was such a gossipmonger.

Stepping out into the street, she couldn't help but wonder what Eimear had done the night before when Ben showed up. Perhaps she should have stayed around but she knew Eimear had to make her own decisions about Ben. She'd done her bit and whatever happened now was beyond her control.

She would concentrate on things that were in her control –

like building on her relationship with her mother or her caring for her daughter or making sure she would do as well as she could at college so that she could eventually work somewhere a little more exotic than the corner shop.

With a smile on her face she pushed open the door of the shop and came face to face with Mrs Quinn who clearly – very clearly – wasn't having nearly as good a day as Ciara. Her face was like thunder – even her frown lines had frown lines which gave her the appearance of a Shar Pei chewing a wasp.

"Morning," Ciara offered, slipping off her coat.

"I think you won't be needed today, Ciara, so just put that coat back on."

She didn't know what to think – either Mrs Quinn was having some sort of mental-illness episode or she had done something to piss her off. In no other circumstances was she ever, ever told she wouldn't be needed. There was always something to be done. There were price stickers to be peeled off old goods, there were tins of pea and ham soup to dust down so they didn't look as if they had been there forever and there was the mouldy dairy cabinet to clear out with a bucket of water and some cheap thin bleach.

"Are you sure?"

"As sure as I've ever been. I don't want liars working for me."

The penny dropped, there and then and Ciara felt tears spring to her eyes. But she was not going to cry in front of this baggage. I can't control what other people do, only how I react, she reminded herself.

"I'm not a liar," she said, as firmly as she could.

"Then why are you telling everyone that my Ben is your baby's father?" Mrs Quinn's nose turned up at the very thought Ciara could ever have come anywhere near to being a member of her family.

"Because he is. It's not a lie and if everyone refuses to believe me there is a very easy way to prove that he is. We'll get a DNA test – I'll even pay for it – because, Mrs Quinn, I'm no tart and your grandson is no angel. Now if you wish to believe him over me, that's fine. I understand you have a loyalty to him more than you ever would to me – but I can promise you now that I have never lied to you, or anyone. Now I'll go home, but you are making a mistake and you will be the one with egg all over your face when this comes out."

Mrs Quinn's mouth flapped open and shut and her eyes darted around the shop, trying to find something that would rescue her or give her a witty response. Ciara felt her heart thump in her chest – she had never stood up to Mrs Quinn, ever, and she was, in all probability, now out of a job but she wasn't going to sneak out the door as if she was at fault. Slipping her coat back on, she lifted her bag and made for the door.

"Ciara," Mrs Quinn said, and Ciara looked around waiting for the final barbed remark. "Take the day off. Come back tomorrow and we'll talk."

Ciara knew she wasn't going to get an apology. There was more chance of Mrs Quinn running off with a teenage toy boy than ever openly admitting she was wrong about anything. But her gesture – small as it was – was proof enough that somewhere deep down in her heart she knew that there was indeed the possibility that her grandson was about as pure as the muck-ridden slush.

* * *

The doors of the community centre swung open and Liam was first to arrive, just as Detta was putting on the kettle and tipping the chocolate biscuits onto the cracked melamine plate with the faded blue rim.

She looked up at him with a warm smile and he felt something in him light up. He hadn't seen much of her since Friday night but they had spoken on the phone and she had met him for coffee the day before in the Country Kitchen. They had walked back to the builder's yard hand in hand and the rumour was, from one of the boys in the office, that Laura had heard all about it and wasn't a bit impressed.

The thing was, though, Liam wasn't a bit bothered what Laura thought about it – or him or anything. She had made her decisions – ones she was happy to stand by even knowing what a monster her chosen paramour was.

He had admitted to both Agnes and Poppy that Detta was his special new friend after their conversation on Saturday morning. While he wasn't normally one to lose the run of himself and shout his secret love from the rooftops he knew this was different. He already knew both Agnes and Poppy approved and he knew that Detta wouldn't try to rush things and they could play this the perfect way so that no one would get hurt. Not that he believed for even one second Detta could hurt him.

Looking at her warm eyes now, her smile, he knew that she wouldn't ever hurt him, or Poppy. He doubted Detta O'Neill could ever hurt anyone.

"Hey, you," she said.

He loved the way she uttered the word "you". The way she said it made it feel more special than any honey, sugar, lamby-poo in the world.

"Hey, yourself," he said, smiling from ear to ear and walking towards her – kissing her gently on the mouth before pulling back. "Is it slightly unethical now that I'm coming here for support when you are the one helping me piece my life together outside of this community centre?"

"We're friends first, Liam," she said, lifting his hand and

kissing it gently. "We're all friends and blast this group, we're always going to be friends – so bugger what anyone but us – and Niamh, Ruth and Ciara – think."

"Did someone take my name in vain?" Niamh asked, closing the door behind her and heading for her seat, second from left in their "semi-circle of trust".

"Not at all, we were just talking about this – us – our, erm, friendship," Liam muttered.

"Couldn't have happened to two nicer people," Niamh said warmly.

"Bless your heart," Detta said.

"Nonsense," Niamh said with a wave of her hand. "Besides I like living my life vicariously through you two at the moment."

"Lady, you have your own share of dramas," Detta said, sitting down at the front of the group.

"Nothing that a great builder and some new gorgeous worktops can't cure," she smiled.

"Yes, I heard about your DIY on Friday night," Liam said.

"Grand. I was hoping you would so you don't have a fit when I decide to double the amount of work I want you to do on the house."

"Double it, or triple it. I don't mind."

The door creaked open and they heard a raucous giggle erupt.

Ruth entered, followed by Ciara and then by Lorraine pushing baby Ella who was soundly asleep in her pram.

"We thought the more, the merrier," Ruth smiled.

"I even bought extra biscuits," Lorraine offered.

"And Ella's been fed, watered and changed and isn't likely to wake up," Ciara added.

"Come in, take a seat and have a cuppa. All are welcome," Detta smiled. "Good thing I always have a spare supply of pens and notepads."

As she handed them out, she knew that tonight's session would be different to any other she had. Her group members already looked completely different to the people who had walked through these doors two months ago. And she knew herself she had undergone the most tremendous of changes.

While she looked at Ruth. Liam, Niamh and Ciara she didn't see people searching for their identity and hiding their secrets any more. She saw people who were getting on with things and finding confidence in themselves that they never even knew existed before.

She knew this because that evening – when she had looked in the mirror before she came out – she had seen a transformed woman staring back at her. One day she would admit to them how they had saved her, just as much as she had saved them.

51

"When was the last time you enjoyed being in the rain?" she asked, stretching her arms wide and tipping her face towards the sky, allowing the cold rain to batter off her face.

Unsure what to think – and wondering if she had finally flipped her lid, Liam answered. "I much prefer the warmth of a fire, a nice rug and some wine. Let's go."

"Don't be such a killjoy, Liam. Feel it, it's amazing – when was the last time you allowed it just to wash over you before running for cover?"

"Not sure I ever have," he replied with a shrug of his shoulders, pulling his jacket closer around him and wiping the rain from his face.

"'Course you have!" Detta replied with a smile. "I bet when you were a wee thing you were always begging to be out in the rain. I bet you liked nothing more than getting your wellies on and jumping in puddles and not giving a ha'penny damn about whether you were soaked through to your skin."

Liam thought of all the times Agnes rolled her eyes to heaven and ordered him into his pyjamas as he walked into the house like a drowned rat and he smiled. Of course, he always got a good dose of castor oil for his troubles too.

"We forget it," she shouted as she walked down the beach spinning in the pouring rain. "We forget to enjoy the small things. We forget to run in the rain, and jump in puddles and laugh until we almost puke."

"I don't know if we forget it or we just grow up," Liam said, slipping his arm around her waist and walking on. He was starting to enjoy the rain now – walking here with Detta along the beach as the sunlight faded into the cold winter evening. The Christmas lights were glistening in the shop windows and he couldn't wait for the big day.

They were all – every last Loony, their kids and even Agnes too – going up to Niamh's house to celebrate her new kitchen and her new life and each of them was bringing something towards the dinner. Niamh had offered to cook but her cooking skills were mostly confined to ringing a caterer and ordering whatever they recommended. She had taken some persuading to allow her friends to contribute to the big dinner, but eventually she had caved in – especially when Lorraine had offered to bring her speciality cheesecake. Most of all though Liam was looking forward to spending it with Detta who had slotted into his life as if she was always meant to be there.

"Growing up is largely overrated," Detta said, her face clouding over. It wasn't the first time he had noticed this sadness in her eyes but he had been afraid to push her – in case he was in some way the source of that sadness.

"Are you okay?" he probed, gently, looking into her eyes.

"This time of year, it brings it back," she said.

"I'll never push you to tell me, Detta, but I'm here when you want to talk."

"I know," she said. "And I should tell you, but I'm not sure how you might react."

"Nothing you could tell me could shock me. Unless, you know, you tell me you once were a man, because that would kind of freak me out. But I don't think that's the case." He smiled softly and she laughed.

"I had a son," she blurted. "Patrick," she whispered his name as if it were a prayer.

"He was with me for thirteen years. And then he died, three years ago now. It was cancer and it was quick." She paused, allowing the words to start to sink in. "I spent a lot of time after that in Dublin, trying to find some hint of him. You know, I went to all the places we used to go – did all the things we used to do, hoping, just hoping to feel his presence, but it was like he was gone entirely. I couldn't find any trace of him – no matter how hard or how long I looked."

"I'm sorry," Liam said, shocked to his core by this revelation. He knew there was something more to Detta, he just never knew it could be something as serious as this.

"Don't be. We had thirteen wonderful, wonderful years filled with such love and happiness. He wasn't with me as long as I would have liked him to have been – I'd have never let him go if I could have got away with it – but he was amazing. You'd have loved him."

"If he was anything like you . . ."

"Oh, he was the total opposite – a wise head on young shoulders, always laughing at me and telling me to grow up. Sometimes I think he was the grown-up and I was the child."

"Sounds like he was a good boy."

"The best."

They walked on a little bit, hand in hand – the grip just that little bit tighter now – lost in their thoughts. Liam wanted to scoop her up into his arms and protect her forever. How could she have gone through so much pain and never let them know? When she was piecing together their lives, how could they not have known her own was in pieces?

"The thing is," Detta started, "after a while I realised I wasn't going to find him in Dublin, or anywhere really, and I wanted to come home. And I wanted to grow up a bit and make a difference. The group was my way of making a difference and finding him in whatever way I could."

"Did you find him?"

"Yes and no. I found peace. I found friendship and I found you. And I realised that I loved walking in the rain and jumping in puddles and acting the eejit and kissing lovely builders and making Hallowe'en costumes and making posters with big markers and glitter pens. He would have wanted this."

"I'm glad," Liam said.

"So am I," Detta said. "Glad and content, and ready for my happy ending."

52

The dining room was a strange combination of opulence and what could only be described as shabby chic. The clean lines of the dining table, which sat ten, were impressive but what was more lovely, more welcoming was the garlands of handmade paper chains hanging across the room. The children, under Detta's carefully skilled guidance, had worked themselves into a sticking and cutting frenzy three days before making decorations for the big Christmas party. Even Thomas and Eimear, who Ruth had assumed would turn their noses up at such things, got into the spirit of it. Ruth had watched proudly as Thomas had helped his little brother link the chains together before lifting Poppy up to BluTac them to the ceiling. She had breathed out then, as she sat on one of the designer chairs sipping mulled wine. Thomas had become so withdrawn after things reached crisis point with James that she was worried he would self-destruct. He had locked himself in his room for a week or two, but then he had emerged – a little more confident and a lot more talkative. It was as if James, and his run-in with the law, had given Thomas some sort of faith in his ability to cope. It helped too, of course, that Ruth had showered him with praise.

She had been so utterly proud of him when he insisted on

coming to court with her for James's case. He had held her hand, his head high, throughout the proceedings and when they were done, and James had his warning and his fine, it was Thomas – along with Dr Donnelly, who had persuaded her not to rest on her laurels and to go the whole hog and use the court system for maintenance.

Thanks to that, and thanks to Dr Donnelly increasing her hours just that little bit, she wasn't so terrified of Christmas any more. That said, knowing that there was no fear of getting hit, or James getting drunk and ruining things, had meant that money or no money this was going to be a pretty impressive Christmas anyway.

"They've done a good job," Ruth said proudly as she carried a stack of plates in to set the table.

"They really did. Although you can tell which ones the twins did," Niamh said with a smile, nodding her head in the direction of a garland which was straggling towards the ground.

"Sure they're only babies. And it's cute."

"It sure is," Niamh said with a smile. "I think that it's going to be a good Christmas. It's important to me they have a good Christmas."

Ruth put her plates down and hugged Niamh. She had changed so much these last few weeks – she was more confident, more assured and looked less and less like she might break if someone looked at her the wrong way. But Ruth knew that she was still grieving and, well, a hug never hurt anyone.

Niamh rubbed a tear from her eye with the cuff of her cardigan. "I'll not be crying," she smiled. "Well, not at least until the kids are in bed and we're all a bit squiffy on the wine!"

"That's a girl," Ruth said gently. "Now lead me back to your gorgeous new kitchen so I can gaze once more with lust and longing at your new kitchen island."

The pair linked arms and walked back to where a rabble of voices greeted them above the hiss and fizz of the Christmas dinner bubbling on the stove while a host of over-excited children ran out through the back door to play on the newly constructed climbing frame and swing set.

Among them on the slide was Ciara – with Ella on her knee – a look of absolute joy and innocence on both their faces as they hurtled towards the bottom. She had also transformed these last few weeks. After visiting the college to discuss night classes she had decided to go the whole hog and take an Access course. Mrs Quinn was kindly allowing her time off during the week so that she could combine work with study. Lorraine had nearly died with shock the day before when the village battleaxe had wandered up her garden path laden with a bag of toys and clothes for the baby.

"I think she deserves something from our side of the family," she had said, gingerly handing over the Santa sack.

Bridges were being built and Lorraine was just delirious to see her daughter not only blossom as a mother but also as a seventeen-year-old child – still able to race to the top of a slide set.

"She's having fun," Detta said with a smile and Lorraine nodded.

"She is indeed and, cunningly, at the same time avoiding doing any cooking or cleaning. She's a genius that one."

"You've got to admire anyone who can avoid cooking and cleaning," Detta said.

"Amen to that," Liam answered. He was perched on a stool at the kitchen island sipping a glass of red wine and making a half hearted attempt to stir a pot of soup.

Detta threw her head back and laughed. "I know, you

poor pet. You're killed there, stirring your soup." She walked over, put her arm around him and kissed his cheek.

The rest of the group hadn't seemed to mind their blossoming relationship at all. In fact they all seemed deliriously happy about it. It hadn't affected their meetings which were now less about writing letters to themselves and more about having a bit of *craic*. Detta had even gone and ceremoniously burned those first letters they had written and locked away in a safety deposit box. Their lives were getting better already – they didn't need letters any more to help them.

Laura hadn't been overly impressed with Liam's new romance, but she had accepted it. She said she wouldn't stand in the way of his happiness and he had thought that was big of her. She was still with James, but they didn't look so happy any more and Liam wondered if it would only be a matter of time before they split up. In a way, it would serve her right, he thought. And then he had let go of that touch of bitterness because he had more than he could ever have wanted right beside him.

He had persuaded Detta to tell the group about her son at their last meeting. There had been tears aplenty and he had felt a bit awkward – aware of his lack of the female knack for saying and doing the right thing when faced with a woman crying her eyes out. But it had been him who walked her home that night and curled up beside her on her bed while her tears subsided and she found her smile again.

Agnes hadn't even commented at the ungodly hour at which he had returned home. He never thought the day would come when his mother would seem happy to be pimping him out.

He looked at his mother, sat like a queen bee on the soft sofa close to the French doors supping on a glass of sherry while reading to Poppy and his heart swelled. The Christmas season was definitely making him an old softie. He'd have to make a point of drinking some extra-strength lager or belching loudly later on just to assure himself he was still a man's man.

"Right, I think we can move through now," Niamh shouted above the chatter and they started to file into the dining room – the children's eyes wide at the seven-foot Christmas tree in the hall decorated to perfection with hosts of crystal angels and glass baubles. The dining table looked glorious, as did the extra table drafted in to cope with the number of guests. Niamh loved the buzz of it all. If Seán had been here they would have been sitting like some stately old couple in relative silence in this massive room eating their dinner, just the two of them and the children.

Now the very rafters of their home rang with laughter and before the day was over, things would be louder still. Her parents, along with Robyn, were calling round for supper and staying over. She planned to keep the twins up until they fell into a sweetie-induced coma-like sleep and then she would let them sleep in her bed where she would stare out of the Velux windows at the stars above.

She didn't think she believed Seán really was a star in heaven now. But she liked to talk to him still. She didn't shout any more. If she was honest she knew what she was getting into when she met him. He wasn't the kind to ever settle with anything – no matter how much that anything was everything he ever wanted. She didn't forgive him as such, but she understood. And occasionally now, she allowed herself to miss him again. Just a little. Because she had to accept that without him she wouldn't be where she was now – and now was okay. Now was good.

Sitting down, once she was sure everyone had a drink, she breathed out as Liam stood to carve the turkey.

"Before we start," Ruth said, standing up and raising her glass, "I just wanted to toast you all. To friends, old and new! And misfits everywhere."

THE END

In Conversation with
Claire Allan

1) Have you always been creative/written or is it a new discovery?

I've always loved writing and making up stories. I was always, and still am, a big daydreamer. Most of the time I'm lost in another world, imagining what people would do or how they would react in a plethora of situations.

At school at Thornhill College in Derry, I loved writing and was a member of the Writers' Workshop. We were very lucky to have a guest teacher for a time in the form of fellow Poolbeg author Anne Dunlop, who I'm now friends with. I still have a signed copy of her book *The Pineapple Tart* in which she wrote that I should be more confident about my writing!

When I started work as a journalist I found I didn't have the time any more to write creatively and the process of writing news is so very different to novel writing. I don't think I'd get away with stringing out news stories to 110,000 words or using the feck word all that much!

But the desire was always there eating away at me and when I was turning 30 I decided it was a 'now or never' crossroads. I had recently lost a dear friend who had always encouraged me to write and I decided to write *Rainy Days and Tuesdays* in her honour. The book is dedicated to her.

Now I'm addicted and love the creative process – even at the times when it feels like very hard work.

2) Tell us about your writing process; where do you write? When? Are you a planner or "ride-the-wave" writer?

Most often I write in the evenings, on my sofa – laptop on my knee on a cushion. I dream of a fabulous study, complete with inbuilt library overlooking a lake or other coastline in which I could while away hours writing at a proper desk. However my house is very much a family home and almost every room is overrun with toys and baby equipment.

Evenings, once my two children are in bed, are sacred to me. It is a brilliant form of relaxation to open the file of my latest book and get writing.

As regards how I write – I'm somewhere in between a planner and a 'ride the wave' author. With all my books I know where I want to start and where I want to end, but I let the characters lead me on their own journey there.

As a book evolves I find the characters form into their own people and often would react differently to what I would have planned for them originally.

For me, seeing a character evolve is one of the most exciting parts of the writing process. It gives me a real buzz to feel the story come to life.

3) Since your first novel *Rainy Days & Tuesdays* was published in July 2007 has your life changed much?

Aspects of my life are very much the same. I still get up the morning, try and make myself look presentable and try to get to work on time and with my sanity intact. I still spend my days working as a journalist and writing in a very factual way and in the evenings I'm still mammy – except now I'm double the mammy as I have a second child in the form of our daughter Cara.

But in others ways things have changed entirely. I feel more complete now – as if a lifetime's ambition has been fulfilled and to an extent it has given me more confidence in myself.

I have done things I could only ever have dreamed of before – appearing on TV, taking part in photoshoots, speaking in public, hosting book signings etc. I'm actually quite a shy person so it has been a challenge to push myself forward and I'm proud that I've survived it all – and enjoyed most of it.

I also think I have improved as a writer with each novel – and I strive to push myself more and more with each book. *Jumping in Puddles* was certainly my biggest challenge as a writer and I'm very proud of it.

4) Do you have a favourite character in *Jumping in Puddles*?

I'm fond of them all in their own way. I think Niamh is very brave – and wonderfully glam. I covet her house and her kick-ass boots! Liam is a great dad and a strong and hunky character – he was great fun to write. Ruth is an exceptionally strong and witty woman and Ciara is wise beyond her years.

In a strange way I think of them all as real people – but if I was to pick a favourite from *Jumping in Puddles*, I would probably opt for Detta O'Neill who brings all four of the lone parents together. She is an enigmatic but golden-hearted creature who is just wonderfully quirky and supportive. She was a delight to write and I especially loved writing in a love interest for her.

5) What character & scene was most difficult to write for you? Why?

Ruth was the most difficult character to write – and the scenes in which she is beaten by her husband were very challenging. I wanted and needed to get it right. I didn't want to patronise anyone who had been through domestic violence and I wanted to make her experiences feel real to the reader.

Over the years I have interviewed many women who have had abusive partners and who have been brave enough to tell their tale. The perception of domestic violence was also something I researched for my thesis in Journalism as part of my Masters Degree.

It was therefore exceptionally important for me to do the storyline justice and also to show just how strong and brave a character Ruth was even when she didn't realise it herself.

On a lighter note, Liam was challenging as he is a man (obviously!) and I had to get inside the male mind – which is not an easy task.

6) Who are your favourite authors and favourite novels and why (worldwide and Irish based authors)?

I have several favourite books I go back to time and time again. The first is *Rachel's Holiday* by Marian Keyes which made me roar with laughter one minute and cry buckets of tears the next. It really was a book which made me sit up and think "I could do this" and inspired me to give it a go.

I also have a great fondness for the early Patricia Scanlan books – especially the *City Girl* trilogy. I dreamed of opening my own 'City

Woman', renaming myself Devlin and being so terribly glamorous. I'd say those were the first real Irish chick-lit books and they were fabulous.

These days I love anything that is witty and sharp. I think my fellow Northern Irish authors – Anne Dunlop and Sharon Owens – carry this off perfectly. Their books are beautifully written, gripping and very funny in places.

If I want a good cry I'll re-read *Queen Mum* by Kate Long which has the most poignant depiction of loss and grief I have ever read.

7) Tell us a bit about your next book – have you started writing it yet?

My next book has a working title of *Finding Annie* and I can't tell you how much fun I'm having writing it!

It's a romantic comedy about a woman who seems set on sabotaging her own life at a time when all she really wants is to have her happy ending. She watches her best friend prepare for her wedding while her own relationship comes crashing around her ears.

It's set in the very glamorous world of PR and features a host of really quirky characters and fun situations.

As with all my books, there is a serious undertone – examining how so many women today feel a little bit lost and unsure of what they should be looking for – but hopefully the reader will enjoy the many laughs along the way.

8) The support group for lone parents is filled with interesting characters – such a great dynamic! Where did the idea come from?

Initially I was going to write the book solely about Niamh – the character who is widowed. I wanted to write a book about someone who chased their dream to find it all went wrong and to show that money does not necessarily buy happiness. I also wanted to focus on the fact she was left behind with two young children – and that spawned the idea of having a support group for lone parents.

People seem to have very set stereotypes of what a single parent is and I thought it would be interesting to show how people can find themselves alone raising kids for a myriad of reasons. The characters kind of formed themselves after that – and it was great fun to write.

9) You've recently had a baby girl – congratulations! Has this influenced your writing or direction the book has taken?

Thank you! Baby Cara was born on March 4 and she has changed our lives completely. I suffered from hyperemesis throughout my pregnancy with her – which meant I was physically sick every day, right until she was born! It was hard going I can tell you but I think it also gave me a new sense of get up and go. If I could get through hyperemesis I can get through anything. I have pushed myself writing this book – dealing with very serious topics but trying to keep humour involved. I think the overdose of hormones helped me write the more emotional scenes!

Since she was born I have been working on my fourth book – and my writing time has become even more important to me. It is my time to be Claire, not just Cara and Joseph's mummy – although being their mummy is the very best job in the world!

10) The village/ rural setting adds so much to the atmosphere of the novel. Why did you pick this setting?

I love Donegal. Some of my happiest memories are holidaying in small coastal villages with my husband and son. I love the village dynamic – how in so many ways these villages have moved with the times but there is something very traditional in their outlook.

I thought it would be interesting to take an issue which is still, in some circles, taboo and put it in a very close-knit community and see what happens.

I also have a dream of relocating to a village just like Rathinch – where I can spend my days writing by the sea, taking the kids for long walks and enjoying a more relaxed lifestyle.

It was also the perfect excuse for many daytrips to the seaside in the name of research!

If you enjoyed *Jumping in Puddles* try
Feels Like Maybe also published by Poolbeg

Here's a sneak preview of Chapter one

Feels Like Maybe

Claire Allan

POOLBEG

1

Aoife

When I die someone will write "Aoife McLaughlin was very good at going it alone" on my headstone. Then again, I will probably have to come back from the dead and write it myself.

That thought crossed my mind as I took yet another shallow breath and felt yet another contraction rip across my rounded, swollen belly. It shouldn't have been like this.

I should have had a loving husband mopping my brow and encouraging me through every wave of increasing pain. We should have jointly decided on a name and painted a nursery together – pausing only to leaf through the Yellow Pages and order pizzas with tuna and banana on them – and yet, here I was alone in a room where everyone spoke in a different accent to my own and struggled to pronounce my name.

There was no husband. There wasn't even a significant other. There was just me and my cervix which, much to my annoyance, was dilating at a painfully slow rate.

The pain came again and I breathed deeply on the gas and

air that was my only salvation. The anaesthetist was busy, or so they had told me, so here I was with not so much as an epidural to make the whole experience more bearable.

All I had was a radio that was blasting out what seemed like the same four songs on a loop. I swore that if I heard the Outhere Brothers sing "Boom, boom, boom, let me hear ya say weyoh" one more time I was going to boom-fecking-boom the radio out the window.

A very cheerful midwife by the name of Peggy walked into the room just as the contraction reached its excruciating crescendo. "How are you doing, my lovely?" she asked, looking at the jumble of peaks and troughs on the monitor beside my bed.

I wondered did she want the honest answer or the polite answer? Was this similar to when you go to the hairdresser's and don't like the disaster they've made of your barnet but you feel compelled to give a thumbs-up anyway?

But I have never been one for bullshit, it was one of the things my clients admired so much about me, so I decided to opt for the honest approach.

"You mean apart from this baby trying to squeeze its way out of my fandango while I lie here twenty hours into labour with no epidural? Just fucking peachy, thanks!"

"Oooh, if you're starting to swear, it must mean Baby is nearly here!" Peggy chirped, disappearing between my splayed legs for a quick look.

I was tempted to point out I had been swearing for most of the last twenty hours – being Irish it was as in-built in me as breathing. I wasn't about to stop now when my genitals were being shredded by a supposedly natural force.

"How far?" I asked, panting as the pain subsided.

Peggy held up a gloved hand, slightly stained with blood, and I felt a wave of nausea wash over me. Throwing up what was left of my breakfast I swore I would never, ever, believe anything that I saw in the movies again. You didn't get bloodstained hands in Hollywood.

"Seven centimetres, my lovely. Shouldn't be too long now. You should have this little one by morning."

I looked at the clock, it was 11.15 p.m. Damn fecking right I would have this baby by morning – even if I had to do the Caesarean myself. Another contraction hit and I sucked hard on the gas and air, sinking my teeth into the plastic mouthpiece, imagining it to be Jake's undersized penis.

"Sweet" – gasp – "Jesus" – gasp – "make" – gasp – "this" – gasp – "fucking" – gasp – "stop!"

Peggy, still smiling despite my clatter of swear-words tapped my knee, as if her gentle tapping held some magic anaesthetic quality.

"There, there, lovely! It will all be worth it when Baby is here." She smiled and walked out of the room, leaving me alone to my growing sense of panic.

Would it be okay when "Baby" – this nameless wriggling creature fighting to get out – was here? Somehow I doubted it. I had made some pretty major mistakes in my life before but this was a fuck-up of immense proportions and as my tummy tightened I knew it was too late to change my mind. What goes up must come down, I thought with a wry smile. I promised myself nothing was ever going up again.

I started to wonder if the gas and air was working any more. It made me feel woozy, that was for sure, but the pain didn't seem relieved in any way. What I really needed – really, really needed – was a king-size Nurofen and a bottle of vodka. That had always killed any pain I had before.

I mean, how much harm could a wee drink of vodka do to the baby now? Surely by the time the alcohol made its way down into my uterus, through the placenta and into the umbilical cord, the baby would be separated from me anyway?

A cigarette would be good too, or a nice big juicy joint. I closed my eyes, inhaling deeply on the Entenox and imagined I could feel the warmth of sweet smoke fill my lungs. Momentarily there was relief from the pain and then, bam, back at point zero. Tummy tightening. Back aching. Fandango fanning. Baby burrowing its way towards the light. There has got to be a more humane way to bring new life into this world. Beam me up, Scotty, I'm in trouble . . .

Much as I'm averse to crying, I started to wail, crying big gulping, snottery tears born of fear, tiredness and pain the like of which I had never known. I'd heard giving birth was at best like having a big poo and at worst like a bad period. What utter shite! I would have cried out for my mother, if she wasn't the most annoying fecker on the planet – so instead I just cried.

Peggy stuck her head back round the corner. "Now what's the matter, lovely? No need for tears."

I tried to tell her what was wrong. How it had all gone horribly pear-shaped and that I had never asked for this – never wanted it. It wasn't in the game plan. I was doing pretty damn okay before this, thank-you-very-much.

But all that came out was a muffled scream.

"I need to push!" I gasped, as soon as the power of speech returned to me.

It's hard to explain, but the feeling was beyond my control. I suddenly understood what bearing down meant. Every inch of my body, from the tips of my toes to the split ends of my auburn mop wanted to bear down and to push.

"No, dearie, you don't. You're only seven centimetres," Peggy replied.

"Yes, I do. I need to fucking push!"

"Now, now, lovely. Baby will come when Baby is ready to come."

"My name is not fucking 'Lovely' it's Aoife – Eee-fa!" I said, emphasising the pronunciation in the hope she would at last get it right, "And I'm telling you this baby is ready to fucking come now!"

I grimaced as my body contorted with pain and pressure. This was beyond my control and yet I felt strangely okay about it. This was my body and, by Christ, this was really happening and I was powerless to stop it.

"I'll go and get someone to check," Peggy said, making for the door.

"No! I need to push now!" I gasped, my body taking over and forcing me to push with every muscle available. "Aaaaarrghhh!" I could feel something move down to my pelvis, could see Peggy's eyes widen as she rushed to the end of the bed.

"I can see Baby's head!" Peggy said.

I took this as encouragement to keep going, and going, and going.

It wasn't so much that I longed to cradle the baby, I just longed for this pain to be over. My tummy tightened and I instinctively pushed again – my exhaustion gone as this primeval force took over.

"Pant now for me," Peggy said and I forced myself to stop pushing, to take small gasping breaths, as I felt this new life emerge from me.

Suddenly, although it had taken twenty-one hours, I felt a surge of relief. The pressure was gone and this little mewling creature was staring at me. The most perfect little girl in the world.

I cried again, but this time it was because I knew that no matter how I had planned not to let this happen, I had already fallen madly in love with my daughter. My baby.

* * *

Ten perfect little fingers, with nails that needed trimming already. Those fragile little hands, curled up close to that button nose. I wondered had I ever felt skin so soft? Rubbing my nose against Maggie's cheek, I whispered my apologies to her.

"I'm sorry I didn't want you before but now that I know you, now that I've seen you, I want you more than anything." No one else could hear our conversation but then it wasn't for anyone else's ears. It was our moment alone and I could hardly believe how fulfilled I felt when just an hour ago I had felt more alone than ever before. I knew, I guessed, that I would never be alone again.

Peggy came back into the room, smiling now, the look of shock at Maggie's speedy arrival replaced by her usual calm demeanour.

"Do you want me to bring the phone in? You can let people know this little poppet is here."

I shook my head. There wasn't really anyone to tell. Beth would find the note in the morning when she returned from her break to Brighton. No one else really mattered, not now anyway.

"I'm okay, thanks," I said, never for one second lifting my gaze from my daughter.

"Well," said Peggy, "I'll be outside if you need me."

"Yes, thank you. Thank you for everything."

"All in a day's work, lovely, all in a day's work."

Peggy was clearly baffled by my reluctance to announce my new arrival. She had seen enough of me for one day. Letting her see my fandango was one thing, explaining my complicated set of circumstances was another. Some things were private.

Exhausted, I placed Maggie in her little plastic crib by the bed and lay down, desperate for sleep but reluctant to let this little one out of my sight. All I could see now was a patch of pink skin, swaddled in blankets with a white hat on her tiny head. I put my hand to my stomach, now a gelatinous mass – like a balloon that has been partially deflated – and wondered had this little creature really been inside me just a few hours ago?

The name Maggie seemed perfect. I had no idea where it had come from. I hadn't allowed myself to think of names before, but as soon as I saw all 6lbs and 9oz of my child, a tuft of dark hair and her face set in a determined little stare, I knew that no other name would suit the same.

No doubt Jake would have wanted something a bit more "out there". He would laugh and tell me that Maggie was "so suburban", "so bland", so "predictable". He could go and scratch himself. I was going to have a big enough problem selling this one to the folks back home without announcing the arrival of baby "Aisha" or "Bluebell". Nope, Maggie was just fine. Absolutely perfect.

POOLBEG WISHES TO
THANK YOU

for buying a Poolbeg book.
As a loyal customer we will give you
10% OFF (and free postage*)
on any book bought on our website
www.poolbeg.com

Select the book(s) you wish to buy
and click to checkout.

Then click on the 'Add a Coupon' button
(located under 'Checkout') and enter
this coupon code

POOLBEG

USMWR15173

(Not valid with any other offer!)

POOLBEG

WHY NOT JOIN OUR MAILING LIST

@ www.poolbeg.com and get some
fantastic offers on Poolbeg books

See website for details

All orders despatched within 24 hours!